The Runaway Debutante

Elizabeth Harmon

Cover Design by Blue Water Books

Also by Elizabeth Harmon

Pairing Off
Turning It On
Getting It Back
Heating It Up
Shining Through

Dedicated with love to my husband Tom, who has always believed in me.

THE RUNAWAY DEBUTANTE

A Victorian Romance

ELIZABETH HARMON

ROSEDALE
PRESS

PART ONE

CHAPTER ONE

August 1873

C onstance Barrett had one last ball to endure before the London season ended and she could embrace her destiny.

She stood before the dressing room mirror as her maid put the finishing touches on her attire. Her dark brown hair was curled into ringlets that tickled when they bobbed against her shoulders. Rather than scratch at the curls, she ran her gloved fingertips over the ruby necklace that lay cold and heavy against her throat. Father's gift to Mother on their wedding day, it was one of Lady Beverly's finest pieces. She'd insisted Constance wear it tonight.

Fletcher fastened the rubies and stepped back. "You look

beautiful, my lady."

Turning her head carefully so as not to disturb her hair, Constance had to agree. Fletcher's skill often amazed her. "I fear you've done far too well with me. I feel like a fancy package, all turned out to attract attention." She fingered the delicate rose-red silk and fine Parisian stitching. One of the most magnificent dresses she'd ever owned, Mother had chosen it in the spring for Constance to wear on the final night of what was sure to be a most successful season.

Poor Mother should have known better.

"If you turn a young man's head tonight, there's nothing wrong with that," said Fletcher. "Make them regret you getting away."

As if any young man would notice. Constance was ignored far more often than she turned heads. Thank God that in a few weeks, it would no longer matter. "They had their chance, Fletcher. Now I shall have what I want."

In the corner, she glimpsed brown leather-bound volumes of history, poetry, and mathematics. She'd already begun to study in anticipation of her first term at Girton College. The books would be better company than what she'd face tonight. "I wish I didn't have to go to this ball. I daresay I'd rather stay home."

"Now, now, my lady. It will make Lord and Lady Beverly so happy to show off their beautiful daughter one last time." Fletcher made a final adjustment to the silk roses on Constance's gown and smiled. "Come now, your parents are waiting in the study."

"Already?" The filigree mantle clock had just chimed half-past six. The ball did not begin until eight o'clock, though perhaps she was mistaken. At university she would keep better track of her appointments.

She followed Fletcher out. One of the mahogany combs in her hair was already loose. She gave it a shove and hoped it stayed. Gathering her monstrous skirts, she squeezed through the bedroom door. At Girton she would dress as she pleased, perhaps even in trousers, like that American lady doctor she'd read about. Scandalous maybe, but the idea had merit.

As Constance entered the foyer, the butler pressed himself into the corner to avoid her enormous clothing. A pity the poor man had to endure such ridiculous conventions. What possible difference did it make if her skirts brushed Martin's boot? Since no one was nearby, she whispered, "Did you read this morning what Mr. Malthus had to say?"

Martin's quick look of disgust said he had. A servant in a fine household knew better than to discuss politics with his employer's daughter, but they'd enjoyed a meeting of the minds since the day she caught him cursing over an editorial that opposed suffrage for the working class. Martin respected her opinions and admired her intellect.

If only her parents felt the same.

They'd agreed to Girton only because she'd failed to attract a proposal after two full seasons. They'd been so excited for her debut, and despite herself, Constance had been too. Foolishly. Outmatched by girls who'd been accomplished coquettes since the nursery, her conversations about a book she'd read, or a pressing issue before Parliament, were ignored or quietly ridiculed. At balls, she'd been a wallflower more often than not. Her parents' disappointment only made it worse.

Though it stung not to have been a success in the marriage mart, she looked forward to using her mind and talents to make a difference in the world. Exactly how, she didn't yet know, but Girton would help her find a way. Like Miss Florence Nightingale, whom she deeply admired, Constance would make her own mark.

Martin inched past to open the door to Father's study, but before doing so said in a hushed voice, "Good luck, my lady."

Good luck? Whatever did he mean? His face held no answers, only a servant's blank expression. He escorted her in to where her parents waited, and left without a word.

Roland Barrett, the Earl of Beverly, looked younger than his fifty years, with bushy brown hair and a robust build. Mother was as delicate and beautiful as her namesake flower. Rose Barrett pressed her palm to her breast, as if to still an excited heart. "Oh, Constance, you look lovely!"

Constance perched on the edge of the closest chair, nervously arranging her skirts. More often, Mother would notice her unruly hair, disheveled dress, or some other flaw. Something strange was going on and it was imperative to keep her wits.

"Indeed, you're quite the picture." Father cleared his throat and sat back down next to Mother. "And as you know, Lord Gaffney has grown quite fond of you."

What did Gaffney have to do with anything? Henry Somerville VI, Earl of Gaffney, had been her polite escort to several parties this past month. He was dull as a butter knife and only slightly more intelligent, but by now, her parents were ecstatic over any man's interest.

"He and his father came to see me this morning," Father

continued. "They have made an offer which we were delighted to accept upon your behalf."

"My behalf?" She touched the heavy collar of bridal rubies at her throat.

"Lord Gaffney asked for your hand in marriage," Mother said. "We will announce your engagement tonight, and you will wed in the spring."

She gripped the arm of the chair as the room and her thoughts spun. Gaffney's interest was only polite, and she had been careful to convey the same. He was thirty-six and rumored to have engaged in a torrid affair with Victoria Stansfield. Surely, she had not heard right. "Marry... Gaffney?" Spoken together, the words repulsed her. Her heart raced, and cold sweat prickled her scalp. "But... we are so different. I am not even sure I... like him."

"Nonsense," said Father. "He is the Duke of Arlington's heir, for God's sake. You will be kept in luxury and security for the rest of your life."

The rest of her life. Her stays, heavy gown, and jewels grew heavier and more restrictive. The future closed in. Years of dull balls, petty gossip, and silly social games she'd never master. She would have to vow to honor and obey Gaffney. Forsake all others unto a man for whom she felt nothing.

"What about Girton? You promised I could attend." She cringed at the shrill desperation in her voice. So much for keeping her wits.

"We agreed when there was a concern you might never..." Mother shuddered, unable to speak the words. "Thank goodness, that's no longer a worry. Your father has already posted a letter to the college, canceling your enrollment."

"But you knew what Girton meant to me!" She stood, gloved fists clenched at her sides. "How could you arrange a marriage and barter me off like some bloody possession?"

"Enough!" Father's roar filled the room, as he also stood, looming, his face scarlet against his starched white shirt. "I shall tolerate no more of your impertinence and vulgar language! We accepted this proposal because frankly, daughter, you are unlikely to get a better one."

Constance stilled, as a sobering reality set in. She was an only child, a daughter. She couldn't inherit her father's title or fortune, that would all go to her uncle Albert. Changing the world was possible only if she had the means to do so. Deep down she'd always known her only true option was marriage.

Father shook his head as he returned to his seat. "Through two seasons you have repelled potential mates with your bizarre ideas and lack of social grace. It is a problem which shall only become worse once your femininity is compromised by too much education."

Mother smiled. "It would please us so much to know that your future is secure, that you will never lack for anything. Nor will our grandchildren."

She shrank back, angry and defiant, yet broken. Constance wanted children too, someday. She wanted to make her parents happy, and refusing meant disappointing them in the only way that mattered. Father spoke, more quietly this time. "There will be no more argument. You will accept Lord Gaffney's proposal, then return home to Sussex to plan your wedding and learn to be a proper wife. Is that clear?"

Her eyes stung. The freedom she'd longed for had been a silly dream, and there wasn't a thing to do other than accept it. Angry, yet powerless, she forced the words out. "Quite clear."

The Duke of Westminster's magnificent home on Grosvenor Square was awash in light. Excitement over the season's last event crackled in the sultry night, but to Constance it might as well have been a funeral. Condemned to her fate, she entered, flanked by her parents. The only victory would be to survive tonight with her dignity intact.

Moments after the Beverlys entered, Gaffney appeared. A large man, he favored mutton-chop sideburns and a full mustache. These, along with his parted and pomaded hair, made him look much older, resembling a guardian rather than a fiancé. Like Cassandra bound for Troy to meet her doom, she followed him into a private salon. He stood stiffly, with his hands behind his back, and chin tilted upward. "Your father has informed you of my intentions."

Numb, she could manage hardly more than, "Yes, my lord."

"And the terms are agreeable." It wasn't a question, but he paused, expecting an answer.

She could say no, but her wishes were irrelevant. She could march out the door, but her parents would stop her. She darted glances left and right, desperate for escape, her heart racing. The tiny window? Her skirts would never fit through. Like an animal, she was trapped.

Dizzy and nauseous, she closed her eyes. Was this how it felt to faint? She'd never fainted in her life and took great pride in it, but obviously no one had much use for a young lady of sturdy constitution. Time stood still, as though she could prevent the inevitable by refusing to answer. Then Gaffney cleared his throat, and in a dull whisper, she replied. "Yes, my lord."

"Of course, you want a bauble to display." From his pocket, he drew out a square black box. Inside was an enormous ring encrusted with pearls and rubies. The ring fit loosely and slipped around to the inside of her palm. Her fate was sealed.

After the engagement announcement at dinner, Constance forced a smile so broad her head ached. Jane Watson was the first to offer congratulations, folding her into a tearful embrace. "Oh, my darling, I'm so happy for you." Jane's pretty face was bright with excitement. Her effervescent blond cousin was the belle of the season, yet never once had Jane lorded her popularity. "I hope one day I'm as fortunate to find true love."

True love? This was a business transaction. Once she'd dreamed of true love, of a handsome Mr. Darcy, captivated by her smart, capable Elizabeth. Instead, she had been auctioned off for the best offer her parents could find. Instead of passion, she must grit her teeth and make the best of it. It was all she could do not to dissolve into a quivering puddle of grief. Fletcher's brisk voice echoed in her mind. Chin up, Lady Constance.

By God, she was trying.

Later, dancing with Gaffney, she watched the couple beside them. A handsome young man and beautiful debutante, captivated by one another. The couple's adoring gazes almost undid her. Why couldn't Constance have had that? Gaffney frowned. "You seem distracted, Constance. Are you already consumed with wedding details?"

How little he knew her. Though like it or not, he was her betrothed and nothing would change that. Yet maybe... just maybe, she could still salvage one small thing.

It was worth a try.

She beamed a coy smile. "Why, everything is perfect, my lord. It's just that..." She dropped her eyes, laying it on thick. "As you may know, I was about to begin my studies at Girton College. While I am over the moon at the thought of becoming your wife, I had looked forward to going. Having been to Oxford yourself, I'm sure you can understand. I wonder if we might extend our engagement. Not long, perhaps a year? That way, I can still attend university."

He sniffed. "Girton is a female academy, not university. While it was necessary for me to attend to cultivate political contacts, I see no reason for you to do so. I know your father agrees. Still, once we are wed, if you would enjoy music or art instruction, I could allow it, as long as it does not interfere with your other duties. I suppose you might also channel your energy into charity work... of the right sort."

Music lessons and charity work. Of the right sort. This would be her future as the Earl of Gaffney's wife. They had rescued her from spinsterhood, but at what cost? Her dreams, her freedom, and her identity.

The night wore on. By midnight, she was lightheaded from three glasses of champagne and at risk for imprudent speech. The safest place to be was at Gaffney's side, as he spoke with his chums. No one paid her the slightest attention.

"All this talk of reform!" Lord Rutherford shook his head in dismay. "Don't these fools understand the workhouses must be harsh? Otherwise, every wretch on the East End would be at the door. These are lazy, shiftless people who choose to live this way!"

"Hear, hear," murmured the others.

Gaffney nodded. "They also cannot see poverty is inevitable. Just this morning, the Times published an essay by Mr. Malthus, arguing that in our society, poverty is part of the natural order. It's just as Herbert Spencer wrote, 'survival of the fittest.'"

Surely, he wasn't serious. She'd read that essay. It was not worth the paper it was printed on. The son of a prominent MP, Gaffney was a future member of the House of Lords. He would have the power to correct injustice and she had a duty to enlighten him. Perhaps this would be her contribution to the greater good. "Why, that's ridiculous!" she said. "No one chooses to be poor. It is our duty to help the disadvantaged. Not just for their sakes, but for the sake of England. Did not Mr. Disraeli speak of the dangers of two nations?"

Gaffney's eyes widened. The other gentlemen stared, their faces reflecting a mixture of distaste and amusement. Rutherford glanced at Gaffney, a smirk playing at his lips. "Appears you will have your hands full with this one, old man."

His tight smile didn't hide his anger. "Yes, quite. Come along, darling."

His grip pinched her arm as he led her back to the salon where he'd proposed. She braced for a vigorous argument, but gathered her thoughts, determined to prevail. Gaffney shut the door firmly. She tried to pull away, but he held her fast, and slapped her hard across the face.

CHAPTER TWO

The force of the blow knocked her sideways. Pain jolted her neck and shoulders. Reeling, she righted herself and tried to pull away, but Gaffney squeezed her arm and shook her. His crimson face was inches away. His cruel eyes were terrifying. "You will never contradict me again. Apologize immediately!"

"No! I meant only that –"

"Say it!" The force of his words sprayed spittle onto her cheeks and she shrank back. He raised his open hand to strike again.

"I'm… I'm…" Her eyes trained on his hand, she cringed, dreading the pain of another blow on her tender cheek. Her throat tightened. She choked back a sob. "I apologize, my lord."

Mercifully, he let go. She staggered backward and grabbed the closest piece of furniture, a small chair. This couldn't be. Even Father, as domineering as he was, had never raised a hand against her or Mother. Her knees buckled and before she crumpled to the floor, she guided herself down onto the seat. Gently, she touched her wounded cheek, dabbing away tears and spit. Fresh pain made her wince.

Gaffney took a menacing step forward and gripped the arms of the chair, crowding her in. Nauseous from the scents of cloves and gin, Constance's stomach rolled. This close, Gaffney was even more grotesque. Who was this monster, to whom she now belonged?

"I understand why your father feared you would never wed, though I had hoped a girl of your breeding would know to hold her tongue. Nevertheless, you will learn. In my household, you shall behave as a lady or be punished as a willful child. You shall obey me completely and provide me with an heir. Nothing else." Quiet menace laced his voice, as he traced a thick fingertip across her tender cheek. When she bit her lip from the pain, he smiled. "Never forget that no one else wanted you."

As if she could. Here was the consequence of her high ideals and tactless tongue— marriage to an ogre to whom she must bow down. She closed her eyes and nodded.

Gaffney dug a handkerchief from his evening coat and tossed it in her lap. "Compose yourself before anyone sees you. You are an undignified mess."

With that, he left.

Muffled music and laughter bled through the closed salon door as Society danced on. She stared down at Gaffney's handkerchief, then flung it to the floor. She hated this vile man whose title and importance disguised a common brute. She hated herself. But shouldn't she have guessed this would be her fate? Why would Gaffney—or any man—put up with someone like her? Women were to decorate the world, not change it. This was the rule which would govern her life from now on.

Look what rebellion had brought.

The next morning, just after the stroke of nine, Fletcher bustled in with a breakfast tray. Constance lay still, eyes closed and breath steady, feigning sleep. Perhaps Fletcher would merely leave the tray and depart. No such luck. Mother pulled her blanket away. "Wake up, darling! You have a busy day ahead. Jane will be here soon."

"Jane?" Constance lifted her aching head and then dropped back onto the pillows. Today was their long-planned outing to the Crystal Palace. A light-hearted excursion was the last thing she wanted. Almost the last thing she wanted. Her cheek no longer throbbed, but the raw humiliation was still fresh.

Full of unusual energy, Mother bent over to rearrange the pillows. There was no choice but to sit up. Hands trembling, Constance took the cup of tea Fletcher offered. "I'm not sure I feel up to it."

"Oh?" Mother furrowed her brow and pressed a cool hand to Constance's forehead. "Are you ill? Do you feel faint? Perhaps we should summon the doctor."

Doctors were Mother's answer to everything. Constance took

a bracing sip of hot tea. "That won't be necessary."

After she'd returned to the ball, the rest of the evening had passed in a blur. Somehow, she smiled through another hour, then pleaded a headache. Mother placed her in the care of their footman, who delivered her home. Fletcher gently escorted her upstairs and brought a cold compress to ease the swelling on her cheek from where she'd collided with a carriage door. At three in the morning, she awoke from a nightmare of being locked behind prison bars encrusted with pearls and rubies.

"What's the matter, then?"

The question hung in the air. Her gaze locked with Mother's. Suppose she revealed everything? "Are you and Father sure Lord Gaffney is a suitable match for me? He seems rather... forceful."

Mother's eyes lingered on her cheek, then dropped to her arm. Constance glanced down. Two finger-shaped bruises marred her skin. She knew! Her heart pounding, she drew a hopeful breath and spoke carefully. "... he doesn't behave as a gentleman should."

The ticking clock filled the silence. Then Mother pursed her lips and turned away. "As wives, it is our responsibility to tame a man's base behavior. It isn't always pleasant, but there are worse things than a strong-willed husband." Her voice was resigned. "Poverty, for one."

An awful realization settled in. Of course, Mother wouldn't take her side. Marriage had turned her from a humble shopkeeper's daughter and governess into a countess. She would rather turn her daughter over to a devil than challenge Father's decision.

Never in her life had she felt more alone.

14

Mother fussed with the lace coverlet. "I'm sure you're merely feeling peaked after you overindulged in champagne. Fletcher tells me you ran into a carriage door. Really, Constance, you must be more careful."

"I'm tired is all," she murmured, and rubbed the bridge of her nose between her eyes. "After a bath, I will be fine."

The lavender and chamomile bath revived her a bit. At least the headache was gone. Fletcher brought out a summer gown of peach cotton, dotted with tiny sprigs of flowers. "This will brighten your color, my lady, and no one will notice your poor face."

Gaffney's ring had left a slight discoloration on her cheek, but so far, her explanation seemed to have satisfied everyone. Did her future hold more collisions with carriage doors? Her throat tightened as Fletcher worked quietly to transform her into a perfect young lady. Whatever her maid might think, she kept it to herself. Yet Constance couldn't bear to be without this kind woman, who cared for her when no one else did. She bit her lip and in the mirror, watched her eyes turn red and shiny. "You'll come with me, won't you, Fletcher? When I... marry Gaffney?"

Fletcher set down her brush and gently touched Constance's shoulders. "Of course, my lady," she said, and tugged the gown's short puffed sleeve down to hide the bruises.

When Jane arrived, Constance was properly turned out in low-heeled slippers, a simple hat, but no engagement ring. The thought of sliding it onto her finger made her skin crawl. Unfortunately, Mother noticed.

"It's much too large for my finger," she protested. "I'm afraid I'll lose it."

15

Mother frowned. "Then take care not to. You must wear it, Constance. It would be most improper if anyone saw you without it."

"I know!" said Jane, smiling. "Why not wear it on a ribbon? It is unconventional, but just for today, no one will mind. That way, it will remind you of your beloved every moment."

⁂

The Crystal Palace, at Sydenham Hill, drew visitors from across London. The enormous glass building held everything from live hippopotamuses to nude male statues. Jane and Mary, her chaperone, insisted on seeing those first. Mary consulted a map and guided them to the anatomy sculpture exhibit in the upper floor's North Gallery.

Though it was doubtful Gaffney bore any resemblance to the statues, the sight of naked men only served as an unwelcome reminder of her impending wedding night. His bulbous frame would crush down, smothering her, while he had his way. Constance shuddered and shifted her gaze, though not because of modesty. "Let's go see the Crystal Fountain," she said, urging her companions away from the statues.

The towering fountain stood at the center of the grand glass Palace, surrounded by full-sized elms and beds of colorful flowers. As they admired the spectacle, Constance spotted Victoria Stansfield and three other women emerging from the China exhibit. She ducked behind the tree. Unfortunately, too late. The women hurried over.

"What a delightful surprise to see London's darling of the

moment," cooed Victoria, now Mrs. Lionel Houston. The voluptuous redhead's sudden marriage to an American railway tycoon was all the talk at Ascot last month. "Come, little one." She coaxed with her fingers. "Show us the ring."

Jane scowled, but Constance cared nothing about the woman's trivial request. She lifted the ring which hung from her neck on a red silk ribbon.

Gaffney's former mistress pursed her scarlet-tinted lips and turned the ring in her thick fingers. "What a curious way to wear it. I can only assume that the band was too large for your delicate little hand?"

One of Victoria's heavily-perfumed friends giggled. Constance's stomach rolled as the dreadful truth became clear. The ring did not fit because Gaffney had purchased it for someone else. His sudden proposal and public announcement were only the spiteful posturing of a spurned lover.

"After I fell in love with Lionel, I feared Henry would… never recover." Victoria's expression was blank and her eyes were dead. "Such a relief he's found a lovely young bride." She studied Constance's face intently. "It also appears he's introduced you to his peculiar style of pleasure."

Constance stilled, her horror growing.

Victoria ran a gloved finger up Constance's bare arm and leaned forward, speaking in a hushed voice. "I advise you to learn to enjoy it. Or find a way out."

Her knees felt weak, and the room seemed to spin. Gaffney's vulgar former mistress was more sympathetic than her own mother! She stepped back. Trembling hands pressed still against her waist, she was vaguely aware of Jane tugging at her elbow.

17

"Come along, Constance. You mustn't listen to another awful word."

She jerked the ring back and on trembling legs, followed Jane and Mary away. Despite her cousin's assurance that Victoria Stansfield was nothing but a jealous trollop, bleak hopelessness unlike anything she'd ever known engulfed her. She didn't want a lonely life under her father's roof, nor did she want to live subject to a brutal husband.

But there seemed to be no escape.

Further into the maze of exhibits, the air was ripe with smells of roasting chestnuts, German sausage, and an exotic mix of voices. The cultured tones of the upper crust mingled with slang-laden Cockney. Mary frowned at the ring, bouncing against Constance's bodice, and cast a wary glance to the left. "You should tuck that out of sight, my lady. This place is crawling with riff-raff."

Constance looked in the same direction. A short distance away, by a ginger-beer stall, were three rough-looking young men. The youngest was a red-haired, freckled urchin, wearing a newsboy cap and ragged pants too large for him. The second was maybe sixteen, with swarthy skin and a muscular build, under his smudged white shirt. He sported close-cropped black hair, and a harsh expression.

The third was by far the most interesting. He looked about her age. Tall and slender, he wore rust-colored checkered trousers, an emerald-green striped waistcoat, and a battered bowler hat. Even more curious was his hair. It was blond, straight, and hung almost to his shoulders.

Jane gasped and grabbed her hand. "What a disreputable-looking person. And he's staring right at you."

She almost laughed in her cousin's face. Men stared at Jane, not bookish, brown-haired Constance. She turned, about to say so, when she met his gaze and gasped as well.

Jane was right.

As their eyes met, he tipped his hat, and a slanted, boyish grin lit his sharp, but handsome features. Though his hair belonged on a highwayman in an old story, there was nothing cruel or threatening in his smile. Instead, it seemed to penetrate the depths of her misery, spreading warmth and light, gently leading her out. A curious, giddy thrill sent her pulse racing. Before she could stop herself, she smiled back.

"This way, my ladies. We need to get away from here," said Mary.

Jane and Mary hurried off. Reluctantly, Constance followed, yet kept looking back over her shoulder to keep him in her sights as long as possible. His hair and clothes were outlandish. No respectable person dressed that way. His attention should have shocked her. Yet his friendly eyes and sweet smile made her want to know him. This wasn't a man who would ever threaten or harm a woman. She was sure of it.

Then a tall girl with jet-black hair and rouged cheeks bounded up beside him. She grabbed his arm, and he laughed, favoring her with his beautiful smile. He drew something from his pocket and gave it to her. She kissed his cheek, stuck out her tongue at the dark-haired fellow, and flounced off again.

Constance's eyes stung as she turned away. How ridiculous to be jealous of one stranger and infatuated with another, even to the point of ascribing noble characteristics, despite much evidence to the contrary. These were poor East Enders with miserable lives. The girl was coarse and hard-looking. As for him, he was sure to be the criminal sort— a pickpocket, most likely. He'd made eyes at Constance even though he had a sweetheart. Not a person with whom she would ever want to associate.

Yet they seemed so happy. If only she could be like that girl, free to kiss a handsome young man. A girl free from fear, able to do as she pleased.

She turned back to where Jane and Mary were a moment ago, but now there were only strangers closing in on all sides. Momentarily disoriented, she looked up at the Crystal Palace's immense domed roof. If she headed back to the center atrium, she would find the Crystal Fountain. From there, she could make her way to the French lace exhibit, which they had planned to see next.

The corridors through the French exhibit were mobbed, but Jane and Mary were nowhere in sight. Perhaps they were looking for Constance. Trying to locate them on her own in this enormous building was futile. She needed to find a constable straight away.

A sign led her to the South Entrance, where the only constable was busy assisting a dowager and her companion. Waiting impatiently for him to finish, she watched the trains come and go from the adjacent railway station.

A well-dressed couple hurried past, the lady's gloved hand caught in the crook of her much-older husband's elbow. She seemed to struggle to keep up, but instead of slowing, her husband jerked his arm forward, nearly knocking her off balance. His threatening gaze quickly silenced her slight cry of protest.

Constance twisted the ribbon that rested against her neck.

Soon that would be her life. Twenty years from now, she would fasten a collar of bridal rubies on her own daughter and tell her, "This is better than poverty."

Unless.

Goosebumps prickled her arms as a terrifying idea suddenly flared to life. What if she were to board one of these trains and ride far away from everything she knew? When she disembarked, she would be just another girl. Not the Earl of Beverly's daughter. Not Lord Gaffney's betrothed. Merely a woman free to control her destiny.

Her eyes grew wide, and she quietly drew in a breath. A shiver danced up her spine. Could she really do it? Find a way out and begin a life on her own?

Her hand went to her bodice, where her ring lay hidden. If she sold it, she would have enough to live on until she found work. But what sort of work? A governess? A lady's maid? Either would put her back into her upper-crust circle. Then it came to her.

She could become a nurse like Florence Nightingale.

It was perfect! Miss Nightingale was well-born and would sympathize with an upper-class girl being forced into marriage. She would understand Constance's predicament and happily give her a job.

She clutched her hands together. First thing tomorrow morning, she would call on Miss Nightingale at St. Thomas Hospital. But returning home was out of the question. Who knew what her parents had planned? No. Tonight she must find lodging and for that, she needed more than the three shillings in her reticule. To get it, she would have to visit a pawnbroker.

She knew of none, but suspected they were plentiful in the

21

East End. A shame the blond pickpocket wasn't here. Surely, he would know where to go.

Queues were forming beneath small black-and-gold signs that marked each railway destination. Victoria Station. Ludgate Hill. Fenchurch Street. Wasn't Fenchurch Street in the eastern part of the city? From there, she could catch an omnibus. At least she hoped so.

Never having been to the East End, she didn't know what to expect. The papers were full of hair-raising stories of thieves, shameless women, and vicious fiends like the Tiger Bay Slasher. Yet the people waiting on the train looked only shabby, not threatening. A forward-thinking person should know there was nothing to fear.

Especially since what awaited back in Mayfair was far more frightening. Her family departed for Sussex in just three days. If she went, she was doomed to marry a monster.

If she were going to flee, it had to be now. She squared her shoulders and took her place in the queue.

⚜

An hour later, she came out of the railway station onto Fenchurch Street to find omnibuses collecting and discharging passengers. She boarded one with "Spitalfields & Whitechapel" painted on the side.

The cramped, sweltering bus crept along at an unbearable pace. Her feet ached, but there was no place to sit. Passengers stepped on her skirts as they pushed past. She worked her way to the rear and tried to peer around a burly workingman who stank of beer and sweat.

If only Jane were along for company, though her sheltered cousin would be utterly beside herself. Perhaps for excellent reason. Conscious of curious looks from the ragged passengers, she glanced down to make sure she'd hidden her ring. A bead of sweat tickled as it rolled down her back. Clutching the overhead bar tighter, she jostled along, as the conductor announced stops in unintelligible language.

She watched through the window for a pawnbroker's sign, but other passengers blocked her view. The sun, what she could see of it, had the soft glow of late afternoon. She needed to have this done by nightfall and find a place to stay. But where? The row of shops stretching north on Commercial Street looked promising, so she disembarked.

The air reeked of horse droppings. She lifted her skirts and stepped quickly around an enormous pile. If she wasn't careful, she would ruin her only pair of shoes.

At the corner of Commercial Street and Whitechapel Road, she considered her next move, baffled by what it might be. Dingy shops lined the street, but none with three gold balls hanging above the door. Ragged children played outside tenements so old they sagged against one another.

Several more passengers had climbed down from the bench atop the omnibus. Perhaps one of them could help. Turning back, her mouth dropped open at the sight of the red-haired boy from the Crystal Palace. Next came the girl and behind her... Constance caught her breath and her spirits soared. The moment the blond spotted her, his eyes widened. "Why, hullo there," he said in a Cockney-flavored voice as warm as sunshine.

He dropped the girl's hand and approached, grinning. Amid rubbish and poverty, he was a cheerful sight. The knot between her shoulder blades relaxed, and she no longer felt so alone. Even better, he seemed just as pleased to see her.

Then the scowling dark-haired boy pushed past him and grabbed the red silk ribbon holding her ring. With a painful tug, he yanked it from her neck and dashed off down the street. In a blink, the others followed.

Stunned, she splayed her hand across her bodice. Good Lord, she'd just been robbed! In desperation, she cried out. "Stop, thief!"

The few people on the street paid no attention. A small boy bounced a rubber ball against a concrete step. A stout woman hauled a wash-basket into a tenement. A costermonger minded his wagon of potatoes. Wouldn't anyone help a lady in distress? Apparently not. Seeing no other choice, she gathered her skirts and ran after them.

They were three streets ahead before she reached the first corner. Pressing on, she made it to one more corner before her heavy skirts and tight stays made it impossible to keep up. Sweating, exhausted and breathless, she collapsed against a stone wall and watched them disappear up Commercial Street.

Her ring, her only means of escape, was gone.

What a fool she was! The blond had seen her interest and used it so his friend could steal from her. If that weren't dreadful enough, she had smiled back, mistaking his greed for something else. She clenched her fist. Damn them. Damn him. In two days, two men had humiliated her, and this one wouldn't get away with it.

A small boy with a smudged face and matted hair scampered over. "'elp ye, Miss?"

She gulped in smelly air and steadied her voice. "Yes. I have just been robbed. Three boys and a girl. I need the constable immediately."

Or did she? The police would ask questions, such as why she was here. They would summon her parents. Father would lock her in the house until her wedding day. No, involving the police was out of the question.

The boy made a face. "Pah. Constable won' do nothin,' but those thieves ain't far. For a penny, I'll tell you where."

Confront the thieves on her own? The idea was outrageous, and potentially life-threatening, but what else could she do? At the moment, she could think of no better alternative, so she paid a penny from her dwindling funds and followed the boy's directions.

Walking north on Commercial Street, she passed shops, taverns, and a church with a soaring steeple. Maybe someone there could help, but the front door was locked. Even the churches had to guard against thieves.

She soldiered on, mentally rehearsing a speech that might persuade the blond pickpocket to return her property. The best approach was an appeal to his basic human decency — assuming he had any. If that didn't work, she would threaten him with the police.

At White Lion Street, she turned left. And stopped. And stared.

The hulking mansion stood three floors and took up most of the row. Peeling shingles curled up the sides of its mansard roof.

Vines clung to the cracked stucco walls. Closed dark shutters, like blackened eyes, covered the first and second-floor windows, but on the top floor, French doors opened onto delicate balconies. A polished brass knocker graced the red front door. An ornate black iron fence, which looked new, surrounded weed-choked gardens. The place had an ominous air of elegance and neglect.

Icy fear gave her pause, but the ring, her ticket to freedom, lay on the other side of that door. She touched her tender cheek. The dull throb was a reminder of her fate if she turned back.

It was a future she would do anything to escape. This was what it meant to be an independent woman. Florence Nightingale solved her own problems. Constance would do the same. The unlocked gate was a positive sign. Summoning her courage, she marched up the steps and knocked on the door.

CHAPTER THREE

A t the corner of Commercial and Dorset, five streets north of Whitechapel Road, Alex and his mates stopped running. Danny was at his heels, red-faced and excited, soaking it all in. Tim and Nancy laughed as they caught their breath. Tim mopped his sweaty face with his sleeve, clutching the girl's ring in his paw. "Didn't I tell you she was an easy mark? Wearin' gravney 'round her neck, just waitin' for me to grab it? Stupid nobs deserve what they get!"

Tim was full of himself as usual, and his boasting lit Alex's temper right up. "Why the bloody hell did you do that? I told you to leave her alone. So what do you do, but blag her jewels, right on the street! You're the stupid one. Tryin' to snatch and run, when there's three people with you?"

"Shut up, Black! I knew what I was doing! What was she going to do? Chase me down in her petticoats? I wasn't going to get caught."

The cocky arse needed to be put in his place. "Ain't about you, bloke. Didja think about Danny? Or Nancy?" And what about the girl? Right classy, she was. Not fit to be alone in this part of town.

At Nancy's name, Tim's scowl grew darker. "Well, ain't you just full o' concern for the ladies? The half-wit nob, and Nancy, too. Ain't one enough for you?"

That's what this was about. Though Tim wasn't one for following orders, he toed the line mostly. Nancy stood with Danny, watching Tim's fit. She'd not let on, but probably loved every minute of this.

Tim sneered. "You're our bleedin' don, an' you tell me I can't hit the easiest mark I seen all day? I oughta tell Count Zuko. He'd be right happy to know you've gone soft. Maybe you'd even take a thrashin' for me when I come back empty-handed!"

But Alex wouldn't be the one thrashed to keep Tim in line. Again, he looked at Nancy. This time, Tim saw it. "You fuckin' arse!" He charged forward. Alex shoved him back.

Nancy grabbed Tim's arm. "Quit it, both you lot! Throwin' fists at each other like a pair o' lushingtons!"

Tim jerked his arm away. "That's right, protect your bloody sweetheart! Go on, stay with him. See if I care!" He spat on the ground and then stormed off down Commercial Street.

Alex fumed at Nancy's little smirk, but he was just as steamed at himself for playing along. "Happy now? Your plan was a smashing success. He's green as hell."

Nancy snorted. "I didn't think he'd lose his head and pull a flimp in the middle of Whitechapel Road! He knows better."

A few streets north, Tim aimed a wide kick at a costermonger's wagon. The old man yelled something; Tim raised his fist and shouted back. Alex heaved a sigh. "He ain't thinking with his head right now. You got to talk to him, Nance, be straight with him. Ain't fair, playin' with him like that. Ain't fair to me, either."

Nancy looked down and kicked a loose brick with her boot. This was the closest he'd get to I'm sorry. "Lucy has my red dress, an' Minerva told me to wear it tonight." She turned east and walked off toward her friend's lodging house on Fashion Street.

Danny stared after her with wide eyes. "Blimey. She sure can cause a lot o' trouble."

Alex tilted his head toward the Count's house. He'd had enough theatrics for one afternoon.

They walked north on Commercial Street. The boy kept pace, but didn't say much. Alex didn't feel like talking, either. Passing the fruit seller's cart, his stomach reminded him he'd not eaten since this morning's bread. Who knew if there would be any supper left? Too banded to chance it, he stopped and dug a penny from his pocket. "Want one?" he asked Danny.

The lad shook his head. "Ain't got money."

No surprise there. "Two," he told the costermonger, pointing out the best apples in the basket. He tossed Danny the bigger one, and they sat down to eat on the front stoop of a nearby shop. The apple was mealy and sour. He looked closely, afraid it might be wormy, but there was no sign of a trail. Maybe it was his mood. A pretty girl he couldn't have put everything in a bad light. The fruit was clean, just bad tasting. He ate it anyway.

Danny wolfed down his like someone would take it if he didn't finish in a hurry. When he finished, he licked his fingers clean and looked over, a vexed expression on his dirty freckled face. "Black? If Tim don't bring in his share, will you get in trouble?"

"'Course not. Besides, Tim made share today."

He chewed his bottom lip. "How about me? Will the Count hurt you if I don' make share?" His voice dropped to a whisper. "'Cos I didn't. I ain't once yet."

The lad looked ready to cry, and Alex blinked in surprise. The boy feared for him. Strange it was, having someone care that way. "I know, but you will," he said, quietly. "Just takes time. 'Til then, I have you covered." He grinned, hoping to put the boy's mind at ease. "An' no one's going to hurt me, all right?"

Danny nodded, though he didn't look so sure. *Makes two of us, lad.* Instead of saying so, Alex clapped Danny on the back and rose to his feet. "Come on, let's get home."

The lad was a worry he didn't know how to solve. Danny had been at the mansion since May Day and still couldn't filch more than handkerchiefs. Alex and Luke had found him in an alley, soaking wet and half-starved. It never crossed their minds the boy might not take to the life. But they'd brought Danny in, so they had to look out for him.

Better to think about the society girl. Not too tall, not too short, and curvy in all the right places. Why the hell had she been on the Whitechapel bus? She'd smiled at him in the Crystal Palace. Maybe it meant something. Poor girls liked him well enough. Why not a rich one?

He had a mad notion of giving the swag back to her. Not that he would. They had to make share and a girl like her probably had twenty more. Not to put too fine a point on things, but he was a thief, a damn good one, thank you very much. He ran a crew; they had to make share, and that was that. The girl would be all right. She'd go to the constable who would do nothing about the theft, but would see to it she found her way back safely to wherever she belonged.

Laughter and music drifted out of the Four Farthings, and he caught the malty scent of ale as they passed. He might have stopped in, but not with Danny along. He couldn't watch the boy every minute and folks liked to give gin to the young ones so they could have a laugh when they got too lush. It had happened to him a few times years back, and he'd woken up in some strange place with his head pounding and his boots gone.

Maybe Spitalfields wasn't the best neighborhood and stealing for the Count not the best life, but he'd known far worse. Nobs like Society Miss would likely judge him for it, but there was a lot to be said for having a dry place to sleep and food to eat.

They went in the mansion's rear door, and downstairs to their room. Luke wasn't back yet. Dan flopped down on his straw mattress. Alex tossed his hat on his own mattress and unbuttoned his waistcoat. He was about to kick off his boots, when he heard voices coming from upstairs. Women's voices.

He returned to the backstairs. Passages that carried sound well connected the entire house. You could learn a lot back here. From the first floor landing, he listened to the raised voices coming from the parlor. There were three — Minerva's, Nancy's, and one he didn't know. The third voice was rich, like red velvet. Elegant. If she looked as good as she sounded, she'd be a fine sight.

The red velvet voice was angry. "How dare you look me in the eye and tell utter lies? You were there! You saw all of it!"

Nancy's stream of cussing meant she was lying. Now Minerva joined in and both were shouting at the third lass who got off a few choice words of her own. He eased open the hidden panel door and slipped into the dining room on the light footsteps that made him such a good thief. He stayed close to the wall to keep out of sight. From here, he had a clear look into the front parlor.

Nancy and Minerva stood side by side. Nancy had her red dress draped over her arm. Minerva stood close to the parlor door. Her tight hair and painted eyes reminded him of a snake he once saw at the London Zoo.

The third woman had her back turned. Her voice wasn't what he expected — older somehow, but he didn't need to see her face to know her. Not too tall, not too short, and curvy in all the right places.

"I insist you return my ring immediately, and if you don't... I shall go to the police."

But she wouldn't. That little pause just gave it away. Scared as she was, she'd come on her own to get the ring back. Society Miss was desperate, and in over her head.

"Will you?" Minerva's voice was as nasty as the woman herself. "Strange you didn't do that first, rather than barge into my home making wild accusations for which you have no proof. Could it be that you would rather not involve the constable?"

"Please return my property and I will leave and never breathe a word of this to anyone." This time, her voice trembled.

Nancy smirked. Minerva moved in like that zoo snake, ready to pounce on a meal. "Even if we had this ring you claim is yours, you don't expect us to simply hand it over, do you? We would want something in return. Do you have money?"

The girl took a slight step backward, but kept her head high and her voice haughty, like she was doing Minerva a favor. "Very well, then. We shall arrange a bargain. What is it you require? A lady's maid? Garden help?"

Garden help. He bit back a laugh. She had brass, he'd give her that, but this wouldn't end well. He kept out of Minerva's business, but knew virgins fetched a top price in the brothel. He wouldn't stand by while that happened.

He stepped out into the open, hands in his pockets and a smile on his face. "Hullo, Minerva. Did I hear your friend say she wants a job?"

The girl whirled around and stared wide-eyed. "You!" She jabbed her finger at him. "You did this. I want my ring back, and I insist you give it to me! Otherwise, I'll have you thrown in gaol."

It pained him to see her so angry, especially since he'd told Tim to leave her alone — not that she'd believe it. "Wish I could, luv. But I ain't got it. Tim's turned it over to our employer, and he'll not give it back. Not to me. Not to anyone."

Minerva's upper lip curled. "What are you doing up here? Don't you have anything better to do than meddle with my business?"

The old bag had no right to talk to him that way. She worked for the Count, same as him. "I say you meddled in mine, when you coaxed Nancy to leave my crew for a fancier line o' work." He stood next to the girl. "Seein' as I'm the one short-handed, I'm sure the Count would say I call dibs on any new employees."

"Employees?" The girl watched with angry brown eyes fringed by long lashes. Up close, she was even prettier, all high

33

cheekbones, pink cheeks, and creamy skin. Her face was heart-shaped, her lips soft red, like summer berries. Her hat and long brown hair hung down her back.

She took a deep breath, trying to get herself under control. She looked up with eyes that were true and honest. "Please, I must have this ring back. It... it means everything to me. I promise, if you give it to me, I will leave and you will never see me again."

She didn't lie or play games, this one. He'd be honest with her in return. "I appreciate that, miss, and if I had it, I would give it to you. But I don't." Her face fell, just a little. "Still, if you're willing, you can earn it back."

She crossed her arms. "Just how am I supposed to do that?"

"Depends. You work for Minerva here, you'll earn it on your back." Her wide-eyed shock made him grin a little. "But if you work for me, you can earn it on your feet."

"As a *pickpocket?*" She didn't seem to like this idea any better.

"I like 'thief', but that pretty much sums it up. You've already seen one of our capers close up, and from the way you took on Minerva here, I'd say you have the guts for it. So what'll it be? Upstairs with Minerva and the girls, or downstairs with me and the lads?"

"Neither. I'm leaving this minute." She hiked her skirts and charged toward the parlor door. It was locked, of course. She pounded on it twice, and whirled around, panicked as a sparrow about to be stuffed in a pie.

Then Max, the Count's ugliest punisher, came in and stood behind Minerva. The old whore arched an eyebrow. "You're not going anywhere."

Max took a step towards the small, scared girl. Alex slipped his hand into his trouser pocket, where his switchblade waited, ready. Her gaze shifted wildly from the hulking, bald brute to Minerva to Alex.

"You," she said. "I'll go with you."

CHAPTER FOUR

S he rushed to his side, standing as close as she could without touching.

Minerva glared, angry he'd won. She would run straight to the Count, but he didn't give a damn. Society Miss didn't belong in a whorehouse. Not that picking pockets was a fancy life, but at least in the basement he could watch over her until she went back to wherever she came from. He cocked his head toward the backstairs. "This way."

She followed him through the dining room. At the dark passage, she drew back. He took a candle from the sideboard to light the way. He went in first and offered his arm. She looked back over her shoulder at Minerva and Max. Deciding he was the lesser of two evils, she took it and let him lead her downstairs. In the dark, she clutched his elbow and stayed close. She smelled like the purple flowers that grew in Victoria Park. He was just glad he'd bothered to wash this morning. They came out in the basement, near the old kitchen, and she quickly let go.

"Here's where we stay. Count Zuko charges us each a pound a week for our rooms and supper. You pay him out of what you bring in." He glanced around to make sure they were alone. No one was close by, but he used a quiet voice, just the same.

"'Course once you make share, if you keep some for yourself, no one has to be the wiser."

"What a strange name, Count Zuko," she said, in a dazed voice. "I doubt he's even gentry, let alone of noble birth."

Alex laughed. "Bloke's no more high-born than me. Claims he's a count from Budapest, but it ain't true. He's from Budapest, all right, but he's just a plain ol' crook. Anyway, there's nine of us down here. All lads, 'cept for you. We share rooms, but you'll have a private place."

She crossed her arms tight across her body and looked scared to death, but nodded, trying to act brave. She fixed her eyes on the front of him. He looked down. With his waistcoat unbuttoned, there was nothing to keep his shirt closed. Society Miss wasn't used to seein' blokes undone. He closed it as best he could. "Sorry. Lost me buttons."

Society types liked it when folks used polite manners. He didn't know any, but cleared his throat and stood stiffly, like the doormen outside the Royal Hotel. "My name's Alexander Blackwood, but everyone calls me Black. I go by Alex, too. If you prefer." He tried to make a proper bow, though he felt like an ass and almost lit his hair on fire with the candle.

For his trouble, he got a brief smile that tugged the corner of her mouth. She stood straighter and seemed to get back some of her moxie. "I am Lady Constance Eleanor Barrett, formerly of Mayfair. My father is Roland Barrett, Earl of Beverly."

How about that? Not just a lady, but an honest-to-goodness Lady. Titled nobility running with him and his crew of street thieves. This strange turn made him laugh out loud. "Well, 'at's right nice, Lady Constance. My mum was Annie, the most prized whore in all of Shadwell. I look forward to us becoming very good friends."

She made a small gasp and covered her mouth. For an awful moment, he thought he'd made her cry, but she was laughing, right along with him.

It made no sense. Here they were in a crook's mansion, with whores above stairs and thieves below. She'd just had everything she owned stolen away. He was going to turn her into a pickpocket. There wasn't much to be happy about. Yet right then, they were. Everything else fell away, and it was just them, Constance the lady and Alex the thief, laughing together. The walls between them weren't gone exactly, but for the moment, they didn't seem to matter much. His gaze met hers in the soft glow of candlelight. And the strangest thought came to him.

He wanted to kiss those berry-red lips of hers, and he didn't think she would mind.

Still, he didn't do it. For one, he meant to send her packing as soon as possible. This was no place for a girl like her, especially if Minerva wanted her, too. Besides, she belonged with fine gents, not the likes of him. He belonged with Spitalfields whores, not

Mayfair society girls. A shame things couldn't be different, but he was what he was. She was what she was. He had no business kissing her, or even thinking about it.

Almost like she'd read his mind, she looked away and tugged at her little lacy gloves. He looked down at his scuffed black boots, not sure what to say next.

Be honest, just like she'd be with you.

He looked her in the eye and did his best. "I'm sorry you ended up here. Tim did what he had to and I'll not apologize for him, but I give you my word. I'll help you earn your money back and be on your way."

She answered with a single nod.

He took her to their room. Luke, back from Sally Browning's, had his fiddle out. Danny lounged on his mattress playing Scratch Cradle. When they laid eyes on Lady Constance, Luke stopped playing and Danny tossed aside his string. "Cor, blimey!" Danny said. "Whas' she doin' here?"

"This is Lady Constance. She'll be stayin' with us, learnin' the life. Luke, you're bunkin' with Jimmy now."

"Aww come on, Black. That glock snores!"

Alex glared, reminding Luke who was in charge. Luke took the hint. Remembering how to treat a lady, he brushed his hair from his eyes and bobbed a greeting to Lady Constance. "Nice to meet you, miss." He turned to Alex. "You want, she can have my spot."

"I'm puttin' her in Danny's," Alex said. The room's left corner was farthest from the door. It wasn't much protection, but it was the best he could do. Soon enough, Count Zuko would find out she was down here. If anyone came after her, they'd have to get

39

past him first. "Danny, go out to the stable and find a blanket for Lady Constance. For a curtain," he added, seeing her shock. Danny left and Luke set to work gathering his things.

"Tim back?" Alex asked.

"Back, an' boasting' 'bout some big swag he filched today. Went straight up to tell the Count about it." Luke, no fool, took in Lady Constance's fancy gown and figured out the rest. "He ain't gonna be happy to see her, is he?"

"Doubt it. Besides that, Nancy tried to make him green by hangin' on me all day. Worked too bloody well."

Luke laughed. "Lookin' to give you a do-down, is he?"

"Like to see him try." From the corner of his eye, he saw Lady Constance hanging on every word. He shrugged. "I'll stay clear of him. He'll cool down soon enough."

Danny brought the horse blanket. Luke found a hammer and some rope. Together they rigged up a curtain for her to sleep behind. Jimmy dragged in a wooden pallet from the alley and they lifted her mattress onto it, to keep some of the vermin away. Alex gave her his spare blanket, folded in a bundle. It wouldn't be easy to sleep with just a curtain between him and her curvy-in-all-the-right-places body. But there was no other place to put her. She needed protection. Most of the lads were all right, but he didn't trust Tim as far as he could throw him.

The rest of the crew was back, so he left her with Luke and went to the kitchen. Pete once said it used to be a servant's hall — back a hundred years ago when a rich Frenchman lived here. He poured a cup of beer, sat down in his usual spot near the fireplace, and took out his ledger.

Little Jack had brought in a handful of coins and two silk

handkerchiefs. One had fine lace trim and would fetch a good price. "Got that off a swell comin' out of St. Paul's," the lad said. "Bloke wasn't too happy 'bout gettin' robbed outside the bloody church!"

Alex laughed, pushing past the guilt that stung every now and again. He noted the take in his ledger. Jack was off to a promising start this week.

One by one, the lads brought their daily take. He wrote the amounts next to the symbol he used for their name. Danny, the last to come forward, had just three billies and none as nice as Little Jack's. Alex said nothing to Danny; he didn't need to. The boy knew he wasn't pulling his weight. Soon enough the Count would catch on, but until then, Alex would let it lie. He noted Danny's take next to the cross that signified his name, since they'd found him behind St. Mary's Church on Whitechapel Road.

Last up was Tim. He tossed a few coins on the table and got down low in Alex's face. "You can write in that little book o' yours that I done made me share… for the bloody week." Big John, Little Jack, and the Irish brothers gathered round, clapping Tim on the back. Tim pulled out his flask, toasted himself and drank. "The Count's got plans for me, away from you lot."

"That so?" He drew a line beside Tim's symbol, a black diamond, then gathered up his ledger and the pile of coins and handkerchiefs. He stuffed the loot into a leather bag. "I'll be sure to ask him about it."

Tim narrowed his eyes, ready for a fight. "Don' believe me, do you?"

He didn't rise to it. "Wasn't what I said. Just plan to ask is all."

He took the backstairs to the attic, staying clear of the whorehouse. Clients would arrive soon and Minerva always said her fine customers didn't want to see the likes of him. Just as well. He didn't want to see them either.

What plans did Count Zuko have for Tim? Probably collections — going round to people who owed money and taking it out in cash or flesh, depending. Nasty business, but if Tim did it, Alex wouldn't have to.

Viktor Zuko sat behind his monstrous desk in a chair that looked just like a throne, heavy and carved, with red cushions. He wore evening clothes, ready for wherever he was off to tonight. The chamber door was open and one of Minerva's girls lounged in the bed, a sheet covering her bare breasts.

The Count was sipping claret and poured some for him. "You will enjoy this," said Zuko in a silky, accented voice. "It's 1855 Chateau Margaux. Quite expensive. Much better than what you have downstairs."

Before he tasted, Alex swirled the wine in his glass to release its smells, just like the Count taught him. He smelled grapes and smoke. He tasted and held the wine in his mouth, letting the flavors spread across his tongue. Rich, almost buttery. Not at all bitter. The Chateaux whatever-it-was, was excellent. His employer knew all about fine things. "I think this would be wasted on the lads," he said.

Zuko snorted. "Your crew doesn't care what's put in front of them, as long as there's enough to get drunk. You, however, appreciate quality and I am pleased to share."

The Count propped his feet on the desk and gazed out the west window that stretched from the floor to the ceiling. There was one on each side of the room. Three of the windows had balconies, but the fourth which faced the rear courtyard, had only a straight drop to the ground.

All the windows opened.

From here, the Count could see his entire kingdom, from the thieves' dens and brothels on the East End to the fancy clubs and gambling hells on the West End. Viktor Zuko ran London, not that the swells would ever admit it. He held up the ring they took from Lady Constance and peered with glittering black eyes. "Tim's take for today was impressive. But you tried to talk him out of it. Why would you do that?"

Alex steadied his breath, though his fingers tensed on the stem of his wineglass. "Too risky. Too many people round. Besides, Nancy and Danny were with us."

"Oh, yes. That would be the boy who likes handkerchiefs." The Count's voice was light, but there was menace behind the words. "He doesn't seem to have much ambition. Perhaps a visit from Max would motivate him."

The threat was clear, either to Danny or to him. His shoulder muscles clenched at the memory of Max's whip, slicing open his skin. But he stayed still and looked the Count in the eye, careful as always to show no fear. "Dan's learnin,'" he said. He lifted the bag from his lap and dropped it on the Count's desk. It landed with a solid thud. "Add it up. We all made share this week."

Zuko counted the loot twice, then smiled. "You don't disappoint me. However, picking pockets is a boy's job. You're about to turn twenty and it's time for bigger responsibilities."

Alex sipped his wine, as if it didn't matter a whit to him. "But I'm good at running your crew. Why not bring Tim up? He's tuggin' at the bit for it. Said he was workin' for you this week."

"I'm sending him out with Ulysses to visit some of our delinquent accounts. Tim is useful when certain skills are required. But for you, Alexander... I have other plans." Zuko steepled his fingers and looked out the west window. "I am a powerful man, but it has come at a price. People are reluctant to trust me." He gave an empty laugh and turned back with a vicious smile. "Yet you are charming, attractive. You behave as a gentleman and appear trustworthy. I can use that to my advantage and yours, provided you do as you are told." The Count poured more wine in Alex's glass. "Minerva tells me this afternoon you brought in a lovely young lady."

"She ain't that lovely."

Zuko's laugh showed he saw through the lie. "Minerva says otherwise. I'm pleased by your effort and want to see more."

"I need her for my crew. With Nancy gone, I'm short-handed."

"And you may keep her. Provided she's productive. But I have plans for her, if she doesn't pull her weight."

"I'll see that she does."

"Good. If I have one concern, it is that you are too soft. There is no room in this world for sentiment. Emotions must never prevent you from acting in your best interests. Or mine."

He returned to the basement, passing the scullery and the heavy wooden door that led to the cellar — where the Count's bashers did their work. He'd been down there only a few times and never by choice. The comfort he gave Danny rang false. If the boy didn't improve, they would haul him or the lad down there for a lashing while the others had to watch. The Count was right. There was no room here for mercy.

Pete hadn't wanted to live that way. The Count saw to it Pete didn't have to.

He pushed aside the black memories and made his way back to the warmth and light of the kitchen. All the lads were here, boxed in for the night, but considering what they'd come from, it was a trade they were willing to make. Outside were poverty, hunger, and the workhouse. Here, they had food, drink, and each other, the closest most of them had to family.

His crew greeted him. Even Tim, soaked in the Count's praise and the good gin that had been his reward, clapped him on the shoulder. No hard feelings mate, though there was spite in Tim's eyes when he looked at Lady Constance. She stayed far away from him, too. Another reason Tim working for the Count this week was a fortunate thing.

He helped himself to victuals. Blood pudding tonight. Between the coppery taste and chewy bits of fat and gristle, it wasn't one of his favorites, but when you were hungry, you ate what they gave you.

Afterward, the cards and dice came out, as they usually did. Luke fetched his fiddle, Jimmy his guitar. Danny grabbed a pair of spoons and rapped out a rhythm on a wooden keg. Lady Constance picked at her supper. Blood pudding probably wasn't on the menu much in Mayfair.

He played a hand of whist with one of the Irish brothers and Little Jack. Little Jack cheated and won. The second hand Alex paid more attention and won, but when he looked up, Lady Constance was gone. He went to their room. Her bed was empty. He found her at the back door, crouched in the dark, trying to pick the lock with a hairpin.

She gasped and whirled around, holding the hairpin like a tiny sword.

The wide-eyed terror he'd seen in the parlor was back. If only things could have stayed the way they were when they laughed in the hallway. He gave her his most fearsome scowl, and with the lightning-fast hands of a good thief, seized her wrist. "Give it to me."

Her sweet lips parted in a small cry. Beneath his grip, he felt delicate bones and soft, clean skin. Her body tensed and she released the hairpin. He loomed over her, but let go of her wrist. "You don't want to do that. Lotta rough characters about. Besides, door's bolted on the outside."

She shrank back, rubbing her wrist. "Why? To keep the rough characters out? Or keep us in?"

Good. He'd scared her. Maybe she'd have the sense to go home. "This is no place for you. In the morning, I'm taking you back to Mayfair."

She tilted her chin and crossed her arms under her breasts. "No, you're not." He stared, surprised, until she turned away and he saw something he missed before. A shadow across her right cheekbone. The dark beginning of a bruise. It matched the ones on her upper left arm, which she tried to cover with her little puffed sleeve. Those bruises were from fingers pressing into her flesh, as someone held her with one hand and struck her with the other.

Whatever she'd run from was bad enough to make her choose a life among thieves rather than go back.

An odd mix of tenderness for her, and black rage at whoever left those marks, came over him. Emotions he quickly squelched.

46

Tender feelings were dangerous for him, and for her. Once more, he set his face into a scowl. "Expect to earn your keep then, starting tomorrow. Off to bed, now."

He reached for her arm, but she pulled away. With guarded eyes, she moved past. She looked at the candle in his hand. "May I have that, please?"

He gave it to her and with the step of a fine lady, she walked down the hall to their room. He waited by the door until the dim light went out. Only then did he return to the kitchen.

CHAPTER FIVE

G et up."

The rough command yanked her from sleep. Constance forced her eyes open. Her neck ached, her back was stiff, and standing over her in the dim room, was the blond pickpocket she had been so mistaken about yesterday.

This wasn't just a dreadful dream.

She pulled the blanket up to her chin, even though she was dressed. "What are you doing here?"

He pushed back the horse blanket they'd hung as a curtain. Behind him, light filtered in through the filthy window above the boy pickpocket's bed. "Time to go to work. You're comin' with me to the city."

The city? What on earth was he talking about? It was hardly past daybreak. Then, becoming fully awake, she gasped. "Good heavens! You want me to steal from people? You can't be serious! I don't have the faintest idea how to —"

"I bloody well knew that," he snapped. "You're not stealing this morning. You'll watch me, then we'll come back here and I'll teach you. Hurry now. We're catching the bus to Princes Street."

"But someone might recognize me! My father's club is nearby. My fiance does business at the Bank of England! No, I can't possibly come with you, at least not there."

He let out an exasperated sigh. She held her breath. Her escape to a new life could be thwarted before it began. Not that she was eager to become a pickpocket. She must treat it as an odious means to an end, something for which she would make restitution through future good deeds. Her zealous commitment to mankind would impress Miss Nightingale.

"Fine," he said, with a terse nod. "You can stay here today. There's wash to be done, and no one's swept the kitchen. Tea's gone, too." He dug a coin from his pocket and tossed it to her. "The shop's on Commercial Street. Buy what you can with that."

She fumbled to keep the sixpence in her hand. "You expect me to be your *maid?*"

"Think you're too good for it, do you? I expect you to earn your keep and since you can't do it on the streets, you'll do it here. Now get to it, so I can teach you when I get back." He went to his mattress, gathered up his sheet and dirty clothes, and tossed them into a pile. "Wash those. I'll tell the others to bring you what they have."

When everyone had left and the basement was quiet, a heap of dirty sheets, shirts, trousers and unmentionables awaited in the middle of the room. She hadn't the faintest idea what to do with them.

She carried the smelly bundle to the kitchen, still cluttered with the remains of last night's meal. Cold blood pudding sounded unspeakably repulsive, so a crust of stale bread would have to do. Chewing on her meager breakfast, she contemplated the problem of the laundry.

A large kettle hung above the fireplace. She could use that to wash the clothes. But there was no fire and no one around to start one, as morning was apparently a splendid time for picking pockets. No one had told her where to find water, either.

The scullery pump turned out to be dry, though perhaps there was water in the cellar. She opened the door and peered down the stone steps, into Stygian darkness. A decayed, coppery stench, like rotten blood pudding, drifted up. She slammed the door and shuddered. Nothing in the world would make her go down there.

There was a pump outside and after laboring in the sweltering sun, she got a trickle of water flowing into the kettle. When it was full, she tried to lug it back downstairs, but could not lift it. Grasping the lip of the kettle with both hands, she dragged it down to the kitchen, spilling water as she went. By the time she reached the fireplace, the kettle was half-empty, but at least she could lift it. Using every ounce of strength, she hoisted it onto the hook. More water slopped out, drenching both her and the inside of the fireplace.

She dumped coal into the burner and struck a safety match to light the fire. One lump smoldered, but the match burned down to her fingers before the rest ignited. She tried again. And again. And again. She tossed the matchbox aside and wiped the perspiration from her brow. No fire, no boiling water.

She would do her best with cold water. She pushed the clothes around in the kettle by hand, spilling more water and soaking the coal beneath. Black water collected on the floor, staining the hem of her gown.

When the clothes seemed clean enough, she wrung out each dingy item and carried as many as she could to the clothesline in the backyard. She stood beneath it, but it was too high to reach. There was a concrete bench beneath a tree, but it was anchored to the ground. Didn't the fiddle-playing pickpocket own a stool? She left the wet clothes on the bench and trudged inside. She found the stool, brought it back to the garden and hung the clothes. Problem solved. She returned to the kitchen for another load. Soon, she was as wet as the laundry.

The broiling sun beat down. The rotten-egg summer stench of the Thames, hardly noticeable in Mayfair, was overwhelming here. Sweat beaded across her bosom and itched inside her stays. The rest of her itched too, from tossing and turning on a straw mattress. Her hair stuck to her neck. She was covered in coal-water and dirt. A cooling lavender bath, a light luncheon, and a nap in her soft bed on Bruton Street sounded like heaven. But she was no longer a lady of leisure and there was work to do.

Rather than traipse back and forth, she hauled the kettle to the courtyard. The blond pickpocket should return soon. Although she had not made it to the grocer's and the kitchen floor was not only dusty but wet, he would surely be impressed by what she'd accomplished.

She could not have been more wrong.

"Bloody hell!" he said in dismay, taking in the kettle and the dripping, dingy laundry hanging everywhere. "Are you too lazy to boil the damned water?"

Lazy? She had worked harder today than she ever had in her life! Every muscle in her body ached. She'd washed most of the laundry. But all he could do was yell and call her lazy.

"How dare you?" she shouted back. "At least I've done honest work, which is more than I can say for you!"

His eyes narrowed with contempt. "Say what you want, Society Miss. It takes guts and smarts to be a good thief. Any half-wit knows you boil water to wash clothes."

"I knew," she muttered through gritted teeth.

His mouth fell open. "Then why the hell didn't you do it?"

His angry face made her want to be anywhere else. Her bottom lip trembled and her eyes burned. "Because I don't know how!" Her voice sounded thick and moist.

He stared, dumbstruck. "You're serious?"

She turned away to hide the tears brimming in her eyes. With a curse, he stalked off.

She fell to her knees beside the kettle. Seething, she pushed the clothes around in the cold gray water. She might as well go back to Mayfair and marry Gaffney. What gave her the preposterous idea she could become a nurse for Florence Nightingale? She couldn't boil water. She couldn't light a fire. She couldn't do anything. She shook the dirty water from her hands and rested her elbows on the kettle. Unable to hold back any longer, she let the tears flow, dripping down her cheeks into the wash water.

After a little while, she sensed someone nearby. She looked up. He stood beside her, his hands shoved in his pockets. She braced for more insults.

They didn't come. Instead, his eyes held sympathy, maybe even compassion. "Why would you know how? You've not had to do it before and no one's ever taught you, have they?"

"No." She sniffed and wiped the lingering tears away, hating that she was so useless.

"Come on, then. I'll show you."

They went inside, following the trail of water on the stone floor. At the hearth, he pushed aside the pile of damp coal, then took a handful of wood and paper scraps from a box beside the fireplace. He laid them in the burner and placed small chunks of coal on top. "This is your small coal and you light it first."

He struck a match and held it to the scraps. Small flames ignited and licked the chunks of coal. He knelt beside the hearth and blew gently on the small blaze. The flames grew. "Once you have it going, you add more coal, a bit at a time." He added a few more pieces and gave her the poker. "When the bigger pieces light, you break them up and add a little more. See how it works?"

She did as he instructed and soon had a steady fire burning. It was simple, really. "I started with a large pile and couldn't get it to light," she said.

"An easy mistake," he said. "Especially if someone's always done it for you."

Maybe she hadn't been wrong about him, though she wasn't sure why it mattered. In a few weeks she would have her money, leave Spitalfields, and never see him again. They stood quietly, watching the fire grow. Then he turned and appeared to study her for a moment. "I'll bring the pot in so you can finish up. Your lessons can wait 'til tomorrow."

He brought the kettle and hung it in the fireplace, then went away again. He returned with a folded bundle. She groaned at the thought of more clothes to wash, but the shirts and trousers were crisp and clean-smelling.

"Those are for you," Alex said. "Nancy wore them when she was down here. You might prefer them to what you have on."

"Thank you," she said, grateful to have something to wear besides her filthy dress. Tired as she was, she felt a little thrill that she would get to wear trousers after all. She set the clothes on the table, and expected him to leave, but he took a seat on the bench.

The room was silent except for the quiet hiss of the fire and the sloshing of the laundry as she stirred. Her face felt warm. Maybe it was from the fire, but maybe not. She was aware of his every breath as he sat on the bench, watching. She remembered the tingling she'd felt when he smiled.

"So, Lady Constance, are you ever going to tell me why you were on the Whitechapel bus?"

Her mind sounded a warning. He had been harsh last night and earlier today. He was a criminal. Yet his regret over the theft seemed genuine. Once he got past his anger about the laundry, he'd tried to help. She recalled his sweet smile in the Crystal Palace. He was not smiling now, yet she detected kindness and humor in his blue eyes and the gentle curve of his mouth.

At least she thought she did. Perhaps it was just wishful thinking, brought on by a silly infatuation.

Who was the real Alex? She didn't know for certain, but considered herself a good judge of character. Initially, he'd seemed trustworthy. She would follow her hunch. "I was looking for a pawnbroker," she said.

His brows shot up. "A jerryshop? What for?"

"Because I had decided to become a nurse. Though now, I'm not so sure."

"Oh?" He shook his head, as if trying to make sense of it. "Must be quite a story."

"I suppose it is."

He leaned forward, his elbows resting on his knees. "Well, then. Let's hear it."

She began with her acceptance to Girton College and ended with her escape from the Crystal Palace. The only thing she didn't mention was Gaffney's slap. As she talked, he helped her move the laundry from the pot to the line. Once they'd hung the clothes, they sat in the shade on the concrete bench. The smell of the river was still heavy in the scorching afternoon, but not as strong as before.

Alex leaned back against the tree and stretched out his long legs. "So you ran away because this Lord Henry bloke wanted someone else?" He shook his head. "What a bloomin' fool."

Did he mean Gaffney? Or her? "It really wasn't about him," she insisted. "It hurt, knowing they had parceled me off to someone who didn't want me, but I didn't want him either. And his proper name is Gaffney, not Henry."

Alex scowled. "Henry? Horace? Don' right care what he's called. Is he the one who bruised your arm and cheek?"

Her cheeks flushed. Despite her efforts, he'd noticed the

marks. "He wasn't a pleasant man," she whispered.

"Then why did your family want you to marry him?"

Because no one else would have her, though she wasn't about to admit that. She shook her head and laughed bitterly. "It's what proper girls are expected to do. Not go off to university, and certainly not become pickpockets!" She pushed back her heavy hair. "People in my world marry for plenty of reasons other than love."

"People in my world don't even bother," he said, tearing a leaf into strips. "What's the point when you only got a good year or two?"

Good heavens! She'd heard East Enders had loose morals and cared little for conventions such as marriage. It must be true. "Well," she said tightly. "I suppose if one enters a union intending to leave whenever they please, there really isn't a point."

He started to reply, but seemed to think better of it. A wise choice, as his position was indefensible. "So you didn't love Horace and Horace didn't love you —"

"Henry," she corrected him.

He rolled his eyes. "Fine. *Henry*. But your family wanted you to be a proper society miss and marry him instead of going off to some fancy school?"

"Yes. And that's why I ran away to become a nurse."

"Except you changed your mind."

"I'm not sure I have the proper temperament, to be honest. I can't do anything practical. I loathe the sight of blood and people who go on about their ailments try my patience." She sighed. "I think I have a better idea of what I don't want than what I do want. I must seem quite foolish."

"Not really. Can't say I know what it's like to want to go to a fancy school or work for Florence Nightingale, but I know what you mean about the rest of it. About knowing what you don't want."

"You do?" This surprised her. She would have thought him content with his lot. "What don't you want?"

Alex shrugged. "This. I don' mean bein' here with the lads, but once I turn twenty, the Count wants me upstairs, bringin' in fresh girls for Minerva, and smooth-talkin' the shopkeeps into payin' protection money."

She flinched. "And you don't want to do that?"

"Don' matter if I do or not. The Count's made up his mind. He thinks I'll be good at it because I can get people to trust me."

She kept staring straight ahead, afraid to even look at him. The Count was obviously a shrewd man. For a dangerous moment, she too had been seduced by Alex's charm and forgot what he was — a criminal who would use his charisma to extort money and lure innocents, just like her, into prostitution. He was not her friend and never would be. Sky-blue eyes and a beautiful smile did not change that.

This was a strange and dangerous place. She must keep her wits if she hoped to survive.

CHAPTER SIX

In the two weeks that had passed since she arrived at the mansion, Constance had done more domestic chores than she ever knew existed. She washed clothes, swept floors, tidied the kitchen, and stocked the cupboards. Her efforts weren't perfect, but the lads were grateful and easy to please. She was exhausted at the end of each day, but also felt an unexpected sense of accomplishment.

Though still angry with her parents, she knew they must be worried sick. Mother never handled trouble well. Father likely had the entire London police searching. Jane surely blamed herself; Fletcher would be equally distraught. She considered posting a letter to Jane or Fletcher, then thought better of it.

Loyalty to her parents, or misplaced concern, might compel them to reveal what they knew.

Even if her family relented and didn't force her to marry Gaffney, it was only a matter of time before they arranged another betrothal. If her prospects had been dim to begin with, jilting Gaffney wouldn't help matters. No, even blood pudding and petty crime were preferable to a miserable marriage.

She did not want to steal, yet saw little choice. She owed room and board to a criminal. Bringing in at least a pound a week would be a challenge, but if she didn't, Alex would send her to the brothel. For now, he was covering her share, but that wouldn't last forever.

She also needed money to begin her new, independent life. Ten pounds ought to give her a comfortable start, and Danny had already shown her the loose brick under his mattress that was the basement's best hiding place. If she tucked away a few coins each day, before long, she could walk away from Spitalfields. As the days went by, she wanted to get started.

One evening after dinner, she told Alex she was ready to begin her apprenticeship.

"You're sure?" His voice carried a note of unease.

She was.

<hr/>

In her boy's disguise, she rode the bus with Alex and Danny to central London, blending into the sea of workers bound for banks, exchanges, and offices. This was a foreign world; the handful of gentlemen she knew who held professions spoke more about lunching at their clubs than what they did during working hours.

Watching Alex relieve bankers of their purses and watches was nothing short of amazing. He was so fast, she barely saw his hands at work. Danny was far less skilled. After he took a purse from a distracted gentleman outside Barclay's Bank, Alex praised him enthusiastically, but the red-haired boy looked miserable. "What if the man needs his purse? What if he can't eat or gets kicked out of his rooms 'cause I took all his money?"

"You didn't take all his money," Alex replied. "Did you see his coat and hat? The gent won't starve 'cause you filched two bob from him. We're just takin' from the rich to help the poor, Dan. Like Robin Hood. There's honor in what we do."

Was that how he justified it? The first night, she'd found a book tucked inside the blanket he gave her, a cheap penny dreadful entitled *The Adventures of Robin Hood and His Merry Men*. The cover showed a handsome young man with long, blond hair.

After a morning of prowling the streets for bounty, they returned to the mansion. That afternoon, Alex began to teach her the tricks of his trade.

They started with handkerchiefs, which she soon mastered. Encouraged, Alex and Luke showed her a scam where one pretended to beg while the other robbed unsuspecting marks. Then Alex hung his black frock coat from the clothesline and she practiced plucking things from the pockets without moving it.

To her surprise, she had a knack for it. But the lessons grew harder.

It was a sweltering Saturday afternoon, the sort of day she would have spent under a shade tree on her family's Sussex estate with a book and a glass of lemonade. Instead, she was in Spitalfields, sweating in an overgrown courtyard as a pickpocket and a prostitute demonstrated the finer points of street theft. Alex played the gent, Nancy the sly pickpocket. Over and over, he stashed a watch case and a small purse into his pockets. Over and over, Nancy retrieved them.

"Go on over there," Alex said, gesturing toward the opposite end of the courtyard. "All you have to do is bump me on the path and take my money like Nancy did. Easy."

Except it wasn't. When her shoulder brushed his arm, she plunged her hand into his frock coat. She was so intent on reaching for the purse; she did not realize he'd stopped walking. "Bloke will notice that, don't you think?" he said, as he watched with a bemused expression.

Next, she tried to take the watch from his waistcoat, but when she fit her fingers into the small front pocket, he jumped back, laughing. "Bloke will definitely notice that!"

Her face burned. Pretending to beg, or pulling a purse from an empty coat was one thing. Invading someone's person was quite another. His next suggestion was even more shocking. "You want me to put my hand where?"

"Right here, luv." He pointed to the side pocket of his trousers and grinned, as if he enjoyed making her uncomfortable. "How are you going to rob me if you won't reach in?"

"But I can't do that! It isn't proper!"

61

Alex ran his hand through his hair. "Of course it's not proper. It's theft, not a bleedin' garden party!"

She rubbed the angry scratch on her arm, left by an untended rose bush. Indeed, this was no garden party. Alex returned to the opposite end of the path. "Back over there now. Let's try it again."

She took a deep breath. She could do this. She marched down the path, concentrating on the task at hand.

"Why are you staring at the ground? Sidewalk ain't goin' anywhere."

His brusque tone wasn't helping. "Perhaps not. But I cannot look at a person I am about to rob."

"You have to, or else you look suspect. Remember, you're robbin' the rich to help the poor."

Actually, she was robbing the rich to help Count Zuko and to some extent herself, but she steadied her hand and continued forward, her head held high. As he approached, she tried not to think about invading him in such an intimate way. Reaching into his trouser pocket would put her hand dangerously close to...

No. Definitely best not to think about it.

Just as he was about to pass, she stepped to the center of the path so that her shoulder collided with the solid wall of his chest. "Oh, excuse me, sir!" She smiled up at him as she dipped her hand in. But there was something in his pocket besides the purse. It was cold and heavy, and when she pulled it out, a long, razor-sharp steel blade sprang forward.

"Good heavens!" She dropped the open switchblade on the ground.

"Damn it! Watch what you're doing!" He snatched it up, looking like the very picture of a vicious criminal. She shrank back, her body tense, fearing his attack.

He muttered another curse and retracted the knife. Then he shoved it in his pocket and walked away, to a small patch of shade beneath a tree. He stared at the ground, his hands shoved in his back pockets. Constance held her breath. What if he gave up teaching her to steal and forced her into the brothel at knifepoint?

Then he turned back and tilted his head, beckoning her. He grasped a branch just above his head. "Pretend we're on the bus. You come up behind me and take the money from my pocket. *This* pocket." He pointed to the one without the knife.

She stood behind him. Somehow, this was easier when she could not see his face. At least it was until she brushed against his back and brought her hand close to his side.

"Good." His hushed voice beckoned. "Now find my money."

Her insides knotted, and her mouth felt dry, but she steadied her hand. Heat seemed to radiate from his body as her fingers hovered above his hip. Extending her thumb and index finger, she dipped delicately into his gaping side pocket. Afraid to even breathe, she pinched the purse and carefully drew it out. If he turned, if he moved, she would leap from her skin. Before she knew it, the purse was free.

Fighting to contain her excitement, she buried it against her skirts and moved away.

When Alex turned, his beautiful smile lit his features. "Very nice, Lady Constance. We'll make a thief of you, yet."

On the bench beneath the shade tree, they shared a cup of low beer. Beside her, Alex rested his back against the tree trunk. Their shoulders brushed as he passed the drink. It wasn't lemonade in

Sussex, but the malty taste wasn't unpleasant. The water here was not safe to drink without boiling it first and seldom did anyone bother.

"You're catching on," he said. "You'll be as good as Nancy before long. Right, Nance?"

"No, but no one's as good as me. 'Cept maybe you, Black." Nancy swung on a knotted rope that hung from one of the tree's large limbs, and took the cup from Constance's outstretched hand. Nancy and Alex didn't appear to be sweethearts, yet she was hard-pressed to define their relationship. "Hope you're a fast runner, so you can get away if you have to."

She wasn't a fast runner at all, and she'd been trying not to dwell on this part of her new profession. The lads were full of tales of whippings, gaol, and worse. She swallowed hard. "They don't hang pickpockets, do they?"

"Forty lashes is the worst you'll get," Alex said. "'Course that's bad enough, but murder's the only thing they hang you for. So when you're stealing luv, try not to kill anyone."

She shivered, recalling the barbaric spectacle of public hangings at Tyburn. They'd ended three years ago, and she'd had no desire to attend one, though many considered them excellent sport.

Nancy glared. "Now look, Black. You scared her."

"A bit o' fear's a smart thing. Keeps you from getting careless," he said quietly, then offered an amiable smile. "But nothing for you to fret over on a Saturday night. It's almost time to go dancin'."

"Dancing?" she asked, as indifferently as possible.

"Luke and Jimmy play for the Saturday night dances at the

Farthing," Nancy said. "I don't get to go anymore, but it's loads of fun."

Fun was seldom a word Constance associated with dancing. Or dances. In polite society, people kept their cutting remarks discreet, but what sort of ridicule would she face at a boisterous East End tavern? She shook her head. "No. I couldn't, possibly. I've never set foot in a tavern."

"Then it's time you did," Alex said.

She could scarcely imagine such a thing and rubbed at a dirty smudge on her peach gown. "I have nothing to wear."

"I have a dress that ought to fit. Go wash up, then come to my room." Nancy hesitated as a look passed between her and Alex. "Or better, I'll come to yours."

Alex smiled. "It's settled, then. Hurry along, now. Tonight I want to dance with the prettiest girl in all o' London."

She was about to ask who he meant, but stopped herself. This was no longer Mayfair, and perhaps it was time to do things differently. "Very well. I suppose trying it once couldn't hurt."

She washed at the crude outdoor shower behind the mansion. Wrapped in a blanket for modesty, she hurried to the cool, dark basement and took refuge behind her curtain. Her skin and hair were blessedly clean. She was grateful for it, just as she was for the coarse suppers offered each night. As Alex often said, "When you're poor, you quit being particular."

Poor. A disconcerting way to describe herself, even if it was only for a little while. She must think of something else—just as disconcerting, but much more pleasing. Alex had called her pretty.

She wasn't used to hearing that. People considered her smart and sensible, but no one ever rhapsodized over her angelic face or perfect figure. He hadn't done that either, but florid odes to beauty did not seem the way of the East End.

Even beyond the unexpected compliment, was the fact it came from him. Each of his smiles brought the same thrill she'd felt in the Crystal Palace. She had yet to grow tired of admiring his silky, shiny hair or the unusual shade of his eyes, which were the deep blue of the sky just before twilight.

Thinking of him made her happier than she wished it did.

She could not afford to forget what he was. Though he stole to survive, he was the product of a brutal environment. There was no doubt he could use that switchblade in his pocket. He could count and manage sums, but drew symbols in his ledger for each pickpocket. Though he owned a book, she'd never seen him read it and suspected he couldn't. His speech, dress, and manners would be unacceptable in her circle. She imagined introducing him to her parents, Jane, or even the servants. They would be appalled.

Hard as it was to admit, she understood. She'd always considered herself forward-thinking and concerned for the poor, but the fact was, the poor lived rather shocking lives. Intellectual discussions with the family butler hadn't prepared her for this hard truth. There was no room in her world for someone like Alex, nor room in his world for her.

"You decent?" Nancy called out.

"I'm just in my chemise. Can you hand me the clothes?" Constance stretched out her arm and took the green plaid dress. Thank goodness, it was modest, with long sleeves and a square neckline. The waist appeared small, so she dug out her stays and laced them, though not as tightly as she had in Mayfair.

"When you're dressed, I can style your hair."

She could style her own hair, but recognized the friendly gesture. Yet another development she couldn't have imagined in her wildest dreams. "I'd like that, thank you."

A plunging neckline made the dress far less modest than she hoped, and the bodice hugged her figure. The black sash and flared skirt emphasized her small waist. Instead of the ruffles she usually wore, this dress was tight and intended to catch a man's eye. She'd have to make the best of it, as she had nothing else. She only hoped she didn't look too foolish.

Once dressed, she sat on a stool and let Nancy dry her hair with a flannel towel. "Does a maid do this for you?" she asked.

"Not any longer," Constance replied, missing Fletcher, though how could she explain leaving a life of privilege to a girl who worked in a brothel? She couldn't, so she distracted Nancy with a question. "How long have you lived here?"

"Been here six years, since Mum came to work for Minerva. She's gone now, but Pete, he used to be the don, he let me stay on. He 'n Black taught me loads, but I got tired o' running 'round London dressed like a boy. When I turned sixteen, Minerva said I could make a lot more money workin' for her, an' look pretty whilst I did it."

So Alex had not forced Nancy into her present line of work. She almost smiled, yet it didn't seem appropriate to the conversation. "Do you like it?" she asked, then felt like a fool the moment the words left her mouth.

Nancy snorted. "Ain't about likin' it, duck. I got to eat and keep a roof o'er me head. Beats workin' Covent Garden."

Too embarrassed to reply, she said nothing else and let Nancy work the comb through her thick curls. The girl had a gentle touch. Then Nancy said, "Black fancies you, you know."

Heat rose in her cheeks. "Aren't you and he… friends?"

"Friends, surely. I love Black. But not in that way. I mean, we've been together an' all."

"You have?"

The girl laughed at her obvious shock. "I been with all of 'em, 'cept for Danny and Little Jack. Count's orders." Her voice softened. "Tim's the one I like best, though. He's got a right bad temper, but what can I say? Guess I like 'em big, dark, an' angry."

An apt description for the surly fellow who glowered at her on his rare visits to the basement. Thank goodness she'd seen little of him lately. "To each her own, I suppose."

"Tim's still all bothered because I asked Black to help me make him green. I told him we were just play-actin'." She sighed and shook her head. "Sometimes, it's hard to figure why you like a person."

"Quite true."

"As far as Black goes, you're more his sort than me. He likes fancy, elegant stuff. In that way, he's different from us. But he's a good bloke, an' you seem all right, so why not, I say?"

Why not? Aside from not trusting him and social differences too many to count, she was not planning to stay in Spitalfields a minute longer than necessary.

"Now, we'll just pin this up." She lifted the sides of Constance's hair and secured it with hairpins on top of her head, but left the rest hanging down. The moment Nancy left, Constance would pin all of it up properly. Then, Nancy brought out a small pot of pink-tinted cream and dabbed some on her finger. Constance drew back.

Nancy rolled her eyes. "Relax, duck. There's nothin' wrong with a little color. I promise I won't use too much."

"I would prefer you did not use any at all."

"You can always wash it off, but why not have a look-see before you decide."

Constance submitted to the paint, then took the mirror Nancy offered. Going to a tavern in a tight dress, done up like a tart, was a ludicrous idea. One look in the mirror would put a stop to this madness.

She caught her breath at the sight of her reflection. Instead of an awkward Mayfair wallflower, staring back was an alluring woman, with saucy brown curls cascading over her shoulders. Nancy had a skilled hand with color; the pink in Constance's cheeks and lips looked natural, not painted on. She lowered the mirror and smoothed her hand over her hourglass curve.

Nancy's lips twitched in a smile. "You like it, don't you?"

At first she wasn't sure. She was a plain, practical girl—not the type to strike a man speechless with desire. Yet a part of her had always longed to be. She was tired of being asked to dance only after the more desirable partners were taken. Tonight, she wanted to be noticed.

"Thought so," Nancy said, with an air of pride. She took the mirror and linked her arm through Constance's. "Come on, I want to show you off."

In the kitchen, Luke, Jimmy and Danny practiced a song on fiddle, guitar and sticks, while in the scullery doorway, Sam, Big John, and Little Jack passed around a flask. Nancy pushed her forward. "Hey, you lot! Have a look!"

Luke's bow halted. His mop of curls bobbed as he lifted his head. "Cor blimey, girl! You clean up nice."

"Here I thought you were fetching in a pair of trousers."

Constance whirled around to see Alex, just back from the Count's, leaning casually against the kitchen doorway.

Mesmerized, she took in every detail. The dim light masked his frayed cuffs and collar, and in a clean white shirt, with his waistcoat buttoned, he made quite the dapper young gentlemen. He came closer, and she caught the clean, crisp smells of soap and citrus shaving tonic. "You're more an East End girl than a Society Miss. Less a Lady Constance, and more of a Connie."

His lingering gaze suggested this was not a bad thing.

On Commercial Street outside the Four Farthings, factory girls in tight dresses flirted with young workingmen and street crooks in colorful waistcoats. Constance looked no different from the rest.

Inside the crowded tavern, Luke, Jimmy, and a pianoforte player performed on a small stage at the far end of the main room. Danny perched atop the piano, rapping out a rhythm with his sticks. This music was much faster than the waltzes played at society balls, and she'd had trouble enough keeping up with those. She would have been content to stand and listen, but Alex took her hand.

"Come on, let's dance."

She shook her head. "I'm not very good."

"Me neither," he said, with a grin and a shrug. Before she could say another word, he was leading her into the crowd of dancers.

He was a better dancer than he admitted. He led with confidence and didn't comment when she stepped on his toes. It was too crowded for anyone to observe, much less criticize, her not-so-graceful dance steps. No one else here seemed especially graceful, either. Like stealing handkerchiefs, she soon had the hang of it.

Tonight, for the first time in her life, she danced more than she watched. Even Tim, who was quite drunk, spun her around the floor in a clumsy polka. When she danced with someone else, Alex chatted with the bartender. Before the musicians took a break, he claimed her again. The ritual was the same as society balls, where a gentleman claimed the last dance before supper in order to dine with the lady of his choice.

From the crowded bar, he brought over two mugs of ale and an order of fish and chips, wrapped in newspaper. Since coming to Spitalfields, she'd acquired a taste for chips, and these were especially good; hot and crispy, generously seasoned with salt and vinegar.

Alex raised his glass. "To Connie's new life as an East Ender. May it be the glorious escape she wanted."

"Cheers." She tapped her mug against his, then noticed he was looking at something over her shoulder. She turned to see a girl approach their table. Her heart sank.

The girl smiled at Alex and tossed back her long red hair. "Hullo, Black."

He nodded politely. "Hullo, Lucy."

71

The band had started again, and she made a pretty pout. "You should dance with me, not stand 'round here." She grabbed his hand. "Come on. I like this song."

Alex drew his hand back. "I'd rather stay here, thanks. Lucy, this is Connie. Connie, this is Lucy."

"It's nice to meet you," Constance said, hoping her disappointment wasn't obvious. The redhead merely scowled. Who was this girl? Then again, what business was it of hers? As much as she enjoyed Alex's attention, she couldn't return his interest. Keeping him to herself wasn't fair. She forced a smile. "Dance with your friend," she said. "I don't mind."

"You're sure?" He sounded surprised. And disappointed.

"I'm sure," she said with a decisive nod. "I believe I'll step outside for a breath of air."

He furrowed his brow and glanced around uneasily. "All right. But don't go too far from the door. Ain't safe for a lady alone."

With a heavy heart, she watched them leave, though she scolded herself at the same time. She was sensible and levelheaded. Falling for a pickpocket was not a sensible, levelheaded thing to do. Lucy was exactly whom Alex belonged with — a brazen working-class girl who wouldn't care if he earned his living as an extortionist or whoremonger.

But the sight of them together only reminded her how wonderful she'd felt in his arms. Lulled by the dim lights, music, and ale, she let her mind roam. He'd called her pretty. More than once, she'd thought — hoped — he might kiss her. She ran the tip of her tongue across her lips, imagining the soft brush of his mouth on hers. Not that it would ever happen. Lucy would be the one to enjoy his kisses.

She rubbed her stinging eyes. Was it the smoky tavern air? Or the bittersweet song of lost love, reminding her of what could never be? She shook off the maudlin thoughts and took her hand from her eyes.

From the dance floor, Alex's gaze found hers. Even as he danced with Lucy, the undisguised longing in his eyes frightened her. She felt it, too.

She had to get out of here.

Outside, the night air was cool and bracing. Still unsteady, she stood just outside the Farthing's front door. Two boys were engaged in a spitting contest, and one of them narrowly missed her shoes. She stepped aside.

Suddenly, a thick arm snaked around her waist. Tim leered over her shoulder. "Lookie what I found."

"Tim? Let me go," she said, trying to push him away.

Instead, he tightened his hold and laughed. "Wha's the matter, girl? Teased me all night, you did. Now I get what's mine."

She did not understand what he meant. Under no circumstances would she have led Tim on. Panic rose in her chest and her heart fluttered like a frantic, trapped bird. She clawed at his muscled arm as he dragged her backward. "Tim! No! Let go of me!"

"Shut up." Just as she was about to scream, he clapped his hand over her mouth and hauled her around the corner into the alley.

In a dark corner, he shoved her against the wall and forced his mouth on hers. The taste of gin and cigars in his mouth made her gag. She tried again to push him away, but he was too strong.

Pinned to the wall by the weight of his body, she turned her face to escape his savage kisses. "Stop it! Get off me!"

His bulk forced the air from her lungs as he crushed her. His hands clamped around her upper arms, rendering her helpless. She braced herself as he smashed his mouth down onto hers. Fighting tears and terror, she fought back the only way she could.

She bit him.

Tim tore his mouth away. "You bitch!" Enraged, he shook her, slamming her against the bricks. Her vision swam, and she tried to scream, but the sound froze in her throat as the blow knocked the breath from her lungs.

Suddenly Tim was pulled off her. Alex had him by the collar and by the hair.

"Keep your filthy paws off her, you bastard." He slammed Tim face-first against the wall.

"Little whore asked for it, she did! Just like a bitch in heat. Ain' my fault," Tim bellowed, his face still smashed against the bricks. He swung one arm wildly to push Alex away, but he dodged it.

"Shut your fuckin' trap." He pushed Tim's face against the wall again, this time smashing his nose. Blood gushed from Tim's nostrils. Alex spoke low into Tim's ear, barely controlling his rage. "You touch her again, I'll hurt you worse than this."

"Piss off, Black!" Tim wrenched himself from Alex's grasp and stood breathing hard, like a bull about to charge. Constance gasped as Alex brought his hand to his pocket, about to go for his knife.

Then a bright light slashed into the shadows. A constable stood at the mouth of the alley, holding a bullseye lantern high. "Here now! What's going on back there?"

Tim's shoulders sagged, and he wiped his bloody nose with the back of his hand. "Ain't nothin' goin' on."

The constable frowned. "Didn't look like nothin'. You all right, miss?"

She paused, unsure how to answer. If she told the truth, the officer might haul Tim off to gaol, but he probably wouldn't stay there. When he returned to the mansion, things could be much worse. "Yes," she said. "I'm quite all right. Thank you."

The man peered, curiously. Did he not believe her... or was her speech too refined for a girl involved in an alley fight? If she wasn't careful, he might realize she was the Earl of Beverly's missing daughter. She tossed her hair back, like Nancy and Lucy did. "Tim's lush, is all. He ought to go home, 'fore he picks a fight with another bloke."

The constable narrowed his eyes, but to her relief, he grabbed Tim by the arm. "All right, you. That's enough trouble for one night. Get on, 'fore I throw your arse inna bridewell."

A beaten man, Tim staggered out of the alley back onto Commercial Street, the constable close behind. Once they left, she was about to leave, too, but stopped short. Alex blocked her way. Her heart pounded. Had she made a terrible mistake not asking the constable for help? What if he pulled out his knife and took over where Tim left off? Cornered, she looked around for anything she could use as a weapon. He stepped forward. She drew back. He reached out his hand. She flinched, and a scream rose in her throat.

Gently, Alex touched her shoulder. "Are you all right? Did he hurt you?"

She took a few deep breaths and hugged her arms across her

body. "I'm fine," she said in a small voice.

"Fine? He slammed your head against the wall. It's not bleeding, is it?"

She touched the lump on the back of her head. It was tender, but nothing was wet. "I'm fine," she repeated, afraid to give him any excuse to send her to the brothel. "I stayed by the door like you said, but he grabbed me and dragged me into the alley. I didn't want to go with him."

"Drunk fool." Alex put his arm around her waist and guided her from the alley. "If he tries to hurt you again, I'll kill him."

She flinched again, but this time it wasn't fear of Alex, so much as fear for him. He could hold his own against Tim, but she dreaded to think of them locked in mortal combat. Being the center of attention wasn't nearly as much fun as she'd first thought. Having power over men was as frightening as it was exhilarating.

Together, they walked to the shop next door to the Farthing. He eased her onto the steps, then took a seat beside her. He moved his arm away, but stayed close enough so that his shoulder brushed hers. The friction sent tendrils of heat from the point of contact. "I doubt he'll bother you again," Alex said. "Tomorrow, he probably won't even remember."

"I hope not." His shoulder was the perfect height to rest her head against and though she didn't do it, it was nice to have him so close. Did he feel the same, or was he only staying out of obligation? Side by side, they watched the Saturday night revelers pass. Finally, she asked, "Why aren't you dancing with Lucy?"

His lopsided grin made her toes curl inside her pointed boots.

76

"She got tired of me. Decided she'd have better luck with another bloke." His eyes held hers for a long moment, in a connection that seemed strong enough to touch. "Do you want me to take you home?"

The buoyant sound of a country dance, accompanied by clapping hands and laughter, beckoned her back to the Farthing. She'd never had as much fun as she'd had earlier tonight and now Tim was gone. She'd even tried to send Alex into the arms of another girl. It wasn't her fault if he didn't want to stay there. "Heavens, no! I want to dance some more."

He laughed a little, then his bright expression faded into one more wistful. "I meant Mayfair. If you want to go home, I'll take you tomorrow."

The crisp night air kissed her skin, and the warmth in his voice caressed her. Tonight, something inside had awakened, and she'd glimpsed the girl she'd longed to be. Alex had seen it. Not only that, he'd been part of it. Return to her safe, empty existence? Unthinkable.

Whatever her doubts and fears, it was easy to ignore them when she gazed into his beautiful, deep blue eyes. "No. I want to stay."

CHAPTER SEVEN

Monday morning, the city streets reeked of dray horses, livestock, and the sewers. Alex tugged at his too-tight collar. Today would be a hot one. Beside him, Connie kept pace and held her head high. Her end of town didn't stink like this, but she seemed to get on just fine. Lady Constance was no fainting flower that was for sure.

With the parish cap pulled low, she passed for a lad. At least she did as long as she kept her shirt pulled out. The tight dress she wore Saturday night gave him a welcome look at what she had, which was as soft, curvy, and tempting as he imagined. He hadn't kissed her, even though he wanted to. Most of all, he was glad she didn't leave after that drunken ass attacked her in the alley.

But this morning, she'd been ready to go after her first mark, so he'd brought her here, where the take would be the best. He'd tried to blend in with the crowds of clerks heading to the banks and offices, by wearing his best black frock coat and topper. Breakfast was a slab of warm gingerbread, swiped from a vendor's cart. The gingerbread was good, but Connie's smile was even better.

As they crossed Bishopsgate Street, he told her how to choose the right mark.

"Him over there you want to stay clear of." He spoke in a quiet voice and nodded toward a big gent walking a few steps ahead. The man wore a dark green coat and kept glancing round. "Do you know why?"

"The way he's looking at everyone. He expects to be robbed."

"Right-o. See a better choice?"

"Him?" She tilted her head toward another fellow.

This one had his nose stuck in a newspaper, but wore a frock coat so old it was shiny, and shoes with heels worn round in the back. "Why?"

"Because he's not paying attention to what's happening around him."

"But look at his clothes."

She studied the man for a moment. "He looks poor and probably doesn't have any money."

"That, or he's one of us and he'll plant a one-two on me the minute I reach for his purse."

She winced, as if feeling the blow herself. "Let's keep looking."

A block from the Exchange, she nudged his arm and glanced

over at a man wearing a maroon tie and carrying a fancy walking stick. His pocket had a telltale bulge. She had chosen well.

Suddenly, he stopped cold in his tracks. He had taught her a little, convinced her she could do this and brought her out here. But what if they caught her? The thought of her arrested and hauled off to gaol brought a mad urge to take her straight back to Mayfair. He grabbed her arm. "Let's run the beggar."

His glare silenced her into doing it his way. She slumped her shoulders and slowed her pace. "Sir! Can ye 'elp me out? I've not 'ad a bite to eat. Please, gov'nor? Can ye find it in yer 'art to 'elp a poor lad?"

Was that how he sounded to her? Dear God, he hoped not. He almost forgot his own part in the flam until the man raised his walking stick to strike her. Alex charged forward. Their meeting was hard, and he hoped, painful for the mark. Connie darted away into the crowd. In a flash, he lifted the man's purse and watch.

"Watch out, you clumsy oaf!"

The cane landed hard across the small of Alex's back. It hurt, but he'd been dealt worse. Connie's whereabouts were the bigger concern. He found her in the doorway of an eel pie shop halfway up the row. Eager to get off Lombard Street before the mark went for his watch, he pulled her into the nearest alley.

"He didn't hurt you, did he?" she asked, looking vexed.

"I'm fine." He shrugged it off, but it was nice she cared. Better than having her afraid of him.

"What a dreadful man! Swinging a cane at a poor beggar child and striking a stranger." She shook her head, then her eyes got big with excitement. "So what did you get?"

The purse held a few shillings, but the watch was right elegant — plain gold, brightly polished. Connie smiled and pressed it into his hand. "You should keep it. Every gentleman needs a watch, and all you have is an empty case."

"You're forgettin' I ain't a gent. I'm a thief who needs to make his share."

"Mine and Danny's, too. Luke told me," she said, answering his surprised look. "He said Danny wasn't good for much more than stealing handkerchiefs... and that you'd been carrying him since May."

He only nodded, but liked the approval in her voice. Come to think of it, he could use a watch, and if Connie thought he was worthy of this one, perhaps he ought to keep it.

"And who says you aren't a gentleman?" she went on. "Being a gentleman's not just about having a title or money, you know."

"Helps a lot." He dropped the watch into his trouser pocket as they returned to Lombard Street.

"I know plenty of rich men who aren't gentlemen."

"Who? Henry?"

Like a pretty song, her laugh floated above the noise of a bus rattling past. "Horace."

<hr />

They stayed in the city until early afternoon, when the bankers and barristers broke away for dinner at their clubs. Thanks to his quick hands and her loud begging, a few got a nasty surprise when it came time to pay the bill. Near the East India Dock Company, he took a handful of smoked beef from a sidewalk stand. They ate in the square by Tower Hill.

"How long have you worked for the Count?" she asked, as she chewed on her beef.

"Came to the mansion when I was thirteen." The beef was salty. He should have grabbed a bottle of ginger beer to wash it down. "Worked in a match factory before that, but I ran away."

"You never went to school?"

"I went. Didn't like it much. All that sitting still and copying things. But I learned figures and sums. I was good at memorizing. I can read and write. A bit," he felt obliged to add.

"Memorizing? Like poetry?"

"Not poetry. School was church-run, so mostly from the Bible. Psalms and such."

"Like the twenty-third Psalm?"

When he gave her his spare blanket, he'd left two things inside — his *Robin Hood* book and the little cross with "Psalm 23" painted on it. "I won a prize for memorizing that one."

"Though I walk through the valley of the shadow of death," she recited, then gave him a long look, almost as if she understood what the verses meant to him. He looked away, but felt her gaze. "Where did you go to school?" she asked.

Thank goodness, a safer question. "The ragged school at St. Paul's."

"Why, I've been to St. Paul's many times, but I never knew it had a charity school. I attended the Countess of Marshfield's wedding there last summer. It's just a magnificent cathedral." When he laughed, she scowled. "What's so funny?"

"Thinkin' about the likes o' me in St. Paul's Cathedral. Don't think they'd let me past the front door. St. Paul's Shadwell is where I went to school."

"I'm not familiar with it."

"Wouldn't expect you to be. Shadwell's north of Wapping, near the docks. Quite the place. I lived on Cutthroat Lane."

"Cutthroat Lane?" She narrowed her eyes. "There's no such thing."

She was so damned pretty; he smiled even as he talked about the rookery. "So you say. An expert on Shadwell, are you? How many times did you say you've been there?"

She crossed her arms. "Well, no one would name a street Cutthroat Lane! Would they?"

"All right," he said, feeling right good about life and the world. So what if the Count thought he was soft? The hell with Zuko. This made him happy. She made him happy. "It had another name, but no one ever called it anything but Cutthroat Lane. I'll take you there sometime. We'll drop by Labour in Vain Street, too."

"Maybe not." Her tight smile told him what she thought of that idea. "You've been stealing since you left?"

"Been stealin' since I could walk. Even when Mum was alive, we never had much, so I learned to get what I needed. It's just takin' from the rich to feed the poor."

"Like Robin Hood."

"Good ol' Robin. Proof a thief can be a man of honor."

"Your hair makes you look just like Robin on the cover of your book, you know," she said, with a saucy smile.

"I like my hair." It shouldn't matter, but he was glad she seemed to like it, too. He shook it loose from the tail he'd tied it into this morning. It was falling out anyway. "'Course I didn't get to be a tip-top thief 'til I came to the Count's."

"Pete taught you. Nancy mentioned him. I haven't met him yet, have I?"

He smoothed down the frayed brim of his hat, as black memories clouded over the sunny ones. "No."

"Will I?"

He stilled, recalling Pete's friendly grin and quick laugh. How Pete had taught him the life, just as he was now teaching Connie. Pete would have liked her. He gripped the bowler's brim, bending it even more out of shape, as another memory invaded. Pete, bloody and still on the cellar floor.

Even after two years, the words felt strange in his mouth. "No, luv. Pete's dead."

<hr />

At the end of the day, Constance presented her take to Alex. He looked up from his ledger and smiled. His cheerful mood seemed to have returned from wherever it went when she mentioned his old friend. Obviously, it was a sensitive topic. Politeness prevented her from asking more, though she was curious.

"What 'ave you got for me?"

"You know what I have. Three handkerchiefs and this." She gave him the purse they took from the mean man with the walking stick.

"Well done, Lady Constance," he said, pretending to see the handkerchiefs for the first time. "These will fetch a good price, though this one needs washing." He held the crumpled linen square by its corner and dropped it in the pile. "But not by you."

"Earning my keep, am I?"

He ran his finger down the column of symbols in his ledger. At the top was an arrow. For Robin Hood, perhaps? After it, a musical note for either Luke or Jimmy and farther down, a cross. The total beside it was smallest, so it probably stood for Danny. A crown, a club and a spade followed, then a diamond with an empty line beside it. That must be for Tim, who wasn't around much these days. The last symbol was a heart. Beside it, he noted her take.

"You are. We'll have you on your way before you know it."

On her way to what? She'd had little time to consider career options beyond the one in front of her. She moved away from the table, so Alex could count Little Jack's take.

This was her favorite time of day, when everyone had returned and the dark thieves' den rang with laughter, music, and conversation. She brought out the newspaper she'd scrounged from a rubbish pile, and read as Luke, Jimmy, and Danny practiced "The Jenny Lind Polka." The second time through, Luke played the fiddle part flawlessly and flashed a wide grin, his eyes hidden by his mop of curly hair. Sam brought her a cup of ale. Soon, she set the paper aside and tapped her toe along with the music.

The longer she stayed, the more she liked her fellow basement dwellers, noisy, smelly, and uncouth as they were. In some ways, they were so foreign, she couldn't believe they were Londoners. They spoke appalling language, much of it vulgar slang she struggled to understand. None were educated and most told harrowing stories of their lives before they came here. Danny's opium-addicted mother abandoned him on the streets. Luke's father sold him to a chimney sweep, who beat him. Jimmy's family had come from Jamaica, seeking a better life, only to eke out a living collecting dung to sell to the tanneries.

Yet, they shared their food and drink with her. Nancy gave her clothes. Jimmy offered to teach her to play the guitar. Danny and Luke were sweet and helpful. Just being with Alex made her happy.

He could have attacked her in the alley Saturday night, but he'd protected her. He was fair with his crew and patient with Danny. Regardless of the Count's plans, Alex's heart seemed to be elsewhere.

It was like she was living amid a strange dream. Some of it was frightening — Minerva, the Count, the decrepit mansion and her fledgling life of crime. Yet, she'd found friendship and generosity when she had not expected it.

Noise at the back door signaled supper. Patrick and Tommy, the Irish brothers, carried in a box of eel pies. Big John followed with a fresh cask of ale. She helped herself to both and took her customary spot near the fireplace. Alex, back from the Count's, brought his food and sat beside her.

After dinner, the music started again. "Champagne Charlie" was a popular music hall song Jimmy wanted to play for sidewalk busking. Alex sang along. His voice wasn't trained, but unlike her, he possessed a natural ability to find the right note. Forgetting ladylike posture, she rested her elbows on the table and let her thoughts drift, pleasantly carried away by Alex's cheerful tenor.

As he drummed his fingers in time to the music, she noticed

the small, faded scars that pitted the backs of his hands. What sort of injury might have caused them? Her gaze roamed over his forearms, dusted with fine hair a shade darker than that on his head. Though she'd tried not to look, his buttonless shirts revealed a swirl of similar hair on his chest. At night she'd laid on the mattress, imagining how it might feel to press her palm against his warm skin and beating heart. Suddenly seized with an overwhelming urge to touch him, she brushed her little finger against his wrist.

The contact startled them both. She jerked her hand back and hoped the dim light hid the blush which burned her cheeks. Jarred from her daydream, she sat up straight. "Excuse me."

"It's all right," he said, softly.

"Alex?" Oh, no. Everyone else called him "Black." She was the only one to use his given name. Immediately, she wanted to disappear.

He smiled a little. "What, Connie?"

What? Good question. Her mind raced and her gaze fell on his open shirt and bare chest. Egad, he needed buttons. Buttons, that was it! She faced him with as much dignity as she could muster. "Tomorrow, I'm going to buy buttons to repair my shirt. If you like, I'll repair yours, too."

"Thought you couldn't do anything practical."

"I can embroider, and this is just a needle and thread. A smart girl like me should be able to figure it out. I'll have you looking like a proper gentleman before you know it."

His teasing grin was hard to resist. "Makin' me into a proper gent, are you? First the watch, now my shirt. What's next? A haircut and a weddin' suit?"

It was only a joke but still, it mortified her. "Of course not. You don't believe in marriage, remember?"

"When did I say that?"

"The day I told you about Gaffney. You said people in your world don't bother with marriage because if you only have a few good years, what's the point?"

His smile faded. "I meant that people 'round here don' live so long. Why marry when you'll only have a little time together?"

Though his tone was matter of fact, the bleak words chilled her. He was no longer joking. "Is that what you believe? That you won't live very long?"

"It's what I've seen. Makes you think, is all. Once I'm workin' upstairs ..." He gave a resigned shrug. "It ain't the safest job."

With those quiet words, she understood what awaited him. A short, brutal life as a crime boss's henchman. Heartache and anger rose like bile, at the thought of Alex transformed into someone savage and cruel. Her throat tightened and her empty arms ached to hold him and soothe his pain away. But she kept her hands still in her lap. "It's hard to picture you doing that."

His blond hair hung like a curtain across his face. "Ain't like I got a choice, luv. Come November, he wants me upstairs."

CHAPTER EIGHT

Alex awoke just past dawn. The room was still dark and Danny still snored, but someone was moving about in the kitchen. He caught the smell of a fire and smiled.

These past weeks, he'd taught Connie plenty he wasn't proud of, but he was glad to have taught her this. Lady Constance might be smart enough to go to a fancy school, but no one had shown her how to survive on her own. He would see to it she knew before she left the East End.

She couldn't go back to her family that was certain. What kind of people forced a smart, gorgeous girl to marry a swine? He didn't know much about high society, but it just seemed wrong. Men hit their wives, he knew that, but he'd been hit enough times and didn't like it. Why should Connie suffer? She deserved a good life, and he would do whatever he could to start her off.

Still, he had to be careful. Something was growing between them. He felt it when they danced. Even when she tried to send him off with Lucy, the sad look in her eyes told him she didn't want him to go. Then last night, she touched him and got embarrassed when he noticed. He hadn't minded. Quite the opposite. In fact, he fell under the same spell just talking to her. Talking to Connie was easy. Too easy. When the talk turned to his future, he said more than he should have and wanted to say even more. But getting attached was a terrible idea. Soon enough, she'd be gone, and odds were good he would be, too.

As the summer ended, he'd come to a crossroads. One path was a future with the Count. Zuko trusted him, but demanded complete loyalty and obedience. Down here, he could do a bit as he pleased. Upstairs, the Count would control his every move. He'd known from the start this would be his future, but years back, he hadn't given it much thought. He never expected to last this long. Yet he had. Now it was time to make good.

To refuse would cost him his life.

Pete had taken that path. Little by little, Alex felt himself moving in the same direction. It scared him in some ways, made him sad in others. But really, what did it change? If he spent his last years doing something that made him feel dead anyway, why stick around? Plenty of blokes didn't see twenty-five. He wouldn't miss much.

Keeping on the straight and narrow brought no guarantees, either. Folks starved to death, froze to death, drank foul water, and died from the cholera, like Mum. In the factories, they got worked to death. He saw all that before he was thirteen and it brought him straight here. This was as good as it got for the likes of him. He'd cast his lot with the Count long ago and knew too many secrets to leave. Alive, anyway.

He found Connie at the kitchen table. She smiled over the rim of her cup, bright-eyed, given the early hour. "I made plenty, if you'd like some."

"I would. Thanks." He seldom bothered with tea in the morning, but since she was offering, he wouldn't turn it down. He found the cup he usually drank from, filled it and sat across from her. For a moment, he pretended they'd shared a bed last night and were starting their day together, like normal people. He took a sip. "Fine tea. Nice and hot."

"I'm a quick study." She saluted with her cup and blew on her tea. "Are you taking me stealing this morning?"

The way she said it, she could have been asking if he was taking her to the Ascot races or to meet the Queen. He smiled and answered like an upper-class gent. "Yes, my lady. I am taking you stealing this morning."

She gave a sure nod. "Good. It's time I got started."

He pushed back his fear. She didn't want him to carry her forever, nor could he. Connie must learn to make her own way.

By late afternoon, they were near Fenchurch Street station and Constance had her eye out for the perfect mark. Someone prosperous, distracted, and unlikely to run fast, should flight be necessary. Men gathered at a newsstand close to the station. A gray-haired man in dark blue pulled out a drawstring purse, paid the vendor, and dropped the purse back in his pocket. The strings hung down the outside.

She nudged Alex's arm. When he turned, she shifted her eyes toward the mark. He gave a subtle nod and started forward. She grabbed his sleeve. He'd taken every mark she'd chosen today. Though he always gave her the money, it couldn't continue. She shook her head and mouthed a single word. "Mine."

His raised brow questioned her. She nodded with more confidence than she felt. Alex looked just as tense, but he stepped to the edge of the crowd. As ready as she would ever be, she squared her shoulders and approached the newsstand.

The mark was talking to the vendor, and his purse strings still dangled. Beside the mark, she steadied her hand. As she'd practiced dozens of times, she grasped the purse strings. Moving only her wrist, she lifted the small suede bag. With a single, quick motion, she cupped it in her hand, then slipped it into her trouser pocket as she moved away.

Alex waited at the edge of the crowd, with a calm expression, but alert eyes. Her heart pounded wildly and her knees threatened to buckle, but once she reached his side, she'd be safe. Five, ten, twenty paces. She'd made it. She released the breath she hadn't realized she held. Lightly, he touched her back and steered her away. Her pulse had almost slowed to normal when a man shouted. "My purse! I've been robbed!"

She gasped.

"Come along, brother, we'll miss our train." Alex took her elbow and hustled her toward the closest of Fenchurch Street station's seven doors. No one was following them. At least she hoped not. When they were almost inside, she looked back over her shoulder to be sure.

The vendor, standing atop a crate, spotted her and pointed. "Him! That boy! You, there! Stop!"

Instinct took over. Panicked, she darted into the station, leaving Alex no choice but to follow. She raced down the stairs, with no thought to where she was going. Trains rumbled in and out, but without tickets, they couldn't board. Frantic, she looked for an exit.

"This way." Alex grabbed her hand, and they ran toward another steep staircase. No police in sight, but seconds later, their luck ran out. A stout railway constable came barreling after them.

"Stop in the name of the law!"

She wasn't about to stop for anything, nor was Alex. Ahead of her now, he led her through the throng of commuters descending from Cooper's Row. Gasping for breath, she stumbled on the slippery marble steps, but he pulled her to her feet. His top hat tumbled from his head and bounced down the steps. He let it go. The constable had reached the steps and mounted them two at a time, huffing like a locomotive that had escaped the rails. Half way up, he bellowed at the top of his lungs. "Stop, thief!"

People turned to stare.

At the top of the stairs were turnstiles. Alex vaulted over the set at the furthest end. They were too tall for her to scale, but he hoisted her over. They pushed their way through the revolving doors, out of the station. Cooper's Row went south toward the Tower, but to her surprise, Alex ran east on John Street. She followed him into a narrow, dark lane lined with dingy shops and tenements. Though her lungs fought for air and sharp pain shot through her legs, she kept running—afraid he might leave her behind.

The shriek of a police whistle echoed off the buildings. Alex grabbed her hand and dragged her into the closest alley. The stench of blood from a butcher shop was thick back here. She covered her mouth and swallowed the bile that rose in her throat. Holding tight to Alex, she let him lead her through the twisted, nameless lane, kicking aside rubbish as they ran. Around a corner, they came face-to-face with a huge barking dog and three boys, armed with sticks.

"Bloody hell!" Alex grabbed her waist and hurled her onto a ladder, bolted to one building, then scrambled up behind. The worn soles of her boots were slick on the rungs, and twice she lost her footing, as the rickety thing swayed under their weight. She ducked into the closest opening on the building's second floor. The tenement hallway reeked of urine, unwashed bodies, and rotting food. Somewhere, a baby cried. Alex pulled her into an alcove and popped open his switchblade. He wrapped a protective arm around her shoulders. His body tensed, ready to fight.

She tucked her head beneath his chin and rested her cheek against his chest. Beneath her ear was the comforting, powerful thump of his heart. The citrus scent of his shaving tonic masked the wretched smells surrounding them. He hadn't abandoned her. He was here and would keep her safe. She closed her eyes, wrapped her arms around him and melted into his embrace.

Sounds rose from the alley. The barking dog. The boys' shouts as they tried to mount the ladder. Then a man's rough voice, heavy with authority. "Go on, you no good lot, an' take that mangy cur, else I drown it."

A policeman. Eyes open and alert, she held her breath, straining to hear if the boys gave them away. But there was only the welcome shuffle of footsteps as they retreated down the alley.

Alex stroked her back in soothing circles. His buttonless shirt had come untucked, and his exposed muscular chest, with its intriguing swirl of hair, was close enough to touch. She swallowed hard. The little thrill she felt whenever she looked at him flared into something intense and unknown. Pressure throbbed at her very center, aching for release.

She gazed up, her sights filled with his handsome face and beautiful eyes. She caught her breath as he lowered his head and brushed his lips across hers.

At first, he hesitated as if gauging her reaction, but when she raised herself on tiptoe, he grew bolder. His arm pressed across her shoulders, even the hand that held the knife became part of the embrace. She brought her hand up to rest on the collar of his coat, tracing her fingertip along the frayed edge. It was an intimate, familiar gesture, yet not enough. Aching to feel his warm skin, she brushed her fingertips over his throat, then his clean-shaven jaw.

The excitement he'd awakened shamed, yet thrilled her. Ladies weren't supposed to behave this way, certainly not with men like him. But as his kiss went on, her fever rose, threatening to consume her already shaky self-control. She threaded her fingers through the heavy, soft silk of his hair. His tongue and teeth played with her lips. He seemed to want her to open her mouth, but she wasn't sure. She'd never kissed this way and openmouthed kisses seemed so provocative. If she did it, and she was wrong, what would he think of her? She kept her puckered lips together.

Then, abruptly, he drew back. She longed to lose herself in his eyes, but in them were emotions that ripped her heart in two. Disappointment and regret. A slight smile tugged at the corner of his mouth. Gently, he removed her arms from around his neck and stepped from the alcove.

He didn't want her after all.

She remained frozen to her spot. Devastating as it was, his rejection came as no surprise. In this respect, Alex was no different from the young gentlemen at society balls. He'd indulged his curiosity and found her lacking.

"Think we lost 'em," he whispered.

On stealthy footsteps, he returned to where they'd come in, and then beckoned her. She followed him onto the ladder, suffering a moment of vertigo as she looked down two floors into the alley. Was she dizzy from the height? His kiss? Or her terrible embarrassment?

Back on solid ground, she followed him out of the alley. By the butcher shop, he peered round the corner. "Bus stop's over there. We can catch it home."

He behaved as if nothing had happened. She must as well. "I can't believe I looked back. I almost got us caught," she said, as they walked to the stop.

"But we didn't get caught. And you won't look back again, right?"

"Right." There was a tailor's shop by the omnibus stop. She sat on the steps. He paced back and forth on the sidewalk, keeping his distance.

It was for the best. Yesterday, he'd all but admitted he couldn't even read. How could she, who so valued learning and education, ever be happy with someone like him? The idea was preposterous. This was infatuation and nothing more. Once she left Spitalfields, she would find a man just as attractive and much more suitable.

If only she weren't so taken with this one.

The purse sat heavy in her pocket. As he reminded her often, it could be full of farthings as easily as crowns, but she had a hopeful feeling about it, anyway. She drew out the small leather bag and cupped it in her hand.

He stood, blocking the view of passersby. "Don' like to count it 'til I get back. Too many thieves about." He grinned. "But you don' want to wait, do you?"

"I have to know." She tugged the strings open and poured the contents into her palm. It was full of farthings and pence, but also contained two crowns. Quite a success for her first actual theft. "I've almost got my share for the week. Is it always this easy?"

"Bit o' beginner's luck, I'd say. But get a few more like it and you'll be out of here in no time."

Of course, he was eager to have her gone. He'd spent most of his time teaching her these past weeks, when he could have been stealing for himself or his employer. It was perfectly reasonable for him to want his life to return to normal. She forced a smile. "Yes, I hope so."

There was an awkward pause. Then he bobbed his head. "Right-o. Stash that away, now. The bus is comin'."

After a silent ride home, she hurried to their room and took refuge behind her horse blanket. She removed her shirt and rubbed her upper body with the linen handkerchief she'd dampened at the pump on the way inside. Cool basement air dried her skin. She was about to change into her other shirt, but remembered her missing buttons. This afternoon, she would fix them. She put on her peach gown and brushed her hair. Taking two pence from the purse to cover the cost of buttons, she stepped from behind the blanket.

Alex stood beside his bed, his back turned and his shirt off. His trim physique was every bit as attractive as she'd imagined. But raised, puckered lines of pink and white sliced across his shoulders and back. Scars. Some old, some more recent.

She gasped and covered her mouth with her hand. The sound gave her away. Alex turned around.

The sight of him rekindled the arousal from his kiss. Now, she could see what she longed to touch. He was lean but strong and beautifully formed, with sinewy muscles that defined his arms, shoulders, and chest. She imagined brushing her fingers over the tight muscles of his stomach. But scars laced his fine build here, too. A vicious, red welt sliced around his side and halfway across his belly.

Horrified, she could only stare. Alex snatched up his shirt and put it back on.

"I'm sorry," she said, not only for catching him half-dressed.

He grinned and shrugged, pretending she did not see what she obviously had. "Not your fault. I forgot you were back there. Just wasn't paying attention is all. Thought I'd go wash up. Hot day, you know?"

Her cheeks burned. "I did the same. It felt good. I was about to go buy buttons for my shirt, and yours too, if you like."

"Don' have to do that."

"I want to. To say thank you for all you've done for me."

His sweet, sad smile almost undid her. "For what? Teaching you to steal?"

"For helping me make share these past weeks, even though you're carrying Danny, too. And teaching me to build a fire."

"I was happy to do it and you needn't thank me. But if you feel you must, I'd love to have my buttons back." A moment passed. He looked down at his bare feet, then back up. "An' I hope you'll forgive me forgettin' my manners, an' kissin' you today. It ain't how a gent should act, and it won't happen again."

She hoped her smile looked convincing. After all, this was the best thing. "I forgive you. Now if you'll excuse me, I need to find the dry goods shop."

"Across from the Farthing, on Commercial Street, just past Christ Church. They ought to have what you need." He dug a coin from his pocket and cut off her protest with a wave of his hand. "I know you got money, but you need to save it so you can get out of here. Don' argue now. Take it."

He pressed the penny into her hand and closed her fingers around it. Her pulse pounded at his touch. His gaze held hers and she felt tears push perilously close to the surface. Then he released her. "Go," he commanded, softly.

She went, glad to be alone. Their kiss had been something for which he felt the need to apologize and never repeat. He didn't desire her, and to repeat it would only embarrass them both. Besides, falling for an illiterate street thief had never been part of her plan. No matter how attractive he was, no matter how kind he was, he belonged here. She did not.

Yet, those terrible scars haunted her. What had he done to deserve such cruelty? Her heart knew the answer—nothing. Gaffney's callous dismissal of the poor had outraged her. Now, one of those poor had a name, a face, and a soul. Could she really leave this place and do nothing to help him?

At the dry goods shop, she bought a card of needles, a spool of thread, and buttons for their shirts. The shopkeeper wrapped them in a newspaper parcel and she started back to the mansion. She took her time, trying to lose herself in the industrious hum of Commercial Street. Passing Christ Church, she admired the steeple that towered over Spitalfields. An enormous porch and soaring portico, supported by elegant Grecian columns, graced the front of the building. The church was even more impressive, given its humble surroundings.

Something tugged at her skirts, and she looked down to see a small, wire-haired dog sniffing around her. What an adorable little fellow! She reached to pet him, but jerked her hand away when the creature erupted with outraged barking.

"Augie! Augustine! Enough of that!" A short, bald man, about her father's age, hurried over and snatched up the dog. "Where are your manners, being so rude to a nice young lady!" He gave an apologetic smile. Friendly brown eyes twinkled behind his rimless spectacles. He stroked the little dog's head until it stopped barking and licked his palm. "I'm sorry, miss. I hope he didn't frighten you."

"Goodness, no. I hope I didn't frighten him. I had just stopped to admire the church. It's lovely."

"That it is," he said fondly, gazing up at the building. She now noticed he wore the somber black suit and white collar of a clergyman. He turned back and smiled. "I am Mr. Charles Lockhurst, the rector here at Christ Church."

"I am ... Miss Eleanor Jones."

He offered his hand in greeting. She shook it and discovered it was damp from Augie's licks. He drew his hand back and wiped it on his coat. "Again, I apologize, Miss Jones." He gestured toward the steps. "I would be honored to show you the inside."

With no polite reason to refuse, she followed him into the church. The soaring ceiling of the sanctuary was immediately familiar. "Why, this looks just like St. James Church at Grosvenor Square. I attended there ... with distant cousins," she quickly added.

"I believe the same architect designed both buildings." Mr. Lockhurst regarded her with interest. "Are you new to the neighborhood, Miss Jones?"

"Yes." She hesitated, and then added, "I'm staying over on White Lion Street."

"Ahh, I see." She half expected him to order her out of the church straight away, but he gave a kind smile. "Are you upstairs?"

"Downstairs."

His brow creased with concern. "Recently, I met a boy who said he lived there. A red-haired lad, about eleven or twelve. A very sweet little fellow who was quite taken with Augie. Perhaps you know him?" The rector's voice had a hopeful lift.

"Yes. His name is Danny and you'll be happy to know he's fine and well cared for. The leader of ... us watches over him. Sometimes Danny has trouble ... doing his part. Alex covers him out of his own pocket."

"Danny's blessed to have such a caring friend," said the rector. They all were. Her throat tightened. She needed to go.

He took a deep breath. "Miss Jones, please know that you or Danny or even your... leader are welcome here. If you ever need help, come to me."

"Thank you, Mr. Lockhurst." She turned to leave, but on her way out, passed a wooden table stacked with small paper booklets. One caught her eye. *Psalms and Proverbs for Every Day.*

She picked it up and flipped through the pages. The words were clearly printed. Easy to read. There were even a few small pictures. A mad thought flashed in her mind — one she couldn't dismiss. Could it work? If there was even the slightest chance, she had to try. She dug a coin from her reticule. "Mr. Lockhurst, would you be willing to sell one of these?"

"Sell one? Of course not, child. You may have it."

She hurried back to the mansion, clutching the booklet. Here was a way to help Alex!

She found him in their room, dressed in clean clothes. "Did you get what you needed?" he asked.

"Yes, and I brought something back for you." She thrust the booklet at him.

He took it and thumbed through the pages. His downcast eyes betrayed his shame. "That's right kind of you, Lady Constance. But I can't read it."

"Yes, you can! It's a book of psalms! You memorized psalms at school. All you have to do is learn to read the words you already know, and I will teach you!" She grasped his hand. "I'm going to teach you to read!"

CHAPTER NINE

No?" She stared, wide-eyed. "Why not?"

Alex hated the disappointment in her eyes. "Just don' want to, is all. Don' see much point to it."

"The point is, you could be something besides a criminal's henchman! You could get an honest job!"

"Really, duck?" Connie was all good intentions and big ideas. Too bad she didn't know what the hell she was talking about. "Who would give an honest job to a thief, even if he can read? Besides, I've had an honest job. Wasn't such a great bargain, you ask me."

"When?" Her tipped chin and crossed arms showed she didn't believe it.

"When I was twelve. Worked at a match factory in Wapping. Couldn't get away fast enough."

"Why? To become a criminal? And now, when you have a chance to better yourself, you refuse?" She shook her head, sad and confounded. "For all your talk about honor, the only thing you seem to have in common with Robin Hood is your hair."

"What do you know about it?" he snapped. Across the room, Danny looked up from his bed and stared. He didn't care. Fueled by anger, his heart raced and his eyes stung. He'd hoped she might see past their differences, but she was just one more high-and-mighty society type, quick to think the worst. "Who are you to judge me, when you're stealing right beside us? Don' forget you're one of us now, and you'd better get used to crime, because when you're poor, it's how you get on in the world."

"That's an excuse. There are plenty of poor people who don't turn to crime. It seems to me you chose to become a pickpocket rather than stay on an honest path!"

"Some choice. You know what I did at that factory?" He thrust out his hands to show her the pitted scars. "Dipped sticks in pots of white poison that ate my skin if it touched me, and stunk like the devil himself. People working there got sick from that rotten stink. Their faces swelled up, their skin glowed green, and the ones who didn't die had to have their jaws sawed off."

Her eyes narrowed. "Glowing green skin?"

"He ain't lyin', Lady Constance! It's phossy jaw! I seen it," said Danny.

"So don't talk about excuses and choices," Alex said. "Not 'til you've had to steal to eat, or live down in the sewer to keep warm." Her eyes got wide with surprise. "Don' look so shocked, luv. People do it. I was one of 'em."

The heat of his anger seemed to put out the fire of hers. She shuddered and gave a quick nod. "I see. I'm sorry. I didn't know."

But he wasn't done. "It's easy to look down on someone like me, ain't it? At the way I talk? How I got no manners and can't read?"

"But I can teach you. You don't have to be ashamed of it anymore."

"I ain't ashamed! An' I ain't a bloody gent, either." He tore the watch from his pocket and flung it on his mattress. "I'm a sewer rat and a thief who's damned proud he's risen so far as to run a crew. Even if it is for a criminal. Sorry if that ain't good enough for you." He stormed out of the room, Danny at his heels.

If the lads in the kitchen heard the ruckus, they said nothing. He poured wine in his cup and sat at the table. The Irish brothers were playing cards, and Danny waited at the edge of the game to be dealt in. Alex wasn't in the mood.

What did Lady Constance know about choices? The biggest one she'd had to make was which flavor of jam to put on her breakfast toast. Kissing her had been bloody stupid. They couldn't be more different. She didn't even know how to kiss, and he'd bedded whores. She was smart enough to study at some fancy school, and he couldn't read a damn word. He was completely unworthy of her. But to know she thought so, too? It was even worse than her pity, and that was bad enough. He'd seen it when he caught her staring at his scars. He drank deeply. The wine was bitter stuff, nothing like the Count's fine claret, but it ought to take the edge off his hurt and rage.

It didn't.

The honest world had nothing to offer a bloke like him. It was a place where little ones slaved for pennies in dark, stinking factories. It was a place where you got watery soup, stale bread, and if you weren't grateful enough, a beating. It was a place where people in fine clothes preached hell and damnation to those in rags.

Everything he'd told her was true and there was plenty he'd left out.

Annie Blackwood drank up most of what she earned whoring on the docks, so he'd learned to steal food when he was small. Home was an unheated room, and a few times it got so cold, they'd had to go underground. Still, life in Shadwell wasn't all bad. There were friends around and places to explore. At school, they were good to him and he got fed a decent meal each day.

All that changed when his mum died. The landlord rented out their room and took Alex to the Mile End Workhouse. The first thing they did was shave his head because they said he had lice. From there, he ended up in the closest thing he could imagine to hell.

After he ran away from the Tru-Light Match factory, and survived by his wits on the streets for a while, the Count's mansion seemed like paradise. Once more, he had friends around and food to eat. No longer did he have to sleep rough. Pete taught him to be a top-drawer thief. When he got a little older, Nancy taught him other things.

And now Lady Constance wanted him to live an honest life? Ha! Too bloody late for that.

She came to the kitchen for supper, but went back to their room when she finished. When he came to bed, she was asleep.

On his bed were his mended shirt, his gent's watch, and the psalm book.

He stared down at them, feeling like a heel. While he'd been stewing, she'd been putting him back together, stitch by stitch. Caring that she did it right. Buttoned and folded, the old shirt could have come from a fine shop, not been stolen from a rag man. She'd laid it beside the polished gold watch she said he deserved to carry. Once, he memorized something about treating others as you wanted to be treated. It made more sense to him than anything he'd ever heard. He sure hadn't done that to Connie. But she'd done it for him.

He flipped through the little book. The words inside meant nothing. What made her think he could learn to read? He never was the best student. He could memorize but that wasn't reading. Was it? He had hazy memories of letters, sounds, and how to write his name. Seemed like there was an "x" in it somewhere, but that was about all he could recall.

❦

The next morning, she was in her lad's clothes and ready to go when he came to the kitchen. "Thanks for mending my shirt," he said. "Didn't expect you to."

She sniffed. "I said I would. I don't go back on my word." She drank her tea, but didn't offer him any.

They went back to the city, and Danny came along. The lad needed extra help — it was true — but if he hadn't been there, he and Connie wouldn't have said a word all morning.

Pickings were slim, even for a sunny, late summer workday.

Danny got a few billies, he got one purse, Connie nothing. They drifted through London, walking west.

They followed Cheapside until it forked. The south fork passed the churchyard at St. Paul's Cathedral — a fine reminder of schools, reading and fancy places he didn't belong. But the north fork turned into Newgate Street and led past the prison. Every once in a while, he passed on hanging day, when the crowds gathered and the black flag flew, to show the crooks were dead. Danny didn't need to see that. None of them did. He chose the southern route, around St. Paul's.

He led them to Blackfriars Bridge, the furthest west he came. Beyond it lay the new Victoria Embankment with its wide, clean streets and fine buildings. Looking east from the bridge was the dome of St. Paul's, the city, the Tower of London, and beyond that, the tenements, docks, and factories of the East End. Smokestacks belching black smoke dotted the eastern skyline as far as he could see.

Connie stood at the bridge rail, far enough away that no one would ever guess they were together, and stared off to the west. Danny sneered. "Bet she's wishin' she was back with all her high society types."

Danny had taken his side in the fight and was giving Connie the cold shoulder out of loyalty. But the more Alex thought about it, the more he saw it was the lad who needed her help. "Don' know about that." he replied. "Been thinkin' it might be good if you learned to read. I'm sure she would teach you."

"Reading's for nobs 'n swells like Lady Constance. An' who needs her?" The boy stuck out his chin. "She was jus' judgin' us right, Black?"

"I might've been quick to judge her. And knowin' how to read would help if you ever want to leave the Count's and work an honest job."

"Like in a match factory?"

Alex shook his head. "Better than that."

"Why would I want to leave? You ain't gonna throw me out, are you?" The lad was scared. Danny's own mum had tossed him into the streets. "I want to stay with you. Learn to be Robin Hood."

The breeze off the river ruffled Danny's hair. It was longer now. Like his. His chest tightened, torn up by it all. No one in his whole sorry life had ever loved him the way Danny did. "I know, and you can stay as long as you want. But think about what I said, all right? An' don' be too hard on Connie. She means well, even if she is a nob."

He brought the idea up to Connie later, when they sat in a little park and watched Danny chase pigeons.

"I'm willing, but I'm not a teacher," she said. "I only thought I could help you because you'd memorized psalms. Why is it so important to you he learns?"

"He ain't cut out for this. He don' belong at the Count's any more than I belong at Buckingham Palace." He swallowed hard, and his eyes stung. "Might come a day when I'm not around to look after him."

She nodded and looked over with that calm, steady gaze. "I want you to know I wasn't judging you last night. I was asking questions. Reasonable ones, I thought. Maybe things you've even thought about."

He had, though he hated to admit it.

"When you treated me like I'm one of those who condemned you, weren't you the one judging me? Have you forgotten I told you that you are indeed a gentleman?"

"Might've," he said, avoiding her eyes.

"I know there are parts of your life that are quite unsettling. Just as I'm sure there are things about me which seem odd to you."

"Your love for school." He smiled a little, as the chill began to thaw.

"Exactly. Neither of us can change what we were born into. Nor can we deny that under different circumstances, we wouldn't even be allowed to speak to one another. But just because those rules exist, doesn't mean they're right. Nor do we have to accept them."

"You think you can look past everything you've ever heard about people like me?"

She paused, thinking. "Yes, I believe so. Can you?"

Honest and true. He'd known it the first time he saw her. She didn't deny their differences, but she wasn't scared of them. Or scared of him. He hated being angry and bitter. To nurse those feelings around Connie was just a waste of precious time, and he didn't have much of that. Even if he left this life as nothing more than a thief ... even if he had to steal for a crook, wouldn't he rather do it beside this girl who saw him as someone good and fine? He bobbed his head. "For certain, it's worth a try."

He stood and held out his hand. She took it and his good mood came back a little more. He pulled her to her feet, and she smiled. He held onto her longer than he needed to, and then put his arm around her shoulders, pulling her close. "Come on, luv. Let's go rob someone."

CHAPTER TEN

B y autumn, Constance's life before the East End felt like a distant memory. One morning as she, Alex, and Danny boarded an omnibus, it occurred to her that by now, she would have been well into her classes at Girton College.

It was remarkable, really. In a matter of months, she'd transformed from prospective university student to apprentice pickpocket, watching for marks from behind the mask of her boy disguise. No one would have imagined that beneath the grime was an earl's daughter, who once lived in an elegant home on Bruton Street.

When she commented on it later, Alex asked, "Do you miss it?"

"Some things, like lavender baths and my old bed. I don't miss silly gossip and being bad at things I'm expected to do well because I'm female."

"Like what?"

"Needlework."

He glanced down at his shirt. "Sewed my buttons on well enough."

"I did, didn't I?" His tailoring standards weren't very high, but his praise felt good all the same. "Playing the pianoforte and singing," she added. "I am dreadful at both."

"No pianofortes 'round here, but Jimmy can teach you guitar. An' who cares if you can't sing? I sing good enough for both of us."

Who cared indeed? Not him.

Never in her life had she known anyone who appreciated her the way Alex did. The things she could do impressed him and he didn't hesitate to say so. What she couldn't do was unimportant. After years of hearing all her shortcomings, it was wonderful that Alex found so much to like.

She found much to like about him, too. In recent weeks, she had been teaching Danny to read and write. It wasn't long before Jimmy decided to learn. At first, Alex kept his distance, but now he joined them each night. His memory was excellent, and he knew more than he realized. He quickly relearned the alphabet, and how to write his name. As she hoped, he recognized words from the psalms when he saw them in other places. She taught him more by pointing out words as she read the newspaper aloud. As time went by, he learned to read street and shop signs. One night, she found him hunched over the *Robin Hood* book, working through it, word by word.

Even better, he wanted to learn more. When she used a word he didn't understand, he asked her to explain it. After hearing her speak French, he'd remarked, "Might like to know some French. Maybe you can teach me."

They were like two halves of a whole, each made better by the other.

Yet the days were bittersweet. Beneath the loose brick in their room, she had almost eight pounds stashed away. Not enough to live on yet, but close. The closer she came to being able to leave, the less she wanted to.

By now, she knew Alex well enough to see the worry behind his carefree demeanor. He tried to reassure her with jokes and smiles, but she hated when he went alone to Count Zuko's attic lair. She'd only seen the Count, a man with thinning hair and cruel eyes, occasionally, but Alex's scars were proof of what he was capable.

As close as they'd become, there was no repeat of the kiss they'd shared. Some nights she lay awake for hours, tormented by desire and heartache. While there were many things he liked about her, her kisses weren't among them. Alex considered her nothing more than a friend. Like a sweet soprano voice, the natural ability to attract a man was another feminine quality she lacked. Soon enough, he would take up with Lucy or a pretty girl from the brothel. When that day came, she would take her money and leave, moving along to the next stage of her life and whatever it held.

Today, they were on Fleet Street. It had taken some doing, but she'd finally persuaded him to venture west of Blackfriars Bridge.

She resorted to jokes about constables standing guard at Ludgate Circus to keep out the riff-raff and Alex's pride all but forced him across. He'd been pleased by the dearth of pickpockets and police, as well as the wealth of the purses. She liked the energy she found in the thick of London's newspaper district.

"Maybe I could be a reporter," she mused, as they passed the offices of the Daily News. "I know they hire lady reporters. I think I would be an excellent one. I like to write, and I've seen a lot since I left home."

"Don' doubt that," Alex said.

"If I wrote about Count Zuko, Scotland Yard would put him out of business. Then none of you would have to steal anymore."

He scoffed. "Zuko's got friends at Scotland Yard. Parliament, too. Gents who protect his crooked arse to keep their own names out of the papers. The Count took me to parties at his gambling hell a time or two. You wouldn't believe who I met there." Ahead of them, Danny filched a handkerchief from an elderly man. "Besides, what else would we do? It wasn't the Count that turned us into thieves." His sideways glance dared her to argue back.

She didn't take the bait. "You should leave him. You could get an honest job. A good honest job," she emphasized, expecting his protest. "You're smart enough. When I leave the East End, you could come with me. We could tell everyone we're brother and sister."

He laughed. "Soon's I open me mouth, I be givin' that one away. What would I do? Ain't no one hirin' a thief to be a footman or a shop assistant." They paused outside the offices of the London Reformer, as a well-dressed man climbed from a carriage. Alex's gaze lingered on the liveried driver who exchanged a capable nod with the departing gentleman. When he spoke again, his voice held the quiet despair he would be quick to deny. "I been with the Count too long. I know too much. He ain't going to let me just walk away."

They passed a vendor selling buns. Danny eyed them longingly and her mouth watered. There had been little to eat last night and nothing left over this morning. The vendor was distracted by a newsboy hawking papers an arm's length away.

Alex strolled up to the cart, slipped something inside his sleeve, and snatched his hand away the moment the vendor turned back. The man scowled from beneath bushy dark eyebrows. "You wan' som'tin?"

Alex flashed his most charming smile. "No, gov, just lookin.'"

The bun man crossed his arms over his dirty apron. "Then look somewhere else."

Alex tipped his bowler, but there was sarcasm in the gesture. As he turned away, the bottom of his tattered frock coat flared, emphasizing his slender, athletic build. Even in rags from a used clothes wagon, Alex carried himself with a grace that defied his circumstances. Her throat caught as she thought of him doomed to a life of crime and poverty.

He lacked the breeding of a gentleman, and most people would never consider him one. But manners could be taught. A pickpocket could be educated. What truly made a gentleman were his character, intelligence, and compassion. Alex possessed these qualities, even more than some noblemen's sons she knew. His quick mind, threadbare dignity, and kind heart made him too good to be exploited by the likes of Viktor Zuko.

By a mere accident of birth, he'd been forced into a life he

116

didn't want, just as she had. She had escaped the future society tried to impose. Somehow, she must help him do the same.

"Get your Daily News 'ere! U.S. and English railways bankrupt! New York Stock Exchange shut down!" The newsboy's cry rose above the rattling cart on the street. Alex took the bun from his sleeve. He only had one. Constance tried not to let her disappointment show. He tore it into three portions and gave the larger to her and Danny.

Danny gobbled his, but it felt wrong to take the bigger portion, when Alex hadn't eaten today, either. "No," she said. "You should have this."

"Ain' hungry. If I want another, I'll get one." He popped the bun in his mouth, ending the discussion.

He had a point. He had been stealing food since boyhood and being able to provide for the people he cared about, even in a small way, meant a great deal to him. Besides, she was hungry, so rather than argue or hurt his feelings, she ate it gratefully.

"Now there's a place I wouldn't have minded goin,'" he said, as they passed another newsboy shouting about stocks and railways.

"Where? New York?"

"America. Don' matter what part. A bloke who wanted to get away... and start over again? Might be a place for him there."

She caught a breath as hope rose. "I'm sure there would be. Why don't you go?"

He grinned. "How am I going to get there, luv? Swim? Trade on me good looks?"

If the ticket agent was female, he definitely had a chance. "That might work," she said with a smile.

He shook his head and looked grim again. "Ain't gonna happen, at least not now. Fare costs close to two month's wages, and I'd need even more to eat and start out once I got there. Unless I wanted to steal to get by." His sardonic tone made it clear he didn't. "On top of all that, I'd have to get up to Liverpool to catch the boat."

His gloom was frustrating. He seemed so resigned to becoming one of the Count's thugs. Yet he'd given it enough thought to know the cost of fare and from where ships left. "But if you could get the money..." she coaxed.

"It's almost winter, Connie. Once it turns cold, anyone with money takes a cab instead of walkin'. An' everybody's got less from spendin' their pennies on coal. From now on, making share will be hard enough. Lucky for you, you've almost got what you need." He tilted his head toward Danny. "There's him to think about, too."

Of course, he wouldn't leave Danny behind. Yet America would give Alex what he needed most—a fresh start. There had to be a solution. As much as it hurt to think of him on the other side of the ocean, she vowed to do whatever she could to get him there.

The gaslight cast eerie shadows across Count Zuko's bony face and bald head. Slowly, he counted the notes, coins, and handkerchiefs piled on his desk. Then he counted it again.

Alex shifted his weight. He knew how much was there— fourteen pounds and ten shillings, plus the one-pound they'd get from the fence for Danny's handkerchiefs. It was his crew's total from the week. He'd counted it and kept track in his ledger. There weren't a lot of honest things he knew how to do, but he was very good at counting money.

The Count sat back in his heavy chair. In his fine evening clothes, he looked powerful. And dangerous. Lottie perched on the arm of the chair. Her red dressing gown showed a glimpse of her curvy body and bare legs. Alex had interrupted something, but the Count never put pleasure ahead of business. The girl pouted and lowered her eyes in an invitation. With a word, she could be his. The Count didn't mind sharing, but he wasn't interested. Not when Connie waited below stairs.

Zuko smiled with good humor that cloaked his vicious nature. "You're short again, Alexander. You aren't holding out on me, are you?"

His mind flashed to the leather bag Connie had hidden beneath the loose brick under Danny's mattress, but he kept his wits. The Count could smell fear. Besides, he wasn't short and his ledger would prove it. Zuko was playing a game. He crossed his arms and challenged his boss. "Count it again. There's fourteen and ten there, plus the handkerchiefs. You can get a pound for those. I have the sums if you want to look."

"There's no need." The Count relaxed, and Alex did, too. Once again, he'd passed a test. Zuko drummed his fingers. "You've done well, Alexander, and tonight, I want to reward you."

"Reward me?" No reward was better than returning to Connie's side, while she practiced guitar with Jimmy or taught Danny his letters.

"I'm giving a small dinner party tonight, for some important and well-connected guests. Men it will do you good to meet." Zuko nodded to Lottie, who went to his bedchamber and returned carrying an evening suit. "I believe that will fit you. You will join us for dinner and entertainment afterward." His stern voice left no room for argument.

The French manservant who worked in the brothel took him to a room on the third floor. Tim, Max, and Ulysses all lived up here and he would too, if he joined up with the Count's bashers. It was clean and comfortable, a far cry from the basement. After the servant had bathed, shaved, and dressed him in the black tailcoat and white tie, Alex decided he made quite the swell.

He straightened his cuffs and admired the onyx studs that held them. A shame Connie couldn't see him. He ought to send word he was safe, but she wouldn't want him going to the Count's party. It didn't matter. Soon she would leave, and it would be time to move into the life he'd been groomed for, ever since the Count chose him from the basement thieves. A life that had its advantages.

He ate the best dinner he'd had in months. The mansion's kitchen served only the brothel and the Count, never the pickpockets. In the basement, they got jellied eel and plonk. Up here, it was a loin of beef so tender it melted in your mouth, mashed potatoes, fresh breads, rich desserts, and a fragrant French claret to wash it all down. He could get used to this.

Too bad he didn't like the company. Aside from the Count, Ulysses, and Tim, were four stuffed-shirt nobs whose names he couldn't remember. Three Sir Somebodys and a Lord Somebody. He caught the given name of Lord Somebody, Henry, which reminded him of Connie's bastard fiancé. But as someone of much lower status, he could only address them as "sir" and "my lord." He dealt with the situation by saying as little as possible.

At dinner, Lottie sat between him and Count Zuko. "You must be countin' the days 'til you're up here, livin' the high life," she said.

He turned away, so he didn't have to look at the half-chewed meat in Lottie's open mouth, or the shine of grease on her chin. "Can't complain about the food."

Lottie shoveled in a spoonful of mashed potatoes. "For your birthday, the Count wants to give you whatever girl you want. He won't be mad when you choose me."

It would be a cold day in hell before that ever happened. A manservant added more wine to their glasses. "All the way to the top," Lottie said, gesturing with her dirty spoon. She raised the brimming glass and slopped claret down the front of her dress.

Quickly he grabbed his napkin, but Lottie just smiled and ran her fingertip through the splash of wine on her chest. She licked the drop away. "Something this good shouldn't go to waste. Come on, Black. Taste what you want so much."

He'd rather taste blood pudding—loads of it, stone cold. But Lottie was offering herself, right at the table, for his pleasure. What man wouldn't take her? A man whose heart belonged to someone else, that was who. Only to let it be known, would put Connie in terrible danger. Everyone at the table burst out with cheers and howls, egging him on. Like a crowd at a cockfight, they were eager to see what they had no business watching. Loving a woman was a private thing, not something to entertain drunks at a party. But the Count and Tim were watching. Lottie put her hand on the back of his neck, to push him face down into her tits.

Alex closed his eyes and lowered his head. As he licked wine from Lottie's ripe-smelling flesh, the ruckus grew louder, swallowing him. Soon, this would be the only love he would know.

After dinner, they moved to the saloon. Nancy was there, and so was a young blond girl he'd never seen before. She wore a tight pink dress and couldn't have been a day over thirteen.

She pouted and posed for the men, but the act seemed put on. She wasn't scared or tearful, like she was being forced to do this, but he sensed she was new at it. Her eyes darted between him and Tim, the only men close to her age, but guests had first dibs. As the highest rank, Lord Somebody, a gent in his thirties with fleshy lips, bushy sideburns, and a big wart on his upper-right cheek, chose her first.

Alex shot billiards with Ulysses and one of the Sirs, but couldn't forget the girl in the pink dress. Soon, it would be his job to bring in more just like her. Could he lure an innocent girl into a whorehouse? He remembered how scared Connie was the first day. Could he have calmed her fear and then turned her over to Minerva?

A manservant refilled his glass with the fine claret he liked so much. As he tasted it, he thought about what paid for all this. Money extorted from hard-working shopowners and publicans who only wanted protection from vultures like Viktor Zuko. That would also be Alex's job — to bully honest people like Mr. Browning, and threaten everything he held dear, just to line the pockets of a crook.

He set down his glass. The girl in the pink dress was back. Her red-rimmed eyes were dead. Alex was overcome by such loathing for what he saw and what he was about to become; he knew he could never do it.

What choice did he have, though? He didn't want to go the way Pete had. Not when there were people he loved and who loved him. Connie believed he could be more than a common crook. Maybe she was right.

There was a touch on his shoulder and behind him, the Count's silky voice. "Time to choose."

Alex's heart stilled. Then he realized what Zuko meant. Minerva's whores, on display for selection. "Perhaps my lovely Lottie, or sweet young Millicent? Tonight was her first time, you know. Lord Gaffney had the pleasure of deflowering her, but she's still fresh," said Zuko.

Millicent thrust her little breasts against her tight pink dress, showing herself to her best advantage. Beside her, Nancy, who'd lost a tooth recently when a drunk client got too rough, looked old and used up. Tim, Max, and Ulysses eyed the merchandise. The entire scene was ugly and brutal. The only thing Alex desired was to leave. Tim shifted his eyes from Nancy to Millicent and leered. "You, Millie. Les' go."

Millie strutted forward to claim Tim. Ulysses chose Maude. The Count's eyes bored into Alex, waiting. He also felt Nancy's eyes, wounded and sad. He smiled at her and held out his hand.

Tonight, her dim, patchouli-scented room felt gloomy in a way it never had before. Nancy knocked back a shot of gin and went to work. She pressed on him a probing, gin-flavored kiss and untied his cravat. He grasped her wrists and gently removed her hands. "I can't do this."

"What, Black?" Her voice shook. "Rather have a go at Millie after all?"

"'Course not," he touched her shoulder. "I can't do any of this, Nance. Lay with you, work for the Count. None of it."

"You ain't got a choice! You know what he did to Pete. You watched it, same as me." Her lower lip trembled, and he remembered how Nancy used to follow Pete around, moon-struck. Her eyes were shiny, but she blinked and got herself under control. "If you don't join him, he'll do the same to you."

"It doesn't matter. I don't want to live this way."

"Don' say that," she snapped. "Look, it don' have to be for long." She looked around, as if someone might overhear, then whispered. "The Count ain't going to be around forever. Tim's got ideas. You and him could run things, you as the brains, and him as the brawn."

"No. I'm done." The words were out, alive now, and he knew down to his soul he couldn't take them back.

Nancy smirked. "It's her, ain't it? Lady Constance. She got to you, made you think above your place in the world. You're East End, Black. She's West End. She ain't like us." She paused then and cocked her head, as if noticing something she hadn't before. She chuckled, sadly. "But I guess in a lot o' ways, you ain't like us either, are you?"

He wasn't. He'd known it a long time, but until Connie, he'd never understood what it meant. He still didn't know for sure, but one thing was certain. He had to leave the Count as soon as possible.

Nancy took his hand. "You've been a true friend, Black. Promise you won't do anything stupid."

He looked her straight in the eye. "I promise."

Nancy hugged him. This might not be the last time he saw her, but it was farewell, nonetheless. She looked him up and down and smiled. "You look right handsome, dressed that way. I say you'll fit in with the nobs just fine."

In the third-floor dressing room, he took off the evening clothes and put on his worn trousers, waistcoat, and shirt. He buttoned the old linen shirt Connie had mended for him. Whatever the future held, he would gladly wear rags as long as they were together.

When he returned to the basement, she was asleep. Pushing the horse blanket aside, he gazed down at her. She was as fine and lovely as a princess, her dark brown hair fanned across the pillow. But even by candlelight, he saw her troubled brow. Had she missed him? He crouched down and without thinking, brushed his fingers across her forehead to soothe the bad away.

Her eyes fluttered open. She squinted in the candlelight and sat up. "Alex? Where have you been?"

"Upstairs at the Count's party. But I'm back now." Where I belong. His mind finished the sentence. "Just wanted you to know, is all. Sorry I woke you up."

Her body relaxed, and he saw how relieved she was. He'd been wrong to worry her. "Don't be. I'm glad you woke me." Then she scooted forward and wrapped him in her arms.

Surprise turned to desire as her soft, tempting body pressed against him. But with Danny snoring just inches away, this was not the right time. He also sensed that what she needed right now was comfort.

He needed it too.

If the Count was the corrupt side of his life, Connie stood for everything good. He clung to her, trying to shut out memories of the girl in pink, and the foul taste of Lottie's skin. Tears burned his eyes. He feared he might lose control and weep like a child. His precious Lady Constance believed in him, and somehow, he would become the man she deserved.

She gently stroked his back, and after a long moment, released him. "Was the party fun?"

"No." He pushed back a lock of hair from her face. "I would have rather been here with you."

She smiled. "I wish you had been. Jimmy taught me to play 'Sing a Song of Sixpence' and I wanted someone to sing with me."

"Tomorrow, I promise. Go on back to sleep now, luv."

She settled back on her pillow, sleepy, beautiful and at peace. "Goodnight, Alex."

He stayed at her bedside, watching over her as she drifted off. When her breathing grew steady and he was sure she'd fallen asleep, he brushed a kiss across her lips. In the dark, he whispered, "I love you."

CHAPTER ELEVEN

Something had definitely changed.

Constance settled into the circle of Alex's arm as they rode atop the omnibus from Smithfield Market, to the financial district. She wore her boy's disguise but since they were the only rooftop passengers, he moved closer

"Cor blimey!" Danny said. "He let you 'ave a whole slice of beef an' two pieces of cake? I never even 'ad one, 'cept for some Christmas cake once. Did it have sugared fruit on top?"

"Don't recall," Alex replied.

All morning, Danny had peppered him with questions about his night at the Count's. But even as he described the lavish meal, there was little enthusiasm in his voice.

Last night, when Alex didn't return from the attic, Constance had feared the worst. Luke shot a glance at the cellar door and told her not to worry. "If Black was in trouble, we'd know. The Count used to invite him to parties. He ain't been to one in a while, but that's probably where he is."

She couldn't imagine why he'd go to one now — other than the possibility of a pretty new whore. She went to bed, woeful and lonely. When she awoke to find him at her bedside, she'd wrapped her arms around him to assure herself he was real. He'd smelled of cigar smoke and sandalwood, but there was something about the way he held her — as if he needed comfort as much as he wanted to give it that convinced her he hadn't been with another girl. Why he'd gone to the party wasn't important. What mattered was that he'd returned.

Alex brushed his fingertips against her shoulder, and she turned to find him smiling back. His sunny mood was catching. When the swaying motion of the bus jostled them, their bodies touched in a friendly, yet intimate way. Danny, sitting on his opposite side, tugged at his sleeve. "Hey, Black? Next time the Count has a party, can I come too?"

"Might not be the best idea, Dan."

This morning, they'd worked their usual Saturday route around the livestock markets, but Alex hadn't stolen a thing. Nor did he choose any marks. When Danny was nearly caught trying to steal a silk topper from a man haggling over the price of a pig, she suggested they try their luck on Princes Street. Alex merely shrugged and smiled.

She had no idea what to make of it.

The bus came to a halt, and they scrambled down the ladder,

taking care to avoid the pile of horse droppings on the street. "Where to, luv?" Alex asked.

Dismayed at suddenly being in charge, she glanced around at the crowded streets. One direction was as good as any. "This way," she said, turning east toward the Bank of England.

Bright golden sunlight bathed the street. The Martin's Summer weather had brought out everyone who could find a reason to escape his office, and they worked around the banks until afternoon. On Lombard Street, near Barclay's Bank, she stopped short. There stood Gaffney, talking with three other gentlemen. His sideburns were bushier than they'd been a few months ago, but his fleshy lips had the same arrogant sneer. The large mole that grew on his upper-right cheek still defined his face. "It's Horace!" she whispered.

Alex gave a wide grin. "The middle one with the big wart? That bastard was at the Count's party last night. Had a roll with a thirteen-year-old whore, he did. Fine gent your parents picked for you. You goin' after him?"

"How could I not?" She tossed back a wicked smile and tugged her cap down low over her eyes. With the jaunty, arm-swinging gait of a carefree lad, she charged forward, crashing into Gaffney with as much force as possible.

"Oops! So sorry, gov'nor!"

"Filthy brat! Watch where you're going." He turned and their gazes met. Suddenly, his eyes narrowed as he peered into her face, as if he knew what he was seeing, yet didn't understand it. She seized on his distraction, plunging her hand into his coat, where she knew he kept his purse. Sure enough, it was there. A handkerchief, too. Maybe the one he'd tossed in her lap at the ball.

She slipped them into her trousers and returned his scowl with a smirk.

He swung his open hand. She dodged it and when she was out of reach, turned back and shouted in her best Cockney, "An' a fine day to you too, arsehole!"

Alex and Danny waited nearby in the alley. The moment he saw her, Alex hooked his arm around her shoulders and planted a friendly kiss on the top of her head. "You might not sing like a lark, but you're a natural-born thief."

"Thank you. I think." Even if it was just a chummy gesture, her spirits soared. Without thinking, she hugged him back.

Danny grabbed her arm. "Let's see what you got!"

"A big one, I'm sure. Gaffney likes to carry a lot of money." She pulled out her ex-fiance's purse and emptied three gold sovereigns into her palm.

Danny's eyes grew wide, as if he had never seen so much money. "Blimey, look at all that. The bloke's bloody rich!"

The boy was right, but the money piled in her hand brought a sobering thought. As of this moment, she had enough to leave Count Zuko's. There was no longer a single reason to stay.

No, there was a reason. Standing beside her in a shabby frock coat and dented bowler, Alex no longer smiled. "That almost makes enough for you, doesn't it?"

"I'm not sure. Maybe not. I still have to add it all up." She tucked the money back in her pocket and said no more about it.

It was almost evening when they returned to the mansion. In

the courtyard, Little Jack and the Irish brothers kicked a ball around, while Sam washed at the pump. Luke and Jimmy, carrying their instruments, met them at the back gate. "Hurry up, Dan," Luke ordered. "Mr. Browning wants us at the pub early. It's going to be a big crowd tonight."

When Alex went to the pump, she took her savings from beneath the loose brick and added today's take. She had a little over twelve pounds.

She gazed up at the dirty window above Danny's bed. Tomorrow, she could leave, go straight to the West End, and rent a room. Monday morning, she could walk into one of the newspapers on Fleet Street and present herself as capable and competent. No longer was she a Mayfair misfit, doomed to spinsterhood or a horrible marriage. She was a young woman who could light her own fire, brew her own tea, and best of all, control her own destiny. She had done it. She had set herself free.

But she couldn't leave Alex behind. She hadn't yet convinced him to leave the Count, though after today, he might reconsider. If he was willing, Constance knew what she would do.

He was waiting in the courtyard, dressed in the striped waistcoat and checkered trousers he had worn the day they met. Never in her wildest dreams would she have believed that one night, she'd be the girl on the arm of the handsome blond pickpocket. As she approached, his blue eyes raked her over, his smile told her he liked what he saw. He brought her hand to his lips and kissed it. "You are lovely, Lady Constance."

His words brought a delicious little shiver.

A true gentleman, Alex offered his arm. She smiled and took it. Walking down Commercial Street they made a striking, if disreputable-looking, pair. Sam and the Irish brothers were flash, in short jackets of the latest style, colorful waistcoats and new bowlers, stolen from who knows where. Even Danny was shined up, wearing a clean shirt and trousers that fit, proudly carrying his drumsticks. People on the sidewalks gave them a wide berth. Everyone in Spitalfields knew Count Zuko and his house of thieves, whores, and cutthroats. Far from ashamed to be in such company, Constance met the eyes of everyone she passed.

What would her parents or Jane think if they saw her now? Without a doubt, they would be shocked, and the thought brought unexpected pleasure. Perhaps a rebel had always lurked beneath her proper facade. A high-born girl shouldn't even know about this world, yet she'd made her way in it. Tonight, she was proud to step out with a dashing young man who wore mismatched clothes and long hair with such panache.

Her first day here, the raucous laughter coming from the Four Farthings had frightened her. Now, she knew the family who owned the place, and especially liked their daughter Sally, who was sweet on a certain curly-haired pickpocket. Inside the crowded tavern, Sally rushed from the kitchen where Mrs. Browning and the cook fried helpings of fish and chips, to the bar where her father and older brother waited on customers. As always, the sign above the bar promised "Free Beer Tomorrow."

"Evenin,' boys! Good evening, Connie." Arlo Browning knew their drinks and set them up with ales and gin. Sam, Tommy, and Patrick went to find girls. Drumsticks in hand, Danny joined Luke, Jimmy, and Jake Browning on the stage. He took his seat atop Jake's pianoforte and the band swung into its first song.

Lucy, here on the arm of a beefy young butcher's assistant,

tossed curious looks their way, but not once did Constance think Alex might prefer another girl. His attention was only on her. His gaze lingered on her face. They danced nearly every dance. When they weren't dancing, he found reasons to touch her. Even the softest brush of his fingers seemed to burn through her clothing.

When the musicians took a break, they joined the crowd outside, where the butcher's assistant's drunk friends sang bawdy songs off-key at the top of their lungs. They laughed and talked with people they knew, and then Alex tilted his head toward the alley. "I want to show you something."

She took his hand and followed him to the back of the building. Beside the kitchen door, a flight of wooden steps led to the roof. The building was only two floors, but tall enough to put them above the glow of the streetlights. Overhead, the stars and full autumn moon hung on a black velvet sky.

The band had started to play, and music drifted up from the tavern's open windows. Alex swung her into a gentle waltz. As they danced on the moonlit rooftop, he sang along. *"I adore her beauty, she's an angel dropped from above. May the fish get legs and the cows lay eggs, if ever I cease to love. May the moonbeams turn to green cream cheese, if ever I cease to love."*

It was a comic song, popular in music halls and taverns, not a romantic ballad. Yet it perfectly suited Alex's playful nature and meant more than a hundred maudlin love songs. The sweet, silly words touched her heart. This was how she wanted to feel in the arms of a young man. Not revulsion or fear. Not a duty to marry for wealth or position. Just this intoxicating combination of heart-pounding desire and unfettered joy. Life would have been much simpler if a well-born man made her feel like this, but it hadn't happened that way. Was that any reason she should be denied happiness?

Her pulse quickened as he moved against her. She rested her cheek against his shoulder, breathing in the crisp scents of his citrus shaving tonic and freshly- laundered shirt. Drawing closer into his embrace, she slid her hand around to his back. Suddenly reminded of the scars that sliced across his skin, she felt a moment's terror he might refuse to leave Count Zuko. Instead, she pushed it aside and gave herself over to the blissful sensation of being in Alex's arms, the sound of his voice as he serenaded her and the way his hand felt, strong and sure, holding hers.

When the song ended, he gazed into her eyes, and stroked her cheek with the tip of his finger. His soft touch lingered. A new, faster song had begun, but they no longer danced. He put his arm around her shoulders. She followed her natural inclination to wrap hers around his waist and rest her head on his shoulder. She leaned against him, liking this very much.

Together, they gazed up at the night sky, and the sea of rooftops, chimneys, and towers of London. Far in the distance were Mayfair and Bruton Street. Were her parents still there, or had they long departed to Sussex, resigning her to her fate?

"Pretty, ain't it? I think about you off that way somewhere, maybe at a fancy ball, lookin' up at the same stars as me. Now you're here, and we're lookin' at them together. All because Tim blagged your ring. Funny how things happen."

"I'm glad they happened."

"Really?" He sounded pleasantly surprised. "Even comin' here and joinin' a gang of thieves? No regrets at all?"

"My only regret would be to leave you behind when I go," she whispered, holding him tighter, determined to rescue him from his dangerous world. No matter what, she would not abandon him to it.

He grinned. "No regrets on Saturday nights, luv. East London rule."

"I've never heard that rule. I think you're lying."

His mischievous chuckle lingered. "I might be."

She closed her eyes. Though she desperately wanted to stay in this perfect moment, the time had come to tell him. Gathering her courage, she stepped from his embrace. "There's something you must know," she said, and took a deep breath. "As of today, I have enough money to leave. Gaffney's purse gave me what I needed."

His joyful expression faded, and he nodded solemnly. "I knew it would come, I'd just hoped not so soon." He forced a smile and took both her hands. "When are you going?"

"That's just it. I don't want to leave without you. I want you to have half of what I've saved." He started to speak. She held up a hand to silence him. "I want to help you escape from the Count and go to America. You and Danny, both."

Her eyes grew wet, and she clenched her jaw to stifle the sob that rose in her throat. She was offering the gift of freedom and if he accepted, she would lose him forever. But if a broken heart was the price to save him, she would pay it. "You're not a criminal, Alex. You say you aren't a gentleman, but that isn't true. You are a gentleman in all the ways that matter. You deserve the life you want, not one forced on you."

Stunned, Alex shifted his gaze from her face, to their joined hands, then back to her. "Guess you know something about that, don't you?"

She laughed sadly. "I'd say I'm an expert. Now, it's not enough for you both to leave immediately, but it's a start. And I intend to stay and build up the rest of my funds, so when the time comes, we can all leave together. I won't take no for an answer."

Alex looked thoughtful. "I've been thinkin' about it since you first brought it up. Then last night, I decided for sure I had to leave, but didn't see how. Now I do. So I accept — on one condition." He gazed into her eyes and smiled. "That you come, too. I love you with all my heart, Connie. Will you do me the honor of being my wife?"

Now she was the one too stunned to speak. She'd been too blind to see it, but the truth was in his eyes. What she'd only dared to dream of was true — Alex loved her, just as she loved him. Happiness floated up like champagne bubbles.

Then burst just as quickly.

"I know it's a lot to ask." His expression grew serious. "Considering what all you'd be givin' up, to be with me."

Marrying Alex meant she could never go back to being the carefree daughter of a wealthy earl. Polite society would scorn her for marrying down. Not only would she never attend college, most likely, she would always have to work. Could she really leave England, her family, and the life she'd known, and sail away with him?

On the other hand, could she remain and watch him sail away from her? That was the easier question to answer. No!

She had always known the sort of man she wanted to marry; he was kind, honorable, smart and handsome. He would do anything for her. She would admire him, not because of his power or wealth, but because of the strength of his character. He would have the same respect for her. She could trust him with her heart, and her life. His smile would coax one from her. His kiss and his touch would make her pulse race.

Never had she considered his fortune, title, or lineage. Was it so surprising a penniless Cockney had turned out to be her perfect man?

"Oh, Alex, yes!"

"You're sure about this, luv?"

"Yes, I'm sure! I want to marry you and go to America. I love you so much, Alex. I never want to be without you!"

She threw her arms around his neck as he lifted her and they spun in a circle, caught up in the night's starlit magic. Then he set her down, and gazed into her eyes, his face filled with love and wonder. He traced her jaw with his fingertip and gently lifted her chin. His thumb brushed across the soft swell of her bottom lip. "You just made me the happiest bloke in all of London." Bending down, he claimed her mouth in a kiss.

What should she do? The first time they kissed, and she responded, he withdrew. Proper women were not supposed to have these wanton feelings, yet she did. Would he think badly of her and regret proposing? Lost in a whirlwind of conflicting thought, she held still, though her self-control was at a breaking point. Then suddenly, he pulled away. She braced for his disgust and disappointment. But when she opened her eyes, the softness in his gaze almost made her cry. "You've not been kissed this way, have you?"

She swallowed and looked away, too embarrassed to do anything but shake her head. He smiled gently and trailed his fingers across her cheek. "Didn't think so. It's not wrong to want me, Connie. I sure want you. Don' worry about doin' it right. Just relax and let me show you how."

She nodded and gazed into his eyes, under his spell. He cupped her head and moved closer. His lips claimed hers with gentle authority. He coaxed her, teased her with his tongue until she relaxed her mouth and parted her lips to let him in. He explored her mouth, nipped her bottom lip as deep inside, heat began to build.

Oh, yes.

His arm went around her, supporting her as she leaned into him and wrapped her arms around his neck. She threaded her fingers through his silky hair, then splayed her hands across his shoulders, feeling the taut muscles beneath his shirt, aching to touch his skin. Every sensation that sparked deep within was familiar, straight from her fevered dreams of romantic passion. But Alex brought them to life, painting her pen-and-ink imaginings with brilliant colors of every hue — the vibrant crimson of passion, the seductive blue of his eyes, the golden promise of their future. His urgent, hungry kisses left her mouth on fire. Unafraid now, she explored the hard planes of his body, her palms gliding over his slender, muscular frame.

"Connie," his whisper was low, hoarse, and he spoke her name like a prayer. She dropped her head back, exposing her neck. He left a scorching trail of kisses down her throat, to the swell of her breasts. He unbuttoned the top of her dress and slipped his hand inside the tight bodice and chemise to cup one of her breasts. She gasped as he stroked her nipple to stand taut, and when he reverently planted a kiss there, she shuddered. Her center felt wet. He held her tightly. Even if she wanted, she would have been powerless to leave. But she wanted nothing more than to stay in his arms. Breathlessly, she whispered his name.

Then loud laughter and voices penetrated the perfect seclusion of the rooftop. Three rowdy boys swung themselves over the parapet, howling at the moon. Alex released her and rested his forehead against hers. "We should go back in," she whispered, and buttoned her dress.

Alex nodded, and with his arm around her, guided her back to the stairs. They passed the rooftop invaders. It was too dark to see their faces, but one tipped his hat and she recognized Sam's husky laugh. "Hullo, Black. Connie. Hope we ain't interruptin' nothin.'"

She smiled to herself, feeling deliciously wicked with the taste of her fiancé's kiss in her mouth.

Back inside, Luke smiled knowingly from the stage and dedicated the next song to them. As the night went on, they sat at a corner table, held hands, talked, and made plans. They agreed not to tell Danny, or anyone else, until they were ready to leave, so word would not get back to the Count. With luck, they could leave before winter. When they reached America, Constance would seek a newspaper job. Danny would go to school. Alex decided he would like to work in one of the fine restaurants they were sure to find. "On the ship, you can teach me French and fancy manners," he said.

When the dancing ended and the crowd thinned out, Luke and Sally, Jimmy and Fan, a seamstress from Barbados he'd taken a fancy to; Jake, and Danny joined them. Arlo brought fresh drinks and helpings of fish and chips. The boys tucked in with gusto.

Jimmy and Jake rehashed their performance. Luke courted Sally. Constance sipped her ale and listened to the conversation, as she and Alex shared secret smiles.

Never had she been happier.

❦

Their room was empty when she awoke the next morning. Danny had gone to visit the rector at Christ Church, as had become his habit in recent weeks. She found Alex in the kitchen, with a pot of freshly-brewed tea and sticky buns from the bakery on Lamb Street. "Thought we should enjoy one last day before we start stashing away every spare penny," he said.

They ate in the kitchen, drinking tea, licking sweet glaze from their fingers. Then Luke joined them and at noon, they went to fetch Sally. She had packed a picnic, which Alex and Luke took turns carrying on the lengthy bus ride from Spitalfields to Victoria Park.

The park was full of families and young lovers enjoying what was likely the last lovely Sunday of the year. Alex and Constance, Luke and Sally ate beside the large pond and watched the rowboats on the water. "Let's rent one," Sally said.

"What do you say, Black?" Luke asked. "Shall we show the ladies what fine oarsmen we are?"

Alex glanced over. Constance replied with a subtle shake of her head. She longed for time alone with him, and the only boat she cared to ride was the enormous one that would carry them to their new lives. He seemed to read her thoughts. "I think Connie and I might take a walk, thanks. You two go on, and Luke, we'll see you back at the Count's."

After parting company with Luke and Sally, she and Alex followed the path around the pond.

"We should go see Danny's rector tomorrow and ask him to read banns for us. We could be married before we leave," Alex said.

"I don't see how we can," she said, experiencing her first less-than-blissful moment today. "We aren't old enough to wed without consent. Your parents aren't living, but mine are." It went without saying her parents would never permit her to marry him. "And if we have banns read, won't the Count find out?"

"Not likely anyone from the mansion besides Danny will be in church, but you're right. It's best Dan not know until it's time to go, that way he can't spill to anyone."

"Perhaps we can get married on the ship. Or right when we arrive. Then no one can say anything about what we do. But it seems such a long time to wait."

They sat on a bench near the water. She took Alex's hand and rested her head against his shoulder. The sun had dipped low in the sky and the shadow of a full moon was already visible. This perfect day was about to end but she smiled, thinking about the lifetime of perfect days ahead.

Suddenly he turned, excitement dancing in his eyes. "Come with me, luv."

The footbridge at the south end of the pond was deep in late afternoon shadow. The white pagoda on the opposite bank already glowed ghostly in the twilight. At the bridge's arch, he faced her and took her hands. "Constance, before God, I promise to love you for the rest of my life. Whatever lies ahead, whatever we face, I will take care of you and be true to you, no matter what."

Her lip trembled, and tears flooded her eyes. She blinked them away so she could see his handsome face as she spoke her own vows. "I love you, Alex, and I will until the day I die. I also promise before God to care for you and be faithful to you, no matter what."

He dug a coin from his pocket. It was a farthing, worth less than a penny. He pressed the coin into her hand and closed her fingers over it. "I don't have a proper ring to give you, only this. Someday, it will be much more. But there's a story that if you toss a coin off the bridge and make a wish, it will come true. I want you to make one." He raised her fist to his lips and kissed it.

"Don't you want to?"

He smiled. "Mine's already come true."

Hers had too, but she faced the pond and Alex stood behind her. She leaned back in his arms and closed her eyes. In that moment, she saw them standing this way on the ship to America, gazing out over the vast ocean. She saw their future. They lived in a city with their children — a boy and girl, in a fine home they'd acquired honestly. How it would come true, she didn't know, but beyond a doubt, she believed it would. She tossed the farthing into the still water. It left a ripple before it disappeared.

Then, she turned in his arms, and they kissed in the deepening dusk. In her heart, from that moment, she and Alex were married.

Leaving the park, they passed a grove of dense hedges. Impulsively, she pulled Alex toward it. Last night, he had claimed her. Now she would claim him. Behind the trees, in a hidden grotto, she kissed him with a boldness and passion that surprised her. He grinned, delighted by her randy appetite. "Whatever happened to my shy Lady Constance? What kind of woman have I taken as my wife?"

"A woman who can't wait to know every inch of her handsome husband." Timid no longer, she kissed him hard and ran her hands through his hair. Her fingers trailed across the rough surface of his jaw. His tie was already loose. She tugged it the rest of the way and unbuttoned his stock. She slid her hand inside his collar to feel the smooth warmth of his neck and shoulders. She opened another button and pressed a kiss to the base of his throat.

"Want to see more?" he whispered.

Oh, yes, she did.

He undid his waistcoat and shirt the rest of the way, then put his hands on her hips and drew her in. She stroked the back of her fingers over the crisp hair at the center of his chest. He was lean but muscular and perfectly male. Bolder now, she pressed her palm to his warm skin, over his heart. Its strong beat traveled like a current, passing through her palm, up her arm and into her body, where it merged with her own pounding heart.

Her man.

"You're mine," she whispered, scarcely believing it. She splayed her fingers wide, brushing them across his nipples. They stiffened, just as hers did. Feathering him with hungry kisses, she wrapped her arms around him and pulled him close. She basked in his warmth and his scent, as heat built within.

He pressed against her, and she felt the hard bulge in his trousers. Curious, she stepped back and touched him lightly. He drew in his breath and tipped his head back. "Connie."

Had she hurt him? Concerned, she pulled her hand away. His head fell forward and a playful expression danced in his eyes. "Come 'ere, luv."

He captured her face between his hands and kissed her with feverish intensity. She let him take control, as he worked loose the buttons, then the sash of her dress. When he pushed her clothing away, instinctively, she brought her arms up to cover herself. They were in a city park and she wore only her stays and chemise. "We could be caught," she whispered, thrilled despite it.

"Makes it more fun." Alex nuzzled her neck and nibbled at her earlobe, sparking a delicious sensation deep within. "God, I want you so much."

Desire edged out fear. They were hidden by fading light and thick trees. All these months, she had ached for him, longed for him. At last, he was hers. Tonight, she would have him.

Reveling in newfound power, she traced her finger down his chest, over his belly to his trousers. When she reached the place she'd touched before, she stopped and spread her hand wide. Wrapping her opposite arm around him, she drew him close. Caught in her embrace, Alex released a low groan of pleasure. He shrugged off his shirt and waistcoat and stood half-naked before her as she continued to explore him with her hands and her lips.

With exquisite tenderness, he laid her back on a soft bed of leaves and moss. Reaching beneath her chemise, he pulled away her most intimate clothing. His touch caused her cheeks to flame as pleasure spread. Now it was her turn to draw a sharp breath. He gazed down and whispered, "Are you sure you're ready?"

She nodded, never more sure of anything.

A rustle drew her eyes down. He shucked aside his trousers, and she stared at him, long and erect. She could not imagine how he would possibly fit inside her, but trusted he would not hurt her. With gentle fingers, he caressed her tender, secret place.

"Does this feel good?" Each circle of his finger seemed to spiral upwards, shimmers of heat and light, that her body answered with a slick response. "Do you like this?"

"Oh, yes," she murmured, before surrendering to the next delicious wave.

He caressed her until every nerve danced and she cried out in short, soft gasps, digging her nails into his skin. He silenced her moans with hungry kisses and positioned himself between her legs. She felt the tip of him brush against her intimate folds, then gasped, as a sudden sharp pain ripped upward. She made a little cry and clutched his shoulders. He pulled her close and whispered, "Shh, easy now, luv. It's all right. You're doin' fine, Connie, just perfect. The most perfect woman I ever dreamed of."

His words soothed, even as the pain lingered. She ignored it and kissed him with womanly confidence, arching her body and pressing her bare breasts against him. He pushed into her deeper, moving faster now, with long, steady strokes that were unexpectedly pleasurable. With every thrust of his hip, she met him, following her body's natural response, as ancient and primal as Eve. Loving every fresh sensation. Loving him.

He released a groan, then a deep sigh of satisfaction. Warmth flooded through her. "Connie," his voice shuddered with ragged relief. She clung to him, burying her face against his throat, feeling his words and hearing them. "I love you. I love you."

After, she lay curled into him, as darkness closed in. Retreating footsteps passed their hiding place; evening birds warbled in the distance. She tucked her head beneath his chin and let out a slow breath. She wasn't a girl anymore. She was a woman now, who knew a man's touch. She closed her eyes and smiled as she rested in her husband's arms.

He squeezed her shoulder and stroked her hair. "Mine," he whispered. "All mine."

She tilted her head to look at him, and when their eyes met, she saw their connection. They were two halves of a whole. She'd long felt like a misfit, unlovely and unlovable. To him, she was beautiful. He'd known only limits; she gave him hope. How amazing that two people, so different and seemingly so unsuitable, could complete one another so perfectly.

They should go, but she craved a few more moments with him, away from the world. Her gaze fell on the scar that sliced across his side and stomach. She traced it with her fingertip and his taut muscles jumped. Her hands slid around to his back, where her fingers touched more scars. Curiosity turned to bitter anger. "Did he do this to you?"

"Not all of it," Alex said, gently stroking her bare shoulder. "Most of what's on my back is from when I got sentenced to forty lashes at Bridewell." He glanced down at the scar on his belly. "That one there's from a fight. The other bloke looked a lot worse." He grinned, looking rather pleased with himself. "But that part of my life is over now."

She gave a teasing smile and nestled closer. "So you're going to be good from now on?"

"Oh, yes. I will be the best you'll ever have." He sealed his promise with a long, languorous kiss. "I'll be a good husband,

Connie, I promise. No more fights. No more stealing. I don't want to do anything that might take me away from you."

She believed him. And she admired him. The fact he had survived this brutal world was proof of his strength. That he'd kept his inner decency could only be a gift from God.

Yet his scars were a terrifying reminder of what lay ahead. They still must escape an evil, ruthless man who would kill Alex without hesitation. Suddenly, she was overcome with a tremendous sense of dread. If only their purse and Danny were here, so they could leave this very night and never look back.

All the way home, she held Alex's hand, drawing comfort and courage from his presence. She tried to think of their life in America, and the letter she would send her parents, telling them of her marriage. She hoped that in time, they would accept her decision.

Fog had rolled in when they returned to the mansion. The back door was still unlocked, and even as Alex led her through it, she fought the impulse to flee. In the kitchen, the fireplace and candles were lit, but the room was deserted. No one was in the hall leading back to the sleeping rooms. Then she looked into the scullery. The cellar door stood open.

A pitiful cry rose from the darkness. "No! Stop! Please don' hurt me!"

It was Danny.

CHAPTER TWELVE

S he and Alex raced downstairs. Her stomach rolled at the rotting stench. Cobwebs clung to her face. She batted them away. The stone cellar was cold as a tomb, but it wasn't empty. All the lads were here, watching a terrible scene unfold. Danny cowered in the far corner, cringing and sobbing. His shirt was torn. Blood covered his body. Max stood over him, brandishing a whip.

"Danny's been holdin' out on the Count," muttered Little Jack. "Ulysses and Tim found a purse full o' money under his mattress. Had near twelve pounds tucked away, an' all the Count ever got from him was billies."

"Black!" Danny cried out. "Don' let 'im hurt me!"

Max turned, his features contorted in a cruel smile. He held out the whip to Alex. "Get over 'ere," he ordered. "This be your job."

For a long moment, Alex didn't move. His profile was grim. Then he stepped forward. Cold, black fear enveloped Constance. They couldn't reveal the money was theirs, yet surely Alex wouldn't attack a defenseless little boy who loved him like a brother. She pressed her hands to her face. She couldn't bear to look. She couldn't look away.

The sight of Alex standing over him with the whip broke Danny completely. The cellar echoed with the boy's heart-wrenching sobs of fear and betrayal. "No, Black! Please don'. I'm sorry. I'm sorry."

Constance drew in her breath as Alex raised his arm. Then suddenly, he turned and charged at Max, taking a wide swing with the whip. His face twisted with rage, his voice was ragged and broken. "Get out, you bastard! Get out before I kill you!"

The Count's punisher scrambled out of the way, pushing boys aside to reach the stairs. Alex cracked the whip again and just missed hitting some bystanders. Constance rushed to Danny, who gazed up with tearful, frightened eyes. "I didn't tell whose it be," he whispered.

Luke and Jimmy joined her, then Alex, who knelt beside them with the whip still in his hand. Danny shrank back when he saw it. Alex tossed it away and reached for Danny's arm. "Don' be scared, Dan. I'd never hurt you."

Tenderly, he helped Danny to his feet, letting the boy lean against him. With Luke on the opposite side, they guided Danny up the steps. Jimmy rushed ahead, urging the others out of the way. From behind, Constance breathed into her hands to ward off the nausea brought on by the coppery scent of Danny's blood.

Someone had ransacked their room. Her horse blanket had been torn down. Their mattresses ripped apart. Straw, clothing, and torn pages from the psalm booklet littered the floor, along with broken pieces of Danny's treasured drumsticks. Even beyond the theft of her money, the brutal attack on Danny and the cruel destruction of this small thing he loved, sickened her. The Count had sensed rebellion in the pickpocket ranks and crushed it.

She folded the blanket into a pallet as Alex and Luke eased Danny down onto his stomach. She sat beside the boy and stroked his sweat-damp head. Jimmy returned with a shirt that Alex used to dab blood from Danny's back. "What happened?" he asked, in a low voice.

Luke shook his head as he took in the damage. "Dunno. I'd jus' got back from Sal's when they came down an' started tearin' up the place, like they was lookin' for somethin'."

"Just our room?"

"Mine and Luke's, too," said Jimmy. "Lucky we left our instruments at the Farthing last night."

From the doorway, the Irish brothers watched with curious concern. "Tore up our room and Sam's, but they left Big John and Little Jack's alone," said Tommy.

Patrick snorted. "'Cause they's Tim's boys, ya know."

"They found Connie's money, but Danny was a champion. Brave as can be." Luke's gaze shifted back to Alex. "Wasn't just Connie's though, was it?"

Shaking his head, Alex looked down at the boy, a haunted

expression in his eyes. "It was passage to America for me, Connie, and Dan. He didn't know yet," he said, his voice heavy with guilt. "We weren't going to tell him until we had enough to leave."

"So the Count couldn't do to you what he did to Pete," said Luke.

Alex nodded. Bending low, he spoke quietly to Danny. "You did good, Dan. Soon as you're cleaned up, we'll get you out of here."

"I don' want to leave you an' Luke," the boy sobbed.

"We can't stay either," said Alex. "We'll take you to the rector. You'll be safe there and you won't have to steal anymore. Connie and I have to leave, but we'll send for you as soon as we can."

Luke crouched low and whispered to Danny. "We're coming with you. Me 'n Jimmy, both."

"Even the work'ouse is better 'n here," Jimmy said, crouching down beside them.

Luke snorted. "Don' need the workhouse. Mr. Browning said today he'd hire me on at the pub, and I'll bet he can find a job for you, too. He don' want to lose his band." He turned to Alex. "The Count will come after you. Do you know where you're going?"

"Liverpool, maybe. Or Scotland. If we go there, me an' Connie can be married right away." He gave her a brief smile, and she returned it, despite her fear. "First though, we've got to get out of here. Connie, find what's left of our things. Get some blankets. Hurry, they'll be back soon."

She sprang into action, glad to be of use and away from Danny's wounds. She gathered her shirt, trousers, and cap, and a change of clothes for Alex. When she lifted his shirt from the floor, beneath was the *Robin Hood* book, still intact. She was about to

151

toss it aside, but reconsidered. She tucked it with their clothes and rolled it all up with the blankets. She tied the bundle with the rope that held her curtain and slung it over her shoulder. The pack was heavy, but they could manage.

The moment Danny stopped bleeding, Alex helped him up and walked him from their room. Luke and Jimmy met them in the hall, each carried a small bundle of clothing. They were almost to the back door, when Max and Tim stepped from the darkness, blocking their escape.

Tim smirked and crossed his arms across his chest. "Where do you think you're goin',' Scotland Yard? It's what you planned all along, ain't it Black? The Count knows the money don' belong to that little shit. It's yours. And you ain't goin' nowhere but upstairs."

"Then let them go. Zuko's quarrel's with me, not them."

If the brutes took Alex to the Count, he was as good as dead. Did he have his knife? Most times, he did. She hadn't found it in their room, so it must be in his pocket. But Danny whimpered and clung to Alex, burying his face against his side. Even if he had the knife, he couldn't reach it.

Max snorted with disgust. "Count's made Big John the new don. He don' need these worthless shops, not when he can 'ave his own boys in a day or less. They can go." He took a step forward and gave a leering smile. "But not her."

Clammy sweat, as foul as the basement air, prickled beneath her clothes. Her fear was nothing compared to her bitter, bottomless rage toward Viktor Zuko. This vile man had ordered a brutal attack on an innocent little boy, and meant to twist Alex into a savage, or kill him. As long as she was breathing, she would not stand by and allow it. She moved closer to Alex.

"Connie — "

"I'm not going anywhere," she said, in a determined voice. "I love you, and I refuse to leave you behind."

With that, she took his hand. Her gaze held his, and for a shining moment, she watched the bright glitter of tears in his eyes and the shade of a bewildered smile lift the corner of his mouth. Whatever doubts he may have harbored about her true feelings were extinguished. They had spoken vows. Come what may, he was her husband; she was his wife.

He gave a quick, affirming nod and turned to Luke. "Take Danny to Christ Church. The rector there will help. Connie and me ... we'll come when we can."

Luke opened his mouth, about to argue, but the sight of the brutes and their heavy sticks stopped him. What chance did two unarmed musicians have against the Count's bashers, especially with a small boy caught in the middle? He took a ragged breath. "All right."

Gently, Alex loosened Danny's grip and handed him off to Jimmy. He clapped Luke's shoulder. "Take care of him."

With Danny between them, Luke and Jimmy struggled through the back door and were gone.

The moment the door closed, Alex went for his right-side pocket. But before he could reach the knife, Tim slammed his nightstick into the back of Alex's head.

He stumbled forward on the stairs.

"No!" Her screams filled the stairway, and she lunged for Tim's arm. Max grabbed her around the waist and hauled her back. Reeling from the blows raining down on him, Alex still tried to reach his switchblade. But Tim pulled out a length of rope, captured Alex's wrists, and bound them. Grabbing him by the collar, he hauled Alex to his feet and shoved him at Max.

She rushed to Alex's side and with the quick hands of a skilled thief, slipped the knife from his pocket into her sleeve, just before Tim pushed her into the stairway, behind Max and Alex. He followed, carrying their abandoned pack. Trapped in the narrow stairway, sandwiched between the brutes, the weapon was cold against her wrist. Even so, she couldn't fight Tim, Max, and their nightsticks all alone. Her only hope was to free Alex. She inched closer, wondering how to get him loose without Tim seeing. Then suddenly, as if he could read her thoughts, Max stopped the procession and pushed Alex to the front. Her heart sank. Their chance to escape was gone.

The Count's attic lair took up the entire fourth floor. Dark and draped with red velvet, it looked like an extension of the brothel. The polished herringbone-patterned floor reminded her of the ballroom in the Westminster's home.

A bizarre thing to remember at a time like this.

On each side of the room were French doors that opened onto the little balconies she'd admired from the outside. Hard to fathom that this was what lay behind. All the doors were closed, except for the one on the back of the house. She'd never noticed before, but this door had no balcony.

Only a straight drop to the courtyard below.

The bashers marched them to the massive desk, positioned near the rear window. Moist night air drifted in, as Count Zuko strolled out from behind and regarded them with cold, reptilian eyes. "You've stolen from me, Alexander," he said, in a heavily accented voice.

Alex kept a defiant air. "Don' know what you're talkin' about."

"Oh, but you do. Your loyalty is compromised. I thought by the boy, but then Tim mentioned your interest in this lovely creature." The Count leered. Constance's tight dress felt even more indecent and revealing. "Temptation I can excuse, but not disloyalty. Especially from a young man I trusted. I regret this, but your lies have left me no choice."

At the Count's nod, Tim and Max seized Alex and pushed him into a wooden chair. Constance sprang forward, but Zuko grabbed her upper arms and pulled her back. Helpless, she watched as the bashers tied Alex to the chair.

"Stop! Leave him alone! Let him go, you can't have him! He's not yours, he never was!" Her screams were as useless as the knife in her sleeve. The Count's iron grip held her fast, preventing her from fighting. When Alex was bound, the brutes dragged the chair to the window and positioned him backward, just inches away from the three-story drop. Her eyes widened as she understood what they meant to do.

"Build a fire in the courtyard. A large one," Zuko ordered. Tim and Max left without a word. The Count spun Constance around and she recoiled, as his face loomed close enough to see every pore. "The flames will destroy the body or finish the job, should Alexander have the misfortune to survive his fall. Of course, that will depend on how hard you push him."

He laughed coldly. "But first, I shall enjoy you myself, as Alexander watches. I'd hoped to profit from your virtue, but he helped himself to that which wasn't his."

Alex strained against the ropes. "Leave her alone! Don't you fuckin' touch her!"

Her mouth went dry. There was no one to rescue them. No time to wait for the police to arrive. Unless she acted, Alex would die. She peered into the merciless, black eyes of a monster, and primal instinct took over. An eerie sense of calm, rational and detached, supplanted her fear. With terrifying clarity, she knew what she must do.

She would save them both, or die trying.

In her best impersonation of Nancy, she gave a low, throaty laugh. "What makes you think I was so bloody pure to start with? You have me, then I'll go to Minerva and make some real money."

Zuko narrowed his eyes, not sure what to believe. His hungry gaze roamed her tight dress and the black sash that defined her hourglass shape. Constance stood straighter to best display the swell of her breasts. His greedy mouth moved as though he were about to devour a tempting, rare fruit. Snared in his grip, Constance tossed back her hair and smiled.

With that, Zuko took the bait. He hauled her against his body, crushing her breasts. His stale breath was suffocating as he plundered her with a foul kiss. Fighting revulsion, she parted her lips, luring him in. Her tongue parried with his, seducing him into distraction. She slid her hand over his silk dressing gown, massaging the bones and gristle of his back, then reached around and tugged at the sash that held the garment closed. The dressing gown fell open to expose his wrinkled, sagging flesh. She slipped one hand inside to stroke his bare torso, ignoring the dampness of his skin, and carefully slipped the knife down her opposite sleeve. She buried her face in the hollow of his neck, then tilted her head, positioning her mouth at his ear. "Tell me where to touch you," she whispered.

"Lower," he murmured. She cupped the hard bulge in his trousers and stroked him with her fingertips. The Count shuddered and groaned with pleasure. "More … just like that."

The knife slid into her palm.

She dropped her head back, as Zuko suckled his way down her neck and across the exposed skin of her décolletage. He moved lower, to bury his face in her breasts, nipping at her tender flesh with sharp teeth. She panted loudly and cried out to cloak the sound of the switchblade springing open.

In one swift motion, she thrust it deep into his belly and with all her strength, sliced downward through his gut.

The Count let out a garbled cry and grabbed the knife to tug it from his body. The moment it came loose, a river of blood gushed from his ruined flesh, drenching them both. He charged forward, the glistening red blade aimed at her heart. She scrambled back. Zuko lunged, then stumbled, as he skidded in the slick blood that pooled on the floor. He lost his footing and fell backward, striking his head on the edge of the desk.

He crashed to the floor, and a cadaverous smile split his face. His eyes locked with hers, daring her to look away. Once more he tried to stand, rising as far as his knees. Constance was rooted to the floor, too frightened to move, as he lurched forward, swinging the knife in wide arcs. "Vengeance will be mine." The words escaped on tortured breath.

"No," she said, her voice trembling. "You're a killer! You deserve to die!"

With a last breath he lunged toward her, swinging the knife.

He lost his balance, and fell again, this time on the knife, driving it back into his body. With a ghastly moan, he was still.

She stared down, waiting for him to move again. Surely, he was only wounded. The man on the floor didn't budge or breathe. The only movement was the steady flow of blood draining from Zuko's body.

She'd just murdered a man.

No, not a man. A beast. A demon. A vicious predator who would have done the same to her and to Alex. A killer.

Just like me.

She brought her hands to her face to stifle the scream rising in her throat. Just before she touched her cheeks, she stopped. Her hands were gloved in glistening red.

She began to shake, no longer in control of her body. Desperate to be clean, she wiped her bloody hands on her skirt. But her dress was soaked as well. The scream returned. "No! No!"

"Connie! Get me loose!"

Alex's voice brought her back. She rushed over and pulled him from the precipice, using every bit of strength she could find. Then she knelt beside the chair and tore at his bonds. Her fingers were clumsy and slick with blood. Tears flooded her eyes until she could no longer see. She brushed them away, only to realize she'd smeared Zuko's gore across her face.

"Oh, God. He's dead, Alex. I killed him, I murdered him!" Her voice was shrill, on the brink of panic.

"Connie! Look at me."

She stilled at his stern command.

"That's better, luv," he said, calmly. "We're all right. Untie me now, and we'll get out of here."

She took a deep breath and tried not to think about the dead man on the floor.

She freed Alex's hands, and then he worked with her to loosen the remaining knots. The moment the ropes fell away, he gathered her close, heedless of the blood that now stained both their clothes. "You saved us. You're a brave one, Connie. I love you so much."

She buried her face against his neck and let his warm embrace comfort her. Regardless of what had happened, Alex was alive and holding her. "I love you, too," she whispered fiercely against him.

She clung to him a moment longer, then with a kiss, he released her. "Come on now, there's no time to waste." He rose from the chair and grabbed the loose rope. He tied one end to a pillar in the middle of the room and tossed the other end out the open window. He dashed to the fireplace and grabbed a bull's-eye lantern from the mantle.

"We'll need extra candles and matches. Look in his desk."

She opened the top drawer. Nothing. Alex disappeared into the bedchamber. She tugged open a deep drawer on the left side. No candles here either, but she found something better.

Her stolen purse.

She snatched it up, just as Alex returned, clutching a small box. "Alex, I found—"

"I found some too," he said, picking up their pack from the floor. He tossed it out the window and gave the rope a tug. "This won't get us to the ground, but we can drop onto the barn roof. They can't see us from the courtyard. Come on, you first."

Her news could wait. She tucked the purse into her bodice and joined him at the window, suddenly dizzy at the thought of climbing down.

Alex touched her shoulder. "Lie on your stomach and go hand over hand. Do you want me to go first?"

She nodded.

He slipped the lantern over his arm and swung himself out the window, moving down the rope with feet braced against the wall. On her knees, she peered out. The peaked stable roof was less than a story below. Max and Tim would come for them at any moment. She laid on her belly, grasped the rope and shimmied over the edge.

At the bottom, Alex grabbed her waist and guided her onto the stable roof. They moved across it, staying in the shadows, and keeping low. Acrid smoke tickled her throat, and she held back a cough. In the dark courtyard, an enormous fire crackled and glowed like a furnace. She shuddered, thinking of its purpose.

At the roof's edge, Alex swung himself over the side and dropped into the alley just outside the iron fence. Constance tossed down the pack, and he held up his arms to catch her.

When she was on the ground, he took her hand and they crept into the shadows of the alley. "Should we go to the church? The constable?" she whispered.

"The church is the first place they'll look. Constable will just put us in gaol. I know where we can hide."

Hand in hand, they ran away into the blanket of fog.

CHAPTER THIRTEEN

Dank air and foul stench surrounded them as they reached the bottom of the ladder. Alex shined the lantern into the gloomy brick tunnel of the main sewer line. From here, they had to go west.

Connie cupped her hand over her mouth and nose. "You get used to the smell," he said and squeezed her other hand.

She only nodded.

He hadn't been down here in ages, but still remembered the way. The sewers never changed. Once, they'd been as familiar as the daylight streets above. This was London too, but down here, it was always night.

"The Lord is my shepherd, I shall not want..."

They'd gone south from the mansion, cutting through Whitechapel, cloaked by the London Particular. This time of night, the streets were all but empty, and thank God for that. His knife was still in Zuko's belly and with their blood-stained clothes, they made quite a sight. Once they were south of the railway tracks, he breathed a little easier, and he'd never been so happy to cross Ratcliff Highway. The fog broke enough to see St. Paul's steeple. The comforting stink of his old neighborhood meant they were almost safe.

"... he leadeth me beside still waters..."

Connie hadn't said a word since they left the mansion, but at the sight of the church and the dingy tenements around it, she'd asked in a small, scared voice, "Where are we?"

"Shadwell."

"Cutthroat Lane?"

He felt a rush of tenderness that she'd remembered his old street. "Not tonight. We'll get there next time."

There was a high fence around the churchyard and the old sailor's graveyard, but the lock on the gate was easy to jimmy, just like years ago. The little ones must still come here to play. Better here than the wharfs around the Basin. At least you couldn't drown in a graveyard. This place never scared him. His grandfather was buried here. His mother showed him once. Samuel Blackwood, sailmaker. His father could be here, too. Mum said he'd been a sailor, but never mentioned his name.

The church and school were both dark and silent now, but they'd been good to him here. He hoped the place would be good to them tonight. The old trap door was on the north side of the schoolhouse, and its rusty iron hinges screeched open. He glanced up, but the rectory was clear at the other end of the churchyard, too far for anyone to hear. An iron ladder led down into the darkness. Connie shrank back.

"I'll go first," he whispered.

At the bottom, he held the lantern up and called to her. As she climbed down, he talked to her, just as he'd done for Mum. It wasn't as scary that way.

Other than a trickle of water at the center, the storm drain was dry. To the right was the faint light that marked where the drain emptied into Shadwell Basin, but they went left, into the endless maze of tunnels and drains that ran beneath London.

He'd been seven years old when he and Mum had come down here. It was winter, they'd had no money for coal, and he knew about the tunnels from the older boys in the neighborhood. It stank of shit and rot down here, but no worse than the Thames in the summer. It was better than freezing to death. Nor were they the only ones living below ground that winter. Even some of his schoolmates at St. Paul's carried the stink on them. The sewer rats learned to stick together.

Connie gagged at first, but seemed to get used to the smell. The rats were another matter. She jumped at every shadow and when they saw an especially big rat, she'd shrieked and tried to climb up his back. There'd been loads of rats in Spitalfields, and he'd never seen her become unhinged over one. He calmed her down and they kept walking, but he needed to get her to safety as soon as possible.

She paid attention and did as he said, but she seemed to have holed up deep inside herself. He'd done the same thing after Pete's murder, but for Connie, this had to be a thousand times worse. Earls' daughters didn't stab fiends to rescue those they loved. He understood, but wished she would say something. Anything. Even if it was to curse the day they met.

Parts of the tunnel were lit with torches and lanterns. Every so often, they passed shantytowns and campsites of toshers, who prowled the tunnels for coins, metal, whatever they could sell up top. They were harmless mostly, but there were others down here, opium dens and brothels, that were best to stay clear of.

"... though I walk through the valley of the shadow of death, I will fear no evil..."

After a few more turns of the tunnel, they came to an open cavern which rose above a cobblestone street. Abandoned storefronts lined both sides. Street lamps burning dried dung lit the cavern. Crooked signs with faded, old-fashioned letters still hung above some shop doors. Connie gasped when she saw it, just as he had the first time. "Good heavens! What is this place?"

"It's an old part of the Strand. It used to flood, so they built the new street right over the top. That's the story, anyway. Happened a long time ago. Me and Mum lived here a while."

In front of the old apothecary were two boys, covered in filth, and a pale small girl with tangled black hair. The taller boy gave them a wary look.

"Know where I can find Moll?" Alex asked.

The girl replied with a wide toothless smile. "Surely, sir! She's — "

"Shut up, Jennie." The boy cuffed the side of her head and she ran off, howling.

He glared at the bully. "No need for that. Don' mean no 'arm. Jus' want a place to stay the night is all. Moll knew me mum. Go tell 'er Annie Blackwood's son wants to see 'er."

The tall boy thought it over, then gave the younger lad a nod. The boy scampered into the nearest building and returned a moment later with a hunched-over crone.

In the twelve years since he last saw Moll, it didn't look like she'd left the tunnels. Or had a bath. Her withered face glowed like a skull in the dark, and she studied them with rat-like eyes. Connie inched closer, and he put his arm around her.

"So you're Annie's boy. I remember you. Got that nice yellow hair, like she did. 'eard she died from the cholera. Guessed you 'ad too. But you're all growed up." She scratched at a sore on her cheek. "Alonzo? Wasn't that your name?"

"Alex. You were good to us back then. I was hoping we could stay here tonight. Me and my wife."

Moll took out a flask and had a nip, mulling it over. She gestured at their bloody clothes. "Looks like you had some trouble. Ain't followed you 'ere, has it?"

"No. We'll be gone in a few hours, but my wife needs to rest. And we need some water to wash with, if you have it."

"Huh. She looks a might fancy to be wed to a whore's son, but I suppose 'at's your business." She cocked her head toward the apothecary shop. "Go on up. You remember the way."

He led Connie up a flight of rickety stairs to the second floor. Cobwebs and tattered curtains hung like shrouds from the arched windows. The only furniture was a wooden table, covered with dust and grime. A fine place this was. He set the lantern on the table and untied their pack.

The crazed laugher of a madman echoed from somewhere deep in the tunnels. Connie's eyes grew wide.

"It's all right. We're safe here." Gently, he guided her back from the window, to the blanket he'd spread on the floor. His stomach growled. He was banded. Stupid that he hadn't thought to bring food. "Sorry, luv. I should have grabbed some victuals."

Connie shook her head. "I'm not hungry."

"We'll rest a few hours, then go to the docks and find a ship to stow away on. At least you'll stow away. I'll hire on as crew and hide you on board."

For the first time in hours, she perked up. "We don't need to do that. We can buy passage." From her bodice, she pulled out the leather bag from their room.

His blood ran cold. "Where did you get that?"

"I found it in the Count's desk while I was looking for candles. I got our money back!" Her face fell as she read his expression and her voice trembled. "Aren't you happy?"

Happy? No. Despair even darker than these tunnels described it better. Any chance of claiming she'd killed in self-defense died the moment she took the money. But he couldn't tell her. Not tonight. She was scared to death, and he was bone tired. He'd deal with it tomorrow. "Sure I am," he said, and gave her a smile.

The boy returned with a bucket of water. It stank, but was clean enough for what they needed. He took off his shirt, dipped it into the water, and wiped away the blood. Connie removed her dress and dabbed at her hands and arms.

He sat on the blanket and wrapped the larger one around his shoulders. With his back to the wall, he held out the long end for Connie. She crawled over and sat between his legs, nestled close like a child. He tossed the blanket over them and wrapped his arms around her. She shivered, either from the cold, fear, or memories of Count Zuko, bleeding at her feet. He couldn't make her forget this horrible night, but she liked to be held, and when he sang to her. So he did those things.

Skin to skin, he felt every point of contact. Yet this desire ran deeper than physical need. Instinct drove him to protect the woman he loved, regardless of the cost. He'd failed to do it at the Count's, and she'd rescued him. Humbled by her courage and strength, he would prove himself worthy of such a fine woman. He would keep her safe, even if he died doing it.

After a while, she stopped shaking and her breathing became slow and steady. He hoped she'd fallen asleep, but then she asked in a thick, wobbly voice, "Do you think I'll go to hell because I killed Count Zuko?"

It broke his heart to hear her so tormented by something she'd done to save his sorry arse. "Oh, Connie, no," he said, caressing her back. "At school, they told us a story 'bout a thief who was sorry for what he'd done, an' Jesus let him into heaven, anyway. Are you sorry for killing the Count?"

She didn't answer at first, but after a long moment said, "I'm not sorry I saved your life, but I am sorry I had to kill the Count to do it."

He kissed the top of her head. "Sounds like you'll be all right, then."

"What if we're caught? Do you think I'll hang?"

This was a much harder question. Zuko had powerful friends. Someone would have to pay for his death. Even high-born women weren't above the law. She had killed the man and taken money. Hanging crimes. If Connie stood trial, she would be found guilty, and sentenced to death.

His life would be over as well.

There was no doubt he'd face the gallows. Despite Connie's high opinion, he was a crook, and that's all he'd ever been. They'd string him up right beside her. But not if he confessed to the murder first. If he told them he kidnapped Connie, murdered the Count and robbed him, he would still hang, but she would go free. He could die knowing that he'd saved her.

If they were caught, Alex knew what he had to do. He brushed a kiss across Connie's forehead, amazed at the good fortune that brought him a girl like this, even if it was only for a little while. "No, luv," he whispered. "You won't hang."

Her eyes closed, she rested in Alex's arms, his skin warm against hers and his comforting words in her ears. This was a man she could trust and depend on. He got them away from the mansion and found a place to hide. Even in this frightening place, she felt cherished. Not because she was a perfect beauty. Not because she was the toast of London society. Because Alex loved her.

Seeing this grim world of rats, stench, and wretched poverty brought his struggles to life in a terrifying way. The crowded tenements in Spitalfields and Whitechapel were bad enough, but this was a glimpse of hell. While she'd been warm in her feather bed, still tasting her bedtime hot chocolate, Alex had been down here, a cold, hungry little boy trying to sleep in a stinking, rat-infested sewer. What kind of world forced a child to live in such a place? If she survived, she would do whatever she could to rescue others from such a fate.

Survival and sleep. Two things she craved. But whenever she drifted off, the ghastly, dying face of Count Zuko haunted her dreams. The madman's laugh rang out again, and she shuddered. Alex stroked her back and whispered gently to her, soothing her fears until she relaxed. She let his presence envelop her—his warm embrace and the steady beat of his heart. If she hadn't acted, Alex would have perished tonight in a three-story fall, or been thrown into a fire and burned alive.

This was why she'd done the unimaginable.

Had it really been just a night ago they'd danced on the Farthing's roof? There'd been so much to look forward to. How had things gone so wrong so fast? Aching for everything they'd lost, she felt tears sting her eyes and spill out, trickling onto Alex's chest.

He stroked her hair. "Shhh, don't cry, luv. I'm here. Try to sleep now."

Only one thing would make that possible. Constance gulped back her tears. "Would you sing to me again?"

He didn't have to ask what song she needed to hear. The cold and dark seemed to fade a bit as he sang. Constance drifted back to when they'd danced under the stars, and the future seemed as bright as the full moon above.

<hr>

When she awoke, Alex was beside her, already dressed.

"Is it morning?" The dark made it impossible to tell, and she was cold and stiff from sleep.

"Close enough." He shined the lantern on a small chunk of bread, sitting on a handkerchief. "Moll's girl brought it. I've already had my share, so you can eat the rest."

She didn't quite believe him, but her empty stomach silenced her protest. The stale bread stuck in her throat, but she felt stronger having eaten it. When she finished, she retrieved their purse from her blood-soaked dress. "I haven't counted it yet, but if he didn't take anything, we should have more than enough for passage."

Alex placed his hand over the purse and looked at her with serious eyes. "I'm afraid it's not that simple, luv."

Then he told her.

Her stomach rolled, and she pressed her trembling hands to her face. It couldn't be true. She couldn't have committed capital murder. Then she thought back to his long-ago warning, on a sunny afternoon in the Count's courtyard. "… *murder's the only thing they hang you for. So when you're stealing, try not to kill anyone …*"

Her heart pounded as tears and panic rose. "But it was our money! He stole it from us! He tried to kill you! I couldn't let him!" Then a desperate hope surfaced. "The police might not even know about it."

"They might not," he agreed. "But if the lads told the rector, and the rector told the constable… you can best believe Tim and Max will see to it the blame points straight to us."

"Then we leave the money. If we don't have it, no one can prove we took it."

"We can't prove we didn't take it either. And if we make it out of England … we'll need it to start over." His grave expression frightened her as much as thoughts of the gallows. "That's why, if we're caught, I will tell them I was the one who murdered the Count."

"Alex, no! You can't! I won't let you!"

"Shh, Connie, listen. If they arrest us, I'm dead either way. Even if they find out you killed him, I'll still hang as your accomplice. If they think I'm the murderer, though, that I took you hostage, robbed Zuko, and killed him, they'll let you go."

She couldn't argue with his logic. He knew a lot more about crime and punishment than she did, but the thought of Alex being executed left her almost speechless. She shook her head at the brutal injustice. "Why is my life worth more than yours? You don't deserve to die, Alex. You cared for Danny. You cared for me," her eyes burned, her voice was thick with tears. "It isn't right!"

He wrapped his arms around her and pulled her close. "Might not be right, but it's how the world works."

"It shouldn't be."

"I know, luv. Call it the price for my thrilling life of crime. But if I have to die, it'll comfort me to know your life will go on." He gently touched her cheek and his sweet smile broke her heart. "Promise me, Connie."

She'd never had more trouble saying a word. "I promise."

They returned to the drain where they'd come in. The plan was for her to hide in one of the warehouses surrounding Shadwell Basin, while he talked, or bribed, his way onto a ship and then hid her on board. They climbed from the sewer and slipped into the churchyard seconds before a swarm of children spilled out of the schoolhouse.

By daylight, the schoolhouse, a two-story building with tall windows and a hipped roof, wasn't the grim pile of bricks she'd envisioned. Ragged but exuberant boys and girls darted around the little grassy yard surrounding it, their squeals and laughter no different from the well-dressed children who frolicked under the watchful eyes of nursemaids in Regent's Park. Despite what the rest of their lives were like, here these children seemed happy.

Alex smiled as he watched, likely remembering his own days here. It seemed he'd known some joy along with the hardship, and that was a very good thing.

They left the churchyard through a gate on the south side and followed a flight of concrete steps down to a row of warehouses, set at the foot of a retaining wall behind the church. This side of the wharf was all but deserted. Alex tried several doors until he found one that opened. The small warehouse was crammed full of barrels and reeked of vinegar.

"You'll be safe here," he said. Using his cuff to wipe away the grime, he peered out the window at the small ships moored on the opposite side of Shadwell Basin. "These boats won't get us to America, but just about any place out of England ought to do." He straightened his posture, transforming himself into a gallant young gentleman. "Where shall we go, my lady? France, perhaps? Or would you prefer a grand tour of Italy?"

He made it sound as though they were travelers embarking on a grand adventure, not fugitives on the run. She laughed a little, despite their dire situation. "Any place, as long as we're together."

His beautiful smile took her back to their first moment in the Crystal Palace. "That we will be," he said, and kissed her. "All right then, Lady Constance, your cap please." She gave it to him. He twisted his hair into a tail and stuffed it underneath. "The blokes on the ships won't ask a lot of questions, but if the police see me, they will." He tugged the bill low over his eyes.

"Better," she said. "You're less conspicuous." Suddenly, she was overcome with a terrible premonition that when he walked out the door, she would never see him again. She threw her arms around him and held him tightly, unwilling to surrender this precious man she loved so much. "Oh Alex, please be careful. Do you really think this is a wise idea? It seems like such a risk."

"It is a risk," he whispered against her hair. "But less of one than trying to escape on foot or hide out in London for any length of time. Now remember what to tell them ... if we're caught."

They'd agreed on a story, but to speak of it now seemed the worst way to tempt fate. Gazing into his eyes, she vowed to stay strong. She was brave Maid Marian, saying goodbye to Robin Hood. Robin had returned. Alex would, too. He must. They had a beautiful life ahead. Surely, fate would not demand such a sacrifice.

"We won't be caught," she said, as confidently as she could.

"That's my girl. I love you, Connie." He kissed her once more, a lingering kiss that spoke of all they had to live for. Then he turned back to the window. Work seemed to be finishing up on the other side of the basin. It was time. "Keep out of sight, now. I'll be back as soon as I can."

He slipped out the door, even as her hands grasped at empty

air and she fought the urge to grab onto him and not let go. He strolled toward the docks as if he had every reason to be there, turned to the left and disappeared behind the moored ships.

From outside came boisterous voices. She drew back from the window and crouched behind a barrel. Just dock hands passing by. She came out of hiding and looked around the warehouse. Her empty stomach growled. She ought to find something to eat. Using a metal handle, she pried open a barrel. It was full of pickles. Not much of a meal, but it would have to do.

As she ate, she imagined their life together. France? America? It didn't matter. Alex would have the fresh start he longed for and they could be together with no one saying it was wrong. It would not be a leisurely life. Her idle days of embroidery and social calls were gone forever. Even so, she wasn't afraid. Having to work wasn't a curse. She would turn it into a blessing.

She'd come to the East End a naive girl, with silly notions of going to work for Florence Nightingale. But purpose had replaced foolishness. She would work so an innocent child did not have to live in a sewer or turn to crime to eat. She could write newspaper articles to draw attention to the plight of the poor. Or, she could teach in a school and help children find a better life. Whatever it was, she would make the most of it. She could not wait to tell Alex.

She ate another pickle and could have eaten more, but the vinegar made her thirsty. She pushed the lid back in place, but didn't close it all the way, so Alex could have some when he returned. Then she went back to the window and watched.

And waited.

She pulled the *Robin Hood* book from the roll of blankets,

174

hoping to distract her anxious thoughts, but there were too many shadows to read. She stuffed the book in her pocket. Daylight was fading and the dock on the opposite side of the basin looked deserted. The church bell had already rung half-past four. It would be dark soon. Perhaps Alex wanted to wait until nightfall before bringing her out of hiding. It was a sensible idea. As nervous as she was, there was nothing to do but wait. She sat on the floor and rested her back against their pack.

⚜

Shouts and blinding light awakened her.

"Over 'ere boys! We found her safe 'n sound!"

Squinting and shielding her eyes, she tried to see beyond the glare. Then she gasped. The man with the lantern was a Metropolitan Police officer.

"Oh…" she tried to stand, but stumbled. Her numb foot prickled.

"Easy now, miss." The constable helped her up, and took her firmly by the arm. He led her outside, where two more officers waited.

Alex…? Her gaze shifted from man to man, her heart fluttered and her mind raced. Breath came in short, panicked gasps. No. No. Stay calm.

Any moment, he would stroll up, smile, flam the officers with a convincing story, and they would be on their way. "Where…?" she murmured, looking out into twilight that was the same deep blue as his eyes.

It was then she spied the black, windowless police wagon

parked a short distance away. An officer finished securing the lock on the wagon's back door and walked around to the driver's seat.

"No!" She lunged toward the wagon.

"Miss! Miss!" The officer grabbed her. "It's all right. He's all boxed up and on 'is way to Newgate, where he belongs. The murderin' fiend can't hurt you anymore."

She stared, suddenly mindful of her terrible promise. The dull thuds of the horses' hooves beat a mournful cadence on the wharf, as the black wagon carried away the man she loved.

Alex wasn't coming back. Fate had demanded a sacrifice. Anguish gushed forth and Constance fell to her knees, sobbing.

CHAPTER FOURTEEN

B eyond confirming she was the long-missing daughter of
Lord Beverly, Constance said nothing on the way to the
police station.

The officer had escorted her to a Metropolitan Police carriage parked near the docks and driven north. The black wagon, with Alex locked inside, had gone west, erasing any hope she might see him again. On the drive through the dark neighborhood, her only intention was to not dissolve into a puddle of tears. That was sorely tested when they passed Alex's old school, and the entrance to the tunnels where he'd cared for her.

At the station house, the officers brought hot tea and blankets, and summoned Father. When he arrived an hour later, he folded her into a tearful embrace. "Constance, my darling! I haven't had a moment's happiness these months you've been gone! I made a terrible mistake, dearest, but thank God you're all right."

Whether she was all right was debatable, but being in Father's arms, surrounded by familiar scents of tobacco and bay rum, made her long for the safe comfort of her old life. Back in Mayfair, every horrible thing that had happened in the last four and twenty hours would seem further away. There, she would be protected and cared for. Father's regret over trying to force her to marry Gaffney seemed genuine. He must see now that he had driven her onto a path that ended in murder.

Then again, if she hadn't run away, she and Alex would never have met, let alone fallen in love.

The police sergeant allowed them a few private moments, then returned. Mr. Morgan, the family's barrister, was with him, having accompanied Father from Mayfair. "The police have some questions, Lady Constance," Mr. Morgan said, in a solicitous tone. "Do you feel up to speaking with them?"

Constance squeezed her eyes shut. She couldn't imagine telling the story she'd promised to tell. "I'm afraid not," she whispered.

The sergeant opened a small notebook. "I know it isn't easy, miss, but it's very important we capture these details while they're still fresh. When the officers arrested the fiend at Shadwell Docks, he said he was taking you to Shanghai. Is that true?"

That she was parroting a story Alex had devised, made her feel no less ashamed. "It's what he told me."

"He also said he lured you away from the Crystal Palace after you became separated from your party, and took you to the East

End, where he put you to work stealing for Viktor Zuko."

This time, she could only nod.

"Do you know why he killed Viktor Zuko, miss?"

According to their story, Alex and the Count had a falling out over Constance. Alex considered her too valuable to whore for Minerva and had killed the Count, then stolen her away to sell to a brothel in the Far East, where a well-bred Englishwoman would fetch a high price. She pressed her trembling hands to her face, unable to speak the lies that would incriminate the man she loved.

"Miss?"

Anguish exploded in her chest, shattering her fragile composure. Tears gushed forth in keening sobs that wracked her body and robbed her of breath and reason. Surely death was the only way to escape this torment.

"Enough of this!" Father shouted at the sergeant. "You said the ruffian confessed to the killing. That should be more than enough to send him to the gallows. Prurient details about my daughter's debasement are unnecessary."

"No!" Her guttural cries drowned out the rest, and she clasped her hands over her ears, unable to bear the news that Alex's false confession had already condemned him. "Please, no more!"

Father gently took her arm and helped her stand. She leaned against him, blinded by tears. "My precious, precious girl," he murmured. "You needn't say another word. Mr. Morgan will handle this. I'm taking you away from here immediately."

Bruton Street felt like a place she'd never lived. An unfamiliar footman greeted them at the door of the dark, quiet house. "Where's Mother?" Constance asked.

"She returned to Sussex weeks ago," Father explained, as the footman took his overcoat. "Considering her health, Dr. Richards felt it was best."

It wasn't hard to picture Mother languishing in bed, pale against the pillows. She'd seen it often enough as a girl, always fearing Mother would succumb to her weak heart. If Constance's actions had made Mother's fragile health worse, she'd never forgive herself. "She isn't ill, is she?"

"Not seriously, but having you gone was very difficult. She worried constantly."

Devastated to think of the fright she'd given her family, Constance closed her eyes. She'd been desperate, and angry over losing Girton, and her forced engagement, but those concerns faded into insignificance, compared to what she'd done to the people she loved most. Her family. Alex.

"As soon as you're well enough to travel, we'll go there too. I'll summon Dr. Richards first thing in the morning."

"No! I have to stay here!" Though she didn't know what good she was to Alex in London, to leave felt as though she was deserting him. "In case I'm needed," she added, thinking of no other way to explain her reasons.

"Nonsense." Father handed his top hat to the footman. "Your mother is pining away for you, and the sooner you're away from London, the better. It's only a matter of time before the papers get wind, and they'll be even worse than the police with their questions. Mr. Morgan will dispose of all the unpleasantness. It's the reason I retain him."

Upstairs, a housekeeper laid out her dressing gown. Constance had hoped it would be Fletcher tending to her, but the regular servants had returned to Sussex with Mother, so even that small comfort was denied. The woman frowned as she lifted a lock of Constance's heavy hair. "You don't mind me sayin', milady, but this all ought to be cut off."

Constance's hands flew to her head. "Please don't! I kept clean as best I could."

"Hmm." The housekeeper seemed unconvinced and flattened her lips into a line. "We'll see what the doctor has to say. For now, I'll run a nit-comb through it and hope for the best. I'll send a girl up to draw your bath."

When the woman left, Constance stood before the mirror and lifted her hair, imagining it no longer tumbling over her shoulders. No longer would she look like Connie. The part of herself she'd grown to love would be shoved back into a stifling, silk-covered box, never again to see the light of day. Slowly, she peeled away the boy's clothing Alex had given her the first day in Spitalfields. The *Robin Hood* book was still in her trouser pocket, so she placed it in the trunk that still sat half-packed for Girton College. Surely that had been the dream of someone else. She carefully folded the garments and placed them by her wardrobe, to be laundered.

The housekeeper returned with towels, a metal comb, and a bowl of foul ointment that reeked of vinegar. She spied the folded clothes. "Is that what they forced you to wear, poor thing?" Gingerly, she gathered them up and handed them off to the maid who had come with her. "Infested, too, no doubt."

"Are you taking them to wash?" Constance asked, as the maid left the room.

The woman replied with a disdainful sniff. "Burned, is more like it. Now then, let's do something about your hair."

Fighting back tears, Constance submitted to having her scalp slathered with the lard and vinegar ointment. Afterward, a maid tugged the nit-comb painfully through her thick hair. When she finally stepped into a warm soothing bath, her exhausted body longed to sink beneath the surface, letting rose-scented water extinguish her breath. But her mind fought against surrender. Her sweet thief was locked in prison. Even if she didn't know exactly how to help him, she couldn't let him die for her crime. If there was ever a time her family's position might allow her to do something good, it was now. She needed Father's help, and as hard as it would be, she must tell him the truth about what had happened.

After Constance bathed, a maid brought a light supper. Though she had no appetite to speak of and the food stuck in her throat, she forced down a few bites. She must keep her strength up for Alex's sake, if not her own. Too exhausted to dress again, she put on her dressing gown. Gathering her courage, she left her room and went downstairs.

The house was quiet, and there were no servants about. She wondered if Father might have gone to bed already, perhaps even half-hoped she could delay this conversation until tomorrow. In the parlor, she found him staring into the fire as he sipped whiskey. He looked up in surprise at the sight of her in a dressing gown and slippers. "My dear." His brow furrowed with concern. "You should be resting."

"I can't, Father." Constance fought a wave of dizziness, letting thoughts of Alex fuel her courage. Father might be stern, but he was just. She was his only child. He might be shocked, but he would not abandon an innocent man to execution. Nor would she. Constance took the chair beside him and stilled her hands in her lap. "There's something you must know. I wasn't kidnapped, and the man they arrested tonight for Count Zuko's murder didn't kill him. I did."

Father's lips parted. "Constance? What the devil are you saying?"

She began her story, and at first, he seemed to believe her. The details of her anger at being forced to marry Gaffney were familiar enough. But when she spoke of stealing on the streets of London for the past three months, his confounded expression returned. "Are you saying you did this voluntarily?"

"That's right. No one forced me. The only one forced was Alex, who had no choice but to join the Count's upstairs henchmen, or else they would kill him."

Father sneered, as if speaking of an enemy. "Surely, you don't mean the murderer?"

"He isn't a murderer! He's innocent. He is..." Though she'd planned to reveal everything, instinct warned her off of saying they were wed. This was difficult enough for Father, not to mention herself. There would be time to tell him this later. "... someone I care for deeply. He's kind and honorable and dreamed of a better life away from the Count. He protected me and now he's facing the gallows. I can't let that happen! I have to free Alex, and I need you and Mr. Morgan to help me do it."

The shadows dancing across Father's face made him look old

and tired. He stared into his now-empty glass. "Morgan will be here in the morning."

Constance exhaled, her body weak with relief. The truth, at least most of it, was out in the open, and Father hadn't disowned her. Yet, his haggard face revealed the toll this was taking. Guilt over what she'd done to her family, and to Alex, laid so heavily, it took all of her strength to rise from the chair. Penitent, she stood before Father, hands clasped at her waist, and nodded. "Good. I wish to speak with him."

She returned to her room, but remained awake all night, writing down every detail she could recall about Count Zuko, the brothel and the pickpockets. She finally collapsed into bed, wracked by guilt and grief so intense her very body ached.

The doctor arrived early the next morning. Constance endured an examination and more questions, aware that she must appear to be in full control of her faculties, lest the physician pack her off to a hospital. It was no easy feat. Her nerves were tight as violin strings. Yet the doctor pronounced her in excellent health and deemed her fit for travel.

Father would be relieved, and though Constance hated to make Mother wait any longer for her return, Alex needed her help now. Shortly after ten, she gathered her notes and waning strength. She found Father in his study with Mr. Morgan. "Come in, my dear."

"Thank you," she said. Father looked more hale and healthy than he'd seemed last night, thank goodness. She took the empty chair and turned to the barrister. "I assume Father told you everything I told him."

The men exchanged glances, and Morgan furrowed his brow. "That you claimed to have willingly joined a gang of ruffians and were involved in Viktor Zuko's death."

"More than involved. Responsible. I put the knife in his belly to save Alex's life." She thrust out the pages, covered front and back, to Morgan. "I've written everything I know about Count Zuko, his businesses, the brothel, and the pickpockets he exploited. Alex was a victim of Zuko's, as much as anyone."

"Which is ample reason for the young man to kill him." Morgan leafed through the pages, then set them on the table beside his chair. "Perhaps you don't realize how dangerous this wild story is to you."

"I do realize, but it isn't right that Alex should hang. I want you to represent him at trial, so that an innocent man doesn't die. I'm sure you can do this without putting me at risk, but if not ..." She shook her head, resigned. "I'm prepared to face the consequences."

Father blanched. "My God, you can't mean that."

"I mean every word. If Alex dies ..." She couldn't put the awful thought into words. "Father, I need to see him today and tell him we will help. It will give him hope, and he needs that right now. Mr. Morgan, do you know where he is?"

"They took him to Newgate, my lady, but I don't think you understand—"

"I do understand!" Impatience thinned into desperation, as she saw that they might refuse to help, leaving her and Alex to face this ordeal alone. "If you won't help us, I'll go to the police and tell them everything I know."

Father slammed his hand down on his desk. "And risk the gallows yourself? Constance, have you gone mad?"

Perhaps so. If her beloved Alex was hanged, her only comfort would be to die with him. In a sense, she already had. The innocent girl who'd left this house on a sunny day in August was gone for good, never to return. The woman she'd become had murdered to protect the man she loved. There was no place for her in the world of Bruton Street. She'd realized it last night, and now Father knew, too.

If that meant prison and execution, so be it.

Once more, Father and Morgan looked at one another, but now their faces held undeniable fear, realizing that this unpleasantness might not be disposed of so easily. Father gave a brisk nod. "Very well. We'll do what we can for your ... friend."

CHAPTER FIFTEEN

I n late afternoon, Mr. Morgan's carriage rolled to a stop in front of Newgate Prison. Densely built, the low building squatted on the corner of Newgate Street, next to Old Bailey, the criminal court building. In all their excursions around London, she didn't recall Alex ever bringing them this way. Had he avoided this corner on purpose, as if he sensed that someday, he would end up locked inside?

Seated beside Father, Constance steadied her trembling hands in her lap.

He looked over, concerned. "My dear, we don't have to do this. Mr. Morgan can relay your message, and I can take you home."

Her courage faltered momentarily, but she squared her shoulders and turned to him, determined. "No, I'm ready."

A man in a severe dark blue suit answered the door of the warden's residence. After Mr. Morgan explained their business, the man escorted them down a paneled corridor that seemed no different from what one saw anyplace. He stopped at a door at the end of the corridor and let them into an equally ordinary-looking office.

"Sign in, please," he said, directing them to a registry book on a table near a heavy door at the opposite end of the room. Constance reached for the pen. Mr. Morgan pushed past and signed for all of them.

The man keyed open a series of locks, and led them into a large room, painted gray. Like the office, the room had a door at the far end. This one was made of black iron. Two rough-looking turnkeys spoke to the gaoler, then disappeared through the black iron door. Mr. Morgan turned to Father. "My lord, the young man will be brought to us here, so Lady Constance can speak with him."

Father nodded.

The sparsely furnished room held two rough wooden benches, and a coal heater that did little to dispel the chill. Shelves lined the walls. On one were three busts, like something one might see in a museum. What in the world were they?

She stepped closer. The busts were of men, with grotesque, slack features. One was particularly fearsome, as if he could kill without a moment's hesitation. Beneath were names — killers she'd read about in the papers. These busts were death masks, cast after the murderers' executions.

A scream rose in her throat, and she cupped her hands to her mouth. The room spun, and her knees threatened to buckle. Just as she thought she might collapse to the stone floor, the iron door creaked open, letting in dank air. She spun around, heart pounding. *Please God, let it be Alex!*

Her hopes fell as two men entered. One wore a dark blue gaoler's suit, the other was tall, gaunt and dressed entirely in black. An undertaker? The tall man carried a notebook, and was jotting something down as the gaoler talked. Wanting to be far from the death masks, she hurried on shaky legs to the opposite side of the room, where Father and Mr. Morgan conferred with their gaoler. She stood alone by the heater, longing for the moment she could free Alex from this horrible place.

She felt the tall man's curious, intent gaze as he wrote in his notebook. Perhaps he was a reporter. If so, he might prove useful, but at the moment, all that mattered was seeing Alex.

The door opened again. The turnkeys returned. Alex walked between them, leg irons hobbling his steps, his hands shackled behind his back. A chain was coiled around his waist; one turnkey grasped it and shoved him into the room.

Constance raced forward and embraced him. "Oh Alex, I was afraid I'd never see you again!" She gazed up and cupped the side of this face with her gloved hand. "Are you all right? Have they hurt you?"

He kissed her palm, and the corner of his mouth lifted in a bleak half smile. "I'm all right, luv. God, it's good to see you, Connie. I miss you so much."

Constance tugged at the chain, wishing she could break it with her bare hands. "You shouldn't be in here ..." Her voice trembled and grew thick with tears. Unable to speak, all she could do was wrap her arms around him once more, and press her cheek to his chest.

Alex's shackles rattled as he fought against them. "Makes me sad I can't hold you now. There's nothin' I want more than to go back to before all this happened."

"I want that, too," she whispered. "And soon, you will be free. I've told my father everything."

"Connie, no! Damn it, you promised."

She shook her head. "It was a terrible promise! I couldn't keep it! I refuse to let you die!"

"I'm going to die, anyway! You can't save me, and even if you try, it's too late. I've already confessed, and no matter what you tell them, I'll just deny it."

"You can't mean that!"

His bleak expression ripped her heart in two. "This would have happened one way or another. At the hands of the Count or the Crown, it ends the same for me. But at least you still have a future."

"We have a future, together, in America! Please don't lose hope, Alex. Mr. Morgan is an excellent barrister, and Father has promised the best defense money can buy."

His gaze shifted in the men's direction and hardened, but when he looked back at her, a heart-wrenching mix of black despair and intense love played across his features. He shut his eyes and clenched his jaw, as if fighting back his own tears. "'Course he has and we'll be together again, just like we planned. 'Til then, do something for me, would you, luv?"

A whisper was all she could manage. "Anything."

"Don't blame yourself for what happened and try not to be too sad. You gave me so much — showed me I could have a future and a beautiful, smart society miss to share it with." His voice had a frayed edge. "You are all I ever wanted, and no matter how this turns out, I'll not regret a day of it. I will always love you, Constance."

"I love you, Alex." She slid her arms around his neck and pressed her lips to his. For a blissful moment, the present slipped away, and they were back on the roof of the Farthing, dancing beneath the stars.

Then Father's angry voice broke the spell, and the turnkey wrenched Alex from her arms.

"No!" Constance cried out as he stumbled, then regained his footing. For a moment Alex seemed to forget his shackles and lunged forward. The other guard pulled a truncheon from his belt and beat Alex across his back and shoulders, forcing him to his knees. The ghastly sounds of the weapon striking his body, and his agonized groans filled the room. "Stop! Stop! You're hurting him!"

The first guard unlocked the iron door. His partner grabbed the chain at the small of Alex's back and hauled him to his feet. In the last moment, as they shoved him through the doorway, she saw the terror and defeat etched on his face.

"Alex!" She charged toward the closing door, as the reeking maw of Newgate Prison swallowed him. She shouted, desperate to make the guards — anyone — show mercy. "Don't take him away from me! He's innocent! I'm his wife! I could be carrying his child!"

"Constance!" Father caught her roughly by the arms and

hauled her back.

She continued to shout over his shoulder. "He didn't kill anyone! It was me, I swear to God it was me!"

"Enough!" Father shouted in her face and shook her. "Mr. Morgan will do all he can, but you're coming with me, immediately!"

The gaoler took them back through the office, then down the corridor to the street. It had been deserted earlier, but now, police officers and men clutching small notebooks milled about. More reporters. Morgan tossed his coat over Constance so no one could see her face and hustled them out of the prison.

No one spoke on the ride back to Bruton Street. The only sound in the carriage was her sobbing.

Weak from exhaustion and bottomless misery, Constance could barely make it into the house. Father would want an explanation about her marriage to Alex, and she wasn't ready to give it. Not tonight.

Mrs. Dobbs, the housekeeper, helped her upstairs to her room, and gently removed her coat and boots. A young chambermaid brought in a tea tray. "I'm not hungry," Constance said.

"I know, miss," said Mrs. Dobbs, as she smoothed a gentle hand over Constance's brow. "But at least have a nice warm cup of tea. It might help you sleep."

The last time she'd slept had been two nights before, and her body yearned for it. Her throat was raw from shouting. Despite the fire burning low in the hearth, creeping cold like she remembered in the tunnels, permeated the room. A deep ache had settled into her bones.

The housekeeper arranged the pillows behind her back and

laid a quilt across her lap. Constance took the tea and drained the cup. It tasted awful, but didn't everything these days? The women gathered the tea things, turned down the gas sconces and left the room.

Constance spiraled down into a deep, comforting fuzz of exhausted sleep and strange dreams. She felt herself being carried out into the cold. There were hushed voices, and she couldn't discern what they were saying. Though she didn't want to go with them, she wasn't frightened. Just terribly sad, and too tired to fight any longer.

Sometime later, there was the moist huff of a steam engine, and more voices. Again, she was lifted and carried, and the commotion almost returned her to consciousness. But comforting fog lured her back to the warm, soft place where anguish was dulled and no one demanded explanations. A door closed, shutting out the cold, and a soft blanket was tucked around her. Once more she surrendered, lulled by the gentle click-clack of wheels on rails, and familiar Father-smells of tobacco and bay rum.

***

She awoke in Sussex.

In the dim light of her childhood bedroom, Constance looked up at Fletcher, who stood over her, blinking away tears. "I knew you'd come back to us."

She stirred, her joints painfully stiff. The bone-deep ache that started in London had grown far worse. "How long have I been here?"

"Three days, now. Don't worry about anything. Let us take care of you."

"Fletcher ... please. I must return to London." Her voice was hoarse and rusty. Her body burned and shivered simultaneously. She didn't have the strength to get out of bed, let alone travel across England.

"It's just the fever talking, milady. Try to rest, now."

"I can't!" Her mind spun with distorted images, like a sinister kaleidoscope. Ghastly plaster masks, gray prison walls, black iron doors, Alex chained inside. "I have to help—"

"Dearest?" Now it was Mother's voice, gentle and soothing. "The doctor says the illness has settled into your lungs. You must rest, so you can get well." Constance tried to sit up, and her chest tightened, triggering a spasm of excruciating coughs. "Lie back down, sweetheart."

Collapsing against the pillows, she did so. Fevered tears burned tracks down her cheeks. "I'm sorry... I'm sorry... I love you..."

***

The days passed in a haze, broken only by the small, comforting meals they brought, and visits from the doctor, who diagnosed pneumonia. Her monthly flow came, more painful than usual, so he prescribed a mild sedative. The rest of the time, Constance slept. One morning she awoke to the sight of a beam of sunlight coming through the drapes. She stirred, and for the first time in memory, felt rested. When a nurse arrived with tea and porridge, Constance asked her to open the curtains. Outside, autumn had turned to the crystal cold of winter.

It seemed as if the seasons had changed within a day. Her head spun, trying to grasp the passage of time. "How long have I been ill?" Constance asked the girl.

"More than a fortnight. Three weeks at least."

Good heavens! Time had stopped for her in early November, and the world had moved on without her. Alex! Was he still in Newgate, or had Mr. Morgan freed him by now? She needed to get to Alex! But first, she needed to see Mother, to explain everything, and apologize properly for the pain and worry she'd caused. When she asked Mother's whereabouts, the nurse shook her head. "Lady Beverly's away, miss, but I'll tell His Lordship you're awake."

Away? Disappointment turned to cold fear. Had Mother's health taken a turn for the worse? Though still weak, Constance needed to speak with Father straight away. The nurse helped her bathe and dress in a simple gown and slippers, her hair tied back with a matching ribbon, and helped her downstairs. Her shaky legs reminded her she still was not fully recovered.

She found Father in the breakfast room, lingering over tea and the papers. "Where's Mother?"

"Visiting your Aunt Iris." Mother's older sister and her husband owned a seaside inn near Hastings. Father turned a page of the paper, spread out in front of him. "Once Dr. Billings determined you were out of danger, I suggested she go for a few days. She'll be back tomorrow afternoon."

Her relief that Mother was all right was tempered by disappointment that she wasn't here to offer moral support. Constance was still separated from Alex and yearned for news.

Good news, she prayed. There was an awkward silence, as unspoken words hung in the air. She and Father were overdue for a conversation, and though Constance wasn't eager to have it, the time had come. She poured a cup of tea at the sideboard, then joined him at the table. Her gaze fell on the newspaper open between them. "Has there been any word from Mr. Morgan?"

Father glanced up, then his gaze returned to the article he was reading. "Morgan is handling the situation, but these things take time, you know."

"I'm sure they do. If he has questions—"

"He says the pages you provided were most informative."

"Good." She twisted the napkin laying on the table. "Father, I want to go back to London. I need to see..." she paused, gathering her courage. This was harder than she'd ever imagined. "... my husband."

She had his full attention now, and his pleasant expression dimmed. "Then it's true, you were wed to him?"

"Yes," she said, in a small voice.

"Legally? In front of witnesses?"

"No," she said, as emotion threatened to swamp her. "There were no witnesses. We exchanged vows only to one another."

"I see." Father's shoulders sagged, and he looked away, fixing his gaze on the opposite side of the room. "The doctor confirmed you're not with child. Your mother was relieved, to say the least."

Constance stilled. "You told her what happened?"

Father dropped his head and rubbed his brow. "Rose feared you had been ... violated by your captors." He turned to look at her, and his face was rigid and angry. "She doesn't know a damn thing about what happened, and I don't intend to tell her. Nor will you."

"Why not?"

"Because it would drive her to the laudanum for good, if it didn't bring on heart failure first. Your mother has never managed trouble well, and I've done my best to protect her from too much ... complexity. You do not understand what these last months have been like. I fear that any more shocks would be too much."

So it had been this bad? Remorse over what she'd put Mother through became as strong as her remorse over leaving Alex behind. "But I can't stay here and do nothing for Alex!" Her chest tightened, triggering a cough. "I love him, and belong in London, close to him."

Father nodded. "Mr. Morgan is at Newgate daily. The situation with your young man is well in hand. Once the doctor feels you're ready to travel, we'll discuss a brief visit. I suppose we can tell your mother that the police wish to interview you again. But for now, travel is out of the question."

Though she wanted to argue, Constance knew he was right. As badly as she wanted to help Alex, there was little she could do. To tax herself physically could mean a relapse. Then she would be no help to anyone. Father rose and went to the sideboard for a fresh cup of tea. "Perhaps you could write to ..." his voice trailed off, as though he couldn't speak her husband's name.

"His name is Alexander Blackwood. Everyone called — I mean calls — him Black. Except for me," Constance said, blinking back tears as she recalled a time and place that were lost to her, and that no one would understand why she missed them.

"Fine, then. Write Alexander a letter. I'll post it to Mr. Morgan, rather than the prison. He'll be more likely to receive it that way."

So she did. "I think of you always, and long for the moment I can hold you once more. Soon, we can begin our life together. Stay strong, my love, as we live for that day."

She could have written pages, but she wanted to make sure Alex could read every word.

◆◆◆◆◆◆◆◆

Weeks passed, and Constance wrote more letters. She tried not to dwell on the troubling fact that Alex hadn't written back. In prison he wouldn't have paper or pencils. Or books. *Robin Hood* was still in her trunk, where she'd tucked it for safekeeping, until they could read it together.

The second week of December, the doctor said that she would be fit to travel once the holidays were over. Though waiting was agony, Constance would follow the doctor's advice. On the day of the winter's first snowfall, Father and Mother told her that a place was available for her to begin her studies in February — at Vassar College in America.

Mother took a dainty bite of dessert. "I know you prefer to be close to home, but if you feel robust enough, you could go for the spring term, then be home by summer."

"We were wrong to deny you an education when it was so important to you," Father said, "and unfortunately, none of the suitable women's institutions here had a place available midway through the term. So we contacted Vassar, in order for you to start as soon as possible."

A shame they couldn't have realized this last summer and not tried to force her to wed an abusive brute. She was about to throw the offer back in their faces, but hesitated. If she were to go to America, she would already be in the place where she and Alex planned to live. A term of university would make her that much more qualified to find employment. Alex could join her as soon as they released him and they could begin their lives together, as hoped.

Constance agreed.

The decision lifted her spirits. As Christmas approached, there was the usual round of merriment in Sussex. Though she and her family didn't attend as many events as in seasons past, the small gatherings they went to surrounded her in love and good cheer. Among their family and closest friends, there were no questions, only kindness. While it tore Constance's heart to watch Jane kiss Sim, her betrothed, under the mistletoe on Christmas Eve, she took comfort knowing that soon, she and Alex would be together.

What would her family think of him? Would they accept him, or not be able to see beyond their obvious differences? She wanted to believe that Mother and Jane, at least, would see the fine man he was and make him feel welcome, but couldn't say for certain. Wondering only made her miss him more.

That night, she went to her bedroom window and gazed out at the sky, bright with stars. Just as he'd once imagined her seeing this sight from Mayfair, she thought of him seeing it now. From a prison cell? Dear God, she hoped not. Perhaps he was on his way to her this very night, in such a hurry that their letters passed in transit. He might arrive in Sussex tomorrow, the best Christmas gift she could ever hope for. But when Christmas Day came and went with no thrilling reunion — no word at all — she'd ached so much she feared her illness had returned. She went to bed early and cried herself to sleep.

As her family celebrated the arrival of 1874, it occurred to her that the precious months she'd spent with Alex belonged to the year now over. She awoke desperate for answers. In twelve days, she sailed for New York. Though she had written to Alex about her decision to go on ahead to America, she couldn't possibly leave without seeing him. That morning, after Mother left for another visit with Aunt Iris, Constance asked Father to arrange a trip to London.

He quickly agreed and even offered to wire Mr. Morgan's office to expedite their plans. She went to his chair and embraced him. "Oh Father, thank you! And will you please ask Mr. Morgan to tell Alex ..."

Father chuckled and patted her back fondly. The warmth of the holidays seemed to have restored his pleasant nature. "I needn't ask him anything. Morgan has seen the bundle of letters you send to your young man each week."

The next afternoon, she was in the drawing room with Father when Martin, the butler, came in. "This just arrived, Lord Beverly."

Father grabbed a folded white page off Martin's tray. Constance rose from her chair so quickly her embroidery hoop fell to the floor. "Is it from Mr. Morgan?" Eager for news, she rushed to Father's side, though she could not easily decipher the letter's spidery script. Father's brow furrowed as he read the letter. Then he closed his eyes and folded it shut, lowering himself to the sofa. Dread rose in her stomach. "Father?"

"My dearest... I'm afraid the news isn't good."

"What's wrong?" Trembling, she sat down beside him and clutched his arm.

He wouldn't look at her, staring at the floor, as the letter hung limply in his hand. "The young man's case went to trial weeks ago. He was found guilty and sentenced. They have carried the sentence out. Mr. Morgan couldn't find the heart to tell you at Christmastime."

Her mind coalesced around a thought too horrible to comprehend. "Are you saying that Alex is ..." She couldn't speak the words. She snatched the letter from Father. Her hands shook so much she could hardly focus. Her eyes skimmed the lines until she found her answer.

"... *executed by hanging at Newgate Prison...*"

"No! No!" The letter fell from her fingers. She brought her hands to her face to stifle the guttural cry that rose like bile in her chest. Alex was gone. Never again would he touch her, hold her, or brighten a moment with his sunny smile. Never again would he sing to her, or call her "luv." He wouldn't be joining her in America, and would never know the honorable life he'd longed for. Her dreams of a blissful future were dead. Alex had sacrificed himself to protect her, she'd let him down, and abandoned him to die alone. As they'd walked him to the scaffold, and placed the noose around his neck, had his final thoughts been of her?

"Alex, I'm sorry. I'm so, so, sorry! I love you, I always will."

Pain sliced through her body as if someone had driven a knife through her spine. Constance collapsed beside Father.

Her anguished sobs filled the room and reached to heaven, where her sweet thief could surely hear them.

PART TWO

CHAPTER SIXTEEN

May 1884

Beneath a full moon, the enormous ship churned soft waves that melted into the black glass surface of the Atlantic and disappeared. On the main deck, Constance Barrett gazed into the night. Other than stars twinkling against the black velvet sky, there was nothing but ocean as far as the eye could see.

Far below, in the bowels of the ship, the giant engines rumbled like far-off thunder. From the dining room came muted voices and the soft clink of china and crystal, as stewards prepared for tomorrow. All else was still. It was well past midnight, and everyone else on board had retired for the night, eager for the

Lady Boston's arrival in Southampton tomorrow.

But Constance wasn't thinking about tomorrow. Not yet. Alone at the railing, she was here to bury the past.

In her hands were two small objects: a pressed tin crucifix with "Psalm 23" painted on the back, and a book, *The Adventures of Robin Hood and His Merry Men*. Its faded paper cover showed a handsome young man with long blond hair.

For the past ten years, she'd kept them safe. She'd read the book just once and found the little cross tucked inside. The tale of the honorable thief and the courageous noblewoman had moved her to tears, especially at the end, when Robin and Marian lived happily ever after.

Her own story had ended much differently.

In the years since, she had accomplished much. She had completed her studies at Vassar College and become a teacher, working in the slums of New York City. In just ten days, she would wed Stuart Logan, Viscount Inglesby, and begin a new life on his ancestral estate near Bath.

But tonight, there were only memories, as the ship traveled across the dark miles of the Atlantic. The black water swirling below made her clutch the cold metal railing against a spell of vertigo. On her first crossing ten years back, the waves had beckoned, seductive and terrifying. Her parents and Fletcher kept a close watch the entire voyage. With excellent reason. On several occasions, she'd longed to hurl herself over the side, but lacked the opportunity.

Yet there had also been times she'd had the opportunity and not the inclination. By the time she reached America, she'd realized that to end her life would be a shameful disregard of

Alex's loving sacrifice. She had a duty to carry on and make the most of her future. Not only of hers, but to improve the futures of others. It had become her life's work. To the surprise of that once-despondent girl, the future held many wonderful things. To fully embrace them, it was time to leave the past behind.

Thus was her intent when she packed Alex's belongings for the return trip to England. They deserved a proper burial, something he'd probably not received. Gently, she traced her finger over the picture of Robin Hood. Once the book was consigned to the waves, there would be nothing to remind her of what Alex had looked like.

Some nights, she swore that if she turned, he would be at her side, wearing the sweet grin that always made her heart skip, his blue eyes soft with love. But when she did turn, there was only the black night. The familiar ache rose in her throat, and she squeezed her eyes shut to stop the tears that leaked out.

Go on, luv. It's all right. Be happy, now.

She wasn't sure that was still possible, at least not the innocent, hopeful sort of happiness she'd known back then. Even if it was, she wasn't sure she deserved it. But the gentle night breeze brushed a ghost-kiss across her lips and dried the tears that lingered on her cheeks. She hoped Alex had forgiven her, even if she'd never forgiven herself. She tucked the cross into the book and hugged it close. They had been young, in love and dreamed of crossing this ocean together. It was the right place to leave his memory.

Following a restless night, she overslept. The cabin was still dim, but there was enough tepid sunlight coming in through the window for her to see her timepiece. They would dock in a few hours. Constance bolted out of bed.

Though she had to rush through her toilette, she wanted to look beautiful. She hadn't seen Stuart for three months; Mother and Jane, not since Father's death two years ago. Her hair went into its customary chignon, but the ruby earrings Stuart gave her at Christmas, when he proposed, added elegance. Her coppery red velveteen waist and silk skirt, striped with green and gold, was her nicest outfit. Fletcher, now wed to Vassar College's head groundskeeper, would approve.

The dining room served a delicious breakfast, and Constance took full advantage. Ahead was a lengthy day of travel, and this was likely her only meal until she reached Stuart's family home, Tarpley Manor, late this afternoon. She enjoyed soft-boiled eggs, sweet Virginia ham, pastries almost as good as those from the bakery near her New York City boardinghouse, and the strong American coffee she missed already.

Returning to her cabin, she checked for stray items. She saw none. She had already packed her most important belongings; she could replace anything else. Once the porter came for her trunk, she grabbed her carpetbag and went to join the other passengers on deck. The banks along the Channel were muddy gray-green, the day was blustery and overcast. Not spring-like in the least. More like the miserable winter day she'd left England for the first time. Were all her comings and goings from her homeland to be under such gloomy conditions?

But the sight of people down on the docks lifted her spirits, particularly when she spotted Stuart, Jane, and Mother, al waving. When Constance disembarked and found her family, Mother was the first to embrace her. Tears welled in Lady Beverly's brown eyes. "Darling, it's wonderful to have you back at last."

Finally, Mother had shed her widow's weeds. The sight cheered Constance even more. Father's death, after a bout of pneumonia, had devastated Mother. Constance knew the pain of widowhood all too well. Though she was still sorting out her own feelings about returning home, seeing Mother so happy helped considerably.

Jane, now Lady Simsford, wrapped her in an exuberant hug. Beside her was Stuart. Tall, square-jawed, and handsome, he was the perfect English gentleman, with a neatly-trimmed dark beard which needed no enhancements from Makassar oil. His fine wool greatcoat and silk top hat were of the latest style, and the breeze ruffled the scarlet-trimmed cape of his coat. Stuart was no dandy, but kept up with fashion. He greeted her with a kiss to her gloved hand. "Welcome home, darling."

"I've missed you." She smiled and took his arm. Though his quiet reserve had taken getting used to, she'd come to appreciate it. Swooning romance was for schoolgirls.

A strapping young footman in dark green-and-black livery waited beside the hired coach that would take them to the railway station in Salisbury. "Edward will see to your luggage," Stuart explained, as the footman turned smartly toward the ship. "If you ladies will excuse me, I wish to visit the smoking lounge before we depart."

"Imagine," Jane sighed, when they were settled in the coach.

"You went all the way to America only to fall in love with an Englishman. So suddenly, too!"

Constance stiffened momentarily, but she had no reason to feel defensive. This wasn't an impulsive decision, driven by a whirlwind romance. It was a rational, reasonable choice, made by two dear friends ready to embrace the next phase of their lives.

They came from similar backgrounds, but the tales that followed her name in London meant nothing to him. Not only did he not consider her damaged goods, he appreciated her intellect and respected her accomplishments. They discussed ideas for how education could improve the lives of the poor, and how they might share that work. After living a bachelor's life in France, Stuart needed to assume responsibility for his family's estate and legacy. She wanted children, and time was running out. Marriage was the logical solution for them both.

Two years ago, she had initially balked at her headmistress's request to correspond with the Brooklyn Academy's generous British benefactor, Viscount Inglesby, though in America, he rarely used the title. She found she enjoyed their letters. When he'd visited the Brooklyn Academy last summer, that he'd turned out to be handsome, as well as intelligent and caring, was a most pleasant surprise. Their friendship deepened into warm regard. When he'd visited this past Christmas, he proposed.

Constance considered herself a very lucky woman.

Mother arranged her skirts. Her clothes were reserved, befitting a dowager countess living on reduced means. "A wise decision to wed a viscount, especially one who will someday inherit the Torrington title."

Yes, you would think of that. That Stuart would one day be a

Marquess was more exciting to Mother than it was to Constance, or even Stuart. Hadn't they tried to marry her off to a duke's heir a decade ago? A shudder snaked across her shoulders. Thank goodness an impressive title was the only thing Stuart and Gaffney had in common. "Well," Constance said, "if it weren't for his older brother's death, Stuart wouldn't be inheriting."

Mother brought her fingers to her lips. "Oh dear. I didn't know. Lady Torrington doesn't wear mourning clothes. This wasn't recent, was it?"

"Eighteen months ago, in a riding accident." Constance, having lost Father not long before, had tried to offer Stuart comfort in their letters. "I believe it's why Stuart's father wishes to move from Tarpley Manor to London. Lord Torrington and Alastair were quite close."

"I see," said Mother, chastened. "I certainly won't mention it."

"That's best." While Mother's fixation on titles and social status could be annoying, Constance was determined to ignore it. Mother had suffered enough, thanks to her. Better to change the subject. "You look so well, Jane. Your happiness speaks well of married life. I look forward to seeing Lord Simsford again."

"Sim will be here next week, and he looks forward to seeing you, too. We've all missed you so much," she said, giving Constance's hand a squeeze. "However, I was delighted to accompany Aunt Rose to Bath."

Blond, green-eyed and still lovely, her cousin looked hardly any older than when she had been the belle of London. Constance felt ages older. She still regretted not returning to England for her cousin's wedding, though Jane had long since put it behind them.

A wave of melancholy washed over Constance. Jane was a

better friend than she deserved. Her cousin's popularity was a large reason her family's name hadn't been further dragged through the mud. "I'm so glad you could, and that we'll have time to catch up. It's been far too long." She turned to Mother. "I'm sure having Jane along made it easier for you to complete all the preparations for the wedding."

"It has," Mother agreed. "My only concern is that your gown will not be delivered until next week."

The wedding would take place before family and friends in the Tarpley Manor chapel, with an intimate wedding breakfast to follow. It would be a small, tasteful celebration, befitting Constance's age and her family's station. Mother had insisted on one concession to bridal pageantry — an elaborate white silk wedding gown designed by the House of Worth. Though Constance felt unworthy, Mother had insisted.

Putting Mother in charge had been the right decision. Not only was she much more attuned to social ritual, planning the wedding had given her something enjoyable to do. Something better than missing Father and her old life, back when the Countess of Beverly was welcome in the homes of the city's best families.

Constance had brought about the end of that.

Stuart returned from the smoking lounge and took the seat beside her. "Edward is securing your trunk and we will be underway. We should reach Salisbury in plenty of time to catch the train."

The carriage pulled away into the crowded streets of Southampton. Mother smiled at Stuart, then Constance. "Lady Torrington has been so gracious in allowing us to hold the wedding at Tarpley Manor," she said, in case Constance wasn't already aware of her future mother-in-law's generosity.

Stuart chuckled and placed his hand on Constance's. "She is so delighted I am at last taking a wife; I daresay it's brought out the best in her. My parents are eager to meet Constance and were most impressed by her accomplishments."

Were they? She hoped so. Even in America, far too many believed her education and accomplishments made her unsuitable for marriage. In one of their early letters, Stuart had joked that his mother seemed determined to pair him with an empty-headed, young debutante whom she could control. Would Lady Torrington approve of her son's chosen bride?

There was also her family's tarnished reputation. Fortunately, Bath society was likely more interested in its own scandals and gossip than something which happened in London a decade ago.

She brushed her fears aside. She and Stuart might not be in love, but they cared for each other. They needed each other. It was a stronger foundation for marriage than a lot of couples had. The scandal was old news, and from what Stuart had told her, Lady Torrington was one of the county's doyennes. If she accepted Constance, there was nothing to worry about.

"I thought Constance was so brave to move far away and attend a university for women," Jane said. "I would never have had the gumption. Not only that, but to live alone in New York City and teach in the slums? Especially after all you went through, you poor dear."

Mother pursed her lips. "Well, yes. The circumstances were most unusual."

Seldom did they mention the scandal that shook London a

decade ago, when Constance was taken from the Crystal Palace by East End ruffians who forced her to steal, in fear for her life. One criminal robbed and murdered a prominent businessman and was attempting to smuggle her to Shanghai when she was rescued. The criminal was tried and executed. Poor Constance, damaged in body and spirit, had no choice but to leave England.

How much of the truth Father ever told Mother, she didn't know. She assumed it wasn't much and never brought it up. Stuart knew she had been in love with a young man who died tragically, but being a gentleman, he never pressed for details. She never offered them. She assumed he had to know about the kidnapping scandal, too, but he never asked about the past. It was one of his most attractive features.

Outside the city, the land was hilly, and the landscape was greener than along the coast. It was lovely countryside, though the quiet would take some getting used to. If she missed the excitement of city life, she could always visit Mother and Jane in London, though she had no desire to set foot there ever again. Bath would suit her fine.

Stuart opened the coach window, letting in the aroma of grass and countryside, then leaned back in his seat and closed his eyes. It seemed early for a nap, yet perhaps he hadn't slept well. Inns could be uncomfortable. The tension in his jaw suggested some worry or another. A ripple of unease came, but quickly went. His concerned, serious nature was something she greatly admired.

Like rural life, he was safe and comfortable, far removed from passions that could bring both joy and unimaginable pain.

At Salisbury, they boarded the first-class compartment for the trip to Bath, while the footman saw to her trunk. He returned with a light snack of tea and biscuits, then departed with a bow, to wherever it was he traveled. Upon arrival, a dark green-and-black carriage, bearing the Torrington crest, was waiting at the Bath depot. A red-cheeked coachman settled them in the carriage and assisted the footman with claiming her trunk.

Warm and comfortable in the immaculate carriage, she found it odd to not have to lift a finger, after so many years of fending for herself. It was a luxury many envied, but it could also render one helpless, as she knew all too well. Finding the right balance would be one of the many adjustments she would have to make in her new life as Lady Inglesby.

It was late afternoon when they pulled up to a gatehouse topped with a medieval clock tower. A caretaker greeted them and opened the gate to a winding macadam road lined by ornate gaslights. On either side were the gardens, lovely even this early in the season. To the left was an enormous yew topiary, where manicured, animal-shaped hedges seemed to move in the lengthening shadows. A path led through it to a low wall and disappeared.

"That leads to the sunken garden," said Stuart. "Mother finds the Orient fascinating and has commissioned several statues and small buildings. You can't see from here, but just beyond is a pond with a footbridge and pagoda. "

A footbridge and pagoda? Like in Victoria Park?

"Over here is the chapel." He pointed to the right. The charming stone church had a steep, medieval-style roof and colorful stained glass windows, surrounded by low hedges. Here she and Stuart would wed, just ten days from now. Seeing the chapel, the idea became that much more real. Her old life, both the good and the bad, was about to end.

The road curved and Tarpley House came into view. It seemed at first of modest size, but as they drew closer, she saw the extensive wings hidden by dusk, trees and hedges. Constructed of salmon-colored brick with a contrasting diamond pattern set into the masonry, it stood three floors. Large double windows, trimmed with decorative black iron, covered the ground and first floors. On the upper floors, at the corners of the house, were charming, private terraces. The house was topped with a steep, gabled roof.

This majestic place was her new home.

They stopped beneath a brightly-lit portico. Great oak doors opened, and two liveried footmen came out to meet them. They helped the women from the carriage, then saw to the trunk. Stuart offered her his arm, Mother and Jane fell in behind.

Inside, another footman took Stuart's coat. "Good evening, John. I trust my father is in the saloon?"

"He is, sir," the footman replied.

"Excellent. Please tell him I shall join him shortly."

A polished oak staircase branching upward like an immense tree, anchored the main hall. The underside of each flight of steps was painted rich shades of gold and deep green. Along the walls, plaster molding formed elaborate diamond-shaped patterns that echoed the masonry outside. Beyond the staircase, the hall extended into the rear of the house. A gallery of enormous portraits, depicting Torrington ancestors, hung from polished, oak-paneled walls. The entire place gleamed with the warm, soft glow of gas-lit sconces and candlelight.

It was breathtaking and utterly grand. Too grand. Her family's former estate in Sussex had been just as beautiful, yet not so imposing. *Well, of course it wasn't, you goose. It was your home.*

But it wasn't any longer. When Father died, Uncle Albert had inherited the estate. Mother lived in the Bruton Street townhouse. Constance's most recent home had been a comfortable, yet plain, rooming house for teachers a few blocks from the Brooklyn Academy. It was only natural to feel overwhelmed.

Three maids appeared and curtsied. "Good evening, my lady," said the oldest of the trio, a plump, friendly-faced woman about her age. "I will be happy to escort you upstairs so you may dress for dinner."

She took Constance to a lovely corner suite at the rear of the house with French doors that opened onto the terrace she'd seen from outside. They had already brought her trunk upstairs. The maid bobbed a curtsy. "My name is Agnes, milady, and if there is anything you need, please let me know. Kennedy will be in momentarily to unpack your things and assist you in dressing for dinner."

"Oh, that's all right, I don't need help. With unpacking, I mean," she said, answering the surprise in Agnes's eyes. Though she hadn't used a lady's maid in years, that was obviously about to change. "I have preferences about where I keep my things. But I would welcome help dressing for dinner."

"Very good, milady."

Constance quickly unpacked, placing small items in drawers before the lady's maid arrived. She removed her dresses from her trunk. She had only one gown nice enough for dinner at an English manor home, a wine-colored taffeta that was several years old. No one expected a spinster teacher to look stylish, but they would expect it of a viscountess. A lady's maid could prove useful. She left the taffeta on the bed and carried her practical teacher's dresses to the wardrobe.

It was already full.

Were these Lady Torrington's? She examined one gown. Its wide, open neckline and fitted bodice didn't seem suitable for a matron in her late sixties. She pushed through the folds of silk, soft wool, and crisp linen. There were gowns, fashionable day dresses, even a riding habit. She closed the wardrobe. Best to wait for the lady's maid. Leaving her old dresses on the bed beside the taffeta, she went out onto the terrace.

In the fading light, she could still make out the pond, though not the footbridge. Beside the pond was a small cottage where the bailiff must live. A road led past the pond and a small farm, into the woods. Stuart said they used the woods for hunting, and hidden deep in the trees, was the ruins of an ancient village dating back to Norman times.

Tarpley Manor was immense, and it was about to become her responsibility. No, not just hers. Stuart's, too. Together, they would transform it into a warm, welcoming home for their family. Wasn't that the reason she'd left New York? For family?

Returning to her room, a young woman in a neat black dress greeted her. "Good evening, Lady Constance. My name is Lorena Kennedy, and Lady Torrington has offered my services, unless you've already hired a lady's maid," she explained.

"I've not used a maid in years and hadn't even thought of

searching for one. I'm sure you'll be perfectly fine. Perhaps you can shed some light on this?" She opened the wardrobe.

Kennedy smiled. "Those are a surprise from Lord Inglesby." She brought out a pale green, short-sleeved silk, trimmed in white lace. "If you have not chosen a gown for dinner, might I suggest this one? I believe it will suit your coloring very well."

After forty minutes in Kennedy's capable hands, Constance was ready. The gown was more ornate than what she would have chosen, with silk blossoms trimming the bodice and skirt, yet she rather liked it. The fit was perfect. Several months back, an old waist and skirt had gone missing from her wardrobe, but she assumed she'd donated them to charity and forgotten. Stuart must have taken them for the dressmaker. What a lovely, considerate man.

Kennedy escorted her to the landing at the top of the grand staircase. Mother and Jane waited below, on a small divan to the left of the main hall. She did not see Stuart at first, then spied him to the right, speaking with a clean-shaven man who stood in the shadows. The butler, most likely. Stuart glanced upward and seeing her, dismissed him. As she descended the stairs, Stuart smiled up at her, and offered his arm when she reached the bottom.

As she turned toward him, she glimpsed their reflection in a large mirror, hanging on the opposite wall. Stuart and Constance, now the future Lord and Lady Inglesby. They felt like strangers she needed to get to know.

"You are a vision, my dear."

A blush warmed her cheeks. "No small thanks to you. The dresses are perfect, Stuart. It was a beautiful surprise."

"I'm so glad you like them. Are you ready to meet my family?"

She tilted her chin, seeking his gaze. "Will they be disappointed that I'm not a teenage debutante?"

He blinked, then chuckled. "I've given them plenty by returning home. I'd say it's only fair that I choose my bride."

She studied him. "You haven't answered my question."

He sighed and took his hands in hers. "You miss little, Constance. It's one of the many things I admire about you. I've made it clear to my family that I wish to wed a woman of substance, rather than some frivolous girl. While my mother is likely to grumble some, she will come round eventually. We're well matched, you and I. We think alike, and aren't afraid to make choices that others might not approve of."

She looked down at their joined hands. "Heaven knows, there are plenty in London who don't approve of me."

"Decade-old gossip has no place in our lives now. Remember, too, that Mother has offered to host our wedding, so she can't be terribly opposed."

"I suppose you have a point." She rewarded his coaxing with a smile.

He smiled back. "And surely a woman who has braved life alone in New York City can hold her own with the grand dame of Somerset County."

Constance chuckled. "Very well, then. I'm ready." Again, she studied their reflections. They were well-matched. Though it had stung to hear the most momentous time of her life dismissed so easily, Stuart was right. What happened back then only continued to exist because she continued to think about it. She owed it to him and to their future to stop doing so, once and for all.

The butler waited, back turned, at the drawing room door, as they lined up behind him. As the highest rank, Stuart would enter first followed by Jane, Mother, and then Constance. She took a deep breath, preparing to meet the strangers who were about to become her family.

"You may announce us," Stuart told the butler.

"Very good, sir."

Time stopped, as the man's voice brought a chilling moment of déjà vu.

Heart pounding, she rose on her toes to peer past Mother, Jane, and Stuart. The man was tall, with hair of a nondescript color, though her impression was of a younger man, rather than a mature, gray-haired servant. Nothing, aside from his voice, was familiar and somehow, that wasn't quite right either. She'd heard it before, yet it was different in a way she couldn't identify.

He opened the doors and stepped into the drawing room. In crisp tones, he announced, "Viscount Inglesby, the Countess of Simsford, the Dowager Countess of Beverly, and her daughter, Lady Constance."

The moment he spoke her name, a shiver ran down her spine. The Cockney accent was gone, but there was no mistake. She was seeing a ghost, or at least hearing one.

It can't be.

He stepped aside, and she followed Stuart, Jane, and Mother into the drawing room. Waiting were Kenneth and Edna Logan, the Marquess and Marchioness of Torrington; Constance's uncle Albert, the new Earl of Beverly; and two women whom she did not know.

The butler remained at the door, his stern gaze not meeting

hers. She glanced up at him as she passed. He was an attractive man of about thirty years, but aloof and unsmiling, descriptions that didn't fit at all with the memories racing through her mind. His hair was combed back, revealing a high forehead.

It's not him.

Intense, heart-wrenching disappointment shattered momentary relief. Then she saw his eyes, which were an unusual shade of deep blue and intimately familiar.

Eyes she'd never expected to see again.

...Alex?

Stuart was speaking as they crossed the room, but to Constance, it seemed the floor had just given way. The room seemed to spin, as a raging flood of memories obliterated everything in the present. Her vision blurred. Her knees went weak. She toppled backward. Someone caught her, and she knew no more.

CHAPTER SEVENTEEN

Constance? Dearest, can you hear me?"

Mother's voice was far away. Constance fought her way through a muffled fog, back to consciousness. Where on earth was she? Not in New York. Aboard ship? No. The air smelled of wood smoke, not the ocean. She forced her eyes open.

Bookshelves rose to a wood-paneled ceiling. This was a library, though one she'd never seen. Yet Mother and Jane were here, sitting beside the divan on which she lay. Mother stroked her forehead and smiled down at Constance. "Thank goodness you're awake. You gave everyone such a fright. Are you well, child?"

"Well? Of course, I'm well." Her limbs felt unsteady as she propped herself on her elbows. She looked down at her gown. Pale green. New. This was Tarpley Manor. She'd arrived this evening, a maid had dressed her, she'd gone to meet Stuart's family, and ...

Constance bolted upright.

"There, there," Mother soothed, patting her shoulder. "You need to rest. The Torringtons have summoned a doctor from the village. He'll arrive momentarily."

Though her stomach rolled so wildly she might be ill at any moment, she asked, "A doctor? Whatever for?"

"Why, you fainted!" Jane exclaimed. "It was the most extraordinary thing. One moment you were fine, but no sooner did we enter the drawing room and the young man announced us, than you toppled over."

She grasped Jane's hands, fighting to contain her distress. "The young man! What was his name?"

Mother shook her head, perplexed. "The butler? He was the one who caught you before you suffered a terrible injury. I don't recall his name." She waved her hand, as if this detail was of no consequence.

But the butler's name was of enormous consequence. As incredible as it seemed, Alex Blackwood appeared to be alive and working as a manservant for the Torringtons. Either that, or she was going mad.

"Stuart had you brought in here and summoned the doctor. He should be here soon." Mother pulled the coverlet over her legs.

Constance shoved it back and swung her legs over the side of the divan. "I don't need a doctor. I need to return to the drawing room!"

"Don't be ridiculous. No one is expecting you at dinner this evening. The Torringtons understand you are in delicate health and must rest."

"I am not in delicate health. I feel fine." If fine meant a heart pounding hard enough to escape her chest. She stilled and blew out a breath. She must get hold of herself. "Please, Jane, bring me my shoes."

At that moment, the doctor arrived. Regaining control as best she could, she followed the elderly physician and Mother upstairs. Once the doctor confirmed what Constance kept insisting, Kennedy came to repair her hair. An agonizing hour later, Constance returned to the drawing room. This time, a footman announced her. The butler was nowhere in sight.

Across from Constance, Lady Torrington pursed her lips. "I'm rather surprised to see you, Lady Constance, as you still look pale. At dinner, you must avoid wine and rich food."

"As if I could eat," she murmured, distracted. Realizing she'd spoken aloud, she released an awkward laugh. Lady Torrington's face tightened into a stiff smile.

In the corner, Stuart watched his father and her uncle play chess. "Actually, I believe Constance should eat and I hope she samples some wine. I want to hear her preferences for the wedding breakfast."

The mention of the wedding solicited polite questions from Lady Torrington's sister, Baroness Philippa Halifax, and her companion, Dame Dorothy Richards, a widow about fifty years old.

Constance fought to keep her mind on the conversation, but it was impossible. All she wanted was for the butler to return.

Could it possibly be true? Was Alex alive, after all this time?

For months after leaving the East End, nightmares about his execution had tormented her. From the scaffold, Alex tried to comfort her one last time with his sweet smile as they tightened the noose around his neck. There was a horrible rattling sound. The trapdoor opened beneath his feet and his body dropped through, killing him instantly. Then men came to cut his body down. She ached for a last touch, though his skin would be cold and his heart still. But before she could reach him, the men had thrown Alex into the back of a cart and driven him away, to be cut apart as a cadaver. As the cart disappeared, she ran after it, screaming, only to awaken drenched in tears and sweat. Even now, the dream still haunted her.

But in truth, she never knew the date of Alex's hanging. She hadn't wanted to know. That way, she wouldn't ever have to think about where she was, or what she had been doing at the moment he died.

Could he have somehow escaped the gallows? Or did the Torrington's butler simply bear an uncanny resemblance to the dashing thief she'd loved so much? That was the most plausible explanation, and the one that would least complicate her life.

Strangely, it was the one she dreaded most of all.

Then the drawing room doors opened, and there he stood.

She held her breath, waiting for some sign of recognition. But again, he looked straight past her. Addressing Lady Torrington, he spoke in proper diction that bore no trace of Alex's cheerful Cockney. "Dinner is served, ma'am."

Her heart sank.

Lord Torrington stood. "Thank you, Blackwood."

She gripped the arms of her chair, just as she sought to keep hold of her sanity. It doesn't mean that it's him. Blackwood isn't an uncommon name. This man could simply be a distant cousin.

The butler stood at attention as everyone rose from their seats. Lord Torrington offered his arm to his wife. Uncle Albert escorted Mother. Constance placed her hand on Stuart's arm and hoped he didn't notice how badly she trembled. Jane, Philippa and Dorothy followed, as Blackwood led them to the dining room.

Lord and Lady Torrington took their places at the opposite ends of the table. Constance was seated in the middle, between Stuart and Mother, across from her uncle. Lord Torrington, Stuart, and Uncle Albert discussed tomorrow morning's hunting trip. The marchioness and Philippa launched into a critique of a recent party given by someone named Harriet. Constance reached for her napkin and noisily dislodged the sterling arranged on top. Mother frowned.

The butler stood at a small sideboard on the right side of the room, where decanted wines were arranged. As footmen carried in covered platters and tureens, Blackwood brought wine to Lord Torrington, pronouncing its name in perfect French. He poured a sample into Lord Torrington's glass and waited as he tasted.

"Very good," Lord Torrington said. "You may pour."

With a crisp nod, he worked his way down her side of the table, stopping at Stuart's place, then hers. Constance gripped her hands in her lap. He stood stiffly, keeping a distance, though she swore she could feel the heat of his body. "Do you care for wine, my lady?" His voice held no hint of recognition.

"Yes, please," she whispered.

He poured the sparkling white wine into her glass and she studied his hand, which was dotted with faint, but still-visible round scars.

Phosphorous burns.

Oh, my God.

Her eyes followed the line of his black-clad arm to his face. Their gazes locked. In the low light of the dining room, his stern expression softened, and rock-solid certainty banished her doubt. The man she'd grieved was alive and standing inches from her.

Alex, it's you. It's really you!

"Thank you... Blackwood." The name felt strange in her mouth. She hadn't spoken it in ten years.

"You're welcome, my lady." As he turned away, the corner of his mouth lifted with the subtle hint of a boyish smile. The moment took her back to a day in the East End, when he'd stolen to feed her and Danny. A shabby frock coat hadn't disguised the gentleman inside.

She gripped the edge of the table to steady herself. Somehow, someway, Alex hadn't gone to the gallows for a crime she'd committed. He hadn't died alone. He hadn't died at all! Not only had he escaped execution, he was a free man, living the honest life he'd wanted so much.

But it was a life that didn't include her. And he'd built that life while she'd grieved his death. The look in his eyes didn't suggest he hated her. Yet the fact he was very much alive and hadn't tried to find her meant something much worse. He hadn't cared enough to look.

Her appetite had vanished, though dinner continued as if

nothing had changed. For everyone else, Alex included, it hadn't.

Her hands trembled as she stirred the food on her plate. Did he know before tonight that she was Stuart's fiancé? How could he not, especially since no one would think to conceal it? Yet, here he was, as if nothing out of the ordinary was happening. *How can he be so calm? Doesn't he care at all?*

She shifted her gaze back. Alex had matured into a conspicuously handsome man with chiseled, patrician features that seemed out of place on a servant. His cheeks bore a healthy tone. Country life agreed with him. He had slicked his hair back with pomade, which disguised its blond color. Though it was shorter than he wore it on the East End, it was long enough to brush against the top of his starched white stock. He stood at attention in the corner with his hands clasped behind his back.

The pose was an eerie reminder of the last time she saw him, chained in Newgate Prison.

She desperately needed a moment to make sense of all this, though conversation swirled like the cacophony of an amateur orchestra tuning up. Lady Torrington hadn't stopped talking since they sat down. Constance gripped her fork so hard it dug into her fingers. Were Stuart and his family aware? No. Neither she nor Alex would be here if they were. He had revealed nothing, nor would she. This was a secret they shared.

"... and considering his fiancé's delicate health, I believe Stuart should reconsider some of this week's strenuous activities. I don't believe the poor girl can make the trip to Chataigne."

Her breathing slowed, and she forced her mind to what was important — making a good first impression on Stuart's parents. She prayed she could utter a coherent sentence, looked up, and smiled. "Oh no, Lady Torrington, I'm fine. Stuart has told me about Tarpley Manor and I look forward to seeing all of it. There's so much to learn."

Lady Torrington frowned at the reminder that Constance was to become mistress of her longtime home. "Yes, there is much to learn. In fact, I have decided to see to your instruction myself. I have spent close to fifty years here, and I do not wish to see Tarpley Manor's beauty ruined by a bride's inexperience."

She blinked, then looked away to cover her shock at the woman's tactlessness. "I look forward to it, Lady Torrington."

As everyone except Constance savored the last bites of dessert, Alex approached Lady Torrington. "The drawing room is ready for tea, my lady," he said.

She rose, a signal for the women to follow, leaving the men to Scotch and cigars. Constance considered bidding everyone good night, but was suddenly more afraid to be alone with her thoughts. She rose and followed the others.

Alex escorted them to the drawing room and held the door. Philippa brushed against him as she passed, eyeing him with undisguised hunger. Constance shifted her gaze away, unable to even look at him. He poured their tea, then left. Philippa turned to Lady Torrington. "I must say, he's a delightful addition to your staff. He must be new. I would have noticed him before."

Lady Torrington sipped her tea. "He came to us in December, from an old school friend of Kenneth's. Jeffries needed to retire, and our previous first footman would never do as a butler. Charles is much too fond of spirits to be entrusted with the wine cellar. Kenneth's friend, Sir Edward, told us that when it comes to selecting wines, this young man has a highly sophisticated tongue."

Philippa gave a languorous smile and twirled a stray tendril around her finger. "I could certainly make use of a sophisticated tongue. I might like to hire a manservant who is ... well-trained and obedient. I don't suppose that one is available?"

Constance stiffened. Surely, that wasn't one of his duties.

The marchioness huffed. "Take him, please. He makes me quite uncomfortable."

"Interesting that you should say so," Mother mused. "Since I arrived, I've had the oddest sense he dislikes me. I can't imagine why, since I never laid eyes on him until two days ago."

Constance stared down into her teacup and squeezed her eyes shut. *Because of what we did to him, that's why. I promised to help him, and he believes I broke that promise.*

"If he is rude or impertinent, I will speak to him. You see, Sir Edward took him on as a reform project. As a boy, he was a common street thief, and even spent time behind bars. Sir Edward gave him a profession and saw to it he learned to read. He's assured us the man is as honest as a vicar." She snorted. "Nevertheless, I loathe having a criminal in my home, reformed or otherwise."

"A thief?" Philippa gave a low, throaty chuckle. "Well, if he worked for me, I'd see to it he was frequently searched. Have you searched him yet, Edna? If not, perhaps Dorothy and I could assist you." Dame Richards tittered.

"You are depraved, Philippa." Lady Torrington waved her hand dismissively. "We'll sort out the terms, if you're interested in acquiring him."

Constance had heard enough. Her teacup rattled against the

saucer as she set it down. "Acquire him? Good heavens, he's a man, not an object!"

The other women stared. Mother quickly intervened. "She means his contract, dearest. I know it has been years since you've lived with staff, but it's perfectly acceptable to transfer a servant's employment from one household to another."

Lady Torrington narrowed her eyes. "Do you take issue with how we treat our domestics, Lady Constance?"

She should say nothing more, but these women considered Alex nothing but a possession to be toyed with and traded round! He was a human being and deserved to be treated with dignity. In America, she'd forgotten the rigid social hierarchy everyone here took for granted. She might live in this world again, but she could no longer mindlessly accept its precepts.

"I apologize for implying that you and Lord Torrington are anything but fair to your staff," she said. "Yet after living in America, which recently fought a war to rid itself of the hideous institution of slavery, I can't help but wonder if English society couldn't benefit from seeing that everyone deserves respect, regardless of their social class."

Jane and Dorothy grew quiet. Mother averted her gaze and fingered the lace on her cuff. Lady Torrington's nostrils flared, but her voice remained pleasant, feigning a gracious manner. "Well, you have gained some unusual ideas during your time in the frontier. From what I've heard, much of America is still quite uncivilized, including the area of New York City in which you lived."

It was clear she'd pushed too far. Rather than a good first impression, she seemed to be making an enemy of her future mother-in-law. How could she have allowed her emotions to get the best of her on such an important night? Then again, how could she have imagined her first love still lived? She smiled, hoping to defuse the tension. "I taught in a school that served a very poor neighborhood. I saw the children's struggles and worked to help them learn despite their poverty. Stuart's patronage was vital to the Brooklyn Academy's success. We hope to continue supporting its efforts and also encouraging other schools with similar missions."

"Really? He's not mentioned it." Lady Torrington turned to Philippa and Dorothy. "Never have I understood my son's interest in such an unsavory place. Thank goodness he only visits occasionally. Lady Constance, on the other hand, lived in the thick of it for five years."

With fortuitous timing, the drawing room doors opened. Blackwood announced the gentlemen were waiting in the saloon, should anyone like to join them for whist.

The mere sight of him brought a deluge of conflicted emotion. How in the world was she going to live in the same house with him? She couldn't make it through a single evening without bringing on disaster. Best to end the night before things got worse. Constance stood. "Again, Lady Torrington, I apologize if I spoke out of turn. It's been a long day, and I'm quite tired. I feel it best if I retire for the night."

"I couldn't agree more." Lady Torrington rose and barked a command. "Blackwood. Tell my son that his fiancée is not well, and to come say good night."

He directed a respectful nod to the marchioness, ignored Constance, turned on his heel and left the room. Philippa and

Dorothy exchanged leering glances.

At the foot of the stairs, Stuart bid Constance good night. She beseeched him with a silent plea that he missed, though she hadn't the slightest idea what she would say. She could scarcely sort out her emotions, let alone explain them to her fiancé.

***

Alone in her room, her thoughts returned to Alex.

A friend of Lord Torrington's, Sir Edward, had apparently freed Alex from Newgate. But once Alex was free, why hadn't he tried to find her? She'd written to tell him she was going to America, to attend Vassar College. He could have at least written to tell her he wasn't dead.

Had he been so angry that he'd wanted nothing more to do with her? It was hard to picture that. Had he been trying to spare her? That seemed more like him. If so, from what?

From the fact that Father abandoned him to the gallows, then lied about it.

The weight of it crashed down, threatening to smother her. Morgan's letter. Vassar College. Had Father and his barrister arranged it all? Her heartbeat seemed to crash in her ears and she shook her head with so much force, the combs in her hair slipped loose. No, that couldn't be true! Father had loved her too much to betray her in such a cruel way.

Ten years lost to grief had been her sentence, for Count Zuko's murder, for ruining her family, and not fighting harder to clear Alex. Yet all along he was alive, going about his days, as if she'd meant ... nothing.

She lurched forward, tripping on her hem. Catching the bedpost to steady herself, she clutched the neckline of her gown. A stiff bit of lace itched her skin. Her skirts felt unbearably tight and heavy. She had to get out of this enormous dress, but didn't see how she could do it without ringing for help. She couldn't possibly face anyone, so she would have to manage on her own. She tugged off her evening gloves.

He was almost certainly not married. Upper servants in fine households rarely were, though romances below stairs were common enough. Did someone here hold his heart? The thought made her physically ill, but it was of no consequence. Alex had chosen his path, and so had she.

In nine days, she would marry Stuart, a man who would give her the children she'd longed for at the end of each school day, when her little students returned to their families, and she to her lonely boarding house.

Together, they would raise their family, providing every advantage, and continue their shared passions for education and altruism. She would also become the mistress of Tarpley Manor. She could dismiss Alex — no, Blackwood, she must call him now. Then her problems would disappear.

Or would they? As she tugged at the buttons down the back of her gown, her gaze fell on the bottom drawer of the bureau. Her fragile heart whispered a reminder that the truth wasn't nearly so simple.

Stuart was a dear, dear friend, but did she love him the way she'd loved Alex? She did not. But while she'd known the joy of true love, she'd also known the searing agony of loss. At an age when most women were becoming brides, Constance had suffered the black, bottomless grief of widowhood. That she'd had to mourn in silence only made it worse. Eventually she'd come to terms with Alex's death, and moved on, yet years later, the sadness lingered.

She suspected it always would. Losing Alex had taught her how frightening love could be. Never again would she make herself vulnerable to that kind of misery.

She draped her gown over the divan, to deal with tomorrow. In her linen chemise, she slid beneath the soft sheets. As exhausted as she was, her thoughts seesawed from Alex, to her family, to the horror of how badly she'd botched things with Lady Torrington.

She flopped onto her opposite side and closed her eyes, but sleep was impossible. Her feet were tangled in the bedding. The room was stuffy and smothering. She kicked off the blankets and rose.

The balcony door was locked. Confined like a caged canary, and desperate for fresh air, she donned her dressing gown and slippers.

Downstairs, the house was quiet. The card party was over, but lights still burned as servants laid out preparations for tomorrow. She dashed through the grand hall — unseen, she hoped — and out the front door.

She followed the moonlit path to the pond. At the bridge, she stopped and rested her elbows against the rail. Across the water was the little pagoda, tucked into a grotto. Breeze, scented with lavender, rustled the drooping branches of the willow on the pond's edge. It was a vivid reminder of the place where she and Alex had pledged themselves to one another. Did he even remember?

The breeze stopped, and all was still, but in the corner of her eye, something moved. She whirled around.

Alex stepped from the shadows.

He still wore his black clothes, but the breeze had blown his hair free from its stiff dressing. Loose strands framed his face, reminding her of how he'd looked at nineteen. Old desire curled at her center as he came to the railing and stood beside her. What should she do? Throw her arms around him? Run away? She did neither. For a long moment, she could only stare.

He took his time before looking her way. Once he did, his sweet smile lifted, then faded before she could tell if it was real. "It's all right," he said, softly. "You aren't seeing a ghost."

CHAPTER EIGHTEEN

How?" Connie's lovely face showed confusion and shock, but her eyes revealed something deeper. Relief that he was alive, or betrayal? He wondered if she even knew. "I always believed you'd gone to the gallows."

Hearing her say it stripped away all the lies he'd told himself that he'd done what was best for Connie. The ugly truth stared him in the face. He'd given in to fear and doubt and deceived her. "You didn't know, then?"

"No." The breeze blew a lock of soft, brown hair across her face. Once, she would have let him brush it away. The pretty girl was now a beautiful, desirable woman, but little else had changed. Intelligent brown eyes and a forthright brow still balanced tempting berry-red lips. The belted silk dressing gown clung to her curves. He clutched the wooden railing to keep his hands still.

"Mr. Morgan wrote that you'd been executed." Her pale throat tightened, and she stared down at her hands. "I ... I didn't want to know the rest."

Moonlight cast a soft glow on the water and the pagoda. When he'd seen her leave the house tonight and followed, it was no surprise that she'd been drawn to this place. He'd stood here himself enough times. "I gathered as much from your reaction. You never were the fainting type."

She wouldn't look up. "At first, I wasn't sure what I'd seen. I tried to convince myself I was only seeing someone who resembled you, perhaps a cousin you never knew about. But over dinner..."

He nodded, recalling the moment he stood at her side, close enough to touch, yet impossibly out of reach.

She turned, her mouth hardened, and arms crossed under her breasts. "How could this be? Lady Torrington mentioned a man, Sir Edward. Did he help my father's barrister to free you?"

The old bitterness flared in a humorless laugh. "Your father's barrister came to see me twice, only to inform me that my situation was hopeless and there was nothing he could do. Even after I told them everything I knew about the Count and his crimes. When my case went to trial, I was alone."

She closed her eyes. "Father took me back to Sussex. I was ill for weeks with pneumonia. I wrote, though. Every day. Father posted my letters to Mr. Morgan, so he could deliver them. Did they not arrive?"

"No. And you never received mine?"

"No."

His heart ached for her. Lord Beverly's deception had cut both ways.

"But if Mr. Morgan didn't defend you, how did you escape hanging?"

"A miracle, to be honest. Since I'd confessed, there was nothing for the judge to do but pronounce guilt and sentence me. They put me in a condemned cell and the lads came to say goodbye."

Constance looked away. He shook off memories of the terror he'd felt, sitting in that cold, dismal place, waiting to die. "But they weren't the only ones."

⚜

When he first saw the gaunt gent outside his cell, Alex decided the Grim Reaper had come early. Dressed in a black suit, with black hair and a pale face, he'd introduced himself as Sir Edward Collins, editor and publisher of the London Reformer. He'd been in the crowd at Old Bailey, but that wasn't the first time Collins had seen him.

"I was at Newgate the day the Earl of Beverly's daughter ... or should I say your wife, came to call," he said.

Alex tensed. The man must have heard Connie's cries as he was being dragged away. What might it mean, if the truth got out? Nothing good. "She ain't my wife. Jus' some lady tryin' to help me out, I guess."

Collins grunted. "I couldn't help notice she did not attend your trial."

"No." He hadn't expected her to, but it hurt all the same. And it cut

to the quick she'd not written once.

Collins said nothing, only watched with dark, unreadable eyes. "You didn't kill Viktor Zuko, did you?"

Shaken, Alex dropped onto the wooden bench that was the cell's only furnishing, and buried his head in his hands. He couldn't answer, despite how badly he wanted to.

"How old are you, Alex?"

"Twenty." His birthday, apparently his last, had passed as he awaited trial

Collins snorted. "That's too young to die, especially for a murder you didn't commit."

Did the bloke know something? If so, what? Alex stood and shot Collins a look full of East End brass. "Confessed to it, din't I?"

"You did. But I can only speculate what might have taken place," he paused, "or whom you might try to protect."

Whether or not he knew anything, the man was a reporter, fishing for a story. To say another word could put Connie in grave danger. "Get the hell out. I got nothin' to say to you."

Collins stayed where he was, peering in as if he could read Alex's mind. Alex turned his back, wishing the hangman would come for him now, if only to escape that dark, probing gaze. "No," Collins said, quietly. "I didn't expect you would."

The man actually sounded respectful.

"Trust me, I have no wish to jeopardize a lovely young lady. However, it is my opinion, and one shared by many, that whoever killed Mr. Zuko, did the citizens of London … a favor."

The word seemed to hang in the air. Alex kept his back turned, but listened anyway.

Collins went on. "The man was involved in every sort of vile crime and there are discrepancies, questions in the evidence a competent barrister would have brought to light — had one been available. I've reviewed your case and discovered sufficient cause for an appeal. Two renowned legal experts, and an adviser to the Home Secretary, concur."

The Home Secretary? That meant something. Could the miracle he'd prayed for be standing outside his cell? He turned back to Collins. "What questions?"

Collins counted them off on his fingers. "No eye-witnesses, circumstantial evidence, and scant investigation, beyond interviewing two men of questionable character. Each had motive and opportunity to kill Zuko, and a stake in seeing someone else accused. Not to mention the countless others who wished the man dead. This morning, I spoke with Sir John Powell, a respected barrister and abolitionist, who has successfully petitioned the Home Office. He believes we can win a pardon for you, as no one wishes to incarcerate, much less execute, an honorable young man."

His hope died right there. He slumped down on the bench. "That wouldn't be me you're talkin' about, then."

"On the contrary. I spoke with the lads who just left here. Luke and Jimmy spoke of your integrity, and young Daniel told me of your kindness. All will testify on your behalf, as will the rector who took the boy in. And we know Lord Beverly's daughter holds you in very high esteem."

"I don' want Connie dragged into this."

"Connie, is it?" The man's lips quirked with a smile. "I understand. And it won't be necessary, I assure you."

"What do you want from me?"

"I wish to chronicle your story for the London Reformer." Collins lifted his hand in dramatic fashion. "A young man from the stews, of *humble prospects but fine character, wrongly convicted and sentenced to die, finds justice through the brilliant work of a crusading journalist."*

This bloke was a fine character, but Alex rather liked him. "S'pose you're the brilliant, crusading journalist?"

Collins chuckled. "I knew you were a bright lad."

"Do you know I was a thief, too?"

"Oh, yes. Your friends told me all about it. It will not be an issue, considering you were orphaned at a tender age, treated cruelly in the workhouse, and then exploited by a criminal. You're a real-life Oliver Twist, my boy. Your story is that of thousands of youths all over London."

He knew the story of the trod-on orphan and didn't like the comparison much, but if it meant his freedom, he could live with it. "So after I'm free, then what?"

"Why, you'll be famous all over England! You could wed the young lady. Surely, her family would not object to her marrying the young man who embodies enlightened legal reform!"

He had to laugh at that. "Surely they would, bloke. An' I don't want to be famous." He closed his eyes and risked a hope it might all come true. "Just livin' in a nice place, an' workin' an honest job. That would suit me fine."

"Very well. We'll give you a pseudonym." Collins tapped his finger against his chin. "Jonas. Jonas Blackstone. I like that. Since publicity does not interest you, a position, then. Something far from London, where you could live anonymously and learn a profession to help you make your way in the world. You say you want to live in a fine home? Perhaps a service position on my family's estate would do." He looked Alex up and down. "I believe you would make an excellent footman. With hard work, you might even be promoted to butler someday."

243

Connie shook her head. "I knew none of this. Never saw the stories. I'm sure I was in America by the time they were published. My parents remained with me for several months, so I'm sure they never knew either."

"Do you honestly believe that?"

Her chin quivered, and she didn't answer. "But why didn't you try to find me? If your Mr. Collins had enough influence to get you out of Newgate, couldn't he have located me?"

Here was the question he dreaded most. His decision had altered both their lives and to this day, he was not convinced it had been the right one. Yet she deserved an honest answer. "I hadn't heard from you since the day you came to Newgate. Sir Edward said anyone interested in my whereabouts would contact the newspaper. When that didn't happen, I asked him to make inquiries. He learned you'd gone to America."

Her eyes widened. "You knew where I was, and you didn't even write? You let me go on believing you were dead?"

"What was I to think, Constance? You'd returned to your family, and for all I knew, you wanted nothing more to do with me. Perhaps you'd decided I was merely … rebellion. You were still high-born, and I wasn't. None of the things that kept us apart in the first place had changed."

"But in America, none of that would have mattered!"

"Oh, no? What if I had shown up on your doorstep at Vassar College, living proof that your father had bloody lied?"

"My father loved me! He wouldn't have … " She shook her head and brought her hands to her face. "No! I won't hear another word of it!"

"Why not? It's the truth," he said, jaw clenched. "But even now, you take their word over mine."

She met his gaze once more. "If you'd come to me, I would have married you in a heartbeat."

"And then? Your family would have cut you off without a penny. You would have had to leave university and go to work. How long before you thought about what you'd lost? Before you hated me for what I couldn't give you?"

She stared, her lips parted in shock. "So even though I'd pledged my undying love for you," her angry voice dropped to a whisper, "even though I killed a man to save your life, you decided I was too shallow and pampered to stand by you? That what I felt was merely a schoolgirl's passion, and wouldn't have survived a few difficult years?"

He couldn't look at her. "Yes."

She shrank from the cruelty in that single word. But he wouldn't take it back. If she hated him, so be it. They could not be friends. She must marry Inglesby and take her place in society. He must leave Tarpley Manor as soon as possible. "I never blamed you," he said.

"You blamed them, though." She blinked away tears and drew herself up with Society Miss poise. "And given your lack of faith in me, I'm sure our silly infatuation wouldn't have lasted." She took a step back and lifted her chin. "I suppose I should be grateful you saw things so clearly, but at the moment, I can only wish you had remained dead."

If she wanted to hurt him as he hurt her, she'd succeeded. Still, Connie was right. Her life would be much easier if he had gone

245

to the gallows ten years ago. All the more reason to keep his distance. Ignoring pain he'd never known the likes of, he put on the stiff formality which now fit like skin. "I apologize if my pardoned death sentence has proved to be such an inconvenience, my lady."

She drew in a breath. "I didn't mean it that way," she whispered, brushing her fingertips against his arm.

Her delicate touch seared through his clothes. Long ago, he'd held her close as they danced on the Farthing's roof. Her kisses had been innocent, eager, and passionate all at once. In Victoria Park, he'd found love and redemption in her arms, and her body. From the distant past came echoes of a funny love song and the phantom scent of lavender.

Now, he could neither touch her, nor hold her. He was no longer her love and despite what they once pretended, he had never been her equal. He was her servant, and must behave with dignity, no matter what. He drew his arm away and clasped his hands behind his back.

Her forlorn gaze nearly crushed him. If only he could wrap his arms around her and love her pain away. But as it had been that awful day in Newgate, words were the only comfort he could offer. "Perhaps not as harshly, but you speak the truth, just the same. My presence creates a most awkward situation. Trust that I am seeking a new post and will leave the moment I am able. Until then, I will serve you faithfully, and respect your position as the future lady of the house."

Connie closed her eyes and nodded, her arms crossed tightly against her body. She turned to go, but before she left the bridge, she paused to gaze across the dark pond. Was she remembering a bridge, a farthing, and vows that once bound them as husband and wife?

She turned back. Tears glittered in her eyes, but her posture was straight and her voice was steady. "Very well. Good night, Blackwood.

Their roles were cast. Whatever they'd shared was gone, and it grieved him more than he ever thought possible. "Good night, my lady."

He remained on the bridge until she was safely inside the house and then returned as well. Most of the staff had retired to their quarters, and he began his nightly rounds.

He went from room to room checking that lamps and fires were extinguished, and the windows and outside doors were locked. The dining room, drawing room, and saloon were in proper order. The breakfast room was ready. In the library, he chose a book. Lord Torrington allowed the upper servants use of the library, and Alex enjoyed the privilege. He picked a sensation novel written by a cousin of Sir Edward. The man told a compelling story. To engage his mind tonight would require one.

His last stop was the pantry. He locked the door behind him and opened the cabinet that contained the family's valuable plate. Lady Torrington insisted he inventory the pieces each night. A strange twist it was, having a former thief in charge of the silver, and he never took his employer's trust for granted. Satisfied all was present, he inspected some serving pieces. They were tarnished and needed polish before Friday evening's ball. He would assign the job to second footman Ned Beamish in the morning.

His office and quarters were next to the pantry. He lit the lamp and dropped into his wooden desk chair. The day he'd dreaded since learning the name of Inglesby's betrothed a month ago, was at last over.

He'd thought he was ready for it. But the sight of her, and the sound of her red-velvet voice, reopened wounds that had never healed. He hated the things he'd said tonight. He wasn't even sure he believed it all. One thing he believed though, beyond a doubt, was that they had no future.

Constance loved her family, flawed and undeserving as they were. He didn't think he could ever forgive them. Lord Beverly's offer of a barrister was only a lie meant to soothe Connie until he could take her away, leaving Alex to die alone.

Would she have chosen him, if he'd come for her? At the time he'd doubted she would, and now he would never know. But for them to have had any hope of a future, he would have had to forgive her parents. He couldn't then. He couldn't now.

He heaved a sigh. It made no difference. She loved Inglesby, and he could give her the life she deserved. Alex was a servant and must remember his place.

From his desk drawer, he took out a folded list of ten names. Three were crossed off. He had been diligently answering advertisements and had listed his name with a large servants' registry. He'd hoped to be gone by now, but since he didn't like to talk about his past, an excellent character letter from the Torringtons was essential for his future prospects. He wouldn't get one if he up and left.

For the moment, he was stuck.

Though butler's posts were hard to find, and at nine and twenty, his youth seemed to work against him, he would consider a footman's post only as a last resort. It was a demanding job, that was for sure, but he was very good at it. So much of what he'd done at the Count's, like keeping track of sums, running a crew, even tasting wine, stood him well now. He bought supplies and paid the vendors. He managed the menservants with authority and fairness. His skill with wine was respected and valued. He was among the highest-paid staff, second only to the estate manager. He dressed as a gentleman, not in livery. To everyone he met, he was trustworthy and respectable.

The job agreed with him on the inside, too. At the end of each day, he could look back and know he'd made someone's life better, not worse. Even when his efforts went unnoticed, he took pride in them. He'd wanted an honorable life, and now he had one.

It sometimes occurred to him that if he'd stayed with the Count, there would be servants taking care of him these days. He liked it better this way. A fine manor home was a long way from a Spitalfields thieves' den or a condemned cell in Newgate. He'd been given a second chance, and not a day went by that he wasn't grateful.

He didn't need a second chance to be hurt by a woman he'd never stopped loving.

CHAPTER NINETEEN

Constance awoke the next morning determined to gain control of the situation. Stuart was gone for the day, thank goodness, on a hunting trip with his father. Blackwood had assured her he was actively seeking another position. Since there was nothing she could do on that end, at least for now, it was time to repair the strained relationship with Lady Torrington.

She'd apologized to the marchioness twice last night and didn't feel the need to do it again. In New York, she'd enjoyed many lively discussions with friends about politics and social issues. Even when they disagreed, they'd refrained from the cutting, personal remarks Lady Torrington made. The woman was tactless and unpleasant. But she was also Stuart's mother, and deserved respect, not to mention sympathy. Because of the loss of her oldest son, and her husband's wish to move to London, she was about to turn her beautiful home over to a stranger. That could not be easy.

Nor was it easy for Constance. In the abstract, Tarpley Manor had been a picturesque backdrop for her married life. The reality was a grand estate with a 200-year-old house, a large staff of servants and acres of gardens, all of which she would be expected to manage. But she'd never backed down from a challenge. Starting today, she would seek Lady Torrington's guidance and embrace her new responsibilities.

She came downstairs to find the ground floor buzzing with activity. In the great hall, the ancestors' portraits looked less dour as housemaids' dusters tickled their scowling faces. An adolescent boy carried a cleaned and filled lamp into the drawing room. The ballroom doors were open and inside, four maids polished the expansive wood floor on their hands and knees. Perched atop a ladder, a maid cleaned the sconces, while another dusted the ornate chairs lining the perimeter of the room.

There were a great many chairs.

Of course, there was an engagement party set for Friday evening, but she'd assumed it would be an intimate reception for the Torringtons' close friends and neighbors, not a grand affair requiring a polished ballroom and dozens of chairs. She would be sure to ask Stuart about it when his shooting party concluded later this afternoon.

She explored more rooms. The study, saloon, and billiard room held the faint, masculine aromas of tobacco, whiskey, and bay rum. The scents triggered memories of Father, and the day Mr. Morgan's letter had come. Father had held her so tenderly, and crooned soft words of comfort, over and over. *"I'm sorry, my darling. I'm so, so sorry."*

She stilled. Instead of sympathy, had he been apologizing?

She brought her fingers to her lips, and her breathing slowed. The possibility he'd had a hand in a man's death — particularly a man she'd loved — was too devastating to contemplate. Alex seemed to believe it, though. It was true Father had tried to marry her off to Gaffney, but in the years since, he'd been so kind, so loving. He'd supported her financially until she could do so on her own. He'd encouraged her to follow her dreams.

Or had he really been trying to keep her far from England, and from ever learning the truth?

She closed her eyes, sickened at the thought, then shook it off. What was the point of even wondering? She would never know the answer. Father was dead, the past was gone, and she'd already spent too many years grieving what might have been.

On the east side of the house, the drawing room, library, and conservatory caught the morning sun, even on this overcast day. Everywhere, servants cleaned, dusted, and polished.

Yet not once, to her profound relief, did she see Blackwood.

By day, she was ashamed of the thoughts which haunted her through the night. Treasured moments, too painful to revisit when she believed him dead, now came back. The sound of his voice. The touch of his hand. Their first kiss. Memories of their lovemaking.

But she could not give into out-of-control emotion. Alex Blackwood had decided years ago that her love wasn't sincere.

He'd moved on and she must do the same. Her charming pickpocket was gone, as surely as if he'd died in Newgate. Blackwood was a servant whom she must tolerate until he was out of her life.

Her future was with Stuart.

In the breakfast room, tea was set out on the sideboard. She poured a cup and went to the window, admiring the hedges, early blooming flowers, and rolling lawn. The beveled glass windows looked out onto a lovely little patio, where she and Stuart might spend pleasant hours as they had in New York, sharing ideas, discussing books, and his many charitable interests.

The parlor door swung open, and a footman entered, pushing a cart of covered serving dishes. "Why, good morning, my lady."

He seemed surprised to see her, but it was only nine o'clock. Fashionable ladies and gentlemen seldom rose before ten. "Good morning... John. Is that right?"

"Yes, my lady. I'm John Meacham, the first footman. It's a pleasure to meet you, and welcome to Tarpley Manor." A pleasant-looking young man with broad shoulders and neat black hair, he went to work arranging the covered dishes and plates on the sideboard. "Cook has prepared the Torringtons' usual breakfast, but if there is anything else you would like, let me know."

The whereabouts of Blackwood crossed her mind, but she refrained from asking. "I'm sure it will be fine. Everything smells delicious. Thank you."

She helped herself to a generous serving of eggs, bacon, toast and jam, and a small bowl of pears. Hearty breakfasts were her habit, as her teaching days were so busy she often had no time to eat.

She carried her plate to the breakfast table, thinking how odd it was not to have lessons to prepare. No Paul O'Halloran coming in early because her classroom was warm and safe, unlike the tenement where he lived.

Would the new teacher even understand? Miss Griffin seemed competent, but competence was only the beginning. Rambunctious Paul could be a handful, yet a few kind words went a long way. What about shy little Maria Rosetti, so easily overlooked, and one of the brightest students Constance had ever taught? Perhaps a letter of advice for Miss Griffin would be helpful? Or were her energies better spent in other ways?

As much as she'd loved teaching, she knew she didn't wish to remain alone for the rest of her life. Paul and Maria, like so many others she'd watched move on, weren't hers. She was tired of loving people, then losing them. She was twenty-nine. She wanted children of her own and a husband to love. Though she'd never cared about housekeeping or the conventions of high society, and feared Lady Torrington suspected as much, those things were about to become central to her new life.

It was time to set her mind to the tasks at hand — making peace with Stuart's mother and learning all there was to know about Tarpley Manor.

She began when Lady Torrington arrived moments later.

"Why, Lady Constance. I am surprised to see you up so early. I would have expected you to rest. Is your room not comfortable?"

"On the contrary. My room is perfect. I'm simply an early riser.

I have been for years."

Lady Torrington pursed her lips. "Yes, you had to work." She spoke as if Constance's work had been something far less respectable than teaching school. She went to the sideboard and returned to the table with a cup of tea and a single scone. "I see your appetite has returned," she said, casting a disdainful glance at Constance's generous portions.

Constance pushed back a thread of annoyance, determined to keep a positive attitude. "How could it not, when everything smells delicious?" She gave a determined smile and took a dainty bite of her enormous breakfast. "On my way to breakfast, I took a few moments to explore the ground floor. Tarpley House is lovely."

The marchioness sipped her tea. "The manor has been in my husband's family for generations. They built the house over the foundation of the original castle. The basement and wine cellar date back to the eleventh century."

"Stuart mentioned that as a boy, he played in the ruins of an ancient village here on the grounds."

"Chataigne. That's what the family has always called it. I don't suppose anyone knows its correct name, as no one has lived there for seven hundred years. All that remain are a peasants' church and the ruins of several buildings. Lord Torrington and I used to picnic there when we were first wed." Lady Torrington looked almost wistful.

"I would love to see it. Could you show it to me?"

Her hard expression returned. "Surely you realize my health does not permit such strenuous activity."

No matter what, she said the wrong thing to Lady Torrington.

"I understand. Please accept my apologies. Perhaps the gardens closer to the house?"

The older woman gazed outside. "I'm afraid the weather looks poor for walking outdoors, but I suppose I could show you the greenhouse."

A minor victory was better than none.

After breakfast, she followed the marchioness through the conservatory into the greenhouse at the house's rear east wing. A stocky manservant with thinning hair, wearing rough work pants and a plain white smock with the sleeves rolled to the elbow, greeted them.

"This is Charles, the greenhouse steward," said Lady Torrington. "He is responsible for the kitchen and indoor gardening and works with the groundskeeper to maintain the beds outside. Charles, this is my son's fiancée, Lady Constance."

"Welcome to Tarpley Manor, Lady Constance," said the steward. He had a plain, but friendly face. His name was familiar, though she could not recall why.

"Thank you. The gardens are beautiful," she said.

The compliment brought a tight smile from Lady Torrington. "Indeed. They result from years of hard work on my behalf and my husband's ancestors. I will entrust you with their care, and I hope you are up to the task."

The greenhouse smelled of wet earth and peat, mingled with lavender, roses and savory herbs. Charles walked them past long tables covered with trays of seedlings and described the ornamental plants, most of which were unfamiliar. There were also vegetables and a mind-boggling array of kitchen herbs. Near the back of the greenhouse, two boys worked at a large bin. One mixed in eggshells and vegetable scraps, while the other took worms from a bucket and dropped them into the soil.

"That's Gabe and Davy," Charles said. Gabe, a small lad of about ten, bobbed a quick bow. Davy, who was maybe a year or two older, looked up with a vacant expression. Gabe nudged him and Davy bowed. Why weren't they in school? She bit the inside of her lip to refrain from asking Lady Torrington.

At the far end of the greenhouse was a delightful surprise: a miniature grove of potted citrus trees arranged around a small concrete bench. She inhaled the plants' heady fragrance. "We will cut a blossom for your bridal gown and place the trees around the dance floor for Friday evening's ball," Lady Torrington said.

A ball, was it? That explained the busy maids and dozens of chairs. Though she didn't enjoy balls particularly, she would need to become accustomed to them. What bothered her more was that neither Mother nor Stuart had said a word about this. Didn't they think she would want to know?

The sun had brightened the overcast morning, so Charles led them outside. They strolled to the sunken garden, adorned with benches, sundials, and a pair of grotesque Asian statues the marchioness referred to as Fu dogs. The path led to a set of stone steps and ended at the footbridge. Across the pond was the miniature Chinese village with its luminous white pagoda. "The pagoda is beautiful in the moonlight," Constance said.

Lady Torrington frowned. "How would you know that? It can't be seen from the upstairs rooms."

"I went for a short walk last night. I needed some fresh air."

"Night air is most unhealthful and decent people should avoid it," she said. "I expressly forbid the doors to remain unlocked at night, and Blackwood needs reminding to be more diligent."

The thought of him being reprimanded by Lady Torrington didn't sit well, especially because of something she'd mentioned. Constance said little else during the rest of the tour.

The last stop was the chapel, which was much larger than it appeared from outside. Subtle color from the stained glass windows brightened the interior. Carved wooden buttresses supported a soaring ceiling, painted with scenes of angels and heaven. It was breathtaking and had room for at least fifty people. "I believe lilies will be lovely here," said Lady Torrington. "They are a symbol of purity, you know."

They were also a reminder of Father's funeral, but Constance doubted Lady Torrington would care. "Lilies will be perfect," she said.

Lady Torrington went on. "It might be a rather tight fit once all the guests are seated, but we can always bring more chairs."

More chairs?

Lady Torrington drew a packet of folded pages from the pocket of her morning dress. "These are the guests who will attend the ball and the wedding. The members of our family will stay here, but the others include the best families from Somerset County, important people for you to know."

Constance leafed through four pages, covered front and back with densely written, ornate script. What had happened to the small, tasteful wedding she and Stuart discussed when they'd become engaged? First, her engagement party had exploded into a ball, now her wedding would be standing room-only? Lady Torrington had disregarded her wishes, and while she could envision Mother capitulating to the force that was Lady

Torrington, how could Stuart stand by and allow it? Though she could not argue with Lady Torrington, and it was too late to disinvite her guests, Stuart must speak with his mother before she commandeered any more of their plans.

"My son can provide you with sufficient details on each of them, but I expect you to have this list committed to memory so that when you are introduced, you will be prepared to carry on pleasant conversation."

Presumably, pleasant conversation did not include her work teaching in the slums of New York City.

❦

After luncheon, she brought her concerns to Mother. Unfortunately, Mother was less than sympathetic. "I knew Lady Torrington invited some additional family members and friends, but my goodness, Constance, it is her home." Mother surveyed herself in the mirror as Celeste, her maid, and Kennedy altered one of her gowns. "She should be able to invite whomever she pleases."

"Perhaps. But why didn't you tell me?"

"There was no opportunity. Nor did I feel it was my place." She ran her hands over the champagne-colored, striped silk. The gown was short-sleeved but modestly cut, as befitting a lady of her age and position. "I pray you have said nothing else to offend her, and implore you to apologize for your comments last night."

"I apologized. Twice. I also made it clear I was not criticizing Lady Torrington's treatment of her servants, only English society's treatment. I meant nothing personal and if anyone said anything to offend, it was she." Kennedy, who knelt on the floor, while attaching a garland of silk flowers to the gown's skirt, glanced up, but returned her eyes to her work. "Really though, I'm more concerned about this." She shuffled through the pages, as if it might suddenly all make sense.

"Just the same ..." Mother pursed her lips and glanced over her shoulder. Jane had left the room for a moment. "You do not want to begin your marriage by making an enemy of your in-laws."

It was only after Father's death that Constance learned how vehemently the Barrett family had opposed her parents' marriage. A shopkeeper's daughter, Rose was employed as a governess by a Barrett cousin when she caught Roland's eye. His parents had hoped for a more suitable match. Irene, the youngest sister and Jane's mother, had hoped Roland would marry her best friend. But Roland wanted no one but Rose. They had eloped to Gretna Green and for years after, the Barrett family considered Rose nothing more than a common fortune-hunter.

Celeste turned her mistress to remove the outdated flounce from the back of the gown and make it more stylish. Now that the Beverly title and the Sussex estate had gone to Uncle Albert, Mother remained in the Bruton Street townhouse, living in genteel frugality on her marriage settlement and a small allowance from Albert. Yet she never complained. What a shame that a woman who cared so much about fashion had to make do with old dresses while Constance, who never cared in the slightest, would wed in an expensive Parisian bridal gown.

She looked forward to the day when she could buy Mother whatever she liked.

Then Jane returned, and Constance patted her mother's hand. "Please don't worry. I'll not do anything to provoke Lady Torrington. In fact, perhaps you can help me get into her good graces. Are any of these families familiar to you?"

Mother studied the guest list and shook her head. "These are all Bath families. Country society can be rather closed, I'm afraid. I suppose I could say the same for London society. I recognize one name, the Viscount Kingsley. His daughter Lucinda attended a London season two years ago. Not an attractive girl, though I believe she married Lord Weatherby's youngest son."

"May I see?" Jane took the sheets from Mother. "The Billingsleys are friends of Sim's family. You might remember them from my wedding, Aunt Rose. Mrs. Billingsley is most enamored with France and speaks the language fluently."

It wasn't much, but Constance made a note on the sheet. "No matter. I'm sure Stuart will know many of them and the rest, I can ask Lady Torrington."

"You will not!" said Rose, shocked at the suggestion.

"Why shouldn't I?"

"Because the marchioness assumes you know them already! It would reflect poorly on our family if you reveal your lack of social connections."

"But I do lack social connections and I expect she already knows that!" Constance gave an exasperated sigh and turned to Jane. Surely, her cousin would take her side. "Isn't it best not to put on pretense?"

Jane looked grim. "You mustn't think of it as pretense. You're just keeping up appearances. I agree with Aunt Rose. If Lady Torrington intended to help you, she would have offered. This is best kept quiet. But don't fret, dear. Stuart will know all of them."

In the late afternoon, as Lady Torrington and the others took tea in the drawing room, Constance slipped into the conservatory to wait for Stuart to return from his hunting trip. He had been looking forward to spending time with his father, after living so long away, and she wanted to hear how it had gone. They also needed to discuss what she'd learned from Lady Torrington.

The windows looked out onto the charming patio she'd noticed this morning. The amber glow of fading daylight and the small fire flickering in the hearth made it warm and inviting. The day's newspaper was neatly folded on a small table beside her chair. In her family's home, the papers were always placed in the saloon or her father's study, yet here they were in a room frequented by women. It was almost as if it had been put here with her in mind. How kind of Stuart to have informed the staff of her habits.

Or had someone else remembered them?

She set the paper down. She had not seen Blackwood all day. He was sure to be busy preparing for tomorrow night's engagement party, or ball, and avoiding her. She eyed the service bell in the corner. If she rang, who might answer?

To no surprise, it was John. "Yes, my lady?"

She felt oddly disappointed. "I would like a cup of coffee, please."

"Certainly." He turned to go.

"And John?" He stopped, awaiting her question. Heat rose in her cheeks as she heard herself asking, "I have not seen Blackwood today. Is he here?"

"Yes, my lady. Mr. Blackwood meets with vendors on

Thursdays and has been thus engaged today. Would you like to speak with him?"

"No! I … I just wondered, that's all." She smoothed her hair, trying to recover her composure. "I need to learn the household routine, you understand."

"Yes, my lady."

He showed no expression, but she felt like a fool. There was no need to explain herself to the servants, and God forbid the footman mentioned this to Blackwood. "Thank you. That will be all for now, but when my fiancé returns, would you please invite him to join me?"

"Actually, Lord Inglesby is in the saloon with his father and Lord Beverly."

Constance flinched at hearing her own father's name, then realized the footman was referring to Uncle Albert.

"I shall deliver your invitation and ask Susanna to bring your coffee." With a brisk turn, he left.

So Stuart had returned, yet hadn't come to find her. She slumped in her chair. First, it had been the unsettling thoughts about Father, then news about the ball, followed by Lady Torrington's extensive guest list. After this unsettling day, she longed for some time alone with him. The truth was, she felt at sea. A bit of reassurance would help immeasurably.

A dark-eyed maid brought Constance her coffee and left without a word. The brew was pale and had a timid, dull flavor. Timid and dull. Just the way she felt right now.

Stuart arrived a moment later. "John said you wished to speak with me?"

His brusque tone sounded as if he were addressing one of the servants. Unnerved, she smiled, hoping to ease the tension. "I wished to hear about the hunt. Did you enjoy the time with your father?"

"Yes, it was fine." He took the opposite seat in front of the fireplace and sat on the edge of his chair. "And your afternoon was pleasant?"

"Quite. Your mother took me on a tour of the greenhouse and gardens. She mentioned the ruins you told me about — Chataigne. Perhaps we could go there Saturday?"

Stuart furrowed his brow. He seemed distant. Troubled, almost. "I doubt either of us will feel up to making the trip the day after the party. But perhaps next week, weather permitting."

"That would be lovely." She sipped her tepid coffee and smiled again in the awkward silence. She would need to state her concerns about Lady Torrington carefully. "Do you care for coffee or tea? I could ring one of the servants."

"No, thank you." She sighed. Perhaps this wasn't the opportune time for a serious conversation, but the matter could not wait. If Stuart didn't speak to Lady Torrington, what else might she do? "Speaking of the party, your mother informed me it is actually a ball with a rather extensive guest list, and that all of them have been invited to our wedding. Were you aware?"

"She may have mentioned it. Mother believes our family's position obligates us to create an impressive show. Otherwise, it looks as if we're hiding something." He ran his finger along the sharp crease in his trousers and gazed out the darkening window. "You should have a proper gown in your trousseau."

"It isn't that, and it's generous of your mother to publicly welcome me into the family." She tugged at the cuff of her sleeve.

"My concern is that you and I agreed we wanted a small wedding, and she changed our plans without consulting us. I fear that if someone doesn't speak with her, she will do so again."

Stuart grunted. "My mother is a most determined woman, Constance. I am afraid it's something you must learn to accept, as Father and I have." He shifted in his seat, eager to leave. "Was there anything else?"

Apparently, that was that. Stuart's only suggestion was that she learn to live with her mother-in-law's meddling. Defeated, she brought out Lady Torrington's list. "Your mother asked that I learn the names of the guests and prepare to converse with them. She suggested you could assist me."

Stuart grimaced and took the pages. "Did she? I can't imagine why. It's been years since I lived in Somerset County and when I did, I was not part of my parents' social circle."

"But you know your relatives."

He sat back in his chair, perusing the names. "Well, the Logans are on Father's side while the Baxters and Prices are Mother's. Francesca Price is Mother's cousin. She was left a spinster years ago when her beloved died from appendicitis."

Constance could not imagine a pleasant conversation on such a topic.

"She has written several volumes of poetry, however, and traveled extensively through India."

"Oh, Stuart, that's exactly what I was hoping you could tell me!" She took the page back and jotted "poetry, India" next to Francesca's name.

"Elliot Whiteside is my father's second cousin. As a boy, I was friends with his son Emmett, though I haven't seen him in years.

He served in the Royal Navy. Or was it the army?" He smiled apologetically. Constance made more notes.

He told her of another relative who was an expert on roses, and a local family, the Charltons, who kept bees. Their daughter, Winifred, was a childhood friend. Then he shook his head. "I'm sorry, Constance. I'm afraid I have been so consumed by my own affairs, I've rather neglected these social ties. Once we settle in, I hope you can remedy that."

He did? Surely he realized that she wasn't socially adept—she never had been. And yet he expected her to cultivate relationships with people who were strangers? Before she could comment, the door opened. She caught her breath as Blackwood entered, carrying a small silver tray that held a single envelope. "This was just delivered for you, my lord."

Stuart frowned as he opened it and read the note inside. His jaw twitched and a stricken expression came and went.

Constance tensed. "Stuart? Is everything all right?"

"Yes. An old school chum is visiting relatives in Bath. He's invited me for luncheon tomorrow."

"How nice," she said, though his reaction suggested something far more significant. "I'd love to meet him. Will he attend the ball?"

"No," came his terse reply. "He never was one for large social gatherings. We'll spend the day discussing the language academy he hopes to establish in Nice. You would be terribly bored."

"Bored? It sounds fascinating. I'm a teacher, for heaven's sake! Haven't we talked about finding worthy schools to support?"

But Stuart was paying no attention. He held out his hand. "May I borrow that, please?"

She wasn't sure what he meant and then realized he wanted her pencil. She gave it to him. He went to the sideboard, and with his back turned, wrote his reply. It was clear he didn't want her along.

Were they destined to become strangers living under the same roof? Even if they were, why should she be upset? It had been a relief that Stuart had never pried into her life, or tried to learn her secrets. Just as there were things she kept to herself, so it was with him. Yet she didn't believe for a moment that the invitation was from an old school chum.

Stuart had a mistress.

It should come as no surprise. There was nothing unusual about a wealthy, handsome gentleman keeping a mistress. Since girlhood, it had been drummed into her head that if she wanted a faithful husband, she must be so beautiful and desirable, her husband would have no wish to stray. Yet part of her fought against the entire idea. Was it so unreasonable to want a man whose love she could trust? Years ago, she had one.

Stuart placed the note on Blackwood's tray. "Please deliver this straight away."

"Yes, my lord. Will there be anything else?"

"No." He turned to her. "If you will excuse me, my dear, I must dress for dinner." He left, leaving her alone with Blackwood.

She tensed in the sudden silence. Why didn't he leave, too? Was he waiting to speak with her again?

Her heart pounded as Blackwood stood beside her, handsome and somber in his black coat and tie. Once, he had been her charming, adorable Robin Hood, who sang funny love songs on a tavern roof. She never doubted he would be faithful. Instead of keeping secrets, he opened his heart.

Another moment passed before she realized he wasn't about to do so now. He was treating her as any servant would, not speaking unless she spoke to him first.

A drop of moisture pooled in the corner of her eye, and she blinked rapidly. While she was grateful he was alive, the boy she'd loved at nineteen was gone forever. In his place was a quiet, serious man who'd been hurt by her family. Perhaps he didn't blame Constance, but the fact was, he no longer cared anything for her. His loss felt fresh once more.

"Blackwood?" There was a slight tremor in her voice.

"Yes, my lady?"

What happened to you? What happened to us? If I'd told the truth that night on the docks ... if we hadn't been kept apart... would we have been happy? She searched for something to say, but came up empty. They'd said everything there was to say last night. "Nothing," she said, quietly. "You may go."

<hr />

When she came to breakfast in the morning, Stuart was gone, but Jane was awake. If anyone could lift her spirits, it was her ever-cheerful cousin. Whether Jane saw anything odd about Stuart's absence the entire two days since their arrival, she was too polite to comment. Instead, she smiled over her teacup. "It is such a beautiful morning. We should take a walk after breakfast."

They spent the morning strolling the gardens, even walking the lane to the gatehouse. An irrepressible romantic, Jane relished every detail of the approaching ball, her only regret being that her beloved Sim wouldn't be there.

Their love seemed so genuine. Perhaps her cousin would have some advice on how to make a happy marriage. Touring the chapel, she considered how to approach the topic, when suddenly, Jane said, "You seem troubled, my dear. Is there anything I can do?"

"Oh, Jane," she sighed, and sank down on an oak pew. "Before you were married, did Sim keep a mistress?"

Jane's pink cheeks grew even pinker, and she covered her mouth to stifle a ladylike giggle. "Oh, heavens, no. Sim swore he came to our marriage bed untouched, and I believe him. The poor man was so shy, I had to teach him."

"Why, Jane!" Constance couldn't help but smile at Jane's unexpected candor.

"Well, it was not as though I had experience either, but I knew enough to ask certain lady friends for advice." She took Constance's hand. "You mustn't forget Stuart is thirty-five years old and has never been married. Men have their needs and it's normal he should turn to a mistress. But he is also an honorable man. Once you wed, I am certain he will cast this woman aside and be a faithful husband. Perhaps that was the reason for his mysterious trip to Bath?"

Maybe Jane was right. Of course, Stuart cared for her. He'd asked her to share his life, hadn't he? Constance hugged her cousin. "That has to be it. Stuart is a good man, and I was foolish to doubt him."

With more hope than she'd felt in days, she returned to Tarpley House. She would become the perfect lady of the manor and together, she and Stuart would build a wonderful life. While Jane went to change into an afternoon dress, Constance sought Lady Torrington. Appearances be damned. She didn't know the Torrington's friends, and it was best to own up to the fact. A woman as pragmatic as her future mother-in-law would understand.

Lady Torrington, Philippa, and Dorothy were in the morning parlor finishing a light luncheon. Constance couldn't help but note the stark difference between the sisters. The marchioness had iron-gray hair, a long horse-like face and looked every bit of her fifty-five years. The baroness was just a year younger, yet her hair was a rich auburn, without a hint of gray. Lady Torrington was tall and angular, the baroness rounded and voluptuous. Edna's mouth seemed to register permanent disapproval. Philippa's bold confidence more than compensated for her rather plain features.

After she was served a small plate of sandwiches, Constance brought out the list. "Stuart was a great help with your relatives, but did not know many of the local families. I've noted the names I am not familiar with."

Lady Torrington frowned, but took the pages. As she sifted through them, her scowl deepened. Philippa craned her neck for a better look. Lady Torrington placed the pages in front of her and peered across the table, her mouth set in a grim line. "Nearly every name is marked. You are not acquainted with any of them?"

She met the older woman's gaze. "No, Lady Torrington, I am not."

Philippa rolled her eyes. Dorothy shook her head. The

marchioness snorted. "And my son claimed he was not either? I find that difficult to believe. Did you bother to ask him?"

"Of course I did." Her cheeks burned at being taken to task in front of Philippa and Dorothy, not to mention the parade of servants going in and out.

"Rubbish. You should have questioned him further. And today, you let him waltz off to Bath, as if he had no responsibilities here!" She rose from her chair. "I find it most inconsiderate that you waited until now to bring this to my attention. I must say, Lady Constance, so far, I am unimpressed by your manners." In a whirl of silk, the women left the room.

Constance sat, too stunned to move. So much for mending fences. Her future mother-in-law hated her. Her fiancé had a mistress. Her lost love was the butler. What the bloody hell was she doing here, and when was the next ship back to New York?

But she couldn't run. Her old life was over. She had made a commitment to Stuart — a commitment that would not only give her the family she longed for, but would also restore a bit of standing to Mother. There was no question she would see it through. Her only mistake had been thinking it would be easy.

She jumped at the quiet clink of silver and china. Blackwood stood at the sideboard.

Their eyes held, then she looked away. He'd heard everything. Quickly she blinked away the welling tears and squared her shoulders. "Why, Blackwood. I had no idea you were there."

"I apologize for startling you, my lady." He turned to go.

"No. It's all right. Please don't let me interrupt." She gathered up the pages and rose from her chair.

"My lady." His intense gaze startled her. "I don't wish to

intrude, but perhaps if you show me the guest list, I can be of help."

She looked down at the pages, then back at him. "Do you know these people?"

His face registered a ghost of the sideways grin she'd once loved. "Not personally. But the gentleman I served before moved in similar circles as Lord and Lady Torrington."

She gave him the list. He studied the pages for a moment, then returned them and clasped his hands behind his back. "I recognize many of the names. What would you like to know?"

Constance let out a breath, scarcely believing her good fortune. "Oh, my goodness, anything you can tell me." She sat back down and took out her pencil. "Lord and Lady Cloverdale?"

Blackwood nodded. "The Cloverdales. He's the Earl of Cloverdale and the distiller of a very fine Scotch. Lady Cloverdale's given name is Diana, and she's a devout Methodist. They are a most interesting match, I assure you." His voice dropped at the wry aside.

"I don't doubt it," she said, warmed by the ghost of a smile, as well. "The Ellsworths?"

"Sir Miles is a barrister. His wife Eloise is German by birth. Their estate is close to here."

She continued down the list. There were a few names he did not know, but not many. Throughout the house, preparations for the ball continued. Servants popped in and out, often with questions for Blackwood. He answered each with the same calm authority, but stayed at her side. Though he never dropped his proper demeanor, his strong, quiet presence soothed her battered spirits. For the moment anyway, she didn't feel like escaping to

New York.

Then a red-haired footman interrupted. "Mr. Blackwood? The musicians have arrived, sir."

Constance looked up. The fading daylight showed how long they had been here. Soon, it would be time to dress, and he still had much to do to prepare for tonight. She rose from her seat. "I apologize, Blackwood. I hadn't realized how much of your time I'd taken."

"It's all right, my lady." He did not smile, but there was warmth in his voice. Then he turned to the footman. "Thank you, Ned. Please direct them to the ballroom and find Calvin. Have him assist the gentlemen bringing in their instruments and invite them to dine with staff in the servants' hall at half-past five."

"Very good, sir." The footman left the parlor.

Blackwood poured the remaining tea into her cup, then returned to the sideboard, keeping his back turned. The closeness was gone. He was a stranger now, but every time she looked at him, she would remember the first man she'd ever loved.

Was it the same for him? Did she remind him of those dangerous, yet sweet days, when every moment brought a fresh adventure? When laughter, music, and love, rather than duty and propriety, filled their lives? Her heart pounded in her throat. She had to know. Gathering her courage, she asked, "Why did you do this?"

"Do what, Lady Constance?" He used the same crisp voice he had with Ned.

"Help me. I know there were other things you needed to do this afternoon."

He turned. "That's true. But you seemed to need assistance,

and I would have been remiss if I hadn't offered to help when I could."

The impersonal reply made her ache for the love they'd once shared. "You take your responsibilities very seriously."

He paused, and though he stood at attention, his stern expression seemed to soften. "Forgive me if I speak out of turn, my lady. I realize much of this seems foreign, and things that are obvious to Lady Torrington, to you, might be ... less so." Gently, he added, "Please know you may ask my help whenever you need it."

She bit the inside of her bottom lip. Years ago, he'd been a true friend, and seemed to sense she needed one now. After Lady Torrington's scolding and Stuart's indifference, Blackwood's kindness meant more than he could know. Even more, it brought a moment's hope that he felt something other than indifference toward her and bitterness toward her family.

"Thank you ..." *Alex.* The name danced on her tongue, but she held it. "... Blackwood."

"You're most welcome ..." he paused. *Please call me Connie, just once more.* "... Lady Constance. Will there be anything else?"

"No." He couldn't call her Connie. Was she daft? "Thank you... for everything."

"Very good, my lady." With a brief bow, he left. The service door swung closed behind him.

Despite the awkwardness, she was no longer eager for him to leave Tarpley Manor.

CHAPTER TWENTY

Mother's delight as she admired herself in the dressing room mirror brought a smile to Constance.

The maids had done a remarkable job. Mother's three-year-old gown looked as current as something made weeks ago in London. The contrasting silk stripes were embellished with maroon ribbons and a garland of silk roses graced the skirt. The dated flounce was transformed into a tiered train, accented with more ribbons.

"We're glad you're pleased, Lady Beverly," said Kennedy.

Constance wore a slim-fitting peacock blue gown from her new wardrobe. Its draped neckline, tiny sleeves and tiered train were the height of fashion. Stuart had chosen well. She hadn't seen him since his return from Bath, but she'd made up her mind. She would make him forget all about his mistress and had no intention of waiting until the wedding. If all went well tonight, she would lure him to her bed. His rapturous expression as she came downstairs bolstered her confidence. He stared as if she were Aphrodite, come to seduce Hephaestus.

An excellent sign.

Everyone gathered in the drawing room to welcome a surprise guest—Jane's beloved Sim had arrived from London late this afternoon. What Sim lacked in good looks, he more than made up for with his kindness and devotion. Beside him in pale blue, Jane glowed. Uncle Albert chatted with Philippa, Dorothy, and Mother. Lord Torrington, a rustic gentleman more comfortable in the woods than the ballroom, was unexpectedly elegant in formal white tie. Even Lady Torrington, lovely in deep mauve, was all smiles. This afternoon's unpleasantness seemed forgotten, at least for now.

Blackwood approached, balancing a tray of champagne glasses. As he served Constance, their gloved fingers touched on the stem. His admiration caressed, and a frisson of attraction flared. She sucked a breath, then looked away. Blackwood dropped his gaze as well. But was it a servant's deference... or a man's desire for a woman he couldn't have?

Lord Torrington cleared his throat and raised his glass. "To my son and his lovely bride-to-be. May they share as much happiness as my wife and I have known at Tarpley Manor."

The ballroom was awash with soft, magical light from lowered gas sconces and hundreds of candles reflecting off the polished parquet floor. The scents of lemon-infused wax, orange blossoms and fine perfumes mingled in the gentle breeze of an unexpectedly balmy spring night. The small orchestra struck up a lilting melody as Constance, Stuart, and the Torringtons took their places near the door.

As the guests arrived, Blackwood announced them, and as he did, she recalled little details he'd imparted. She greeted Eloise Ellsworth in German, and charmed an elderly professor by mentioning his yet-to-be-completed literary masterpiece. Twice from the reception line, Constance caught Blackwood's eye, expressing gratitude with a quiet smile. He replied with a discrete nod and carried on with his duties.

Across the ballroom, Mother and Uncle Albert chatted intimately. She seemed to enjoy the older man's company. Did he remind her of Father? The two looked nothing alike. Father had been large and robust. Albert was fair and slender, but the new Earl of Beverly was witty, well-read, and an excellent conversationalist. Then another man joined them. A friend of the Torringtons, Sir Charles was the author of several books on the desert lands of Egypt. Mother turned toward the rugged adventurer, her smile as bright as a schoolgirl's.

Among their friends, Lord and Lady Torrington seemed so suited to their lives of country gentility it was hard to picture them fitting into London society. Lord Torrington was pleasant enough, but his interest in horses and hunting seemed out-of-place for city life. How would Lady Torrington adapt once she was no longer the grande dame of Somerset County?

Her gaze shifted to Jane and Sim. Even though they had been married nine years, they still flirted and danced like newlyweds. It was hard not to be envious. While her relationship with Stuart was different, she hoped that a decade in, their marriage would be as happy and strong as the Simfords'.

She had much to be thankful for, starting with the man beside her. Stuart was handsome, intelligent, wealthy, and tonight, perfectly attentive. Whatever took him to Bath appeared to be over. It was time to simply enjoy this wonderful night and set aside worries about mistresses, Lady Torrington, and... other things.

More guests arrived, including Lord and Lady Charlton. Their daughter Winifred, a rather plain woman in her middle twenties, seemed enthralled by her dashing French escort. Handsome, dark-haired, and exquisitely dressed, Jean-Claude was delightful.

Stuart's reaction was much less so.

His smile suddenly faded, and he grew quiet. Something was definitely wrong. Beneath her corset, Constance's stomach clenched. Could this plain, awkward woman be his Bath mistress?

The orchestra began to play her favorite Strauss waltz. "Come," she said, taking Stuart's hand. "Let's dance."

She was aware of everyone's gaze, as they circled the ballroom floor. Her heart pounded as if she were dancing a polka, not a waltz. Stuart led with confident grace, but his eyes were on Winifred and Jean-Claude.

She followed his gaze. "Miss Charlton's Frenchman is charming."

Stuart's mouth twisted in a wry smile. "Charming, yes. Though I fear he's not what he seems. But then again, who is?"

The cryptic comment was chilling, but she tapped his shoulder with her fan. "Why you are, silly. And I am. We are about to wed and tonight we are attending a beautiful ball in our honor. We should treasure every moment."

"You're right, my dear." He smiled, but it never touched his eyes. When the waltz ended, he escorted her from the floor. As a footman passed with a tray, he grabbed a glass of champagne for Constance. "If you'll excuse me, I think I will pay a visit to the saloon."

She saw little of him the rest of the evening, and what she did see was far from reassuring. He rarely smiled. His manner was abrupt, almost rude. He drank more than usual. As midnight approached, she realized she hadn't set eyes on him in almost an hour. Nor had she seen Winifred or Jean-Claude.

She craved a few moments alone, but on the terrace outside the ballroom, guests vied for her attention. In the drawing room, Lady Torrington held court. In the saloon, Lord Torrington and several gentlemen sipped whiskey and shot billiards. Even the library was occupied by a trio of girls who had slipped away to gossip. Constance made polite conversation with them all, but retreated as soon as she could to the deserted hall at the rear of the house. The portraits glowered down with new ferociousness. Perhaps the conservatory was empty.

She started in, but paused at the sound of voices. A man and a woman. The woman's laugh was low and seductive. Constance froze as she recognized them. Blackwood and Philippa.

Knowing she shouldn't look, yet unable to walk away, she peered in. The only light came from a small lamp and the moonlight shining through the wall of windows, but it was enough. Philippa had Blackwood pinned to the wall near the fireplace. One white-gloved hand was clasped around his upper arm; the other was splayed across his black waistcoat. His posture was rigid, his expression stern. Constance's mouth dropped open as Philippa smoothed her hand over the butler's stomach, to rest at the top of his trousers. Holding him in place, the Baroness rose on tiptoe to kiss Blackwood's unsmiling lips.

Constance clenched her hands and gathered her skirts, ready to march in and rescue Blackwood from the woman's clutches.

"Constance? What the devil are you doing?"

She whirled around.

Stuart approached. "What's going on?" He peered into the dark conservatory, then chuckled softly and closed the door. "Ah, Philippa…"

Constance stared in shock.

"Well, it's none of our concern," he replied, guiding her away. "Philippa's a grown woman and the butler can fend for himself. Assuming he hasn't succumbed to her charms. Men find my aunt irresistible. Come, we should return to the ball. I've been looking everywhere for you."

The thought of Blackwood in Philippa's bed was even more disturbing than imagining him with the dark-eyed kitchen maid. But Stuart was right; this was none of their concern. More importantly, he'd been looking for her, and his dour mood seemed to have passed. There was still hope for tonight. Perhaps she needed a little of Philippa's moxie.

"Maybe I don't want to go back to the ball just yet," she whispered, giving him a seductive smile.

Taking his hand, she guided him into the shadows beneath the stairway, positioning him against the wall. Then she leaned in and caressed his face with her gloved hand. Using the tip of her finger, she turned his face to hers. She rose to meet him and their lips connected, hesitantly.

Too hesitantly.

Perhaps he didn't want to frighten her. She moved closer, determined to show that not only was she unafraid, she was eager. But when the conservatory door was wrenched open, he pulled away.

Philippa stormed into the hall, anger seething in each step. She marched across to the saloon and slammed the door behind her. A moment later, Blackwood emerged, cool and collected. He straightened his tailcoat, retrieved a tray from a hall table and headed toward the ballroom.

Stuart arched an eyebrow. "Apparently that did not end well." Then he glanced around the dark hall. Muted voices and laughter drifted from the party. "I'm not sure we should do this, dearest. It's hardly the right time."

"Nonsense," she whispered, silencing him by touching her finger to his lips. She wrapped her arms around his neck and flattened her body against him.

He took her in his arms, and she felt him sigh as his reserve melted.

"Constance…"

She smiled and kissed him lightly, ending with a teasing nip on his bottom lip. "Yes, my dear?"

Suddenly, his lips crushed down in urgent, hungry need. His kisses were hard, bruising almost, without concern for her supposed delicate femininity. Aroused, she dug her fingers into the hard muscles of his shoulders. She arched her body as the intensity in her kisses rose to match his. Yes! Oh, yes!

There was no reason to hold back and a thousand reasons not to. Whatever pleasures he found with another woman, he could find in the arms of his wife. *This is how it should be between a husband and wife. Forget Winifred, or whoever your mistress is, and love me. Love me tonight.*

His beard left abrasions on her cheeks, and he held her so tightly her breasts crushed against his chest, threatening to tumble out of her low-cut gown. She broke their kiss long enough to whisper in his ear a breathless invitation. "Come upstairs with me."

It was as if they had been drenched with ice water.

His eyes widened, and his embrace fell away. "Good Lord, Constance, have you lost your mind? The house is full of people! What's come over you?"

What had come over her? She gaped and stepped back, reeling with anger and embarrassment. Was propriety a concern in the arms of his mistress? Or did he adhere to the galling notion that wives should be modest, while bedroom pleasures were reserved for whores?

To his credit, he looked ashamed. "Constance, I'm sorry. I shouldn't have said that. You caught me unaware. Your behavior was quite out of character, perhaps the result of too much champagne or the tawdry scene we just witnessed?"

Cheeks burning, she turned away, hugging her arms to her chest. "Yes, I'm sure that's it. You're right, this is not the time. Please accept my apology," she said, through gritted teeth.

Stuart sighed and put his hands on her shoulders, turning her gently. "No, Constance, the apology should be mine." He pressed his lips together. "I've been distracted these past days. My father has made me aware of business problems involving Tarpley Manor." He put his hand up to silence her question. "Nothing to concern you, but still an issue that has occupied my thoughts of late. And I know my mother can be difficult. I should not have left you alone today." He shook his head. "Can you forgive me?"

In his troubled gray-green eyes was the warm sincerity of the man she'd agreed to marry. Once again, her dear friend stood before her. "Of course, I can."

Yet another question lingered, an unnerving one that must be asked nonetheless. "But please, Stuart, be honest. Are you having second thoughts about our marriage?"

"No, darling," he said, quickly. Almost too quickly. "We need time together, that's all. I've missed the way we were in New York."

She leaned into him and let his comforting arms banish her worry. Everything would be fine, just fine. "I've missed it too."

He smiled and patted her shoulder. "Let's ride to Chataigne on Sunday, just the two of us. How does that sound?"

It sounded perfect, exactly what they needed to find their way back to one another. She flashed her eyes at him. "Why, Lord Inglesby. Are you suggesting I go without a chaperone?"

He wiggled his eyebrows and dropped a kiss on the corner of her mouth. "That, my lady, is precisely what I'm suggesting."

Feeling more confident than she had in days, Constance took his arm and walked with him back to the ballroom.

CHAPTER TWENTY-ONE

On Sunday afternoon, Constance and Stuart rode away from Tarpley House, following the service road north.

In their own way, the utilitarian grounds behind the house were as lovely as the elaborate landscapes in front. There were extensive kitchen gardens, a smokehouse, and farmyard. Past the carriage house and barn was a Tudor-style stone farmhouse.

"It's charming," she said, admiring the old, but neatly-kept home.

"The Kennedys live there," Stuart said. "They've served my parents for years."

"Lorena Kennedy's family?"

"I believe she's the oldest child. The father is the coachman and Mrs. Kennedy is the cook. There are also several boys."

"I think I met them in the greenhouse. Do they attend school?"

"I don't think so. I would imagine they're taught at home, as there's no school nearby."

"No? Why, I think we should do something about that right away, don't you? Establishing a small school for the local children shouldn't be that difficult. Perhaps we could hold classes here until we're able to find a suitable building."

Stuart shifted in his saddle. "We'll see. Why don't we get through the wedding and my parents' move to London first?"

She sighed, wishing he were more enthusiastic. Then she imagined Lady Torrington's reaction to the idea. "I suppose that's probably best."

On the opposite side of the road was a pond, and beside it, another Tudor house, this one home to the estate manager and his wife, Stuart said. A small rowboat was moored to a dock nearby. Beyond were orchards and tenant farms dotted with small barns and laborers' cottages. The moist aroma of freshly-turned earth rose from a field where a man and boy worked a plow, drawn by a brawny horse. The man raised a hand in greeting as they passed.

She waved back. "Who are they?"

Stuart looked grim. "Part of the business problem I don't wish to think about today."

Around a curve in the road, they came to an unmarked bridle trail that led into the woods. Ancient oaks, hickories, evergreens, and chestnut trees towered overhead, blocking the sun. The damp chill made her burrow into the warmth of her wool riding habit. "I suppose they named the village for the trees?" Châtaigne was the French word for "chestnut."

Stuart nodded. "The Norman invaders supposedly built it. My great-grandfather told me stories about it and as boys, Alastair and I played here often. We were certain it was haunted, but not once did we see ghosts."

She laughed. "That must have been disappointing."

Stuart laughed, too. "It was."

These were the first light-hearted words they'd shared in days. But why wouldn't he be in poor humor? He was a philanthropist who loved learning. Now he must solve business problems involving tenant farmers. His life was changing too, and he deserved patience and understanding, as much as she.

They came to a clearing, about fifty meters across. An ancient church, built of gray stone and as solid as a fortress, stood at the eastern edge, surrounded by bleached white headstones, leaning this way and that. At the center of the clearing was an old well, and at the far end, stood the remains of a tall stone wall. Its single round window stared like a one-eyed watchman, standing guard over the centuries. It was eerie, yet beautiful. She shivered, but not from the temperature.

They dismounted, and Stuart tethered the horses to a nearby chestnut tree. As they crossed the clearing, he pointed out the mounds of earth marking the locations of long-vanished cottages. Behind the stone wall, another wall extended back. Protruding from it were the remains of thick timbers, suggesting compartments of some sort. "We think this might have been a stable," Stuart said.

The stone floor beneath the cover of leaves was a reminder that this ghostly place had once been alive with villagers and animals. Now they were gone, their home abandoned to lonely centuries. Stuart stroked one log, looking pensive. Was he remembering boyhood games with his brother, who was also gone? She went to his side and placed her hand on his. He smiled wistfully. "I'll show you the church."

Though empty, it remained in good repair. Its slate roof was intact and the narrow, medieval windows let in little light, but kept out debris. Bare stone steps led to where an altar once stood. She sensed they were not the only ones to visit. Perhaps Stuart and his brother had been right. There were ghosts here.

She felt his gaze as she moved about the room. When she turned, he smiled and held out his hand. She stepped into his arms and gazed up into his hooded eyes. Through her thick clothes, his hands bracketed her waist. Her pulse didn't race, but this was a man she could learn to love.

It was time to begin their future.

He drew her close, brushing his lips lightly across hers. His urgency was gone, now he was nervous and tentative. Understandable. Though he knew she was not a virgin, she was still inexperienced. A gentleman would go slowly, so as not to frighten her. Yet his mild kisses did nothing to arouse her. As Jane had done for Sim, Constance would have to show Stuart.

Molding her body against him, she wrapped her arms around his neck and deepened her kiss, urging his lips open. Finally he did, softly probing her mouth. She threaded her gloved fingers through his hair, determined to stoke his passion.

Bringing one arm around her waist, he held her tightly, while his opposite hand stroked her curves. But her thick jacket muffled the sensation. She needed to feel his lips on her skin, kissing and teasing. Tilting her head backward, she exposed her throat. He broke their kiss to press his mouth to her neck, moving downward. She closed her eyes, waiting for the quickening in her center and the pleasure it would bring.

Instead, she felt nothing.

Bringing her hands to her collar, she unbuttoned her jacket, then the starched white shirtwaist underneath. Exposed, her full breasts pillowed against the top of her lace-edged corset. Her nipples stiffened in the cool air. It was a sight to tempt any man. Stuart didn't even smile.

Still, he seemed to know what was expected and planted kisses across her exposed collarbone and chest. Again, she dropped her head back in surrender, yet was more aware of the tickling of his whiskers than any feeling of desire. Desperate, she drifted back to a wooded grotto in a city park at sunset.

Suddenly it was Alex who held her, as his lips scorched a trail across her throat. She ran her hands over the contours of his lean, athletic form; exploring his muscular arms, shoulders, and taut, rippled belly. She recalled the silky hair on his chest and the ridged scars that marked him. In her mind, she caressed them with her fingertips. The throbbing between her legs echoed the beat of her heart. Sinuous threads uncurled deep within. Cradled in Alex's arms, she rode waves of desire that rose and crested, and she softly moaned as his name danced on her lips.

Jolted back to the present, her eyes flew open. Dear God, had she whispered his name?

Apparently not, as Stuart soldiered on, intent on his duty. She forced herself back into the moment, but though she willed it, her body did not respond.

Her first time with another man was bound to be bittersweet, but not like this. Her visions of Alex were so vivid and his presence so strong, it was as if he was standing beside her. She couldn't summon any desire for the man in her arms. Though she had pushed Stuart into this, and to stop might destroy her hopes of winning him away from his mistress, there was nothing to be gained in distressed, distracted intimacy.

She stepped back, crossing her arms over her chest. "I'm sorry, Stuart. It's chilly out here, and we did not bring a blanket. I fear the stone floor will be uncomfortable."

Rather than frustration, or disappointment, his face registered relief. "No darling, you're absolutely right." Something else flickered in his eyes and he lowered his gaze. "You deserve ..." his voice grew thick and dropped to a whisper. "... so much better than this."

It seemed as though he was about to weep. Stuart was genuinely hurting, and though she couldn't be certain of the cause, she rushed to soothe his pain. "Oh, Stuart, no. This place is beautiful. It's just that —"

His lips thinned, and he pressed them into a line. He stepped away, and tugged his clothes back into place. "Say no more Constance. Your first night as a bride should be spent in beauty and luxury. That, at least, I can give you."

All the way back, he was silent.

What was he hiding? He claimed not to harbor second thoughts, yet intuition told her otherwise. Not only had he seemed sad and hurt today, but also guilt-ridden. And what had he meant about "the least" he could give? Was he so in love with his mistress that there was no room in his heart for Constance? Though they shared a cordial relationship, his stone wall of reserve seemed impenetrable. In the two years they'd known one another, they'd yet to share intimate, soul-baring conversations. Something was wrong, and she had no idea how to reach him.

Back at Tarpley House, he quickly excused himself to join the other men in the saloon. She went to the dining room, where a cold buffet supper waited. She wasn't hungry, but took a few slices of meat, bread and cheese, lingering alone, ashamed of the reason.

Seeing Alex would not improve the situation, yet she needed to, desperately. She craved a moment of the warm connection they'd shared the afternoon of the ball. Long ago, he'd helped her find her way, and it seemed he was doing the same now. But it was the servants' day out, and the only one present was a junior maid who waited quietly to take her plate. Finally, she pushed it away and retreated to her room.

Her balcony door was unlocked, and she stepped out, gazing up at the first stars. It was a balmy spring evening, perfect for lovers. Unfortunately, she was alone.

The breeze carried muffled sounds of laughter and music. Strolling the length of the balcony, she took a seat on a wrought-iron bench. At the horizon, the inky silhouette of the woods shrouded the ghost village, but closer in, the grounds were dotted with light. Lanterns flickered outside the barn, and people were going in and out.

The servants were having a party.

That must be where Alex was. He was probably circling the dance floor with the dark-eyed kitchen maid at this very moment.

When the music stopped, he would escort her outside to gaze up at the stars. When the music started again, they would remain outdoors, and he would serenade her as they danced in the moonlight.

Her eyes burned, and a lump rose in her throat. Why couldn't she stop thinking about him? She was engaged to another man, and even if she were free, she could not be with a servant. Once, she'd believed such things did not matter, but there were terrible consequences to defying convention.

She and Alex had suffered greatly because they'd dared to fall in love. As awful as it was to admit, Father would never have accepted her marriage. Most likely, he had conspired with Morgan to send Alex to the gallows. Though the scheme had failed, it had succeeded in destroying Alex's love for her. Ten years later, he'd moved on, but she was still paying the price. Never again would she risk that kind of pain. She ought to forget him. She shouldn't want him.

Yet despite everything, she did.

She folded her arms on the stone balustrade, dropped her head, and cried.

CHAPTER TWENTY-TWO

Alex tapped his foot to the music until a withering look from Mrs. Miller made him stop. Such breeches of decorum weren't proper.

There were times he keenly felt the weight of his position, and tonight was one of them. All around, Tarpley Manor's footmen, maids, stable hands, scullery girls, hallboys, and tweenies shook off the hard work of the past week. The Torringtons and their guests had retired early, but those who cooked for them, served them and spent long hours cleaning up after them, were ready for some much-deserved fun.

He'd worked as hard as the rest of the staff. A part of him longed to cast off his formal coat, pour a beer, and ask a maid to dance. He was a young man and there were plenty of eager partners. But he couldn't do it. He and Mrs. Miller were grim, black-clad chaperones, here only to see that the party did not get out of hand. He glanced over at the housekeeper, a stout woman with gray hair. He couldn't imagine her ever engaging in the shenanigans she was determined to prevent. Just as Mrs. Miller guarded the virtue of the maids, it was his job to see the menservants behaved as gentlemen.

With the doors closed to avoid disturbing anyone at the house, the old barn shook with the noise of dancing feet, clapping hands and music. Mary Kennedy banged away on the old pianoforte the stable boys dragged out from the servants' hall late this afternoon. Her husband sawed on his fiddle, and third footman George Ferguson rounded out the trio on concertina. What they lacked in skill, they made up for in volume.

There was even a singer. Agnes Crawford, the unassuming head chambermaid, had a lovely voice. Her song of cockles and mussels, *"alive, alive oh...alive, alive oh!"* brought fond memories of London. He smiled slightly, earning a scathing look from Mrs. Miller.

When the musicians took a break, everyone swarmed the food tables, tucking into the cold supper of leftovers from the Torringtons' weekend festivities. There was chicken and ham, egg salad sandwiches, relishes, and an array of cakes. The footmen had pooled their beer money to purchase a keg from the wine cellar. There was also cold lemonade for those who preferred it. Someone had opened the doors to let in the breeze, and Alex moved to the edge of the barn. The dance would be over soon and he ought to check in with Charles Hill, who was up at the house, watching the bell board.

Agnes Crawford approached, dabbing her cheeks with a handkerchief and carrying a glass of lemonade. She smiled shyly. "Good evening, Mr. Blackwood. Are you enjoyin' the music?"

It was no secret Agnes fancied him. He couldn't miss her admiring looks as he presided over meals in the servants' hall. Some of the staff laughed about it openly, and true enough, she stood no chance with him, though not for the reasons everyone thought. He smiled as much as he allowed himself. "Very much. I had no idea such talent existed among our maid staff."

She blushed. "That's nice of you to say, sir. I've been singing since I was a girl but never had the nerve to sing for anyone else,'til the laundry girls told me I ought to give it a try."

Her smile faded as Susanna Dawson strolled over. The dark-eyed maid carried two glasses of beer and Alex could guess who one of them was for. She'd tugged the neckline of her gown lower than usual to show off the swell of her breasts, which were dewy with perspiration from dancing. He looked away, but it was too late. She gave a knowing smile and shot a withering glance at Agnes. Assuming she wasn't wanted, Agnes turned to go.

Susanna acted as though her attractive looks entitled her to dismiss the plainer girl. After five days of the baroness, he'd had his fill of women who believed their pretty faces gave them the right to mistreat others. "You needn't leave, Agnes," he said.

Undeterred, Susanna flashed her dimples, and stood a bit too close. "Why, Mr. Blackwood," she cooed. "You ain't had a drink or a dance all night. Don' tell me you're one o' them Methodists, who don' hold with havin' a little fun now and then?"

A fair assumption, given his straight-laced behavior since

arriving in December. "I'm on duty this evening. Therefore, no drinking and no dancing. But Giles over there looks thirsty." He nodded toward the groom. "I believe he would appreciate this more than I."

Susanna shook back her hair and pushed the glass forward. He made no move to take it. "Oh, he'd appreciate it all right, but it's you I want to give it to."

"And I'm afraid I must decline. If you'll both excuse me, I should return to the house to see that all is in order." He nodded to the maids and turned to go.

Agnes cast him a longing look. "Good night, sir."

"Good night, Mr. Blackwood." Susanna sauntered off after Giles, but tossed a saucy glance over her shoulder. "When you change your mind, you know where to find me."

He wouldn't change his mind. Though several of the maids had shown an interest in him, and a few, like Susanna, were rather bold about it, the hierarchy below stairs must be maintained. When he entered service ten years ago, as a lowly third footman on Sir Edward Collins' estate, the idea had shocked him. But over time, he accepted it. Just as pickpockets and nobleman's daughters could not be together, neither could upper and lower servants.

Even tonight, the valets who attended Lord Torrington and Lord Inglesby weren't here. Kennedy, the lady's maid, was, but only to watch over her brothers while her parents played music.

Or maybe that wasn't the only thing that brought Lorena Kennedy to the dance. In the corner, she and John Meacham shared a plate of sweets. Alex glared sternly, fitting his role as chaperone, but inside, applauded his first footman. Kennedy was one of the most attractive women at Tarpley Manor. Not only because of her pretty face and figure, she was also poised and intelligent.

He hoped love worked out better for Meacham and Kennedy than it had for him and Connie. With a nod to Mrs. Miller, he left the barn.

✄❦✄

As he followed the path through the kitchen garden to the house, he thought of Connie, just as he'd been doing for much of the last few days.

She'd made eye contact at the ball, but he was sure it was nothing more than gratitude for taking time to help her. It had been his pleasure. Particularly sweet moments from that afternoon still flitted through his mind.

Then last night, he dreamed of finding her on the other side of the green baize service door, where no lady of the house belonged. He'd stripped away her blue silk ball gown and smoothed his hands over the tempting curves of her breasts, belly and hips. Desire glittered in her eyes as he carried her, warm and naked, to his bed.

He'd awakened just after sunrise and gone for a ride, hoping to purge the dream from his mind. After a decade of living in the country, he'd become a competent rider, if he said so himself. The chestnut bay wasn't young, but still tugged at the reins, eager for the freedom of a run. At the service road, he coaxed the horse to a cantor. The moment they passed Phelps' cottage, he pressed the horse to a gallop. As they thundered down the dawn-lit road,

296

their muscles worked in tandem, and the impact of Lightning's hooves pounded through Alex's body. The air was as bracing as icy water and Tarpley House disappeared in the mist.

He rode into the woods to the abandoned village. Here, things were simpler.

On the steps of the old church, he'd prayed for the strength to fight this attraction to a woman he couldn't have, and relief from his bitterness toward the Beverlys, who'd gone to such lengths to keep them apart. But his anger at Lord and Lady Beverly didn't extend to Connie. How could it? She'd been deceived, too, and then he'd made everything worse by letting her think he was dead. He had distrusted her and lost her. Now she was engaged to a viscount. He was the viscount's servant. There was nothing more to say.

If only he could stop wanting her.

Now, he stood outside Tarpley House in the moonlight, gazing up at the soft glow of lamplight in a third-floor window. Connie's room. He knew she'd spent the afternoon riding with Inglesby. Was he with her now?

The sound of footsteps broke that disturbing train of thought. He turned to see Davy Kennedy coming up the path.

"Evenin' Mr. Blackwood, sir." Davy made an awkward bow which wasn't necessary, though Alex didn't correct him. Better the lad bow to those who didn't expect it, than not bow to those who did.

"You're not staying for the dance, David?"

"No, sir. Got to see to the worms."

"Ah, yes. The worms." Hill had put the lad in charge of the worm bin, where kitchen scraps rotted into fertilizer. "Good of you to remember your duties. Do your parents know where you are?" Mary Kennedy fretted constantly that one of her sons, this one in particular, would fall into the pond and drown.

"Yes, sir, and Mr. Hill knows I'm comin.'"

"Very good. Let's go find Mr. Hill."

In the kitchen, a low fire burned in the enormous old fireplace. Hill sat in a corner by the hearth, reading a book. Davy grabbed the bucket of vegetable scraps the scullery maids had collected through the day and headed for the greenhouse. Alex glanced at the bell board mounted on the wall. Small brass bells, one for each of Tarpley Manor's rooms, hung silent. "I gather it's been quiet?"

"Not a peep from our betters." Hill grinned as he said the word. He closed his book and tipped back his old wooden chair. "Go on back to the barn. I'm sure Susanna Dawson will clear her dance card for you."

Alex chuckled and shook his head, then pulled over another rickety wooden chair.

"No?" Hill feigned shocked surprise. "Perhaps the comely Kennedy, then?"

Again, Alex shook his head. "Meacham."

"Oh, yes. Wouldn't want to pull rank, would we? Well then, the warm-hearted and capable Agnes Crawford." Hill's eyes twinkled as he pulled out his flask and twisted off the cap.

Alex grinned. "You."

Hill laughed. "I suppose I should be grateful you're an ethical man. Otherwise, I'd fear you poaching my beloved Agnes away, given my humble position, relative to you, sir." He lifted his flask in a salute.

The comment brought a moment's tension, though Hill meant

nothing by it. They had let bygones be bygones, and Hill had kept his end of the bargain. The gardener took a swig from his flask and passed it. Alex caught a whiff of the stuff inside—cheap, workingman's rotgut, the smell of which had caused Lady Torrington to jump to conclusions about Hill's supposed intemperance. He took a single sip. He didn't want to offend his friend, nor did he care to have the stink on his breath. His next order from Lord Cloverdale's excellent distillery would include some for Hill.

From the adjoining greenhouse came a loud bang, followed by a boy's curse.

"David?" Hill called out.

"Sorry, sir. Didn't mean to disturb you an' Mr. Blackwood. I'll be turning in now, if that's all right."

"You may do so. Good night," Hill said.

The boy shuffled off to his cot in the storage room that separated the greenhouse from the kitchen. "Hard worker, that one," Alex said, in a quiet voice. "I expect you'll need plenty of help this week."

"Ain't that the truth? Her ladyship brought the daughter-in-law down for the grand tour a couple of days ago."

"Oh? What did you think of her?" Alex was careful to not seem overly interested.

"Nice enough, though the poor thing seemed cowed by the old battle-axe. In over her head, if you ask me. None of these high-born girls have much practical sense, though I hear this one taught school and even graduated from some fancy American college just for females." Hill shook his head, as if he could scarce imagine such a thing.

"She's accomplished, then."

Hill snorted. "For what that's worth. Everyone knows she's just a brood mare so Inglesby can carry on the line."

He considered this. Inglesby seemed indifferent, and Lady Torrington belittled her. It made no sense. "Odd, that she would leave behind an established life to be Inglesby's ... brood mare."

Hill chuckled. "Why does a woman do anything? Titles and money! Which is why a handsome bloke such as myself is all alone tonight."

"There's always Agnes."

"Aye, that there is," Hill smiled. "And someday, I hope to make an honest woman out of her, once she quits moonin' over you."

"I don't encourage it."

Hill shrugged it off. "You're quite the catch, my friend. Go on back to the barn, and tomorrow I want to hear you danced with at least three of Tarpley's loveliest."

He left through the service door that led into the conservatory. Two nights ago, he found the baroness lurking in the shadows, but fortunately, not tonight. The fire was out, and he extinguished a lamp before going out to the patio, locking the door behind him.

Faint music and laughter came from the barn, but he was in no hurry to get there. Instead, he lingered on the patio, gazing up at the moon and the stars. The cool evening breeze ruffled his hair and carried a scent from long ago. The smell of the purple flowers that grew in Victoria Park. They grew here, too, and always reminded him of Connie.

Along with the scent was a sound, not of music or laughter, but a woman crying.

He froze, listening. The muted sobs came from two floors up, directly above where he stood. The balcony outside Connie's room.

It took every ounce of self-control not to race to her side. But he couldn't go charging into her room. What if Inglesby was there? Besides, what business did he have trying to comfort her when he'd hurt her so badly?

Why was she marrying Inglesby? For a woman supposedly in love, she seemed terribly unhappy. Money and titles meant nothing to her before. At least he'd never thought so. Did they now?

There was no denying she had changed. The downcast, hesitant woman bore no resemblance to the spirited lass he once knew. What had happened to the Society Miss who became a pickpocket so she could live as she pleased? The debutante ready to cast her lot with an East London bloke without a penny to his name? The courageous girl who'd killed a man to save him?

He didn't know, nor did he know how to ease her sadness. Regardless, he couldn't leave her to cry alone. So for the next quarter hour he remained there, unseen yet connected to her. Only when her sobs quieted and he heard her door open and close, did he leave the patio.

Despite his promise to Hill, he did not return to the party.

CHAPTER TWENTY-THREE

The next morning, when John Meacham brought the mail, Alex noticed a curious look in the footman's eye.

He sifted through the envelopes. There were the usual letters for the Torringtons, a statement from the coal company that should go to Mr. Phelps, and a letter postmarked Boston, Massachusetts ... addressed to Alex.

Meacham watched as he examined the letter, though he knew better than to ask about private matters. Even so, Alex slipped the letter into the pocket of his tailcoat. "Thank you, John. I'll take these to Lord Torrington. Please remind everyone of the staff meeting below stairs at ten o'clock."

Lord Torrington liked his mail delivered as soon as it arrived.

The lord was meeting with Jasper Phelps this morning; he could pass along the coal statement at the same time. The study door was closed, but Lord Torrington had given standing permission to enter. But the moment he did so, Alex knew he had made a mistake.

Lord Inglesby had claimed his father's desk, while Phelps and Lord Torrington sat on the opposite side. All three looked up. Inglesby glared.

Alex gave the viscount a polite nod. "I apologize for the interruption, my lord. The morning mail has arrived. Shall I leave it here?" Lord Torrington always kept a tray for incoming mail on the small table near the door. But the tray was gone.

Annoyed, Inglesby thrust out his hand. "Bring it here." He sorted through the letters, frowned at the coal statement, and tossed it to Phelps. Then he looked up with a cold eye. "In the future, do not presume you are free to interrupt when the office door is closed. Is that clear?"

Alex bristled, but kept his tone even. It was a professional skill he'd worked hard to acquire. "Certainly, my lord. Will there be anything else?"

"Yes, I would like that removed promptly."

Inglesby gestured towards a pile of papers which had accumulated atop the cabinet on the left side of the room. Beside it was an overflowing dust bin. The fireplace screen needed blacking and the coal scuttle was almost empty. George Ferguson, the third footman, and Caroline, the maid charged with caring for the room, had been negligent. Unfortunately, it reflected poorly on him.

As he gathered the discarded newspapers and periodicals, ink smudged on his fingers. These papers weren't properly ironed, nor had the pages been separated. Ferguson was to have trained the hallboy to do this job, but it appeared the lad needed more instruction. He would speak to all of them this morning, but wished Inglesby hadn't called him out in front of Phelps, his boss. The viscount had moved back from London only a month before, but thus far, Alex didn't like him much. The fact he was engaged to Connie had plenty to do with it, but conversations like this one only reinforced his bad first impression.

Inglesby heaved an exasperated sigh. "Father, it makes no difference how long Willoughby has farmed here. His rent is far below what other landowners charge, and raising his rent is a reasonable solution. Surely you agree, Phelps."

"I do, considering our present circumstances, at least until the debt—"

Inglesby cut him off. "I'm glad you agree, but I must remind you that matters concerning our family should not be discussed in front of the help. We don't want gossip spread," he said, shooting a glance in Alex's direction.

Phelps looked down. "Yes, my lord." It was clear there was only one acceptable response from Phelps, who had to get along with the new lord, as did they all. Yet Inglesby considered Alex no more trustworthy than a hallboy who hadn't learned to guard his tongue.

Arrogant swell.

He'd known for months about the large sum of back taxes the Torringtons owed, when Phelps asked him to convey the need for economy to the household staff. He'd done so without spilling a word -- though servants were no more likely to gossip than a gent's fine friends and neighbors.

Phelps shifted awkwardly in his chair. "A higher rent could have the added benefit of making Mr. Willoughby more ambitious and industrious."

Or it could make him poorer and resentful. Alex didn't know the farmer well, but he seemed like a decent bloke. The farm was well kept; the fields planted and harvested. The Torringtons could do worse. A shame Willoughby had to pay for someone else's mistake.

Lord Torrington was not convinced, and the discussion went on.

What did Connie see in Inglesby, anyway? He was like that pompous bit of snuff she'd run away from all those years ago. Educated and respectable, rich enough, but not an agreeable man at all. When Connie needed him, he took off for Bath, most likely to dab it up with a mistress. When he was here, he ignored her. Now he was arguing with his father about how to squeeze more money out of a poor cottager.

Phelps and Inglesby decided to pay Willoughby a visit the next day. Lord Torrington left in a huff. His arms full of papers, Alex turned to leave as well. A sharp command stopped him.

Inglesby glared from behind the desk. "My mother tells me you have not yet ordered wine for the wedding breakfast. I am concerned the merchant cannot provide what we need in time. You do understand the wedding is in just six days?"

As if he could forget. "The cellar is well-stocked, my lord. I am confident we are supplied with whichever wines you and Lady Constance select."

Inglesby's brows shot up. "We select?"

"You mentioned that you wished your betrothed to taste the wines I am recommending."

Inglesby scowled, as though he did not appreciate a servant reminding him of an obligation he'd forgotten. Or never intended to keep. "Right, right. But I don't suppose we have time for that now."

Once again, Inglesby dismissed Connie as one more item on his too-busy schedule. Alex forced the edge from his voice. For her sake, he needed to appear helpful. "On the contrary. I am happy to meet with you and Lady Constance whenever you like. In fact, if you are free this afternoon at three, I could offer a tasting in the wine cellar."

Left with no good reason to refuse, Inglesby grunted. "Very well. Three o'clock will do. Please inform my fiancée."

Alex left the papers in the cleaning room for the footmen and maids and went in search of Connie. He found her in the morning parlor gazing out the window, an open book in her lap. Her slumped posture echoed last night's tears and his jaw clenched with irritation at Inglesby. Still, she perked a bit at the sight of him, and he told her about the three o'clock wine tasting.

"Do you know if my fiancé plans to attend, Blackwood?"

He'd damn well better. "Yes, my lady. I believe that he does."

As he passed through the great hall, the long case clock read ten minutes before ten. Time enough for the letter in his pocket. He went straight to his office and grabbed the penknife on his desk.

The letter was from an attorney representing Mr. Oswald Willard. He knew the name. Willard owned the Boston Beacon, the newspaper that his benefactor and former employer, Sir

Edward Collins, had moved to America to run. Alex had written to Sir Edward, though the gentleman currently lived in a fine hotel and had no need for servants. Still, he hoped Collins might recommend him to someone else.

Mr. Willard, the letter explained, was constructing a home in New York City and sought an experienced man to hire, train, and manage the staff. The position included room, board and an annual salary almost twice what the Torringtons paid him. Based on Mr. Collins' impressive recommendation, the position was his, if he wanted it.

He reread the letter slowly, to be sure he'd made no mistake. He hadn't. It was everything he'd hoped for—the answer to all of his problems. Yet all he could think about was Connie's soft weeping, and the haunted look in her eyes.

"There you are, Mr. Blackwood." Henrietta Miller stood in the doorway. "It's five minutes until ten, sir. Everyone is assembled in the servants' hall."

The woman was as thrifty with time as she was with leftover roast. "Excellent, Mrs. Miller. Thank you for letting me know." He returned the letter to his pocket and directed his thoughts toward matters at hand.

❧❦❧

The basement of Tarpley House housed the wine cellar, larder, root cellar, laundry, coal rooms, footman's quarters, and the servants' hall. The hall held a long worktable surrounded by benches and high-backed chairs, where the staff took their meals and tea. The rest of the time, it functioned as the bakery. A fieldstone fireplace, containing a monstrous black range, took up most of one wall. The hall still smelled of the bread baked this morning, now cooling on racks beneath the window. The basement was the oldest part of the house and dated back to the time of Robin Hood. Legend had it the wine cellar was once a dungeon. Some village girls who worked in the laundry swore there were ghosts down here.

But on this busy Monday morning, there were no ghosts. Instead, most of Tarpley's indoor staff, save the valets and ladies maids, stood round the table. Mrs. Miller stood immediately to his right. Alex took his place at the head of the table, but also remained standing. No one could sit until he did, and this first piece of business deserved the full weight of his authority.

"Lord Inglesby has informed me he does not wish staff to interrupt when his study door is closed. Am I to assume this is the reason for the neglected condition of the room?" He fixed a cold eye on George Ferguson, who looked shame-faced, as did Caroline, the parlor maid.

"Yes, sir," Ferguson replied. "His lordship told me not to come in if the door's shut, and the door's shut near all the time."

"He got powerful angry when I took his coal in, sir," Caroline added.

Alex nodded. "You should have informed me or Mrs. Miller of the situation straight away." He looked round the table, making eye contact with many of them. "Everyone must do this, as we learn the new lord and lady's habits. I will ask Lord Inglesby's preference as to when you may service his study. After that, there will be no more neglect."

Ferguson shifted his big farm-boy frame. "No, Mr.

Blackwood."

"No, sir." Caroline echoed.

"Very good." Alex turned his chair so he could sit without wrinkling his coat tails. The rest of the staff sat as well, the footmen choosing stools or turning their chairs as he had. Mrs. Miller frowned. She believed sitting promoted slothfulness, but deferred to him and took her seat. While he and the housekeeper were of equal status, in the servants' hall, he was in charge. In his opinion, it was unnecessary to stand during a meeting, as each of them spent almost every waking hour on their feet.

He reviewed the status of the wedding preparations. Ned Beamish and Ferguson had cleaned about half of the Torringtons' five hundred-thirty-six pieces of plate. Alex also told Beamish to instruct Calvin, the hallboy, in the proper way to iron papers and use a penknife. Agnes Crawford and her crew of chambermaids had upstairs preparations well in hand for the additional guests who would arrive over the next three days. Beginning Wednesday, the public areas of the house would be cleaned during the night, so as not to disturb the festivities.

Mary Kennedy reported that because of a shortage of spring mushrooms, she would serve asparagus with the lamb cutlets as a first course entrée for the wedding breakfast. Alex made a note, as that might call for a different wine rather than the Chateau Allouette he was considering. "Mrs. Kennedy? When we finish here I'll need the most recent menu written out, please," he said. He would review it before this afternoon's tasting with Inglesby and Connie.

The next to speak was John Meacham. "Sir, I would like to escort Lorena Kennedy to Bath on Wednesday to purchase supplies for Lady Beverly's dress alterations."

"You have much to do here, Meacham. Given that Miss Kennedy's father is the coachman, surely it would be appropriate for him to escort her to Bath."

"Yes, sir. But the farrier comes that day and Mr. Kennedy must remain here. Our trip would not take more than a half-day, and I would be happy to attend to any other errands the staff or the Torringtons might have."

Meacham was all but begging to take Lorena Kennedy to Bath. Nothing against love, but having the first footman gone most of Wednesday was highly inconvenient. "What about Ferguson?"

In a nervous voice, Mary Kennedy spoke up. "If you don't mind sir, I would prefer Mr. Meacham escort my Lorena rather than one of the younger footmen. There's talk of a gang of robbers along the Bath road. It's dangerous for a young lady without adequate protection."

Mrs. Kennedy had a valid concern, and she would be much less distracted if she didn't have to worry about her daughter. Not only that, Meacham had offered to attend to other errands. Perhaps posting a letter to Boston? "Very well," Alex said. "Meacham, you may escort Miss Kennedy into Bath on Wednesday. Mrs. Miller, please prepare a list of errands you need run by the end of tomorrow."

The meeting concluded, the servants returned to work. Alex accompanied Mrs. Kennedy to the kitchen, where she and Susanna described the wedding breakfast in loving detail. Such an elegant feast called for exquisite wines. Connie deserved the best on her wedding day, and painful as it was, it was his job to provide it.

At quarter-past two that afternoon, he returned to the kitchen for a pitcher of water and a basket of bread cut into bite-sized portions. He carried both to the wine cellar.

Taking out his large ring of keys, he unlocked the heavy oak door, reinforced with old-fashioned iron bands. The well-oiled hinges opened without a sound. Propping the door, he carried the basket and pitcher inside and set them on the table in the center of the room. There were no gaslights down here, so he found the box of safety matches and lit the wall sconces. When the room was illuminated with a golden, candlelit glow, he shut the door and went to work.

The room was not large, but held an impressive quantity of bottles. Notched wooden racks lined the walls. Whites and kegs of beer were on the outer wall where the temperature was coolest, reds were on the inside. In between was a large cupboard where other spirits were stored. From the cupboard's top drawer, he took out the ledger that inventoried the cellar's contents. Comparing it to Mrs. Kennedy's most recent menu, he made his choices.

He lit another candle and over it, carefully poured an 1873 red Bordeaux into a decanter, using the flame to see that sediment did not drain out of the bottle. He decanted each of the reds, as they needed to be exposed to air for a good half-hour to bring out their subtle flavors. Then he located his sparkling and white wine selections, set aside the water and basin to rinse the glasses, and sat down to wait for Inglesby and Connie.

He took out the letter and read it again, shaking his head. He'd dreamed of a fresh start in America since he was a lad, but now that he had the opportunity, he didn't want to go. Leaving England meant leaving Connie. Though that had been his intention all along, each day he liked the idea less.

Staying wasn't necessarily the answer, either. If he remained as Connie's butler, was it only a matter of time before he became her backstairs lover? It was better than never seeing her again, but how was he supposed to stand by and see her trapped in a miserable marriage? If he lost control of his emotions for even a moment, Inglesby would sack him. Then he would have to leave her behind.

Nor could he afford to leave service and support her properly, not yet anyway. One day, he planned to go into business as a wine merchant, and he had been faithfully banking his wages. So far, he had saved only about half of what he would need. Even if he could walk out of here tomorrow, and set them up in the fine home she deserved, would she choose him over her family and high society? At one time, he'd thought so, but now he wasn't so sure. There were so many questions, and so few answers. He shoved the letter back in his pocket.

Connie and Inglesby arrived precisely at three. The sight of her brown eyes, reflecting the soft glow of the candles, reminded him so much of their nights in the Count's basement, he felt as if he'd been kicked in the gut.

She gave a hesitant smile. "Lord Inglesby has requested my opinions on the wines, but I doubt I will be much help."

"There's nothing complicated about it, Lady Constance. For each course, we'll serve a different wine, chosen to complement the menu. It's merely a matter of choosing what you like."

"I'm afraid I don't know what I like. My life in New York..." Her familiar little shrug caused a stir deep inside. "I seldom dined in restaurants and lived in a boarding house with other teachers where strong drink wasn't allowed. I'm embarrassed to admit I'm rather unsophisticated."

"Don't be," he said, ready to lose himself in her soft eyes. "The wines follow a similar pattern as the food. We'll start with lighter wines, move to more robust choices for the second course, and end with something sweet."

Like your lips. He pushed the silly notion away and looked down at Mary Kennedy's menu. "For the first course, champagne is an excellent choice with both the spring soup and the seafood. We shall also serve this for your bridal toast." He uncorked an 1871 Veuve Clicquot, dry but not too sharp, and poured two small glasses.

Connie sipped the wine. "It's rather tart, but rich. Like biting into a plum."

"Exactly," Alex said, holding back a smile. "What do you think, my lord?"

Inglesby had drained his glass and popped a piece of bread into his mouth. "I want to try the other one."

The second was a younger Gosset, sweeter, with peach undertones. Inglesby took a single sip and set his glass down. "This one. This is the one I want you to serve."

True, the Gosset was the better of the two wines, but Inglesby had settled the question with no regard for Connie's opinion. She tasted the Gosset. "It's good," she said, with little enthusiasm.

"But you prefer the first one?" Alex asked.

"Well, I— "

Inglesby cut her off. "There's no comparison. The second one is complex, the Veuve Clicquot is bland. Dull." Connie turned away, embarrassed by her bland, dull choice. Inglesby pointed to the bottle on the table. "You will serve that one. Let's move along, shall we?"

"Very well, my lord." He brought the next wines. "For the entrees, either a white or a light red will do. I have two of each for you to choose from."

"May we choose both a red and a white wine?" she asked.

Inglesby shook his head. "It's too confusing."

"It need not be. Each guest will have the bill of fare and the footmen can ask their preference. But it is up to you," he paused, then added, "and Lady Constance."

He hadn't intended the subtle reproof to slip into his voice, but Inglesby noticed. The new master said nothing, but his glare carried a warning. Further impertinence would not be tolerated.

Alex offered tastes of a dry Riesling and a Pouilly Fumé; both preferred the smoky flavor of the Pouilly Fumé. The wine would complement the oyster and lobster dishes, yet still work with the lamb cutlets and asparagus, or the grenadines de veal. The final white was the sweet Sauternes-Barsac the Torringtons liked with third course.

They moved onto the reds. With the entrees, Inglesby had a decided preference for the Vacqueyras Syrah over the Cabernet Franc. Of course, Connie acquiesced. But it was the second-course Bordeaux wines, an 1873 Chateaux Lafite-Rothschild and an 1875 Chateaux Latour, he was eager for her to try. After pouring small quantities of both, he turned to her. "Before you drink, take a moment to smell it, my lady. A fine Bordeaux, such as this one, will have five or six unique flavors present, but most people can only taste three or four. Smelling it first will help you detect them."

She swirled the wine in her glass as Inglesby had done, and held it beneath her nose, deeply inhaling the aromas. "I smell fruit. Berries of some sort. And wood." She laughed a little. "It sounds silly, but it smells like..." she shook her head, reluctant to speak.

"Like what?" he prompted her.

She wrinkled her pert little nose. "A cigar box? I'm sure that's a ridiculous thing to say."

"No, that's exactly right. The scent comes from the oak barrels used to age the wine. You don't give yourself enough credit. You're quite good at this." He gave her a long look, her eyes drawing him in. Now he allowed himself to smile and didn't care who noticed.

With that, a startling change came over her. The melancholy she wore like a cape seemed to fall away. She brightened, her eyes dancing with the glow from the candles. Suddenly, there was no wedding breakfast, no Inglesby. No longer were they the butler and the mistress of the house. They were young and in love, the clever thief and his beautiful lady, whose hearts belonged completely to each other.

The night of the ball, he'd sensed deeper emotions in her, but dismissed them as mere gratitude. Could there be something more? The idea thrilled and terrified him. He still loved her, there was no denying it. But it wasn't enough. Not only was she engaged to another man, Inglesby could provide her with a life Alex never could.

The wine had left a garnet stain on her bottom lip. If he kissed her, she would taste of bittersweet berries, oak, and chocolate.

"What is this wine?" she asked.

"A Chateaux Lafite-Rothschild's Bordeaux, from 1873," he said, unable to look at anything but her beautiful face. "A most excellent year."

"Indeed, it was." Her mouth lifted in a slight smile and there was a faraway look in her eyes as she stared into the depths of her glass.

His heart pounded, and his palms felt slick with sweat. Was she back in that magical time, when they'd fallen in love on the streets of London? She twisted the stem between her fingers, then looked up. "Your French pronunciation is very good. Have you ever been there?"

He'd asked her to teach him the language on their voyage to America. What he wouldn't give for their lives to have turned out differently. His throat tightened. "No, my lady. I'm just a quick study."

Inglesby slammed his hand down on the table, rattling the glasses and breaking the spell. "I think we've spent enough time on this." His brusque tone was a reminder of the present and their respective places in it. Connie dropped her gaze. The viscount rose from his chair. "Make certain there are sufficient quantities of the wines we have selected and submit any additional orders to me no later than six o'clock today. Come along, Constance."

Connie rose, her expression grave. As she left the wine cellar, she turned back and smiled. Moisture glistened in her eyes. "Thank you, Blackwood."

Her delicate hand lingered in the air, daring him to take it and brush his thumb across her soft skin. The temptation was unbearable. Behind his back, he clasped his hands together. "It was my pleasure, Lady Constance."

The small exchange stopped Inglesby in his tracks. The lord turned back, and his face registered such anger, Alex expected the man to strike him. He stood still, prepared for the blow, but the viscount regained his composure. Tilting his head back, Inglesby peered down his nose; an impressive feat, as they were the same height.

"Blackwood." His voice dripped with contempt. "Your hair is too long and I insist my domestics be properly groomed. I shall inform my valet he is to cut it before Saturday. Understand that if you appear unkempt again, there will be consequences. Is that clear?"

Alex remained silent. There was nothing improper about his hair, nor did he appreciate being spoken to as if he were less than human. But Inglesby was throwing his weight around. His kind always did, and there was nothing to be done about it. Far worse was the shock and sadness on Connie's face. It was torture not to rush to her side and hold her close, assuring her there was nothing to fear from Inglesby or his consequences. He despised the man all the more for attempting to humiliate him, but it came with a stunning realization.

The sparkle in Connie's eyes was real. Inglesby had seen it and was using his power and position to vanquish a threat. Lord Inglesby was an aristocrat with wealth and title. Alex had nothing to offer but love. Yet for the first time, in that moment, he dared to hope it might still be enough. He leveled his gaze at Inglesby. "Quite clear, my lord."

"Et, la!"

Stuart lunged forward. When his sword pierced his opponent's heart, he enjoyed a moment's satisfaction. A fatal hit, aimed just right.

But the feeling died quickly. He set down his weapon. It was a fencing foil. His target? A stuffed canvas mat with the painted outline of a man. The problems he'd hoped to vanquish through physical exertion still weighed.

This afternoon, he'd come close to inflicting violence on a servant—something he'd never dreamed he was capable of. He was no elitist who viewed the servants as less than human. The man had infuriated him, but if cheeky domestics were his biggest worry, Stuart would count himself lucky.

He peeled off the thick leather gauntlet that protected his weapon hand. He'd taken up fencing at Oxford. Though he would never be as skilled as Jean-Claude, who'd learned as a boy, it was an excellent way to burn off everything that had been building inside since he returned to England. The frustration. The anger. He was losing control. Not only of himself, but of the entire situation.

To start, there was the tangled array of tax and credit issues Father had dropped in his lap. Father had never paid much attention to money, and losing Alastair had made him that much more careless. If that wasn't bad enough, now Father was behaving like a child, sulking over reasonable solutions, such as a modest increase in the tenant farmer's rent. If they were careful, they could save the estate, but it was impossible to erase years of irresponsibility without some sacrifice. Unfortunately, the one person Father might have listened to was dead, and it was up to Stuart to convince him.

Mother was no help, either. Without a word, she had planned an extravagant wedding neither he nor Constance wanted. Never mind that the money could have been spent paying their back taxes. She only wanted to celebrate a day she thought would never come, and establish them in local society. But now Constance was angry. She expected him to intervene and somehow control his mother. He laughed bitterly. Poor Constance had much to learn.

A sudden stab pierced him, tightening in his chest. Had he strained a muscle, or was it something worse? He rubbed the place between his left shoulder and breast, and felt no small measure of relief when the pain subsided. He was fine, it was merely the stress of all that weighed on him. He poured a glass of chilled water, wiped the sweat from his brow with a linen handkerchief, and sighed. Such was life for the heir to the Marquess of Torrington.

It was a life he never wanted. Alastair had been groomed from birth to inherit the Torrington land and title, along with the expectations that came with them. As the second son, Stuart had never mattered much in Father's eyes, but there was a benefit to being ignored. He could live as he chose, and if he never married, no one beyond his mother would care.

When Alastair died in a riding accident, Stuart's life ended as well. Not only had he lost his brother, but also Paris, and the precious freedom it had given him. Not merely freedom, but also love. His very identity. Yet there was never any question of what he would do. Preserving the legacy of his family was bigger than one man's desires. He'd learned that even on the periphery. Now was his time to step forward. Dutifully, he moved to London.

His parents hoped he would find a wife there, but the women he met were shallow and empty-headed, consumed with society and their standing in it. Constance's letters from America had been a breath of fresh air. She came from his world, but had already freed herself from its constraints. She was open-minded, and cared more about people than convention. She became a dear friend, someone he hoped would be agreeable to the mutually convenient, marriage-in-name-only he had in mind. She'd been hurt once, and implied she wasn't interested in love.

What he'd seen since she arrived, proved he'd been mistaken. Constance clearly wasn't done with love, and she wanted a husband, in every sense of the word. As that became impossible to deny, he'd tried to put distance between them. But her sadness and disappointment only grew, fueling his shame. He'd done her a great injustice when he stopped seeing her as a person, and only as the solution to a problem. He hadn't been honest, and now she'd sacrificed her life's calling for the promise of something he could never give her. She deserved to know the truth, but how could he possibly tell her? Even once he did, then what? Her life in New York was over. Her hopes for children of her own would be over. She would be destroyed and disgraced, and the fault would be his.

He shoved his hand back into his glove, and reached for a new weapon. The saber had a satisfying heft. He assumed the en garde position, preparing for attack. Now, there was a new wrinkle. Constance appeared almost smitten with Blackwood. Her conduct in the wine cellar suggested something more than mere regard for a skilled servant.

On one hand, having Blackwood available to meet his wife's needs would free Stuart to pursue other pleasures. Yet the young butler was quite protective of Constance, as though he sensed something wrong between the future Lord and Lady Inglesby. His disrespect left little doubt where his sympathies lay. Frankly, Stuart felt guilty enough without the reproach of a man who brought his mail.

While it was not unheard of for matrons to take menservants as lovers, for a newlywed to do so would invite gossip … and speculation. This he must avoid at all costs. Mother had mentioned that Philippa intended to hire Blackwood away after the wedding, and that was definitely for the best.

Though he felt like even more of an ogre, about to take away a lonely child's favorite pet, Constance would recover. Especially once he became her doting husband, and gave her the children she longed for. He owed her that much at least, just as he owed his family an heir to continue the Torrington line. Then one day, when the blush had faded from their marriage, he would confide the truth. Content in a comfortable life, with her dreams fulfilled, he hoped Constance would understand his need to return to the life he was meant to live. It was by far the most merciful approach.

He stretched out his arm and lunged into an attack.

"*Et, la!*"

CHAPTER TWENTY-FOUR

A lone in her room the next morning, Constance paced the floor. The headache, which provided a convenient excuse to beg off Lady Torrington's shopping excursion to Bath, was gone. Stuart was with the land steward, attending to business. For once, it was a relief to have him away.

Last evening, she'd passed tense hours under his scrutiny, wrestling with tormented emotions while trying to present a carefree, serene face. When she'd finally escaped to her room, sleep offered no refuge—only dreams of Alex Blackwood.

She'd been back in the Count's basement, where boisterous teenage pickpockets shared a jug of cheap wine. The room rang with Luke's fiddle, Jimmy's guitar, and rude laughter from the lads as they wagered at whist. But most vivid was Alex's smile, warm and bright in the dim room. She'd longed for him, ached for him, so she'd sat in his lap and kissed him, hard. Her boldness surprised him, but he responded eagerly, gliding his hands over her body, caressing every curve. His touch stoked her desire, and she buried her hands in his hair, urging harder, deeper kisses.

He lifted her onto the table, and she leaned back, pulling him down on top of her. All around, the room echoed with loud whistles and applause. He slipped his hand into her open bodice and as his lips left a burning trail across her skin, she'd cried out... only to realize they were in Tarpley House's wine cellar. Alex wore butler's black, and Stuart watched with murderous rage.

Jolted awake, eyes wide open, she sat up and raked trembling hands through her hair. It was a dream, only a dream. Breaking the stillness of her moonlit bedroom, the mantle clock chimed once. She threw herself back against her pillows. This had to stop! Her wedding was five days — no, four days — away. She had no business dreaming of a man who'd cut her out of his life, especially one who could not provide the financial security to support a family. Even upper servants were modestly paid, and marrying was grounds for dismissal, making it impossible to obtain another position.

Though she'd never thought about it, this common arrangement insured that servants' loyalty was to their employer, and obliged them to do whatever their employer demanded. Philippa planned to hire Alex away after the wedding, and the baroness's reasons for wanting him were disturbingly clear. As the new mistress of Tarpley Manor, Constance could refuse to release his contract, but how would Stuart react?

After her behavior in the wine cellar, Blackwood's presence was sure to be a point of contention. Seeing him subjected to Stuart's anger had been horrible. Even if she kept him at Tarpley Manor, how long could she resist the temptation and remain faithful? How long could he? An affair with the married mistress of the house would destroy his reputation and his life. If that happened, she would never forgive herself. Perhaps it would be best to send him away with Philippa, but the thought of that was practically unbearable. She couldn't have him, but she couldn't let him go. Tossing and turning, she succumbed to fitful sleep just before dawn.

After a late breakfast and hours alone, she was desperate for something to occupy her thoughts. Brushing up on roses or discussing housekeeping with stern-faced Mrs. Miller held no appeal. Beside the dainty writing desk was her bulging carpetbag, untouched since the night she'd arrived. Inside were books and articles she'd brought from New York. She spread them out on the bed.

An article by an Italian educator stressed the importance of using students' personal experience to teach, a brilliant insight that would interest Cornelia Wentworth, the Brooklyn Academy's headmistress. As Constance made notes in the margins, more ideas sprang forth. Cornelia could apply these techniques in so many ways! Quickly, Constance donned a simple amber-colored dress from her teaching days, gathered her materials, and went down to the library.

She was engrossed in a lengthy letter to Cornelia when the door opened and Blackwood came in. His midnight-blue coat complemented his eyes.

"Why, Lady Constance. I did not know anyone was here. I apologize for disturbing you."

"No, no. It's all right. Please come in."

"Thank you. I won't be long." He carried two books, and she caught the title of one. "The Principles of Successful Business." Was he returning books left out by others, or had he read them? He paused at her table. "May I return any of these for you?"

"They're mine." She gave a guilty laugh. "I know education theory isn't what I should spend my time on these days. Not when I have so much to learn about rose gardens."

"There's nothing wrong with having broader interests." Her cheeks grew warm. His admiration felt as good as it had years ago. "I'll leave you to it, then."

She returned to her letter, but kept glancing up to watch his lean, athletic form on the tall ladder as he replaced the books, knowing precisely where they went. He must have taken them out himself. Not only could he read, he seemed to enjoy it. His task completed, he returned to her side. "May I bring you anything?"

Tempting as it was to keep him close by, it wasn't a wise idea. Nor was it fair to him. Her gaze shifted toward the open library window, as a grass-scented breeze drifted into the room. The sun was out, at least for the moment, and it seemed a shame to waste it. She closed her book. "No, thank you. I think I will take a walk."

"It is a beautiful day," he said, a hint of longing in his voice.

Her mind went back to the sun-drenched afternoons they'd spent in the little park on Tower Hill. How much fun they'd had, roaming the streets of London. "Will you have any time to enjoy it?"

"I'm afraid not, my lady. We have much to do before Saturday."

It made her sad that his days were filled with so much responsibility, and little else. As they left the library, he held the door for her. They were alone, and she turned, needing to say what had been on her mind since yesterday. Her cheeks grew hot, but she steeled herself and looked him in the eye. "Blackwood, I wish to apologize for Lord Inglesby's anger in the wine cellar. I fear it was my behavior which caused him to react so."

A quiet smile graced his features. "I don't blame you in the least, and accept my own responsibility in the matter. But you are very kind to consider my feelings, Lady Constance."

Her heart hammered wildly. It had been the same yesterday, when she glimpsed his sweet smile for the first time in a decade. She was nineteen again, captivated by a beautiful stranger in the Crystal Palace.

He took a step closer.

Alex. The name danced on her tongue.

"Mr. Blackwood?" A boy of about fourteen came out of Stuart's study. "I'm done trimming the wicks and filling the lamps. Is there anything else you want me to do?" He glanced over his shoulder toward the sounds of shouts and laughter of children playing somewhere on the grounds.

Blackwood's deep blue eyes shifted in the same direction. "Why, yes, Calvin there is. Lady Constance wishes to take a walk outside. I'd like you to assist her around the puddles. Then I suppose I can spare you until after luncheon. Come find me at half-past one and I'll assign your afternoon duties."

Calvin's face brightened with a smile. "Yes, sir, I can do that.

Thank you, Mr. Blackwood."

Outside, she and Calvin made their way along the damp macadam path. Heavy clouds were gathering on the horizon, but the sun was warm, and she would enjoy it while it lasted. As they strolled the sunken garden, Calvin was quiet, keeping with his servant's training not to speak unless spoken to. But he responded to her questions. She soon learned he was the oldest Kennedy son, and had spent his entire life at Tarpley Manor. Given the opportunity, he would have enjoyed attending school.

Behind the house, a half-dozen children played on a wide expanse of lawn. She recognized two as the sons of Stuart's cousin, who had arrived yesterday. Calvin's brothers, David and Gabriel, were here too, and a boy and girl she'd never seen before. Perhaps they were the tenant farmer's children.

A cricket bat and ball lay on the grass and her fingers twitched with a most unladylike impulse. If Lady Torrington or Mother were here, they would be appalled. Ladies did not engage in outdoor sports with children. But in New York, she had played her share of schoolyard games, and was rather good with a bat. When would she get another chance like this?

She grabbed the bat, tossed the ball into the air, and swatted it to Calvin. The children turned and stared. He caught the ball and threw it back. She hit it again, high into the air this time, and the girl raced to catch it.

"Do you want to learn an American game?" Constance asked. They did.

She organized them into teams and explained the basic rules of baseball. The English children took to it with as much enthusiasm as her New York students. She pitched, letting the children's enjoyment and the sunshine lift her spirits, like a well-swatted ball rising into a brilliant blue sky. This was so much better than shopping in Bath.

Gabriel wanted to pitch, so she tossed him the ball and took his place in the outfield. She gathered her skirts above her ankles and walked on tiptoe so her heels didn't sink into the soft ground. She hoped no one hit anything her way.

At bat, Calvin swung hard and sent a ball high into the air, right to her.

"Drat!" She moved backward awkwardly, dropped her skirts and raised her arms to catch the ball. She stumbled as her heel stuck into the soft ground. She tumbled backward and rolled her ankle inward, as sharp pain shot up through her calf. "Oww!"

"Lady Constance!" Calvin ran over, wide-eyed. His brothers followed close behind. "Go get someone," he shouted, and Davy and Gabriel raced toward the house. The Torrington nephews watched with curiosity, while the farmer's children exchanged worried glances and scurried away.

The Kennedy boys returned a moment later with Blackwood. He rushed to her side, his brow creased with concern. "Lady Constance, are you all right?"

"Yes, I'm fine. I can walk." She stood, but grimaced at the pain when she took a step.

"No, you cannot," he admonished, and before she could argue, he'd scooped her into his arms. Cradled against him, Constance forgot about her throbbing ankle.

They came in the rear door, passing through the warren of rooms which made up the service areas. Back here it was noisy and hot, permeated with the aroma of roasting chicken. In the kitchen, Susanna, the dark-eyed maid, and a scullery girl looked up from chopping vegetables. Mrs. Miller came out of her office, and her mouth dropped open. "Good heavens!" she bellowed at Calvin. "What have you done to her?"

"Nothin' Mrs. Miller! I swear I — "

"Calvin! The door, please!" Blackwood nodded pointedly at the green baize door. The boy rushed to open it. He carried Constance into the hall and headed toward the stairs. "Send a maid to assist us, then ride into the village and fetch Dr. Foster."

"No!" she protested. "This is the second time in a week someone has brought that doctor out to examine me. I told you, I'm fine! I've twisted my ankle before. I only need rest and I'll be good as new. Please don't take me upstairs. I'd much rather be in the drawing room."

Blackwood gave an exasperated sigh. "Very well, my lady. We'll do it your way first. But if the swelling continues, I summon the doctor. Agreed?"

"Agreed." She settled against him, her head on his shoulder.

In the drawing room he placed her on the sofa nearest the fireplace. When she bent to unbutton her shoe, her swollen ankle throbbed inside the tight leather. Calvin returned. "Agnes is comin' with a poultice, sir. Should I fetch the doctor?"

"Not yet. I'll tell you when it's time." He dismissed the boy and brought an ottoman to the side of the sofa. "Allow me, my lady." Carefully, he unfastened the buttons on her shoe. "What on earth were you doing out there?"

"Teaching them baseball. My students in New York loved it."

"Obviously you do, too," he said, with the trace of a smile. She winced as he fumbled with the tiny buttons. "I'm sorry, Lady Constance. Perhaps we should wait for Agnes."

"No. You're doing fine."

He said nothing else as he concentrated on freeing her swollen ankle from the shoe. Gently, he lifted her leg to place a pillow beneath her injured foot. "May I bring you anything? A cup of tea, perhaps?"

She thought for a moment. "Not tea. I'd rather have a cup of coffee, brewed strong. Much stronger than Lady Torrington likes. Please tell the cook to use twice — no, three times — as much coffee as usual."

He raised his eyebrows. "Three times as much? I will tell her, my lady."

He left, and she settled against the cushions, reliving the sensation of being in his arms. He still wore citrus-scented shaving tonic, though a more sophisticated version with notes of wood and spice. But the charming boy was now a reserved man, whose eyes held sadness where none had been before. Was he miserable being at the Torringtons' beck and call? She touched the puffy flesh surrounding her ankle bone. If the poultice didn't help, she would let him bring the doctor, if only to prevent the Torringtons from becoming angry with him.

He returned, bearing a tray with a coffee cup. Behind him came Agnes, the chambermaid, with flannel towels and a small bowl of strong-smelling poultice. Perhaps it would have been more proper to go upstairs. But the maid went right to work. She spread a flannel cloth on the pillow, slopped a spoonful of the rotten apples and flowers on Constance's swollen ankle, and wrapped it tightly with the cloth.

Alex brought the cup and saucer. "Cook followed your instructions, though our housekeeper was scandalized by the amount of coffee she used."

The rich scent rising from the cup confirmed the cook had it right. Constance took a sip and let the dark, bitter taste she'd missed fill her mouth. "It's perfect. Exactly what I wanted."

His eyes were warm and held hers. "I'll tell Cook you were pleased. Is that all, my lady?"

Was it just her imagination, or did it appear he wanted to stay? She looked around for any reason to keep him here. "Would you please draw the drapes? It feels chilly."

"Certainly. It appears the rain has returned."

The maid still fussed with towels and pillows, but Constance was eager to have her gone. "Thank you," she said. "I'm comfortable now."

"Very good, my lady." She glanced at Alex at the window.

"Thank you, Agnes. I will see to Lady Constance." She left, and he turned, offering a slight smile. "Will there be anything else?"

"Would you mind building up the fire?"

He gave a quick bow and went to the fireplace. Kneeling beside the hearth, he added coal from the scuttle. The only sound was the patter of rain against the windows and the soft roll of far-away thunder. "I see you've become reaccustomed to ordering about the servants," he said in a quiet voice.

"I took care of myself in New York," she said.

"You seem to have enjoyed your life there." He looked up from the hearth. "What was it like?"

"Wonderful. There were restaurants and even music halls. Not that I was allowed in any of them. Teachers were held to a very high standard of behavior."

A glint of humor flashed in his eyes. "Much like butlers."

"In some ways, my neighborhood reminded me of Spitalfields. Most everyone was poor, but they made the best of it. They'd come from far worse places to find a better life."

"Did they find one?"

"Well, the streets of New York City aren't paved with gold, though some children were told that. I think many of them found what they came for, though. A new beginning, a chance for a better future. And the city..." she sighed. "Oh, Alex! The city is beautiful."

She paused, realizing she'd used his given name. Their eyes held. A line had irrevocably been crossed. The corner of his mouth lifted with quiet pleasure. "Tell me about it."

"Well, it's like London, but new and big and wide open. All around are lovely homes and tall buildings, skyscrapers they call them, going up all the time. There are theaters and a big, beautiful park."

"And baseball," he added.

"Yes, baseball, too. You'd love it there." So many times, she'd longed to have him at her side, as she discovered the joys and wonders of the city.

"Perhaps I'll go someday." He turned away, poking the coals as the larger chunks ignited. "Why did you leave?" he asked, quietly.

"Why, Stuart's proposal, of course!" But her merry laugh rang as false as her answer, even though she'd given it dozens of times. Her voice softened as she spoke from the heart. "It was the promise of sharing my life with someone, of having children. I'm twenty-nine. If not now, when?"

Yes, she'd hoped Stuart's proposal would give her the life she wanted. But would it? The answer to that question didn't come as easily. She forced a smile and steered to a safer topic. "And you, why you're a country gentleman now! It must have been a big change after living in London all your life."

He stood and watched the fire as it flickered. "At first, it was. But I like the country. It certainly smells better than London. I've learned to ride. There's lots to explore here. When I have a chance, I like to ride into the woods."

"Have you visited Chataigne?"

"The old village? Yes, several times. I didn't know it had a name."

"It's French, for 'chestnut.' Because of the trees."

He repeated the word with flawless pronunciation. He looked up. Their eyes met and a dangerous attraction threatened to engulf her. She dropped her gaze to her hands, folded in her lap. "Do you ever hear from Luke, Jimmy, or Danny?"

"As a matter of fact, I do. Luke and Sally are married and run the Farthing with her family. Jimmy works there, too. Dan's a curate in Cornwall."

"Is he? A clergyman? What a perfect career for Danny!"

"It is." Alex agreed. "The rector at Christ Church took Danny in and raised him as his own. He even sent him to Oxford. Dan was married last year. Luke and Jimmy and I traveled down for the wedding." He gave a brief laugh and shook his head. "We've all changed a bit."

"You certainly have. The way you look and speak now, it's hard to believe you were once the best pickpocket in the East End."

"Even with the nice clothes and proper manners, it's still me underneath." When he looked up, there was a playful look in his eye. "But don't tell the footmen. My authority would never recover."

"Your secret is safe. So you aren't as somber as you appear? You're still allowed to sing and laugh occasionally? You had me worried."

His grin widened, fully visible now. "You know how butlers are expected to behave. But if it will ease your mind, I'll serenade everyone with a few bars of 'Champagne Charlie' next dinner service."

She chuckled, imagining Lady Torrington's shocked face. "That would be memorable."

Their smiles and easy laughter seemed to wrap them in a blissful cloud where no one else existed. Her cheeks flushed, and she ran the tip of her tongue across her bottom lip. Of course he couldn't kiss her. Could he?

He glanced toward the open drawing-room door. Servants moved through the hall, but no one paid them any attention. He returned to the sofa and pulled the ottoman closer. Taking care not to wrinkle his coattails, he sat beside her. His warm hand closed gently around hers and she swallowed hard, her heart pounding a rapid rhythm. Then in a voice as soft as his gaze, he said, "Be straight with me, Connie. Does it upset you that I'm a servant?"

Connie. The girl she hadn't been for years. The girl she missed almost as much as she missed him. Her brave, clever Robin Hood, reduced to serving those he'd once outwitted. Seeing it troubled her, as much as she wanted to deny it. Yet he wasn't to blame, nor did it lessen her pride in what he'd accomplished. Unsure what to say, she gave the most honest answer she could. "It does when I see you treated badly."

The stroke of his thumb across her knuckles made her skin tingle. He nodded, understanding. "Serving doesn't make me any less, because I don't let it. I used to take from people, now I give to them, and every day I'm thankful for that. And I have ambitions beyond it. I'm saving to open my own business someday — as a wine merchant. I believe I'll be quite good at it."

In his smile, she saw a glimmer of his cocky charm. "I'm sure you will be."

Her heart swelled, proud of the fine man he'd become. Rather than being ashamed of his humble position, he'd found purpose … and honor. For that, he deserved as much respect as a titled lord. Even so, her cheeks burned as she tried to ask a question that had plagued her since the first night. "But are you …"

"Am I what?"

She sighed. She had raised the subject; she might as well know the truth. "The baroness wants to hire you … for another reason. When I lived in Mayfair, there used to be talk about certain ladies and their footmen. Are you made to …" she swallowed hard, too embarrassed to finish.

She didn't know what reaction she expected, but couldn't have been more surprised when he laughed. "You want to know if my duties include after-hours work, is that it?"

"Yes," she whispered, ready to sink into the cushions and disappear.

"Good God, no!" Then, sensing her embarrassment, he stopped laughing. He brought his opposite hand to her cheek, brushing his fingers gently down the side of her face. With the tip of his finger beneath her chin, he guided her gaze back to his. She sat perfectly still, afraid the slightest movement would shatter their fragile connection, like a breeze blowing petals from a flower. The tenderness in his eyes soothed her troubled heart. "This isn't the Count's house, and no one forces me to do things I don't want to do. I'm not a slave. I can refuse a thing if I want, and I would absolutely refuse that. I'm fine. Truly, I am, luv."

With that single word, the last barriers tumbled. Alex had returned.

Tears sprang to her eyes, but sadness blossomed into relief and joy. Not only was her sweet thief alive and well, he had become the honorable man he'd always longed to be. Despite her family trying to keep them apart, it hadn't been enough to extinguish their feelings for one another. Never would she love a man the way she loved Alex Blackwood. Their joined hands bridged a chasm it had taken a decade to build. But it wasn't enough. She wanted to throw her arms around him, kiss him with abandon, rejoice as they were united once more.

"As for yesterday," he whispered. "I'd say it had little to do with Inglesby's position relative to mine."

Her eyes grew wide as he'd dared acknowledge it, but before she could respond, voices came from the hall. The Bath party had returned. They froze, momentarily caught in shame. Alex squeezed her hand one last time and rose from his seat. All too soon, he was gone, and she rubbed her fingers together, wondering if she would ever touch his skin again. A respectable distance away, he straightened his tailcoat and once again became reserved, dignified Blackwood.

Someone must have told the women of Constance's accident, because they flocked into the drawing room, clucking with concern. Mother was the first to her side. Constance fell into her outstretched arms and buried her face against her shoulder, desperate for comfort. Mother patted her back, just as she did when Constance was a little girl. "My goodness, darling! Are you all right? I shouldn't have left you alone today."

"Good Lord, Constance! Can you walk?" Stuart and his father followed the women into the drawing room. He pointed an accusing finger at Alex, who now stood at the fireplace, a respectable distance away. "And you. Have you fetched the doctor?"

Constance took a deep breath and let go of Mother. It was imperative she compose herself. "I'm fine and I can walk," she assured them. "I twisted my ankle, as I have before. Blackwood wanted to summon the doctor straight away, but I insisted we try to reduce the swelling first. One of the maids applied a poultice and the swelling is all but gone. The staff has taken wonderful care of me."

Mother smiled warmly at Alex. "Thank you for caring for my daughter, Blackwood."

He blinked, caught off guard. "You're most welcome, Lady Beverly. It's been my pleasure."

Stuart cleared his throat. "Um yes, well, then. Thank you, Blackwood." He paused. "Have you spoken with my valet about the matter we discussed yesterday?"

Alex gave him a stony look. "Monsieur Doyen assures me he will have time Thursday afternoon."

Stuart nodded. "Good. You may go."

As he turned to leave, she caught his eye. Stuart was back, but he wasn't the one she wanted close by. She beseeched him silently. *Please don't go. Stay with me.*

Alex paused, as if he'd heard. "Lord Torrington," he said, with a respectful nod to the older gentleman. "Might I serve refreshments? Perhaps tea or brandy to warm this chilly afternoon?"

"Why, yes." Stuart sat on the ottoman Alex vacated moments before and claimed his rightful place beside her. "That's an excellent idea."

CHAPTER TWENTY-FIVE

L ady Torrington insisted Constance rest her injured ankle and take dinner in her room. Alone again, she nibbled at chicken fricassee with little enthusiasm. She picked up the Tolstoy novel which was so engrossing on the ship, but set it aside after three pages. The story of a woman married to one man but in love with another was too haunting to entertain.

Her gaze fell on the bureau. Kneeling beside it, she reached in and brushed her fingertips against a small object tucked way in back. She shouldn't have it. She ought to get rid of it. But she couldn't. She'd already tried.

She went to the window and gazed out at the rain splashing on the terrace. What she felt had no place in her life. Alex was part of the past, when she'd been a naive young woman. He'd broken his commitment, and that decision had changed everything. Now she was committed to another man.

She threw herself down on the soft surface of her bed and stared up at the canopy. What would their life together have been like? Would her vision of them living in a fine city home have come true, or would they have struggled to survive?

She saw the grim reality of poverty on the faces of her students and would never want her own children to live that way. If she had married Alex, she never would have gone to Vassar College. She wouldn't have become a teacher. He would have had to support their family on a small salary. Would poverty and hopelessness have torn them apart?

Or would they have found the happiness which seemed to be missing from their lives? She suspected it wasn't coincidence they had both chosen careers where marriage was frowned upon. Constance held no illusions; she was twenty-nine years old and wanted a family of her own. Marrying Stuart gave her a way to have it. Her loyalty must be to him, and that meant being supportive in times of trouble. She put on soft-soled shoes and ventured downstairs.

Jane was at the pianoforte, performing a lovely rendition of "Stars of a Summer Night" as Constance slipped into the drawing room. Stuart was not there, but she felt Alex's gaze as she took a seat. Just hours ago, they'd held hands in this very room and acknowledged a truth that might have changed everything — though they both knew it couldn't. For him to love her meant risking all he'd achieved. For her to love him meant risking her very soul. Thank goodness everyone had returned before they'd made a terrible mistake. As soon as Jane finished her song, Constance left to find Stuart.

He was in his study, staring out at the rain, a glass of scotch in his hand. The room was unlit, except for the glow of a desk lamp and the low-burning fire. A ledger was open on his desk. He gave a quizzical look when she came in. "My dear, shouldn't you be in bed?"

She waved away his concern and sat in the chair opposite the desk. "I'm fine, Stuart. I was tired of being in my room when there is no need for it. I wanted to speak with you."

"Oh?" His brows rose.

She looked into his eyes. "I know something is troubling you. You haven't been yourself since we arrived. Whatever it is, I want to help. There's no reason to carry your burdens alone. I'm about to become your wife, but just as importantly, I've always been your friend."

He smiled sadly as he looked into her eyes. "A friend who respects my privacy. As I respect yours."

"Yes, and it's something I appreciate. But as husband and wife, we shouldn't keep secrets from one another. Please, Stuart. It hurts to see you so distressed. You mentioned business problems. If you tell me what they are, perhaps I can help."

He sighed. "You're kind to want to share my troubles, Constance, and if I've worried you, I apologize. But unfortunately, these concerns are mine alone. While I can tell you that my father is no businessman, and it's up to me to repair the damage, I must defer to his wishes that it remain in the family."

"I'm about to become part of your family."

Stuart pressed his lips together. "You will share my name and

341

home. Someday, you shall be the mother of my children. However, as the only surviving heir to the Torrington land and title, the responsibility for preserving them falls to me. Once we are wed, you will have your realms as mistress of the house and I will defer to your judgment in those areas. Please extend the same courtesy to me."

His words, kind yet firm, felt like a slap. His expectations were clear. She was to produce an heir and run his household, not share his life. Loyalty to his family's land and legacy would always come first. Their marriage would be a practical arrangement, no different from many others, and exactly what she'd thought she'd wanted. Emotionally safe. Instead of safe, the prospect left her feeling terribly alone.

She also suspected finances weren't his only concern. "Very well, Stuart. I will ask you no more about it. Though I fear there is more on your mind than this."

She could scarce believe she was about to open this door. But it needed to be done. If Stuart was unsure ... perhaps she could prevent a mistake they would regret for years to come. "When I asked before, you claimed to have no second thoughts about marriage. But if you do ... if there's someone else, you must tell me. We're both adults and I'm sure you agree it's better to be honest now than have regrets later. Please tell me the truth. Is there another woman?"

For a long moment, they held each other's gaze. Waiting for him to speak, she could hardly breathe. If he were to admit his love for a mistress, would she be disappointed — or relieved? Rain drummed on the windows and thunder rumbled. Then he lowered his eyes and gave a resigned smile.

"No, Constance. When we take our marriage vows, you may feel confident that you are the only woman who will ever share my bed." He sipped his drink. "Why don't you go back to the drawing room, dearest? I have almost finished and then I will join you. Don't let my pensive mood rob you of an enjoyable evening."

Enjoyable? Not quite, but there was nothing to do but return to the party. The evening's entertainment was just concluding, and she felt no small relief when Dame Richards closed the lid on the pianoforte. Her own command performance would come soon enough, but thank God, not tonight. Blackwood announced the saloon was ready for cards. For the next hour, everyone engaged in a lively game of euchre, but she kept forgetting trump, as her gaze followed him around the room.

It was strange. When she'd questioned Stuart, she harbored a dangerous hope he might end their engagement, leaving her free to be with Alex. But the idea was preposterous. Once, she'd been willing to ignore social dictates and marry beneath her class, but now she knew better. He'd paid dearly for loving her. She wouldn't hurt him that way again. Nor would she risk her own heart. Losing Alex ten years ago had been devastating. To risk that kind of heartbreak again was the worst thing she could imagine. Defying convention only brought disaster. She'd not make the same mistake.

At last, the games ended, and everyone retired for the night. Everyone except her. "I believe I will complete my letter to Miss Wentworth, as I'd like to post it with tomorrow morning's mail," she said, and bid them all good night.

Returning to the library, she set her mind to work once again. After an hour, she finished but remained at the table, drumming her fingers. The last thing she wanted was to return to her room. She should find a different book, as the Tolstoy would no longer do.

Tarpley House had an extensive library. There were volumes of classic literature, popular novels, books on history, poetry and many other topics. She perused a tome of Nordic folktales, then spotted an oversized book with a scarlet cover entitled, "The Artistry of the Country Garden."

Now here was something useful. Just the thing to put her thoughts where they belonged. The book was full of elaborate garden designs and intricate botanical drawings. Maybe some of these plants grew in the greenhouse. She would go and look.

Charles Hill was nowhere to be found, but there was a small office just off the entrance from the kitchen. Perhaps he was there. She was about to knock, but reconsidered. It was late, and the servants deserved rest. She could find her way around without help.

To the right were the worm bin and tool room, to the left were shelves of pots and boxes. The middle of the room held long tables of seedlings. For a workroom, it was surprisingly clean. There was a little wooden marker in the corner of each tray. She started with the first one — geraniums — and opened her book.

Just then, there were voices. She turned to see Hill and Alex come out of the office.

The steward's tie and waistcoat hung loose, but Alex was still in his formal clothes. They were laughing quietly, two friends sharing a nightcap and conversation. But when they saw her, their relaxed manner disappeared and they assumed the demeanor of servants on duty. Hill slipped a metal flask into his pocket.

"Don't mind me," she said. "I couldn't sleep, so I thought I'd come down and learn about plants."

Hill cast a sideways glance. The excuse must sound as ridiculous to him as it did to her. "Well, my lady, I'll be happy to show you around, if you like."

"Oh, no! That isn't necessary. It's late."

"It's all right, Hill," said Alex. "Go on and turn in. I still have my rounds and will be glad to assist Lady Constance."

"You're sure?" Hill shrugged. "All right, then. Good night to you both."

When Hill had gone to his room, Constance asked quietly, "Lady Torrington mentioned a previous footman named Hill. Is that him?"

They walked toward the far end of the greenhouse. Alex nodded. "He took over the greenhouse after the Torringtons hired me."

"That must have been awkward."

"It was. He resented me at first. No surprise, as he expected to take this post when Jeffries retired. I couldn't tolerate a hostile first footman, but he had nowhere to go, so I asked if there was other work he might consider. He chose this, and it's worked out well." He furrowed his brow, puzzled. "Why are you looking at me that way?"

Because his story reminded her that he was the kindest man

she'd ever known. Alex's compassion drove everything he did. His choices weren't always the right ones, but he never acted maliciously. These past few days she'd remembered how much she loved this part of him, though she couldn't say so. "I was just thinking you're quite good at what you do," she said.

He flashed his sweet grin. "Announcing dinner impresses you? You really must get out more."

"I mean how you treated Hill," she said, feeling warm inside. "Instead of sacking him, you found a way for him to stay. Now, he's your friend. It says a lot about the sort of man you are."

He shrugged it off, but she could tell the comment pleased him. "Come on, I'm supposed to be showing you plants. What is it you want to see?"

"I'm not sure." She moved to the first table of seedlings. "What's this one?"

He removed the wooden marker and held it close to his eyes, trying to read it in the dim light. "Sunflower."

She found the listing and skimmed the text. "This is interesting. Some species of sunflowers grow taller than a man and have flowers as large as a dinner plate. Sunflowers symbolize pure and lofty thoughts."

"Something we can all appreciate," said Alex.

He pulled a marker from one of three large pots that held small shrubs with gray-green leaves. "This one is acacia."

'Acacia,' wasn't an easy word, but he had no trouble with it. She consulted her book. "It's a fast-growing shrub native to Australia. I wonder how Lady Torrington came to have one."

"I assume Lord Inglesby brought it back from his trip there last year."

Stuart had gone to Australia? This was the first she'd heard of it, though she should probably become used to such things. "Oh, yes. I'm sure you're right."

Alex plucked a yellow acacia flower and turned it in his fingers. "Does acacia have a meaning too?"

The words on the page brought a flutter to her stomach, but she shrugged, as if they meant nothing at all. "Secret love."

They continued down the rows. There were marigolds, lobelia, nasturtium, and buttercups. There were even miniature rose bushes, laden with deep orange flowers that faded to a delicate yellow at the edge of the petal. The roses were called "Sunrise."

They moved onto the herbs. She plucked a sprig of lavender and gave it to him. "This is one of my favorites."

He smiled fondly. "You wore this scent the day you came to the Count's. What is it?"

"Lavender. It stands for devotion," she read, then gave him a penetrating look. "Or distrust."

"Won't forget that one," he muttered under his breath.

Suddenly, a flash of lightening bathed everything in ghostly silver light. A deafening roar of thunder followed seconds later and rattled the glass panes of the greenhouse. Constance gave a startled gasp. Captivated, Alex gazed up at the light show. "It's almost like you're standing outside, isn't it?"

"A bit too much."

"Stand over here." He touched her elbow, and she followed him to the end of the greenhouse. Behind the grove of potted miniature orange trees, the windowed roof formed a glass dome that surrounded them on three sides with the storm-filled sky. It was darker here, but when the lightening flashed, she saw his

347

delighted expression. "Here comes another one."

She tensed for the next crash and when it came she cried out, and grabbed the first thing she touched. His sleeve. The fine wool was soft beneath her fingertips, but her hand gripped the firm, muscular arm inside. She ought to let go, but remained as she was, holding onto him.

The flickering lights in the sky danced across his features. Her heart thrummed. Her lips parted. Slowly Alex took the gardening book, which she held against her body like a shield, and set it aside. He rested his hands on her waist and drew closer.

The moment his lips brushed across hers, it was as if she'd been struck by lightning. Her knees buckled, her heart fluttered, and she surrendered to desire, powerless to resist. She looped her arms around his neck and pressed herself against him. His kiss was a melody she'd heard once and never forgotten, evoking memories of rooftop dances, young love, and how life looked at nineteen. But boyish exuberance had matured into a man's confidence. His kiss was the perfect balance of assurance and gentleness. His tongue explored the recesses of her mouth, and she responded with a soft sigh, riding waves of ecstasy that rolled and tossed her like the storm. Between them coursed a current of charged passion too long denied, between a man and woman who had never stopped loving each other.

When they broke contact, she gazed up at him, momentarily robbed of reason or breath. Alex smiled and a lock of blond hair, loosened from its stiff dressing by the humidity, framed his face. Once again, she was Maid Marian, in the arms of her dashing thief. She brushed the lock aside. Her throat tightened. "Robin Hood," she whispered.

He touched his forehead to hers. "Until Thursday, anyway."

She smoothed her hands over his wool-clad shoulders. Being with him was wrong, yet the fact that she loved him was one of the few things of which she was certain. Though they could never go further than this, there was one small thing she could confess. "I still have your book, and the little cross you stuck inside it."

He tilted his head, eying her with wonder, and caressed her temple with the backs of his fingers. "After all this time?"

Pressing her lips together, she nodded. "I took them with me to America. One night, I was so despondent and angry that you gave up your life and our future; I was about to burn them. But something stopped me. I cried myself to sleep instead."

She stepped from his arms and turned away, gazing out at the stormy night. "When I returned to marry Stuart, I knew it was wrong to keep reminders of another man, so I decided to bury you at sea. I put it off until the night before we docked. I went out to the deck, but when I looked down at Robin ..." She took a deep breath and turned to face him. "I realized these meager objects were all I had left of you, and once they were gone, it would be as though you'd never existed." Her voice trembled, and she blinked back the tears which kept her from seeing him. "I couldn't do it. I couldn't bear to lose you forever."

With that, a torrent of decade-old grief gushed forth. Her words collapsed into harsh, violent sobs that shook her body, and her pain was fresh as the night he was torn from her embrace. She hugged herself in a futile effort to find comfort, as she had on so many lonely nights.

Then Alex's arms were around her, warm and strong. He drew her close and tenderly stroked her hair. Cradled against him, she closed her eyes and rested her head on his chest. His lips brushed across her forehead, his heart thumped beneath her ear.

When she'd cried that last day in Newgate, she'd longed for him to hold her this way, but his shackled hands prevented it. Now he was free and for this moment, no one could take him away.

"You haven't lost me, luv. I'm not gone. I'm here with you, and it's where I'm meant to be, always."

But he couldn't stay, and his promise only reminded her that soon, he would be gone once more. Phillipa would claim him, and the pain cut through to her soul. After years of grieving, she thought she'd overcome his loss, but only now did she realize he would always be a part of her. She clung to Alex, and let her tears soak the front of his coat, as he did his best to comfort her. When her tears subsided, she dabbed her eyes with his handkerchief.

"God, Connie, I should have told you. I should have trusted you the way you deserved to be trusted. I was afraid you didn't love me enough to leave everything behind. I was afraid, and I'm sorry."

The pain in his eyes matched hers. Though it changed nothing, she couldn't harbor any anger toward him. "It's in the past," she whispered.

He touched his forehead to hers. Outside, the raging storm had subsided to a steady rain. He took both her hands and gazed into her eyes. "Do you love him?"

"I'm engaged to him."

"That isn't what I asked. If there was a way for us to be together, would you leave him?"

More than anything, she longed to say yes. But it was

350

impossible. Alex was part of her past, a past filled with sweet moments and unbearable anguish. A past neither of them could return to. A future with Stuart would give her children the best life she could provide. She'd made a commitment and left her old life behind. She pulled away, shaking her head. "I made a promise, Alex. I can't walk away from a promise."

"He doesn't treat you well."

"He wasn't always like this. Something has changed since we came here." She fingered a dead leaf on one of the orange trees. "After the wedding, I hope the old Stuart returns. Even if he doesn't," she shrugged. "He's no worse than other men in society."

"You're settling, Connie, and you didn't before." He touched her shoulder, and she turned to face him. "As I recall, you once chose life as a thief over an awful marriage."

"I'm a different person now," she said, resigned.

"Is that so?" His half smile revealed his doubt. "Is this the life you want, Connie? Is he the man you want?"

Before she could stop herself, she was in his arms again, her lips crushed to his in feverish possession. This was the man she loved, even if they could never be together. She would have this moment of happiness before they took him from her.

She arched her body against the hard contours of his chest, greedy for his kiss. Her tongue danced with his, she nipped the soft fullness of his bottom lip. A low groan escaped him and her body shuddered. She ached to feel him inside her, for their bodies to be joined, the same as their souls.

A crash of thunder brought her to her senses. She stepped back and pushed him away. "No! We can't do this. I can't do this." Her hands rose to her face. "It's too late, Alex."

"It doesn't have to be, Connie. I've never stopped loving you, not for a day. You feel the same, I can see it. Say yes to what you want, luv, and let's start over again."

Composure cracking, she grabbed the red book from the worktable and hugged it to her chest. "I can't. I'm marrying Stuart in four days."

She swept from the greenhouse before she changed her mind.

CHAPTER TWENTY-SIX

I n the stillness of late night, Alex stared out his office window. He loved Connie, plain and simple. It was the reason no woman he'd met since had ever captured his heart. It was the reason he'd chosen a profession incompatible with marriage. He'd never stopped loving her. He never would.

It was the same for Connie, even if she couldn't bring herself to say it. Though he struggled to understand, it was likely that accepting his love also meant accepting her family's role in keeping them apart. It definitely meant disappointing Lady Beverly now. It was possible she would never be able to put her desires ahead of her family's.

Connie believed she had a duty to help those in need, whether that was a struggling child or an older lady fallen on hard times, and she would sacrifice to do it. It was one thing he loved about her. Nevertheless, even if her heart was torn, the sparkle in her eyes when they were together, and the heat in her kiss, revealed a deeper truth. So did her sadness.

Who could blame her for being sad, though? Inglesby was indifferent and kept secrets. She was ill-suited to what the Torringtons expected from her. He couldn't see the smart, vibrant girl he remembered finding fulfillment in the shallow posturing of high society. Much of the time, he couldn't see that girl at all.

He turned back to his desk, where the American lawyer's letter waited, along with his half-finished response. He needed to complete it for Meacham to post in Bath tomorrow. Unfortunately, he still didn't know what his reply would be.

A week ago, the answer would have been clear. Accept the position, move to America, and leave Constance to a merry life as Lady Inglesby, mistress of Tarpley Manor.

Much had changed since then.

That terrible night ten years ago, when she could have escaped with Luke and the others, she'd chosen to stay, rather than abandon him. It was the same situation now. He couldn't possibly leave her.

At least he'd thought so, when he began his response to the lawyer.

"Dear Mr. Foster, I am writing in reply to your offer of a house steward's position, serving Mr. Oswald Willard of New York City. While I appreciate your consideration, unfortunately..."

He read what he'd written and spotted a word he might have misspelled. As with all of his formal correspondence, he wrote a working copy first, then checked his spelling and grammar, correcting the mistakes, so as not to reveal himself as an uneducated man. He looked up the word in his dictionary. "Appreciate" had two p's, just as he had written it. He set aside his pen and leaned back in his chair.

Perhaps the problem with this letter wasn't the spelling.

If he remained here after Connie's marriage, it seemed inevitable that they would become lovers. If they were lucky, Inglesby would turn a blind eye. If he didn't? How long would Inglesby tolerate Alex's presence before sacking him? What might he do to Connie once Alex was gone? Even now, he sensed his days here were numbered. Yet even if Inglesby never suspected a thing, reducing the truest love he'd ever known to a dodgy backstairs affair, and forcing Connie to live tangled in lies, sickened him.

He took the fine gent's watch from his waistcoat pocket, the same watch Connie insisted he keep all those years ago. It was after one in the morning, and his duties began at seven. Worse, the wedding was a day closer.

He rose and went to the window, watching the rain soak the dark lawn. This afternoon, from this very spot, he'd seen her teaching the children a game. She must have been a wonderful teacher. Her love for it showed whenever she spoke of her old life. What a shame that she'd had to give it all up, to marry and have a family.

But what if...

He stood perfectly still, as if moving might chase the thought away. A position in New York City meant a new life for him ... could it mean a new life for Connie, too?

His heartbeat quickened as he reread the letter. There was no requirement he be unmarried. It was true the English preferred bachelor menservants, but an American might not care. Even if Willard cared, being with Connie mattered more than any position. He sat back down, sent up a silent prayer, and took out a clean sheet of paper. He wrote quickly, checked his spelling and copied the letter before he turned in for the night. When he awoke at six, he reread it. There were no mistakes in his spelling or his intentions.

❦

But in the bright light of morning, doubts weighed.

Connie avoided his glances at breakfast, but the baroness eyed him as if he were a pastry she couldn't wait to devour. Though he'd told Connie the truth, that he was free to refuse an employer's demand, the reality was not so simple. Still, if things worked the way he hoped, he would soon have a new position, and a new life with the woman he loved.

He desperately needed to talk with her alone. Meacham would leave for Bath by noon. If she turned him down, Alex wanted time to write another letter and refuse the position. But someone was with her every minute. Inglesby seemed anchored to her side today, as if making up for his neglect.

Nor was it easy to remain close by and wait for an opportunity. Wedding preparations and his staff's questions kept him busy. Inglesby even asked him to deliver a message to the Phelps' cottage. Ordinarily, he would delegate such a task to Calvin, but when he heard Lady Beverly invite Connie on a walk in the garden, and Inglesby declined to go, Alex changed his mind. Outside, he could intercept them, and offer a plausible reason to speak with Connie alone.

It was a brilliant, sunny day and most of the puddles from last night's rain had dried. At the top of the stairs, he surveyed the sunken garden, a maze of tall hedges that began at the center knot garden with its sundial and benches, and branched off into secluded nooks. Connie and her mother could be anywhere. As he wondered where to look first, Connie's voice floated up from behind a hedge to the right. He raced down the steps.

"A tour of Egypt?" Connie said, a touch of laughter in her voice. "Why Mother, that's a wonderful idea! You should definitely go. Stuart and I will assist with whatever arrangements you need. Such a daring woman you've become. Imagine what Father would think."

Lady Beverly's voice was grave. "Your father had far too much control over what I did."

There was a pause. "What do you mean? I always thought you and Father were happy."

Lady Beverly offered a small, sad laugh. "When I was young, there was nothing I wanted more than to wed an earl. Except, perhaps, a duke or marquess. I loved Roland, but there were things about him that troubled me. Though he always believed he was acting in my best interest, he could be quite overbearing. When I disagreed with him, he seldom listened. Eventually, I stopped trying, even when I should have spoken up … such as when he arranged your marriage to Lord Gaffney."

On the other side of the hedge, Alex remained still. As badly as he wanted to speak with Connie, this didn't seem like the best time.

"Roland feared that if you never married, you and I would become impoverished should the estate pass to Albert. I feared it, too. Marriage to Gaffney seemed like a reasonable solution. We were tragically wrong."

"You didn't realize the sort of man he was. No one did," Connie said.

"Alas, I knew the sort of girl you were, a delightful and unusual one. When you disappeared, I blamed myself for not doing more, and took refuge in my bed and laudanum. After you were rescued, you seemed a shadow of yourself. I could scarcely imagine what you went through. Only when your father was dying, did I learn the truth."

Constance drew in a breath, and her voice trembled. "Father told you what he and Mr. Morgan did to Alex?"

"Alex," Lady Beverly said, quietly. "Roland never told me the young man's name. But he told me you'd loved him, and were willing to risk your own life to save him. Your father had wanted only to protect you, but as the years passed, and you never married, never wanted to come home, he understood the terrible thing he'd done. For the rest of his life, he was haunted by the fact he'd sent the man you loved to the gallows. One of the last things he said before he died was that he loved you, and was so proud of all that you accomplished, despite everything."

A soft gasp and a choked sob came from Connie. "I'd always wondered," she said, in a trembling voice. "I only hoped it wasn't true."

"I know, dearest." Skirts rustled as Lady Beverly took a weeping Constance into her arms. "I wish it weren't true, either.

You suffered so much, and it breaks my heart to think of all the pain we caused. I'm so deeply sorry."

Now both women cried, and Alex stood rooted in place, trying to comprehend what he'd just heard. Despite his doubts, Connie had loved him. In all the years he'd spent being angry at her family, not once had he stopped to consider their reasons. Lord Beverly wasn't a monster. He had wanted to protect his wife and daughter. The man had made a terrible mistake, but so had Alex, when he let Connie believe he was dead. In his heart, he forgave Lord Beverly, and let unexpected peace cleanse the last remnants of the past.

Lady Beverly cleared her throat and sniffed, as her tears subsided. "I suppose I'm an odd one to be giving advice about marriage. But years ago, I stood by and tried to force you into a disastrous union." She took a deep breath. "I won't do that now."

"Mother?" There was another pause. "What are you saying?"

"I'm saying that if you love Stuart and wish to be his wife, I wish you all the happiness in the world. But if not, don't go through with this because of some imagined debt you feel you owe."

"I do owe it. Because of me, you lost your place in society, your financial security, everything! Regardless of what Father did, you didn't deserve that! And if I ever wish to have a family of my own, what choice do I have?"

Her choice was standing on the other side of this bloody hedge, with a ticket to their future burning a hole in his pocket! Though he wanted to march in and propose to Connie this very moment, her mother had only blessed a break with Inglesby, not marriage to the butler instead. He could only guess how that would affect Lady Beverly's place in society. This needed to be done carefully, so he could assure Connie that she could have everything she wanted in life — with him.

He stepped away quietly, before the women knew he was there. Passing the knot garden, he glanced at the sundial. The dial had no shadow. The sun was overhead. Meacham was leaving at noon!

He raced up the steps two at a time, and when he reached the top, spotted the footman and Lorena Kennedy walking toward the carriage house.

"John!"

Damn that he couldn't have spoken with Connie first. After what he'd overheard, he doubted she would say no, but those nagging doubts lingered. Last night, she'd seemed determined to stand by her commitment to Inglesby. Would she even be able to return to her teaching position? This was presumptuous, risky and impulsive. But he'd spent ten years haunted by a terrible decision. If he let this chance slip away, he would always regret it.

He caught up to them near the chestnut trees. Taking a leap of faith, he gave the letter to John, along with sufficient coin to cover the postage. The footman glanced at the address, but made no comment. "Certainly, Mr. Blackwood."

Someday soon, Meacham would make a fine butler.

CHAPTER TWENTY-SEVEN

All through luncheon, as Mother's story ran through her mind, Constance struggled to maintain a calm demeanor, and make polite conversation. Lady Torrington cast a suspicious glance at Constance's barely-touched Brown Windsor soup, but said nothing. After the meal, Constance retreated to her room. At least here, she could pace and fidget unobserved.

She'd never considered Mother unhappy. Yet she'd had doubts about marrying Father and ignored them. Far from being indifferent to Constance's pain over an arranged marriage, she blamed herself. Now, she had all but given Constance permission to end her engagement.

But Constance wasn't marrying Stuart to please her mother. She was ready to have a family and wanted to give her children the best life possible. Stuart would provide it.

Alex would be a wonderful father too, but if she left Stuart to marry him, it would ruin his prospects. The Torringtons would see to it he never found another position. If he tried to open his business, they could see that it failed. Alex would hate her for ruining his dreams. Their children would know the poverty she saw on the faces of her students.

While she couldn't be certain of this, it wasn't hard to picture. One thing she knew—following one's heart had dire consequences.

She was no longer a reckless girl. She was a woman who'd made a rational decision. Love had not been part of it and it mustn't cloud her thinking, now. There were excellent reasons an upper-class woman could not marry a man from a lower class. It was time to accept life as it was and stop pining for something that couldn't be.

Yet at the heart of it was an even greater fear than upending social propriety.

While she cared for Stuart, if something were to happen to him, she would survive it. Losing Alex had been much different—bottomless, black despair that had brought her to the brink of ending her own life. She couldn't go through that again, ever. Though she would lose him in one sense when he went to Phillipa's, it was preferable to having him suddenly taken. The thought of allowing herself to be vulnerable, only to have her heart shattered again, was terrifying, and reason enough to protect herself at all costs.

This evening, she took her turn at the pianoforte, soldiering through "Beautiful Dreamer" and a Mozart piece she'd heard children perform better. Her audience listened to the first song, then carried on muted conversation during the second. Only Alex, standing at the sideboard, gave her his full attention.

Life at Tarpley Manor would feel much emptier without him. Knowing he would not be forced into Phillipa's bed brought some comfort. He would live nearby, working for a member of her extended family. But she would miss his quiet strength, kindness, and beautiful smile. He understood her in a way no one else did. The minor-key song Jane performed next brought her perilously close to tears. Claiming a headache, she bid everyone goodnight.

Waiting on her bed was the small silver tray Alex used when he delivered messages. Beneath a white linen cloth was a chestnut, a rose from the greenhouse, and a sprig of acacia. It only took a moment to decipher the meaning.

Chataigne. Sunrise. Secret love.

There was no question she would go. They deserved this last moment together before they had to say goodbye. After another sleepless night, she donned a simple dress and tied back her hair with a ribbon, the way she wore it as a young woman. At the stable, a sleepy boy saddled a horse for her. Declining his escort, she rode north into the forest.

⚜

The old village was cloaked in light mist, giving it a ghostly, surreal appearance. Only the sight of a horse, tethered to a nearby tree, anchored it in the present. Constance dismounted and tied her own horse nearby. As she walked into the clearing, Alex stepped out from behind the crumbling barn wall.

It was as if Robin Hood stood before her in the flesh. His white shirt hung loose, his sleeves were rolled back and his collar unbuttoned. A lock of blond hair fell softly around his face. The corner of his mouth lifted in the sweet, rakish grin she'd loved from the first moment.

She rushed into his arms.

Their kiss was desperate in its passion, as if they both knew this time together would be their last. She wrapped her arms around his neck and he lifted her against him until her toes no longer touched the ground. She clung to him as her body molded to his. Tilting her head so they fit perfectly together, she welcomed his kiss, giving over to the desire that surged within.

"I wasn't sure you'd come," he whispered.

"I couldn't stay away."

"Connie, there's something I need to tell you."

She knew what it was, but couldn't bear to hear it. Not yet. Instead, she captured his lips with her own in a heated kiss that smothered the words. Yielding to her, Alex resumed his fervent explorations of her mouth, drugging her with languorous kisses that left her nerves jangled and her knees weak. She dropped her head back as he moved his lips to her neck. Her soft gasps blended with the early morning sounds of the clearing.

He lifted her, cradling her as he had when he carried her into Tarpley House. She would treasure that memory forever, but now they were no longer confined to their roles of lady and servant. She was free to nuzzle her cheek against his neck, kiss the line of his jaw, still rough with morning stubble. She caught the faint scents of citrus and spice. She buried her face in the heavy silk of his hair, desperate to capture every detail and store it away. She slid one hand inside the open front of his shirt. Finding his heart, she spread her hand so the powerful beat throbbed beneath her palm and merged with her own heartbeat.

After he was gone, at least she would have these memories.

He carried her to the other side of the wall where he'd spread a blanket on the ground. Slowly, reverently, he set her down, then stretched out beside her. The ground crunched beneath them. This soft cushion of dried leaves, a reminder of their lovemaking in Victoria Park, was the only bed they would ever share.

Indoors, there had never been a place for them.

As her kisses grew more passionate, his hands smoothed over her curves. Deftly, he opened the buttons of her dress and gave a low groan of pleasure when he discovered she wore nothing underneath. His lips claimed each part of her as it was revealed. First her throat, then her collarbone, the tops of her breasts.

She unbuttoned his shirt, then his trousers, reveling in the delicious friction of his skin against hers, as they freed each other from their clothing. Her hands explored his lean, muscular arms and shoulders. Pulling him down onto her, she splayed her hands across his back. Her fingertips caressed the ridges that still laced his skin. Once, his scars had angered and shocked her. Now she loved them because they were a testimony to all that he'd overcome.

Constance stretched out beside him, the morning air crisp and cool on her skin. She writhed with pleasure as he licked and teased her breasts. Jolts of sensation danced along her spine and every nerve was alive as he swirled his tongue around her nipples, coaxing them erect. The cool air kissed the moisture on her skin, but the heat building within warmed her as though she lay beside a fire. His mouth seared a path down her body, across her ribs and stomach, stopping to dip into the delicate cup of her navel. The light probe of his tongue at her center brought forth sensation from deep inside. She caught her breath, rendered helpless against the shocks that surged through her.

Then his hand slid lower to the secret place that knew no other man's touch. Her desire drenched them both as he gently slid one finger inside. She cried out and shuddered, aching for release, but desperate to savor every moment to its fullest.

Alex lifted himself on one elbow and cupped the side of her face. She smiled, losing herself in the deep blue of his eyes, and pushed back heavy golden strands from his face. With his eyes not leaving hers, he positioned himself between her legs.

It had been so long since she had been with a man. When he entered, the tightness recalled their first time. He moved slowly, gently, exercising perfect control. Pleasure replaced pain as she relaxed and rediscovered the feeling of him inside her. Amid the ruins of a village frozen in time, they were rejoined in a connection that transcended miles, years, and circumstance. She rode with him, rocking together as she basked in the joy on his face.

Their release was simultaneous, and so powerful it shook her physically and emotionally. Once this stolen moment ended, it would never come again. For a few precious days, Alex had returned, but it could not last. She clung to him, her wet eyes buried against his shoulder. She let his weight crush down, shutting out everything beyond this clearing and this moment.

Even as he withdrew, she felt the ghost of him inside. Though it was a dangerous thing, a part of her hoped something of him remained behind. She would love him until the day she died, no matter who she was married to.

Alex gave her a final, lingering kiss. Stretched out beside her, he glided his fingertip across her cheek. "I wanted to make love to you here. I got my wish," he whispered.

A final wish before he said goodbye. Tears welled in her eyes, she blinked them away. "You're leaving," she whispered, her voice unsteady.

He nodded. "That's what I wanted to tell you."

"Philippa." The name stuck in her throat and her cheeks grew warm.

"No, luv," He smiled with such tenderness it broke her heart. "America."

The word was so unexpected, it didn't register at first. Then it hit her. Alex was leaving England to begin a new life in the place she'd left behind. At least at Philippa's, she might have seen him now and again. Instead, they would be permanently separated, not by tens of miles, but thousands.

He reached for his trousers. "I've accepted a position in New York City, working for a gentleman who's building a home there. His name's Oswald Willard. Perhaps you've heard of him."

"Yes," she murmured. Her body felt numb. "He's very rich, though he's not known for being a gentleman."

Alex responded with a cocky grin and excitement danced in his eyes. "Must be why he was willing to hire the likes of me, then. But here's the best part. When I took the job, I told him I'd be bringing my wife." He took both her hands. "Connie, will you marry me and come to America?"

A terrifying sense of déjà vu rocked Constance. Her mouth went dry and her bare skin prickled with sweat, even in the chill of dawn. She'd stood in this moment before. Heard Alex speak these very words. Joyfully accepted his proposal. Intoxicated with hope and promise, she'd seen their lives destroyed within hours. Fate was playing the cruelest game possible.

She struggled to pull words out of her turmoil. "But ... will he still want to hire you, if you're married?"

His joyful laugh filled the clearing. "The bloke knows I was in Newgate. I doubt he'll mind if I have a wife. But even if he does Connie, I don't care. I'll find something else. The only thing I want is to be with you." He moved closer and gazed into her eyes. "You can go back to teaching, if you like. I know how much it meant to you. You can show me your favorite places in New York City. Teach me about baseball. We'll start a family. You, me, and a little one of our own. We can do it, luv. It's the life we were meant to have. All you have to do is say yes."

With a single word, she could have everything. The man she adored, and the promise of a family. The work that gave her purpose. Even the city life she thrived on. But to take that step, to say that word, would surely open the door to disaster, just as it had before. A chill snaked across her shoulders and she shook uncontrollably. Desperate to escape before she awakened the sleeping monster that had begun to stir, she pulled her hands from his. Shaking, she grabbed her dress, keeping her back turned. "I can't."

His sharp intake of breath showed this wasn't the answer he

expected. "Why not?"

With trembling fingers, she buttoned her dress as best she could. "Because I've made a commitment to Stuart, that's why."

His laugh had a bitter edge. "That's bloody nonsense, Connie. You came here and made love to me. How's that honoring your commitment?"

She turned to look at him and wished she hadn't. The shock and disappointment on his face would haunt her always.

"You don't love him." Alex pushed his hand through his hair. "It's not honor or loyalty that ties you to him. It's fear."

Hearing him say it, she shrank back, as though he'd peered into her mind. She squeezed her eyes shut and wrapped her arms around her body. "Stop! Just stop!"

"What are you afraid of?" he asked, dumbfounded. "Not being the lady of the manor? Not having Inglesby's fortune?"

"No!" An anguished cry burst from her lungs and echoed in the clearing's stillness.

"What, then?"

Heartbreaking as it was, she owed him the truth. Even as she'd tried to convince herself otherwise, it wasn't fear of poverty that held her back. It wasn't the thought of disappointing everyone.

It was the fear of losing Alex again and being left to grieve alone for the rest of her life.

Once, she'd given her heart to him and dreamed of a beautiful future, only to have it ripped away. She'd relived that tragic, horrible night, and the hollow months afterward, too many times. To risk it again? She shuddered and took a deep breath to rein in her tears. "How can you even ask? Look what happened before! I killed a man. They sentenced you to die!"

He furrowed his brow and shook his head. "So you'll never let yourself be happy, because of what happened ten years ago?"

"You don't know what it was like! You knew I was alive, but I thought you were dead! Dead, because of me!" She clenched her fist to her chest. "Because we'd dared to love each other, they took you away from me! If it happened again, I couldn't bear it."

He put his hands on her shoulders. "Connie, you can't live your life that way. It's true, something bad could happen if you leave Stuart for me. And something bad could happen if you stay. You don't know what the future holds. No one does. That's why it's a leap of faith. You were willing to make one before. Do it again, luv, for us."

She shook her head and pulled away. Why was he making this so hard? "You don't understand. I'm not that person anymore."

Their gazes held for a long, awful moment. A moment she wished she could take back every word and nearly did. Until Alex looked away. "You're right," he said, his voice empty. "I don't understand. I don't understand what happened to the woman I love, and what's worse, I don't understand how to bring her back. But even if I did, it isn't up to me. You're the only one who can do that. And if you aren't willing, then you really are lost to me."

Grief overwhelmed her as she backed away, clutching her fist to her lips, trying to contain her tears. "I can't marry you, Alex. We paid a terrible price and I can't go through that again. I wish things were different, but we're not meant to be together. We never were."

She ran from the clearing, and the sobs she'd held back broke free. Leaving him in the crumbling remains of the medieval village, she rode at breakneck speed back to Tarpley Manor.

CHAPTER TWENTY-EIGHT

H alf-past ten found Alex in the pantry, listening to the bell board ring... over and over and over.

Where the bloody hell was Ferguson?

All morning, he'd held his temper and was doing damn well under the circumstances. But just now, he'd discovered that Beamish, whom he'd assigned to polish the plate, had not finished. What's more, no one was answering the front door.

Cursing, he set aside a tarnished serving fork. Meacham had gone with Lady Torrington to the Cloverdale estate, and in his absence, Ferguson was supposed to answer the door. Except he wasn't. Ferguson was only eighteen, and not the brightest of footmen, yet surely he could be trusted with this! Apparently,

Alex was wrong.

Lately, he'd been wrong about a lot of things.

Gritting his teeth, he went to answer, passing the empty footman's chair in the great hall. At the door stood a man in royal blue livery, holding a gigantic box. "Delivery for Lady Constance Barrett, m' lord."

I'm not the lord, you dolt. He ushered the man inside without commenting on his obvious slip of the tongue and took the box. It was tied with a golden bow and bore the insignia of the House of Worth, Paris.

Connie's wedding dress.

He wanted to send the bloke and his box on their merry way, but what good would that do? If she had to, Connie would wed Inglesby in her dressing gown. He signed for the delivery and the man left. He rang for an upstairs maid. He waited. He rang again. Instead of a housemaid, George Ferguson ambled up.

"Who was that?" Sweaty and disheveled, his face and livery smudged with dirt, Ferguson looked more like a plow-boy than a footman.

"Lazy hob! If you had been at your post, you would have known who it was! Look at you. You're not fit to receive visitors."

Ferguson stuck out his big chin. "Ain't my fault. Mr. Hill needed help haulin' plants to the chapel. That's all I was doin'."

"Enough of your brass!" He landed a solid cuff on Ferguson's left ear. "You don't answer to Hill, you answer to me, and I told you to remain here!"

"Sir?" came a timid voice. He turned to find Agnes Crawford watching, wide-eyed.

"And what took you so bloody long? I rang for a maid nearly

five minutes ago. Are you deaf, Miss Crawford?"

Her jaw dropped, giving her a dull, bovine expression that was irritating in the extreme. She shrank back, as if he might hit her as well. Of course, he would never strike a woman. How dare she even think it? He thrust the box forward. "Deliver this to Lady Constance's room immediately. Unless that's too difficult, foolish cow."

She took the box, as her face crumpled. "No, sir. I'm sorry, sir," she said, and hurried away.

Ferguson shuffled his big feet. "I'm sorry, too, sir. I'll clean up and get back to the hall."

Alone now, Alex was disgusted by his behavior. He'd made it a point to treat his staff with respect. Disciplining subordinates was part of his job, but this morning, he'd reacted out of a pure anger that had nothing to do with them. A headache throbbed behind his brow. Outside on the front step, he deeply inhaled fresh air, and gazed at the long driveway that led to the main road. All he wanted was to ride away from here with Connie at his side.

But it wasn't going to happen. Her wedding was just two days away and as much as he'd believed she would choose him over Inglesby, he'd been wrong. Whatever they felt for one another was too little, too late. It was time to face the bitter truth. There would be no second chance. He would spend the rest of his life without her and had only himself to blame.

He sighed, resigned to his bleak fate, and returned to the house. There was work to do and even if it didn't console him, duty called. In the hall, Ferguson sat backward on the footman's chair, his posture rigid and his coattails hanging off the back of the seat. They exchanged nods, but Ferguson kept his eyes straight ahead. He did not apologize to Ferguson, nor did Ferguson expect it. It was a young footman's lot to get the occasional cuff from an upper servant, and the smart ones learned from it.

Agnes was another matter. There were plenty of maids who could have answered the bell; she'd just had the rotten luck to arrive at the same time as Connie's wedding gown. Worse, he'd called her a name he knew cut deeply. Before anything else, he must make this right.

She was in the greenhouse, sitting in the chair he often used when he visited Hill. The steward knelt before her. Both looked up. Hill glared.

"Agnes," he said, quietly. "My conduct just now was inexcusable."

Hill stroked her arm. "Damn right it was."

The reprimand stung, and he deserved it. "I am terribly sorry and promise to never speak to you in such a way again. I hope you'll forgive me."

Agnes blew her nose and dabbed her eyes. "I forgive you, Mr. Blackwood. You aren't a hateful man by nature, not at all. Maybe that's why it was such a shock, comin' from you."

"I don't know what came over me," he lied.

Charles lifted a thick brow. "You don' mind me sayin,' Mr. Blackwood, you ain't been yourself of late. It's this wedding, ain't it?"

It wouldn't do to let the staff believe he could not handle the pressure of a major event, yet this went far beyond concerns over the supply of Bordeaux. He imagined standing behind Connie and Inglesby, pouring the champagne that would toast their future happiness. He nodded briskly, before either of them could see his pain. "We've all been working hard."

Agnes stood and straightened her apron. "Isn't that the truth? Now if you'll excuse me, there's linens to bring upstairs from the laundry. The girls need them put on the guest beds."

He took a deep breath. "I'll carry a basket for you. It will save you making a trip back downstairs."

This was a lower servant's job, but at the moment he didn't give a damn about protocol, only about staying as busy as possible. Charles and Agnes, on the other hand, stared as if he'd gone raving mad. "Why, that's right kind of you, Mr. Blackwood," she said, with a sideways glance at Charles. His friend shook his head in dismay.

He followed her to the basement laundry, then back upstairs. As they passed the kitchen, each carrying a wicker laundry basket, Susanna Dawson rushed to open the service door. He gave her a curt nod as they passed through. Susanna gaped, and it was surely a matter of hours before wild rumors spread that he and the head chambermaid were engaged in a secret love affair. Agnes held her head high, making it no secret how much she enjoyed this.

At the second floor landing, she stopped. "My basket goes here, yours goes to Mary-Margaret in the third-floor guest wing."

Mary-Margaret in the third floor guest wing. Simple enough. On the top floor, he opened the hidden service door and stepped into the hall. The guest rooms were at the east end. Those working in the lavender-colored chamber known as the Hyacinth Suite were stunned to see the butler hauling bed sheets. He delivered his basket and left the room with an air of crisp authority. After all, everyone must do their part.

He was almost to the service stairs, but froze at the sound of Connie's elegant, red velvet voice coming from the dressing room next to Lady Beverly's suite.

If he were smart, he would slip into the service stairs and disappear. The last thing he needed was to see her trying on her wedding dress. Yet it might lessen the blow of seeing her in it Saturday. In the end, morbid curiosity won. He crept to the open dressing room door, stopping a respectful distance away so as not to be seen.

The girl who once picked pockets by his side was now a beautiful and unattainable society bride. The ivory silk hugged her hourglass curves like skin, then flared at the floor and ended in a long train. Two seamstresses knelt beside her, stitching. Wearing a pincushion on her wrist, Kennedy was doing something to the gown's enormous puffed sleeves. Perched on small chairs, Lady Beverly and Lady Simsford watched.

His beloved Connie was gone, replaced by Lady Constance, soon to be Viscountess Inglesby. How could he have been so stupid to hope she would give up her birthright to marry the likes of him?

It was equally mad to stay another minute. The hell with the wedding, Inglesby, and Tarpley Manor. He had a new position and no need of a character from the Torringtons. The wines were stocked. Meacham was capable. He was leaving. Immediately.

But just before he turned away, Kennedy stepped back and Alex saw his reflection in the dressing room mirror. Startled, he moved out of sight, praying Constance hadn't noticed, and vanished behind the hidden panel to the service stairs.

⬦⬦⬦⬦⬦

Constance caught her breath. One of seamstresses at her feet looked up. "I'm sorry, my lady. Did I stick you?"

"No," she said, still shaken by what she'd seen for a split second in the mirror. Alex, dressed in his customary black tailcoat, but instead of a servant, Constance saw a bridegroom. Was the vision real, or merely the longing of a shattered heart? There was no logical reason for him to have been standing there. He spent his time on the main floor, not up here in the domain of women and maids.

Yet he'd left the salver on her bed last night.

She ran her hands over the fine ivory fabric, smooth beneath her palms. Seeing herself in this beautiful dress brought no joy, only a dawning realization that she'd come full circle. This was precisely where she'd been ten years ago, on the verge of marrying a man she did not love and assuming a role she did not want.

Back then, she hadn't known the sort of woman she wanted to be. She had been confused and unsure. But not afraid. Escape had been her only hope of seizing control of her life, and she hadn't let fear hold her back. What she'd found had been more beautiful than anything she could have imagined — all because she'd been willing to take a risk.

Now, it seemed she was on the back of a runaway horse, riding at breakneck speed toward a lonely future. Her heart pounded, and she feared her knees would buckle, but life continued on. The maids worked. Mother and Jane chatted. When Mother remarked on Sim's devotion, Jane blushed and smiled.

Strange. As girls, she and Jane had dreamed of handsome men who would sweep them off their feet. Others settled for practical matches, but Jane had married for love. She could have chosen a wealthier or more handsome man, yet she'd picked shy, big-hearted Sim. They were the happiest couple Constance knew.

Though it was true Sim and Jane came from wealthy, titled families, that wasn't why they were happy. Such things mattered little to her, as well. Yes, she wanted children, and she wanted them to have every advantage. But most of all, she wanted them to grow up surrounded by love. Love was something she and Alex could provide in abundance.

As awful as it had been to lose him, and although the thought of it happening again terrified her, she'd survived it. Despite her pain, she'd pursued an education and found a calling, dedicating herself to helping poor children. It was a humble life, but a rewarding one. She'd found comfort in the people around her, joy in the simple pleasures of daily life, and fulfilling work. Work at which she'd once earned a good living. Work which made a difference. Work Alex encouraged her to continue.

At nineteen, Constance hadn't known what she wanted, but with unshakable certainty, she knew now. She didn't want to live ruled by fear; she wanted the courage to embrace her heart's desire — to build a life and family with the man she loved. To make a difference in the world. To marry Alex and return to New York.

She looked in the mirror at her ivory-clad reflection and thought of Alex standing behind her. Everything was within her grasp. All she had to do was claim it.

Now.

Like a small bird ready to take flight for the first time, she gathered her courage, and stepped into the unknown. "Miss Kennedy, I need for you to stop."

The maid drew her hands away. "Of course, my lady."

Mother gave her a quizzical look. "Dear? Are you ill?"

Constance reached for the buttons at the back of the gown, frantic to undress. "Will you help me out of this, please?"

Kennedy hurried to help as Mother and Jane looked on, flabbergasted. "Constance, what's come over you?" Mother's voice sounded a thousand miles away.

"I can't do this," she said, as the buttons came loose.

"Do what?"

"I can't marry Stuart."

Soft, feminine gasps greeted her announcement, along with questions she did not have time to answer. As soon as the bodice was open, she stepped from the gown, almost tripping over it in her haste, and tossed on the simple green dress she'd worn earlier. "I'll explain everything as soon as I can, but there's something I must do first."

She rushed down to the great hall. Servants were everywhere, but she did not see Alex. A young footman sat upright on a chair near the front door.

"Have you seen Blackwood?" she demanded.

"Yes, my lady. He went into Lord Inglesby's office."

She dreaded an encounter with Stuart, but luckily, the office was empty. A folded note, addressed in careful hand to Lord Inglesby, waited on the desk. It was Alex's resignation, effective immediately.

No! Where could he be? She hurried to the back of the house and through the service doors. Surrounded by cooking aromas and a warren of unfamiliar rooms, she looked to her right and left. She ran into the kitchen, and came face-to-face with the dark-eyed maid, rolling out pastry at a marble counter.

"I must find Blackwood. Have you seen him?"

Susanna stared at her new mistress. "He just went out to the barn, my lady. But he's acting right strange today. I'd stay clear if I was you."

Constance had no intention of doing anything of the sort. She rushed through the kitchen and out the back door, just in time to see Alex disappear into the carriage house. She picked up her skirts and ran after him.

She reached the carriage house and found him with Mr. Kennedy. Ignoring propriety or consequence, she blurted out, "Alex, don't go!"

The coachman lowered his eyes. Though he'd shed his tail coat and loosened his tie, Alex maintained his dignified bearing. "Mr. Kennedy, would you allow us a moment, please?"

"Certainly, sir."

The moment he left, she rushed to Alex. "I found your letter! I was afraid you were already gone!"

He held her awkwardly. "I can't stay, Connie. I love you too much to watch you marry another man. You've made your choice; now I have to make mine."

"Alex, my choice is you!"

He tensed and she clutched his upper arms as her words gushed out. "I was too blind to see it before, but there is no other choice for me. I've spent ten years without you and I don't want to spend the rest of my life that way! I was so afraid of what might happen if I went with you, I couldn't see the terrible thing that will happen if I stay!

"You were wrong when you said there's no way to be certain of the future. The only thing I'm certain of is I don't want to spend another day without you. I want to marry you and go with you to America! Whatever lies ahead, I want to face it with you at my side. I love you so much, Alex. Will you still have me?"

His stunned expression turned to sheer delight, and his beautiful, sunny smile bathed her in warmth. "Of course I'll have you! Do you even need to ask? I'll treasure every minute we have together. I made mistakes I will always regret but the entire time we were apart, never for a moment did I stop loving you. You are the only one for me, Connie. I love you with all of my heart."

In an instant, she was in his arms and her heart sang with joy as she kissed him. She felt alive, fearless, and invincible. She and Alex belonged to one another and now, the future was theirs. No more separation, no more heartache.

A sudden gasp made them turn toward the carriage house door.

Watching in shocked silence were Stuart and Philippa.

CHAPTER TWENTY-NINE

O h, my," Philippa purred, with a lascivious smile. "Isn't this an interesting turn? Blackwood, so resistant to my charms." She pouted. "And Lady Constance, full of lofty pronouncements about dignity and equality, all to hide a tawdry little affair."

Constance stepped into the protective circle of Alex's arms. Stuart glowered with burning intensity. She'd never felt afraid of him, but she was now.

He took a menacing step forward. "Blackwood. I accept your resignation. I want you gone at once. Otherwise, I will have you horsewhipped to within an inch of your life."

"I'm not leavin' without Connie."

Stuart grabbed a mallet from a nearby wall. Constance gasped as he came closer. He could murder Alex in cold blood and no one would fault him. His lips were pressed thin and his nostrils flared. His fingers twitched on the handle.

Alex pushed her behind him and reached for the pocket where he'd once kept his switchblade. His knife was long gone, but the instincts honed in the dangerous alleys of Whitechapel remained. His body tensed; his fists clenched. He would protect her to the end, even if Stuart killed him.

"No!" She would not let Alex sacrifice himself, not again. She would not lose him. She moved in front of him, spreading her arms to keep them apart. "Alex, it's all right."

His eyes clouded with anger and confusion. "Connie —"

"Listen to me. I have to make this right. I'm the only one who can. I'm not afraid of him. I'm not afraid of anything anymore." As she spoke, she knew deep in her soul it was true.

His gaze shifted from her to Stuart. "You lay a hand on her, I swear I'll kill you."

Stuart sneered. "Oh, for God's sake. I won't touch a hair on her precious head."

"Drop the hammer, then."

Stuart did so, and it hit the concrete floor with a clang. He stood with his arms akimbo.

In her grasp, Alex's tense muscles relaxed slightly. "I'll be right outside," he said. "If he so much as lifts a finger —"

"I'll be all right," she whispered. "Go."

As he passed Stuart, Alex gave the mallet a solid kick out the door. When he was gone, Stuart turned, his face a study in righteous indignation. "Do you wish to explain your adulterous dalliance with my servant?"

From the corner, Philippa chuckled. "I know I can't wait to hear it."

"Out, Philippa!" Stuart roared, pointing to the door. "This is not your affair!"

Laughing, she strutted from the carriage house. Silence settled like dense fog.

"It's not how it appears," Constance said. "This was not some sordid tryst carried on under your nose. We knew it was wrong to be together. But love is not a rational thing."

"Love?" His voice rose in disbelief. "You claim to love a man you've known all of a week?"

"No," she whispered, hating the pain she was about to inflict. But it had to be done. "Do you recall when I told you of the man I loved and lost years ago?"

"The one who died before you were wed." He paused and then snorted in disgust. "I suppose Blackwood reminds you of that man?"

She shook her head. "Alex Blackwood is that man."

She began with the night of her engagement to Gaffney. It took nearly half the hour to tell him everything. "My father's barrister said Alex had been convicted and sentenced to die. I was never told the date of his hanging, only that he'd been executed.

"At first I didn't think I could go on, but after his sacrifice, how could I not? Teaching in the slums seemed the best way to honor his memory. As for him, he believed I'd sided with my family. When Sir Edward won his pardon, he decided not to disrupt my life again."

"And although he is thoroughly unsuitable," said Stuart,

"your feelings have not changed."

"No. Nor have his. I know our life will be very different from what I would have had with you. I'm not afraid of it. Especially when the alternative is to live without him. I've already done that. I never wanted to hurt you, Stuart. You are a fine man and deserve a woman who loves you completely."

Despair etched on his face, Stuart pressed his lips together and was still. In the lengthy silence, she held her breath. Finally, he spoke. "You are right when you say that love is not a rational thing. I also know what it is to want someone who is forbidden. Someone I love to the core of my being, yet can never be with."

His mistress. Constance smiled gently. "I'd suspected as much. Is she also of lower birth?"

His voice was thick with unshed tears, and so quiet she strained to hear it. "It's someone I've known since my school days. I only wish social position was the barrier which kept us apart."

Suddenly, she understood who'd captured Stuart's heart. It all made sense—his change of mood, his reluctance to kiss her, his lack of interest. Just as she had hidden her deepest secret, Stuart had kept his. Her initial shock turned to sympathy for her old friend, who also knew the torment of forbidden love. "It's your school chum," she whispered. "The one you went to see in Bath."

His nod was almost imperceptible. "You met him when he came to the ball with Winifred, who has known about us for years. Jean-Claude is witty, brilliant, and the perfect match for me … in every way but one." Stuart raked his hand through his hair. "I thought I could go forward with our marriage. My family expects it. The truth would devastate them, especially Father …

having already lost Alastair."

She swallowed hard before she could speak. "Oh, Stuart, I'm sorry. I didn't want to hurt you. Please know that I care for you."

"I care for you as well." He paused and held her gaze. "But not in the way a husband should love his wife. We would base our marriage on lies, and I will not force that upon you. So I free you from your obligation. Marry the man you love and never forget how blessed you are."

Stuart's eyes revealed the reserved, yet good-hearted man she knew. Constance went to him and wrapped her arms around his neck. "Thank you, my dear, dear friend."

He released her and gave a short, resigned laugh. "However, as I must continue to maintain a presence in society, not to mention peace in my family, I trust you will consent to play the rejected party?"

Without hesitation, she agreed. "What will you … and Jean-Claude do?"

His face softened with a sad, yet hopeful smile. "We'll continue on, as we always have. True love finds a way."

"That it does." She squeezed his hand. "Goodbye, Stuart, and good luck."

Outside the carriage house, Alex waited beneath a chestnut tree. Constance threw herself into his arms.

CHAPTER THIRTY

U pstairs, Constance told Mother and Jane about Alex. Her cousin wept for joy. Mother wept for other reasons.

"Of course I want you to be happy, but Constance ..." She gulped and dabbed at her eyes. "Good heavens, do you have any idea what hardship you'll face?"

"No worse than the hardship of living without him." She hugged Mother, trying her best to comfort her. Despite Mother's humble origins — or perhaps because of them — she would struggle with this for some time to come.

By early afternoon, Constance and her family were ready to depart. They waited beneath the portico as footmen loaded their trunks onto the carriage. Alex, attending to his final duties, supervised. He'd hoped to leave with them, but had agreed to the Torringtons' request that he remain one more day to instruct Meacham in his new responsibilities. Though Alex would join her in London tomorrow, the fear she'd known while waiting in vain in a dockside warehouse haunted her.

"Where will you go once you arrive?" she asked, in a hushed voice, mindful of curious glances from the footmen and her family.

His formal manner didn't mask the love in his eyes. "I don't know just yet. Luke and Sally have extended an open invitation. I also have a friend in service as a footman in Knightsbridge. His employer may allow me to stay in exchange for a week's work."

Jane stepped forward. "Don't even think of it. You must stay with us. Lord Simsford and I have a lovely home on Albemarle Street."

Sim and Uncle Albert's surprised expressions didn't take away from Constance's immense relief. "Why, that's a wonderful idea! Jane and Sim live just streets from my mother."

Mother sniffed and muttered to Uncle Albert. "Jane's had such problems finding quality help. Perhaps Blackwood can provide it."

Constance's cheeks burned. Alex pressed his lips together and looked down. Then Jane broke the awkward silence. "Nonsense," she said, with a warm smile. "You shall be our guest. You are about to become part of our family."

Her heart swelled with love for her sweet cousin and for Sim, who behaved as a true gentleman and followed her lead. "Quite so," he said, extending his right hand. "We look forward to getting to know you."

Uncle Albert stepped forward, stiff and proper, yet making an effort. "Yes, of course, young man. Congratulations to you and Constance."

Alex's stern expression softened as he shook Sim's hand, then Albert's. "Thank you, Lord Beverly, and Lord and Lady Simsford. I look forward to getting to know you as well, and I'm pleased to accept your kind invitation."

Yet leaving Alex was one of the hardest things she'd ever done. They could not kiss. Their only contact was a prolonged touch of hands as he helped her into the carriage. As it pulled away, she held his gaze until the carriage crossed over a small rise and he disappeared from view. Then she closed her eyes so she could see his face a few moments longer.

<hr />

Back in Mayfair, hours passed with excruciating slowness. She spent the day in her room, remembering the long-ago summer morning when she left for the Crystal Palace and her life changed forever. After dinner, some of Mother's friends dropped by. Constance sat in the drawing room, nerves taut. Each ring of the doorbell brought anticipation … and disappointment. Where could he be? Then at ten o'clock, the bell rang again and moments later, the parlor maid announced, "Mr. Alexander Blackwood is here for Lady Constance."

Unmindful of proper etiquette, she sprang from her seat and raced to the door. When Alex entered her family home for the first time, she walked proudly at his side.

Two days before they sailed to America, Constance and Alex were wed.

In the Mayfair church she'd attended as a child, they stood hand in hand as Danny, now the Reverend Daniel Lockhurst, pronounced them husband and wife. Constance's heart swelled at the loving faces surrounding them. Jane and Sim. Uncle Albert. Luke, Sally, Danny, Jimmy, Charles Hill, and most of all, Mother.

Since their return to London, Mother had realized that while Alex was not a wealthy man, he was a good one who would care for Constance and their future children. Though it was true Constance might always have to work, she had found purpose as a teacher. Only one thing had been missing from her life. Now she had it.

Afterward, everyone gathered in the dining room on Bruton Street for an elegant wedding breakfast. She and Alex drank their bridal toast from a pair of crystal champagne glasses that were a gift from Nancy, who sent her congratulations. Out of polite society's hearing, Luke confided that their old friend now ran Minerva's business and was quite a success. Tim, on the other hand, was serving a 20-year sentence in Newgate, for killing a rival East End crime boss.

As the official host, Albert, the fourth Earl of Beverly, welcomed the son of a Shadwell prostitute into the family. Constance's ears rang with tasteful best wishes and boisterous good cheer. She couldn't have asked for a more beautiful wedding day.

On the last day of May, she and Alex stood on the main deck of the S.S. Celtic and waved farewell to their homeland. Once Liverpool was out of sight, they went to the first-class cabin that was a wedding gift from Sir Edward Collins. In the narrow passageway outside the door, Alex scooped her into his arms and carried her over the threshold. "We're not home yet, but for a week it's the place we'll share as husband and wife. I think we should claim it properly."

A porter had opened a porthole to let in the crisp sea air, and a bottle of champagne was chilling in a silver bucket beside the bed. "My goodness," said Constance, "what a lovely surprise!"

Alex smiled. "It's the Veuve Clicquot you like. The one that tastes like plums. It's not properly chilled yet." He placed her on the bed and tugged loose the silk ribbon of her straw traveling hat. He tossed the hat on the bureau and stretched out beside her, tracing his finger across the swell of her bottom lip. "We must find something to do while we wait."

She could think of no better way to pass the afternoon.

That evening, they dined in the luxurious first-class dining room. Wearing the white tie and waistcoat of a gentleman, Alex conversed with their high-born table mates, perfectly at ease. When asked about his profession, he answered that he was beginning a career in New York City, managing the affairs of Mr. Oswald Willard, and left it at that.

After dinner, she and Alex strolled the main deck, hand in hand. They paused at the stern and looked out at the vast ocean. When they reached America, they would face their first challenge as husband and wife. Oswald Willard might not want a married steward. The Brooklyn Academy had never employed a married female teacher.

But though she couldn't know the future, she knew herself. She'd weathered a devastating loss, and built a life in a new land, living it on her own terms. When she'd felt it slipping away, she fought her fear and took it back. And she knew Alex. He had survived an East End thieves' den, cared for her in a terrifying subterranean world, offered his life to save hers, and for ten years, never stopped loving her. Together, they would be fine.

The moon was full and the breeze cool. She shivered a little in her low-cut evening gown, and he slipped his arm around her.

"This reminds me of the night on the Farthing's roof," he said. "That night I didn't think life could get any better, but it has." He laughed a little. "Not quite the way I expected, mind you, but I'm not complaining. In fact, I think it will be better than we ever imagined."

She wrapped her arms around him and rested her head against his chest. "I think you're right. Would you do something for me?"

"What might that be?"

She smiled up at him. "I think you know."

"Think I do, luv." His lopsided grin made her heart melt. Then he sang. *"If ever I cease to love, if ever I cease to love, may the moonbeams turn to green cream cheese, if ever I cease to love. May the fish get legs and the cows lay eggs, if ever I cease to love."*

His voice blended with the gentle sounds of the ocean and the night breeze. The starry sky above was bright with possibility.

EPILOGUE

New York City, 1888

The carriage parked at the rear of the mansion, just east of Central Park. The coachman opened the carriage door and Constance Blackwood stepped out.

The walkway leading into the house was clear, despite the snow that had been falling all afternoon. Having retrieved her satchel from the coach, the young man offered his arm. Paul O'Halloran was no longer the cold, hungry boy who'd taken refuge in her classroom. She'd recognized his potential and believed that in a better environment, he could flourish. Her hunch had been right, as it often was.

"Thank you, Paul. You were very prompt this afternoon."

"My pleasure, ma'am," he said, with the hint of an Irish brogue. "If you'd think to mention it to the boss, I'd be grateful."

Constance laughed. "Quite the taskmaster, is he?"

Paul shrugged and smiled. "He's not so bad. Better'n most, I'd say. Will you be needin' anything else tonight, ma'am?"

"No. I'm home for the evening."

"Good night for it." He tipped his hat and a shower of snowflakes fell from the brim. "I'll be seein' you, Mrs. Blackwood."

As she came in the service entrance, the smells of roast beef and fresh-baked bread made her stomach growl. She'd hardly eaten today, much too nervous about the lecture she'd delivered an hour ago. Thank goodness it was over, and she could enjoy a quiet evening at home.

Mrs. Becker called hello from the kitchen, where she and two helpers worked side by side. Constance left her cloak in the vestibule outside Alex's office. His suit coat hung from the back of his chair and his desk was open, with papers and bills organized in the storage partitions. A half-finished letter sat on the blotter, alongside a well-used dictionary.

She found him in the adjacent pantry. All the cabinets were open and dozens of silver serving pieces were spread out on the counter. Why Oswald kept all of this, she did not understand. It was much more than he ever used, even for his largest parties. But it was her husband's responsibility to keep track of it all, and this was what he was doing now. His back was turned, but he raised his hand in greeting. She came up behind him and wrapped one arm around his waist, then dipped her hand into his side pocket.

"Have I caught the butler pilfering the plate? Trustworthy help is so hard to find these days." She drew a ring of keys from his pocket and jingled them. "What have we here? The keys to the safe?"

Alex turned in her embrace and brought her close for a kiss that warmed her down to her toes. "Key to my heart, luv. Were you trying to distract me just now?"

She smiled as a stray lock of hair fell alongside his face. At thirty-five, he still possessed the rakish charm she loved. "Perhaps. Aren't I more interesting than cabinets full of tea trays?"

"Infinitely," he replied, using a word he'd recently learned. "And how was your day?"

"It just got much better."

"Mine, too. Did your lecture to the school board transform public education in New York City?"

The Brooklyn Academy's success had attracted the attention of the public schools' superintendent. Constance, who served as assistant headmistress, and Cornelia Wentworth were invited to lecture on the Academy's methods. But their audience turned out to be three stone-faced gentlemen, who sat cross-armed and glared through the entire presentation. "Hardly," she said, with a sigh. "Mr. Meyer felt our ideas were too conservative. Mr. Davis thought them too radical. Mr. Poole won't consider any new curriculum until next year, and they all agreed it was too expensive."

Alex smiled. "You do important work, Connie. Never forget that. Even if things didn't turn out the way you hoped this time, just remember I'm proud of you every single day."

She nestled against him, thinking there was no place she felt happier than in her husband's arms. At one time, she couldn't imagine how he would ever fit into her life. Now she couldn't imagine life without him. He celebrated her accomplishments and her shortcomings did nothing to diminish his love.

As proud as he was of her, she was just as proud of him.

He had little formal education, but read voraciously, sprinkling his speech and correspondence with new words he learned. He managed a staff that respected him and worked hard to meet his approval. His employer was a multi-millionaire who provided them with a comfortable apartment in his mansion. Most important, he was a loving, faithful husband and father.

There were people who looked askance at them. As a respected educator, she was a frequent guest at Mr. Willard's dinner parties and Alex attended them with her. But there were other evenings when he supervised the staff and served the wine. After five years, enough people had observed him in both roles that their unusual match was common knowledge. Some found it intriguing. Others were appalled. Neither she nor Alex gave a damn. The life they'd built didn't look like anyone else's. The last five years had not been easy, but she would not have traded them for anything.

Oswald Willard hadn't cared a whit that Alex was married, but the Brooklyn Academy was far less accommodating. Cornelia Wentworth grudgingly offered a substitute teaching post, expecting Constance would quit once she became pregnant.

No one imagined that day would never come.

"Paul was quite prompt with the carriage this afternoon," she said, as she and Alex returned to his office. "He even remembered to fetch my valise. It appears you've brought him into line."

"Paul brought himself into line. He's a good lad, and you were right, he just needed better influences." He handed Constance a letter from the stack of mail on his desk. It was addressed in her mother's ornate script. "This arrived this afternoon. I assume it's details about Rose's arrival for the holidays."

"I'll read it later this evening. It's wonderful that she's finally decided to make the trip."

Alex grinned. "I'd say we've finally given her the perfect reason."

On the floor beside his desk was a crate of wine bottles. "Was Mr. Solomon here today?" she asked, carefully.

Alex continued to sort through the mail and didn't look up. "Yes, he came about Oswald's Christmas wine order."

"Did he mention the job offer?"

"He did." He set the letters aside and turned to her. "I told him exactly what I said to you last night. That accepting a new position which would require us to move out of here, simply isn't the right thing to do at the moment." Alex shook his head. "It's too much, after everything they've been through."

"I agree," Constance said, though she was disappointed that he had to sacrifice an opportunity he'd long hoped for. She took his hand. "It's a shame the offer came when it did. Working in the wine business is something you've always wanted."

"Connie, what I've always wanted is what I have right now. You and our family, to care for and love. There will be other opportunities. Oswald keeps asking me to look over his business ledgers." He smiled. "He says he trusts me more than the bloke he hired to do the job. So no matter what business I work in, I'm a very happy man."

Footsteps from the hallway interrupted them, as dark-haired Nicholas toddled into the room. Seven-year-old Anna remained just outside the door.

Constance scooped up the warm little boy and planted a kiss on his downy head. She smiled at Anna, who stood beside Sarah the nanny, clutching the notepad and box of pencils and crayons she carried everywhere. Constance had not given birth to them, but she could not imagine loving any children more.

The Brooklyn Academy was not an orphanage, but every so often, children were abandoned at its door. When Anna and Nicholas were found three months ago, Constance had known these children were meant to be theirs. The agonizing years of doctors and disappointment, the heartbreak of being unable to do something that came naturally to every other woman, suddenly had a reason.

Constance reached out her hand to the girl and at Sarah's prompting, Anna stepped into the room. "Hello, Anna," she said. "I missed you today. Have you drawn a new picture?"

The girl replied with a solemn nod, but did not offer to show it. Constance fought the impulse to ask.

Though she worked with children every day, motherhood was a new challenge all together. Nicholas was sunny and loving, but for the first month Anna lived with them, she hid behind her long hair and said hardly a word. Constance's instinct was to be cheerful and positive, but when Anna didn't respond, she became discouraged. Alex urged her to be patient. Watching his gentle way with Anna, she sensed a connection and followed his example. Anna was still quiet, but was slowly emerging from her shell.

"Has it stopped snowing yet, Mrs. Blackwood?" Sarah asked, her deep voice flavored with a Southern drawl.

"No, and I wish you'd consider staying here tonight."

Sarah wound an oversized wool shawl around her head and shoulders. "That's kind of you to offer, but I have to get home. I'll see you tomorrow."

"I've asked Paul to take you in the carriage," Alex said.

"Thank you, I appreciate that. Good night, everyone."

As she left, Isaac, who worked in the kitchen, knocked on the open door. "Pardon me, sir, Mr. Willard's dinner is ready. Mrs. Becker said you had wine to go with it?"

Alex took two bottles from the crate and handed one to Constance. She studied the label, a late 1870s Bordeaux. "Oswald's having this one with his dinner. We must sample it as well. Perhaps tonight, in front of the fire, after everyone is asleep?"

She smiled. "That sounds like a splendid idea."

Alex placed his bottle on the cart Isaac had wheeled into the service hallway. He touched Anna's shoulder. "Do you want to come with me to see Mr. Willard?" She nodded and went to stand beside Isaac. Alex ruffled Nicky's hair, then donned his suit coat. "We'll be back soon."

Constance gave Alex a quick kiss. "Take your time. I know he likes to talk."

⁂

Alex and Anna followed Isaac as he wheeled the cart through

Elizabeth Harmon

the mansion's quiet halls. This was a far cry from their early years here, when Oswald entertained almost every night. But last year, his employer had fallen seriously ill, and though the doctors insisted his health had returned, the man's abrasive, hard-driving personality had not. His brush with death made Oswald turn thoughtful. Life was changing at the mansion.

He glanced down at Anna, still finding it difficult to believe he was a father. He never knew his own father and barely knew his mother. When Anna and Nicholas arrived, he felt completely unprepared. But Connie never doubted he would be an excellent father, so he followed his heart and did his best.

Now, providing for his family gave new meaning to what he did. The work wasn't prestigious, but it kept an extremely nice roof over their heads. His old plan of becoming a successful wine merchant seemed less important, when he considered the many other splendid things in his life. He was married to a beautiful, brilliant woman he adored. His children were loved, safe and fed. No one had to steal. No one had to live in a sewer.

In the luxurious, oak-paneled study, Oswald Willard was reading the Sentinel, his New York paper. Isaac rolled the cart before him and removed the covers from the food. Alex went to the sideboard and poured two glasses of wine. He brought one to Oswald and took the opposite chair, while Anna sprawled on the rug, drawing in her book. Alex swirled the wine in his glass and tasted. It was a full-bodied red, with hints of oak, berry and vanilla. Potent presence, smooth finish. Connie would like it.

Some nights Oswald was talkative. Other nights he wasn't, but the fact that Alex was sitting by the fire, rather than standing in the corner, was another remarkable change.

In the early days, their relationship had been that of employer and servant. But when the parties stopped, Oswald's circle dwindled to just a few elderly gentlemen. One night Alex brought dinner and stood at attention while Oswald ate. He'd sensed the man's gaze, but protocol did not allow him to speak unless spoken to. The following night was the same, and the night after that. Finally, at the end of his meal, Oswald crumpled his linen napkin and shouted in frustration. "Is that all you do? Just stand there?"

"I beg your pardon, sir?" In all of his years in service, this was a first. "Would you prefer that I leave?"

"No!" Oswald barked. "But instead of standing there like a post, the least you could do is strike up a conversation. And fetch me a drink while you're at it."

In England, a servant would be sacked for such behavior, but Oswald didn't know or care, so Alex did as he asked. He poured Oswald a brandy and asked his opinion of New York City's newest professional baseball team. As he handed Oswald the crystal snifter, the man glared. "Aren't you having one with me?"

He'd realized then that the millionaire who loved to surround himself with people, and once entertained every night for six straight months, was lonely. Oswald had many acquaintances but few friends and no family. Now he was sick, eating alone, with no one to talk to except the staff. Alex wasn't about to refuse him. "I'd be delighted to, sir."

"Quit calling me that," Oswald had snapped, and their unlikely friendship began.

Over time, Oswald asked his thoughts on various business matters. Though Alex had never worked in the newspaper business, he understood money and balance sheets, and possessed common sense. His employer appreciated his insights and seemed to enjoy sharing what he'd learned over a lifetime of building his empire. When Anna arrived, Oswald took to her right away and despite the old man's noisy bluster, the feeling seemed mutual. Tonight, he gushed over her artwork. "This girl of yours has talent," he said.

Anna's subjects were childlike, animals mostly, but her drawings had a sophisticated depth. The newest was a rabbit with a pocket watch, inspired by the book Constance was reading at bedtime. "It's beautiful, Anna," Alex said. "I know your mum would love to see it."

Anna nodded and returned to her drawing, while Oswald continued his effusive praise. "She should have the best training. Paris! That's where she should go!"

He was hardly ready to think about his daughter studying in Paris, not to mention how he would ever afford it, but that was a concern for another day.

In the kitchen, the Blackwood family, Isaac, Paul, and Mrs. Becker dined together. Constance was delighted with Anna's drawing. She hugged her daughter, and for the first time, Anna returned it. Then she and Alex gathered their tired children and returned to their third-floor apartment.

When the children were in their nightclothes, Constance read from *Alice's Adventures in Wonderland*. Anna sat between them while Nicholas settled in Alex's lap and fell asleep. Alex stretched his arm across the back of the sofa and brushed his fingers over Constance's shoulder. She looked up, and they shared a smile over Anna's bowed head.

After the children were in bed, Alex made his rounds through the house, while Constance lit a fire in their bedroom fireplace. When he returned, she sat on the rug before it, wearing the peach silk gown he'd given her for her last birthday. He sat down beside her and lifted her into his lap. Her deep kiss was ripe with the taste of wine, the love they shared, and their hopes for the future.

Neither could guess what it held, but Constance, the lady, and Alex, the thief who stole her heart, would meet it together.

ACKNOWLEDGEMENTS

A huge thank you to Tom, Arlo, Gabe, my mom, and extended family, for your constant support during this book, and those that came before. Thank you to beta readers Max and Patty, and to Cheryl, Tory, and Janice for critiques and encouragement, not only as I worked on this book, but as we work on life as writers, friends, and women living in really strange times. To my editor Alicia, your insights made me see this story in new ways, and to "Comma Cops" Tom and Janice, thanks for catching all the stuff I missed!

To the readers who followed me from my contemporary series, and to new readers who are finding me for the first time, an enormous and heartfelt thank you. Every author has a book of their heart, and this one is mine. I hope you loved Alex and Constance's story as much as I do. I look forward to sharing more stories of the past, in the future.

Most of all, I thank God, who always brings the words.

ABOUT THE AUTHOR

A life-long fan of cats, tacos and happy endings, Elizabeth Harmon makes her home in the Midwest. A graduate of the University of Illinois, she has worked as a library associate, a community college instructor, and as a journalist. When she's not writing, teaching or talking books with library patrons, she loves to spend time with family and friends– especially when a good Chianti is involved. Her five-book Red Hot Russians sports romance series is set in the world of competitive figure skating. The first book in the series, Pairing Off, is a RITA® Award Finalist.

Find her online at elizabethharmonauthor.com

Made in the USA
Monee, IL
10 March 2021